tv
little
girls

BOOKS BY FRANCES VICK

two little girls

Frances Vick

bookouture

Published by Bookouture in 2019

An imprint of StoryFire Ltd.

Carmelite House
50 Victoria Embankment
London EC4Y 0DZ

www.bookouture.com

ISBN: 978-1-78681-820-1
eBook ISBN: 978-1-78681-819-5

For my family

'We do not see things as they are. We see things as we are.'

Talmudic saying

CHAPTER ONE

March 1985

The two little girls, bright specks of blue and pink, leave the school gates, wiggling through the scrum of parents, toddlers, shouting swaggering classmates. Most of the children display that strangely exhausted excitement peculiar to Fridays, when the weekend stretches far ahead like a road through the desert, with scarcely a hint of anything but absolute freedom ahead. Car doors slam, babies shriek, parents chat, doggedly ignoring tugging, bored children who are anxious to get home and play.

It's starting to rain, just a little, and the air feels sticky, tacky with moisture. The weather forecast says there might be a storm tonight. Someone's umbrella is forced inside out, and people chuckle. Rubbish is already spread across the street and baffled, resentful cats hide under cars and sheltered doorsteps.

In the middle of all this, the two girls are a bubble of apparent calm. They're neither smiling nor talking, and when you look closer, they're not even walking together. The girl in blue is slightly ahead, her face set in an expression of self-conscious tragedy. The girl in pink lags deliberately behind and she looks at the ground, but her face is tight with suppressed, confused emotion.

No-one talks to them, no-one looks at them, but everyone knows who they are: Lisa Cook and Kirsty Cooper. They're Best Friends Forever. They're almost one entity. The only difference between them is that Lisa is a liar, and Kirsty… Kirsty is…? Nobody knows what Kirsty is really like any more. She's been under Lisa's shadow for such a long time that when (and if) anyone thinks of Kirsty, they think first of Lisa. It's been like that for a long time, and it will carry on being that way, even after Lisa is declared dead.

But that hasn't happened yet. That doesn't happen for a while.

*

It took Kirsty ages to persuade her mum to let her walk home. She wouldn't cross any main roads, or talk to strangers, or anything like that! Come on! Come *on*! *Everyone* walks home, why couldn't she? And it's not like she'd be alone, she'd be with Lisa! What was the problem?

Part of the problem was just that: she'd be with Lisa. Sometimes Sarah Cooper would watch her daughter, her face angled up at her friend like a drowsy flower to the sun, and wonder if they were a little *too* close. There were times, though Sarah couldn't be sure if she saw more what she feared than what existed, when Kirsty seemed embattled by the closeness of this friendship.

'I just think you should make some more friends,' she'd tell Kirsty sometimes. 'There's plenty of fish in the sea!' There was something about Lisa that made all her platitudes rise to the surface like drowned things. 'You can't put all your eggs in one basket.'

But it did no good. In fact, it had the opposite effect; Kirsty was at the foothills of adolescence now, and everything Sarah said was Wrong, and everything Lisa said was, by definition, Right. They'd go to the same school, and live next door to each other when they were older and carry on being Best Friends Forever – it was all worked out. And so Sarah gave ground, agreed to let them walk home together, so long as They Were Sensible and Came Straight Back with No Dawdling and they weren't to go through the park or by the canal, all right? Do you promise? Promise me? Sarah's private belief was that, perhaps – no, *not* perhaps, *of course* – when they got to secondary school, Kirsty would make more friends, blossom, come into her own, and September was only six months away. Six months is no time, is it?

Despite her intense lobbying, her hard won victory, Kirsty felt a little bit scared on the first walk home. Mindful of the No Park, No Canal rule, she suggested walking through the Marne Way industrial park – it'd take longer, but… And they did it for a week until Lisa said that was a stupid way to walk because it was boring and *long* and anyway everyone knew that there was quicksand in Marne Way. 'And that'll kill you, sure as cancer. I saw it on *The A-Team.*'

Kirsty wasn't sure that England even had quicksand, but she'd learned not to argue with Lisa, and so they started taking the different, forbidden path – over the Iron Bridge, over the train tracks, past the secondary school, over the canal bridge and through the park.

'Your mum'll never find out,' Lisa assured her. 'They *never* find out. And if she asks just lie. You don't even *have* to lie, just kind of nod and smile, or get her talking about something else.'

Lisa had mastered this kind of Jesuitical logic years ago, and her own mother, Denise, was none the wiser. Lisa did all sorts of things that Denise didn't know about… She stole make-up testers from Boots, magazines from the newsagents. She watched horror films and claimed that they had a video recorder at home – but Kirsty doubted that because those things were expensive and nobody she knew had one. That was the problem with Lisa; she tended to make things up, but finding out exactly what she *had* made up and what she *hadn't* was pretty much impossible, and if she was challenged, she raged. Kirsty feared conflict, would do anything to avoid it. Other kids in school didn't have her scruples though; they knew Lisa's uncle didn't have a plane; that the twittery nonsense she claimed was Japanese was just gibberish she made up on the spot. They had all lost patience, and as a result, Lisa had become steadily more and more unpopular, until she was practically a pariah.

The Iron Bridge – a dark, rusting hulk that wobbled over the train tracks – was frightening. Kirsty couldn't help imagining falling through the open metal slats of the steps, and, when on the partially enclosed metal walkway, the noise of the trains below rushed up in one angry, animal bellow, she shivered and closed her eyes. Perhaps Lisa was a bit scared too, because it was her idea to bring back an old game they used to play when they were little – they imagined trolls under the bridge, trolls who would reach out to grab them if they didn't move quickly, trolls they had to escape by running the length of the bridge in ten seconds or less. They'd stop at the last step, count to three, and run screaming across the walkway, collapsing, mock-exhausted at the other end, loudly congratulating each other for surviving yet another day. The thrill of besting the Iron Bridge almost obscured the guilt Kirsty felt every time they walked down the canal path and through the park.

'What your mum doesn't see won't hurt her,' Lisa said. 'Don't be a baby.'

'Don't be a baby.' That had been the refrain all school year. Lots of things were babyish now, it seemed... Everything on TV was babyish apart from *Grange Hill* and that was only good *sometimes*. Care Bears and skipping games were babyish, and so were fish fingers, having a pet rabbit or a hamster (although gerbils were excluded from that list because Lisa owned a gerbil named Funshine) and knee socks. They should wear tights, Lisa said, like ladies did. Denise and Sarah didn't buy either girl tights, however, so they had to get the look by stretching their knee socks until the elastic cracked and securing the tops around their thighs with rubber bands. They dug in something awful, but complaining about that was babyish too, so Kirsty didn't any more.

If the Iron Bridge was scary, the canal and the park beyond were scarier still. The water looked like black oil, and it lapped against the concrete bank with a slapping, sucking noise that was faintly lascivious. And then there was the huge, flat expanse of park with the plane trees rustling, looming so high… it was spooky. There were sudden dips in the grass that made you stumble, and sound carried differently – things could seem closer or further away than they were; traffic from the distant road or little wisps of conversation were borne by the wind from far away. Sometimes the opposite happened, and there was no sound at all, just each other and the dark, as if they were floating on the River Styx. Kirsty felt as if the park was a sentient thing, that it played tricks with the sound and the light, simply to frighten little girls who lied to their mothers.

On the walk back home, Lisa would prattle about all the usual things she prattled about – the cerise lipstick she'd nicked from the market, how she was definitely getting a puppy for her birthday (this last was almost certainly a lie, but Kirsty wasn't going to pick her up on it). Lately though, she'd started using these familiar tropes as a way of introducing her new favourite subject: Boys and How to Get Them to Like You. Walking this hypothetical dog would help her get fit because the ideal measurements for a girl were 34–22–34 and both of them had better start aiming for that now. The lipstick was important – everyone wore lipstick and you had to learn how to kiss so it didn't smear all over your face. Lisa was practising by kissing the wall next to her mirror. Kirsty should too. She wondered aloud if she had the right kind of face for a perm? She pinched her cheeks to make them pink – because it made you look cute and excited, and men liked it when you look excited. She took to flapping her arms in a mysterious and ungainly chest exercise designed to make her breasts grow, and she bunched up her skirt, doubling it up at the waistband, trying to make it into a miniskirt. It gave her a strange silhouette, like a half-cooked dumpling, but she didn't seem to notice and Kirsty certainly wasn't going to tell her.

Kirsty, shamefully, hadn't made any inroads yet into Making Boys Like Her but secretly she didn't really want to. She might have succumbed to the knee-sock torture, but she still wore the regulation knee-length skirt and her hair was more often than not cajoled into bunches or held back with plastic hair grips. Lisa had started rolling her eyes at the bunches, so Kirsty surmised that they too were now babyish.

'We should get matching perms. Maybe I should be the blonde one and you could be, like, a redhead? And I could always wear blue, and you could wear black? Or cerise?'

Lisa had a new plan. They were going to start a girl band together – like Pepsi & Shirlie or Mel and Kim. She even had a name – Angels Times Two – and had painstakingly, and with many rubbings-out, designed a logo of two winged fairies pecking at each other's lips, their outsized wings all gilded. Well, almost all gilded; Lisa's gold marker had run out halfway through and she had to colour the rest in with yellow pencil. 'But it looks ace, doesn't it?' Together they wrote song lyrics and laboured over their answers to imaginary interviews in *Smash Hits*. Angels Times Two demanded synchronised dance routines and crop tops and make-up, and Kirsty better get good at those things and quick, especially the make-up bit, and not just for the band, but for school too because everyone in secondary school wore lipstick and eyeliner and you had to be good at that if you wanted a boyfriend. Wanting a boyfriend was in the natural order of things. Kirsty had been excited about secondary school but now she knew it would be populated by make-up-wearing sophisticates and leering boys that excitement had soured into queasy terror.

She scolded herself for this fear, and hoped against hope that, come secondary school, she'd have changed. She was bitterly ashamed of her ignorance; an ignorance she hadn't even known she was guilty of until last October, when Lisa got that ring and started telling her all these baffling things that seemed too weird to be true, and quite possibly weren't... but... what if they were?

CHAPTER TWO

October 1984, and Lisa was waiting just outside the school gates. Normally she swung in late, the crust of cornflakes still between her teeth, a smear of breakfast jam on her cheek. Today though, she was early, waving at Kirsty with a gleeful urgency. Her whisper was theatrical, designed to be overheard.

'I've got something to show you!' She was wearing lipstick. There was a bit on her teeth.

'You've got to wipe that off before Miss Gillgrass sees you.'

'What? Oh, this?' Lisa opened her eyes wide, dapped one slick lip with a chewed, stubby finger. 'Oh, it must still be on since last night. I was out last night. Till late.'

She smiled significantly, and this smile had its predictable effect on Kirsty: a little tug of excitement, a corresponding pinch of anxiety.

'Where?'

'That's for me to know and you to find out!' Lisa chanted.

The bell rang. 'Let's go,' said Kirsty.

'Don't you want to know? You're *dying* to know!'

Kirsty hesitated, letting herself be jostled by the other kids filing into class. 'Why can't you tell me now?'

'Meet me in the toilets at break.'

'Why can't you tell me now though?'

'Because I *can't*, that's why. Meet me in the toilets at break!'

Lisa was given to intrigue. She was exciting that way.

*

During first break, they hid in the toilets, huddled together in a smelly little cubicle, the shrieks from the playground seeping through the toughened glass of the high windows, but still they whispered.

'Look.' Lisa pointed one stubby index finger out and wiggled it inches from Kirsty's face. 'It's an antique.' It was a brass ring, awkwardly twisted into the shape of a snake, taking up most of the finger – all the way up to the knuckle. 'It came all the way from Oman. And the eyes? Real rubies.' She nodded significantly. 'From Oman.'

'Is Oman like Argos?' Kirsty asked after a while.

Lisa rolled her eyes. 'Oman is a *country*. Our lodgers, Tokki and Mohammed? They're *from* Oman.'

Kirsty had heard about the lodgers, but she'd never met any of them. Where was Oman? It didn't sound like a real place even. It sounded like a planet from *Star Trek* or something. Maybe she could go to the library at lunchtime and look it up in the atlas.

'Can I try it on?' Kirsty asked.

'Only if you promise not to tell *anybody*, all right? *No-one*.'

'Tell anyone what? About going to the cinema?'

'That. And the ring and stuff. Promise!' This was a tricky thing to respond to. Lisa might mean what she said, or she might mean just the opposite, hoping the word would spread... Kirsty knew from experience that it was better to promise now and reassess later.

'OK. I promise.' Lisa pulled the ring over one grimy knuckle and passed it over. Kirsty's fingers were slimmer, and the ring rattled to the base of her finger. It was an ugly, cheap-looking thing and the eyes were set crookedly. It gave her a nasty feeling somehow, as if she was touching slime. She gave it back hurriedly.

'Isn't it *gorgeous*?' Lisa breathed.

'How come you've got it?'

'*Tokki* gave it me because...' Lisa struggled to push it on her own finger again, 'and you can't tell *anyone*, about this, *ever*, all right?'

'All right.'

'Promise! Cross your heart!' She made Kirsty slash at the air in front of her chest. 'OK.' She paused dramatically. 'We're engaged.'

Kirsty laughed. 'No you're not!'

Lisa frowned furiously. 'I *am* so!'

'Kids don't get engaged... *old* people get engaged!'

'Well, maybe I'm *not* a kid. Unlike *you*.' Lisa was all supercilious dignity. 'No-one'll ever give you a ring with rubies in it.'

Indignation pushed Kirsty into answering back. 'They're not rubies,' she told her flatly and followed up with something she knew would hit hard: 'And I bet it's from Argos really. We've got the catalogue at home and when I look I bet it's there.'

Lisa scowled. 'It *is* from Oman. He said I'm not allowed to wear it at home in case Mum sees it, but I asked if I could take it to school with me to show you, and he said yes. He didn't *want* to say yes either. He *said* you'd be jealous and you *are*.' She paused to assess Kirsty's lack of enthusiasm. 'You're *jealous*.'

'I'm not,' Kirsty replied. She really wasn't.

'Well you will be soon.' Lisa twirled the ring. 'He says he's going to give me a matching necklace too. For my birthday. And you know Harvest Festival? They say they're going to come. Him and Mo. I *asked* them to come.'

The bell rang then. 'What? Why?'

Lisa rolled her eyes. 'To meet *you*. I *told* them about you and showed them your picture, and Mo said you were really pretty and he wanted to *meet* you. In Oman they're royal, they're real actual princes, and anyone who marries them will be a princess. I wanted us both to be princesses, but maybe I don't now, because you're too *babyish*.'

Kirsty couldn't help feeling a shy pride... someone thought she was pretty? A *boy* thought she was pretty! OK, not a boy, a man, but still...

'You can't just *become* a princess though.'

'Princess Di did,' Lisa replied smartly.

That was true. 'Yeah, but—'

'She married a *prince*, and now she's a *princess*.'

'But, she's grown up! I mean, we're in *school* and you can't get married when you're in school—'

Lisa flapped a dismissive hand. 'Yes you can. You can in Oman. It's *different* there. They told me, they can have lots of wives and you don't get married like in a *church*, but you just kind of say you're married and you *are*.'

Kirsty thought about this for a minute. It could be true. 'How? How can you just say you're married?'

Lisa made that irritated gesture again. 'You *fall* in *love* and then you *kiss* and then you say some words and stuff and then you're *married*. He told me. Things are *different* there.' Her face creased with annoyance. 'I *knew* you wouldn't get it!'

And she tossed her head, pushed past her, and left the toilets with great dignity.

Kirsty shuffled about by herself for a while feeling doubtful and confused. When she got back to class Lisa had installed Jackie Johnson in Kirsty's seat, so she had to sit at the back between Alexandra Wass, who was from a weird religious family who didn't even own a TV, and David Briggs, who ate his own earwax. It was humiliating.

Lisa punished Kirsty for her insubordination all day. They walked home in silence until, on the Iron Bridge, Kirsty eventually cracked and apologised. After that, all the way past the secondary school, under the canal bridge, through the park, Lisa talked incessantly about Tokki, about the desert and oases and flying carpets and showers of gold. To Kirsty it just sounded like she'd watched a lot of movies, and she even recognised huge chunks of one of her breathless tales had been lifted from *The Golden Voyage of Sinbad* because she'd watched it herself with her parents only that weekend. Still, it was so nice to be friends again that she didn't challenge her.

They were nearly at the park gate when Lisa started yawning, stretching, yawning again, before finally mock-stumbling, halting altogether.

'I'm so *tired*.'

'Come on, we'll be late for *Crackerjack*. It's the Spooky Special today.'

'I know all about spooky stuff.' Lisa drawled. Kirsty kept walking. '*Wait!*' Lisa commanded. Kirsty, reluctantly, stopped, turned. Lisa yawned yet again, meaningfully. 'I hardly got any sleep last night. We got back so late I slept in my make-up!'

'Why were you wearing make-up?'

'Because Tokki took me to the cinema last night? That's why I was wearing make-up 'cause it was an 18? And we watched a horror film and it was about this man? Who killed this other man? And then they buried him but he kept coming back? It was scary. And when we got home I didn't want to go to the bathroom and wash my face even, and I couldn't be alone I was so scared, so Tokki stayed with me until I wasn't frightened any more.'

'What d'you mean, he stayed with you?' They were approaching the park gates now, leading to the car park of Kwik Save. From here it was only ten minutes from home. There was no-one around.

'Oh, I shouldn't! I promised I wouldn't tell!'

Kirsty didn't want to miss *Crackerjack*, she was going to have to muster up an appropriate level of interest, otherwise Lisa wouldn't move.

'Lise! *Lisa*, come on, tell me!'

That did it. Lisa was ready to deliver her prepared killer line. 'OK, earlier? I lied. We're not engaged... we're *married!*' she squealed. 'Me and Tokki!'

'What d'you *mean*, you're married?'

'I can't tell you because it's a ritual? From Oman? And it's secret, but when you get engaged to Mo he'll explain it all and then we can talk all about it. You can get the same ring as me, too, but with emerald eyes so they won't get mixed up.' She punched Kirsty lightly on the arm. 'We'll be princesses together! He's *gorgeous*, is Mo. I said to Tokki that he'd better watch out 'cause I might marry Mo too!'

'Can you do that in Oman?' Kirsty, dazed, asked.

'Oh yeah. You can do that in Oman. You can do *anything* in Oman.'

*

The phrase stuck with Kirsty. *You can do anything in Oman.* Anything? Perhaps you could eat whatever you wanted, and watch whatever you wanted on TV, and stay up late and wear make-up (or not). Being a princess didn't seem very interesting, but maybe princesses were different in Oman too. Maybe they didn't have to wear Peter Pan collars and sensible shoes and smile emptily at lines of old ladies and cradle crying babies, like Princess Di had to. Maybe being a princess in Oman was… exciting?

She closed her eyes, trying to summon a suitably appealing image – herself and Lisa on a yacht, brown and lean as those girls in that Duran Duran video, their eyes hidden by enormous sunglasses, holding glasses of cool-looking liquids with their elegant, unbitten fingers. It was a nice image. Tokki and Mo weren't in it because she didn't know what they looked like – it was just her and Lisa. Chink-chink went the ice in the glasses as the sun dipped down into the waves turning them orange, red. And they would finish their drinks and… then what? Dress for dinner? She imagined them slipping into identical slinky outfits, applying sugary lip gloss and emerging into the twilight even more languidly beautiful, taking the arms of their faceless husbands, and then… and then… what? S.E.X.?

You can do anything in Oman.

'Mum, have you ever been to Oman?'

'Isn't it a Scottish island or something?' Sarah Cooper was pulling steaming wet clothes out of the washing machine. 'The bloody spin's broken again.'

'No, it's *abroad*. It's deserts and stuff. Camels.'

'No, I've not been to Oman. What d'you want to know about Oman for?'

'Lisa's new lodgers are from Oman. They're princes.'

Mum peered irritably at the washing machine dial. 'They won't be princes.'

'They *are*, Lisa said so.'

'If they're princes, why're they lodging at Denise Cook's house then? Why're they living in Beacon Hill? Why aren't they living at The Ritz or something?'

'What's The Ritz?'

'A posh hotel in London.'

'Well they couldn't stay in London, 'cause they're learning English at college here.'

Mum gave the washing machine a little kick and that seemed to start its juddery spin cycle. 'Now it does it! After I've got the bloody washing out!'

'They're learning English at Marlborough House.'

'Lisa's having you on, love. She's joking.'

Kirsty was indignant. 'She's not! They're princes and they even want to make her into a princess! They're—'

'Kirsty, look!' Mum interrupted urgently.

'What?'

'Look, there, out of the window! Can you *see* it?'

Kirsty trotted to the window excitedly. 'What? What is it?'

'A pig! Can you see it?'

'A *pig*?'

'Yeah. Flying. Can you see it?'

Kirsty frowned. 'That's not funny.'

'I bet if Lisa told you that, you'd make out you saw it.' Mum smiled a bit grimly. 'You believe everything that girl says. You need to watch that.'

'But—'

'Lisa Cook is no princess, and whoever Denise is letting that room to, they're no princes either. Have some sense. Lisa lies like a rug.'

'She does *not*!'

'Oh, for God's sake!' The washing machine was making a wheezing, clunking sound as the spin cycle slowed. 'This thing is on its last legs.'

'She's *not* lying!' Kirsty insisted.

'Really?' Mum swung to face her, her hands on her hips, her tired eyes narrowed. 'What about that time she was here for a sleepover and she stole your Care Bear and tried to say she didn't, even though I *saw* her put it in her bag? And when she told us her uncle had died in the Falklands and she doesn't even have an uncle?'

Mum didn't like Lisa much. She once said that everyone who lived in the Beacon Hill estate was a bunch of pikeys. Kirsty didn't know what pikey meant and had looked it up in the dictionary, but it wasn't in there, and any word that wasn't in the dictionary had to be Very Bad.

'There's lots of girls you could hang around with. Nicola? Or that new girl, Lorraine? She does horse riding.' Sarah left a little pause, as if horse riding proved Lorraine's superiority over the lumpen proletariat populating St Joseph's Primary. 'I'm not sure you should be walking back with Lisa after all. Maybe you can stay at the school until five and I can pick you up?'

Kirsty's heart stuttered. Walking home from school had been a hard-won victory – it had taken *weeks* to talk Mum round! If she changed her mind she'd have to wait in the empty school for ages, and creepy Mr Ferabee the caretaker might *talk* to her, or try to make her help clean up or something… And so she reached for a reassuring lie.

'I walk part of the way with Nicola now too, and yeah, you're right, I think Lisa's joking, I really do. She has a big imagination.'

'That's one way of putting it,' Mum snorted.

'What's for tea?'

'Fish fingers and chips.' She kicked the washing machine again. 'This bloody thing! Life of its own!'

And that was the end of their first and only conversation about Toqueer Mohammed Al-Balushi. At least until Lisa disappeared.

CHAPTER THREE

That sly, scary doggerel haunted her all night: *You can do anything in Oman… You fall in love and then you kiss and then…* And then what? S.E.X. It had to mean that, surely? She could ask Mum but what if she got embarrassed, started one of those earnest, confusing, blushing conversations, like the one they'd had about 'periods'? Kirsty still didn't know what a 'period' was, but she knew she never wanted to feel that mortified ever again.

And so she sat upstairs in her room, cuddling her Cheer Care Bear, telling herself she didn't need to worry about the princess thing. The engagement thing. It was just Lisa lying. Silly. It was all just silly lies. Like the uncle in the Falklands, or the dolphins she'd swum with in Majorca, Tokki and Mo probably didn't even exist. Of course they didn't! Mum was right, as if a prince would live in Beacon Hill! And if they didn't even exist, they couldn't show up at Harvest Festival, could they?

But they did show up. And that's when everything started to go wrong.

*

Pink cut-out letters, stuck on the low proscenium, proclaimed, 'Thank You God, for the Harvest!' Below were arranged the sad little pyramids of canned peas and corned beef, retrieved by harassed parents from the back of cupboards and shoved into school bags at the last minute. Reverend Gary, the local vicar, having already led the children through a confusing, boring talk about loaves and fishes, was now hobnobbing with the few parents who'd attended as well as the odd pensioner who never missed one of Gary's performances wherever it was. Mrs Butler was grimly pounding out her small repertoire of hymns on the piano and Kirsty was revelling in the relief that the princes hadn't come after all. She was back in class, putting on her coat, looking forward to going outside to take advantage of the baggy half hour after Harvest Festival to hunt for conkers. She knew where the best ones were, and if she was quick she could grab them all. Last year she'd been the conker-fight queen – and she'd kept her winning weapon – a 25-er – scarred and dented, the string running through it ragged and stained, in one of her treasure boxes at home. Just then a kid from the infants tugged on her sleeve.

'Gottercometothehall,' he said. 'Gottercomenow.'

'Why?' she asked, but the child just shrugged, shoved a finger in one crusty nostril and wandered away.

Back in the hall Lisa was waving extravagantly, squealing, 'Kirsty! *Kir*stee!' Beside her stood two men, dark-skinned, impossibly, confusingly, real. They were both quite short, and Tokki – it had to be Tokki because Lisa was trying to hold his hand in a proprietorial way – in particular was slump-shouldered and had a little pot belly that strained against his polo shirt. It seemed weird for a prince to wear something like a polo shirt… Mo was taller, skinnier; his shiny grey trousers barely grazed his thighs, falling in polyester puddles to his tan plastic shoes. Both men were smiling, and their smiles were nice enough, though their teeth were brown and small, like bad baby teeth.

They didn't look like princes.

Both men held a gnarly-looking loaf. 'Special bread! From Oman!' Lisa told her. Kirsty didn't see how it could be edible after being sent all that way, but she just nodded, blushed, and stared at the floor.

There was an awkward pause. Lisa let out a silly little titter.
'She's shy,' she told the men.

Kirsty kept her eyes on the floor, sodden with shame at her own timidity, angry with Lisa for putting her in this position in the first place, shocked that this most ridiculous of lies wasn't a lie after all. And if they were real, maybe Lisa *was* married? Maybe they were here to marry her too! The world swam and she felt suddenly very sick and very scared and very, very young.

'Me and Kirsty, we're going to live together, aren't we? We're going to live right next door to each other, and we'll have one big garden, won't we? And…' Lisa had run out of things to say. The silence stretched. Even Mrs Butler had stopped murdering the piano and was struggling into her fawn-coloured coat. 'Say something!' Lisa hissed at Kirsty. To the men she tittered.

'Is it hot in Oman?' Kirsty muttered. They didn't understand her. A furious blush spread over her cheeks. There was another long pause.

Tokki spoke then. He said, 'You like sport?'

Somehow that seemed to unfreeze Kirsty. She even managed to look up at them. Both men were smiling and Mo made a running movement with his arms and said, 'Athletics. You like sports?'

'No,' Kirsty managed, and she backed away. 'Nicetomeetyou.'

She saw Lisa frowning, saw the men's smiles stay static, she felt her wobbling legs carry her to the double doors, and then she ran to the toilets and cried.

'I told them how you were my best friend and I'd only be a princess if *you* were too, and you made me look *awful*!' Lisa's thin, petulant little voice bounced around in the tiled room. 'Boys don't *like* shy girls.'

'Well they're not boys anyway,' Kirsty muttered.

'You're a baby,' Lisa told her scornfully.

'At least I'm not some... stupid... *cow*, who likes ugly weird men with bad teeth!' Kirsty pushed past her then, out into the corridor, and Lisa came barrelling out after her, chased her into the playground, and soon the school thrummed with the excitement of a fight! Now! Excited kids washed up onto the playing field behind the trees (the traditional place for all fights to be held) like so much flotsam and gasped as Lisa smacked Kirsty in the face with a plastic skittle gone astray from the infants'. Kirsty retaliated by shoving her fingers deep into Lisa's hair, grabbing at the roots and pulling hard. They struggled, and tore and kicked and thrashed for a few minutes, before the breathless chant of 'Fight! Fight! Fight!' from the crowd drew the attention of the dinner ladies who pulled them away from each other with their slab-like arms and sent them straight to Miss Farnell's office where they were told that Ladies-Don't-Fight-and-Enough-of-this-Nonsense-and-Set-an-Example-for-the-Smaller-Children.

True to code, both girls were silent and remorseful in the office, but once they were outside, Lisa thumped Kirsty on the back, and Kirsty kicked Lisa in the shin. Lisa hissed that she didn't want to be friends any more and she didn't want to go to secondary school with her and she could forget about them living next door to each other too. That stung, because Kirsty had always liked the idea of them being neighbours when they were old, old ladies in their forties or fifties... She said in a wobbly voice that that was *just fine*, and Lisa flashed her new sharp, nasty smile, but her eyes were a bit wet too.

For the next week, Kirsty played with other people, the girls she used to play with before Lisa monopolised her. They were happy to have her back; they seemed to see it as their Christian duty, nodded forgivingly, knowingly at her, and included her in their skipping games which Lisa said were babyish, but that was probably because she was bad at them. These girls were the serious, hair-combed, sedate types that Kirsty's mum liked.

In the meantime, Lisa scampered about on her own, pretending to have fun. She smiled a lot, but every now and again she'd forget to, and her face was so desolate, so lonely. There were big sleepless smudges under her eyes, and she didn't wear the snake ring any more. It wasn't long before Kirsty relented, started saying the odd word to her, walking a little closer to her over the Iron Bridge. They got back together, like an old couple, or a bad band, and the sensible, well-groomed girls who skipped watched the process with a kind of adult sorrow. Lisa was A Bad Lot. Kirsty was Too Nice. But, such was life. What could you do?

Soon Lisa started wearing the snake ring again, even after one of the ruby eyes fell out. But she didn't speak about Tokki and Mo and Kirsty didn't ask anything either. She only asked questions on the last day, that terrible last day when they'd argued, and Kirsty had run away and left Lisa alone in the park. If she hadn't, Lisa would still be alive. It was Kirsty's fault. All of it was her fault.

CHAPTER FOUR

March 1985

Kirsty didn't notice that Lisa was crying until they were by the canal. It was only when she half turned to skip over something nasty, a weird skin-coloured, gelatinous thing that she squashed down on the path, that she saw Lisa's wet, red face, her shuddering shoulders. She went to her, threaded one thin, hesitant arm around her waist and asked, 'What's wrong?'

Kirsty's concern seemed to make Lisa sadder still. Soon she was crying too hard to talk, and they clung together under the bridge while her sobs carried on, her breath coming out in little spasmodic puffs. Kirsty found a cleanish bit of path, away from the dark, smelly water, and made her friend sit, patting her on her shuddering back, smoothing her soft hair. It was a long time before she could speak, and a long time before she made much sense.

'I didn't mean it,' Lisa managed eventually. 'About school. About not wanting to go to the same school as you.'

'That was ages ago! I know you didn't mean that!' Kirsty answered warmly. 'Don't be daft!'

'I'm sorry I was mean. I've been mean for ages.' Her breathing was calm now, just the odd little twitch and hitch.

'S'all right. You haven't, but, you know, it's all right—'

'And we'll live next door to each other, won't we? Always?' Lisa turned wet eyes on Kirsty. The mascara she'd taken to wearing was smudged and shiny clots stuck to her lashes, like mud on bicycle spokes. 'And name our kids after each other, and… We'll always be friends, won't we?'

'You'll be living in Oman, though.' Kirsty dared a joke. They hadn't spoken about Harvest Festival or Tokki and Mohammed or any of that for months – after their humiliating fight on the sports field, there had been a careful, tacit detente.

Lisa answered flatly, 'I'm not going to Oman. That was never going to happen. I made all that up.'

To hear the truth stated so baldly was unsettling. Something Very Bad must have happened for Lisa to abandon this fantasy and to be so honest about it.

'What d'you mean, it's not going to happen?'

'Tokki thinks I'm silly.' Her voice was flat with humiliation. 'He told me he'd tell my mum if I carried on… *chasing him*.'

Huge, physical relief hit Kirsty hard. All the kissing and the cinema dates and the rituals and… it was all lies. She couldn't help smiling.

'Don't laugh at me!' Lisa said.

'I'm not laughing. I'm sorry… I just, it's… I'm happy, that's all.'

'Why're you happy? I'm *sad*!'

But Kirsty couldn't explain herself without spilling her own shame – that she was a little girl who didn't want a boyfriend; that she was scared of growing up, that the idea of Lisa knowing anything about S.E.X. was kind of *awful* and frightening and it made her strangely sad. All she said was, 'You don't have to feel, like, embarrassed.'

Lisa stiffened, but Kirsty, drunk with relief, carried on, 'And, well, maybe it's not Tokki that's really made you cry? Maybe it's the making things up that made you sad?' Lisa stayed stiff, silent, and Kirsty, stupidly taking that silence for acquiescence, carried on, warming further to her theme. 'I mean, people know, you know? They know that you… tell stories and… when we go to secondary school, you have to be… well, if you get a bad reputation, you know, if people think you're silly and you lie, then people will think that all the way until you're sixteen and that would be awful, wouldn't it?… So, I just think, maybe, it's not a bad thing? Tokki saying this?' She trailed off. There was a short silence.

'You're right.' Lisa nodded, sighing a little melodramatically. 'It wasn't going to work out with Tokki anyway. We're too different. And Bryan would kill him when he found out. He's such a *racialist*.'

Bryan was Lisa's brother, a wiry skinhead of sixteen who was already something of a local menace. Kirsty felt something in her harden. Bryan didn't even live with Lisa anyway, Denise had thrown him out when he stole the gas money. He lived in one of those creepy houses by the train station with a bunch of other weirdos. Bryan held no sway with Lisa, so this star-crossed-lovers narrative she was working up, hot on the heels of one moment of actual honesty, was just silly. Not just silly, but infuriating, insulting! Lisa was already turning from fact and romancing herself back into her comforting fiction. The small window into truth her tears had opened, was closed.

'People are so against mixed marriage in this country. Maybe we should elope? We could go to America? People are more open-minded there. When Bryan heard I was engaged he went mad! He tried to take my ring! That's how one of the rubies fell out.'

Just a second before, Lisa had hinted Bryan didn't know about this supposed engagement, and now she was saying he'd known for weeks! A month ago Lisa told her that one of the snake's eyes fell out when she was in the bath, and now here she was claiming that Bryan had damaged it in a fit of racist violence. Did she hear herself? Kirsty felt a cold weariness, an adult fatigue. She got up and started to walk away.

'Where're you going?' Lisa demanded.

'I'm going home.'

'I'm telling you about Tokki though!' Lisa scrambled up. She sounded angry. Kirsty still didn't turn round. 'It's important!'

'It's not true,' Kirsty managed. To her surprise she was almost crying. 'You're just making things up again like you always do. And it doesn't even make *sense*!'

'Kirsty!' Lisa's voice was peremptory. 'Wait!'

Just then a sudden wind blew through the tunnel, strong enough to dislodge the squashed jellyfish-type thing stuck to the walkway. It blew onto Kirsty's school shoe. She knew what it was now, and it *definitely* was something to do with S.E.X. It was a – what were they called? A *condemn*? *Cordon*? Something like that, and, ew, just looking at it now and knowing what it was was… *awful*. She could see something leaking out of the top like pus, and it threw her into a sudden panic. She kicked her foot wildly, trying to dislodge it, giving a little whimper. Lisa was laughing at her now. Finally the thing unstuck, fell into the canal, and floated there like something dead.

'I bet you don't know what that is!' Lisa crowed from beside her.

'Yes I do,' Kirsty muttered.

'What is it then?'

'It's one of those *condor* things,' Kirsty muttered.

Lisa's laugh was sudden and very loud. 'A *condor*!'

'Well, whatever they're called.' Kirsty's cheeks burned hot with humiliation.

'*CONDOR!*' Lisa shrieked. 'God! You're such a *baby*!'

Kirsty started to walk away again, just like her mum had taught her. *Walk away, don't get into a fight. Walk away.* She made it as far as the gate to the park before she heard Lisa running behind her, telling her to wait up.

'What time is it?' Lisa asked.

'Don't know.'

'I need to know the *time*! I've got a *date*.'

'No you haven't!' Kirsty yelled, all Mum's advice forgotten. 'You *haven't*! You're such a *liar*! And your lies are *stupid*! Everyone think so and that's why you don't have any friends any more except me! You… you *lie like a rug.*'

Lisa dropped the pout, narrowed her eyes. 'I've got lots of friends,' she said quietly.

'No you don't! You've only got me because everyone thinks you're *stupid*! And you *are*!' Never in her life had Kirsty said anything like this to Lisa, or to anyone else for that matter. Throughout their whole friendship there had been a tacit agreement that, while they were equals, Lisa was the most equal.

Lisa's eyes were going a bit red again. She looked like she was going to cry. Still, she tried to summon up a supercilious smile. 'You're jealous 'cause I've got a boyfriend and you haven't.'

'I'm *not*,' Kirsty told her. 'I'm really, really *not*. I don't *want* a boyfriend, and if I did? It wouldn't be someone like Tokki 'cause he's weird and Mo is weird and… you made it all *up* anyway! That ring's from Argos!'

'It's from OMAN!'

'It's from ARGOS!' Kirsty screamed. 'You probably bought it yourself and it's ugly anyway and so are YOU!'

Lisa was weeping now, making noises that might have been words. The wind howled, blew rubbish around her ankles. Kirsty relented, came forward.

'You're not ugly. That was mean.'

Lisa snuffled, kept her face down.

'But the other stuff? About the lying? I'm just saying what's true, Lise. You'll get into trouble if you carry on like this, you know you will. And what if something *does* happen – something bad, and nobody believes you 'cause you lie so much?'

Lisa was still crying. Kirsty took her arm. 'Come on. Let's go home.'

But Lisa didn't want to go home. She swiped angrily at Kirsty's hand, shook herself upright and shouted, 'Fuck *you*!'

No-one said the f-word. Even Marc Maclean in their class didn't say the f-word – and it was rumoured that he had Something Wrong with Him. The only person Kirsty had heard use the f-word was Bryan and he definitely Had Something Wrong with Him. She waited, her mouth a little *O* of shock, for her friend to blink, to realise that the f-word was Going Too Far.

But Lisa didn't do that. They stood, metres apart, the air cooling, the long-threatened rain starting to fall. Then Lisa said it again, softly and with great malice, and Kirsty shouted, 'I hate you!' and she meant it. She hated Lisa's silly face and her crooked teeth and her scary sex talk and her lies and her… She started to run away.

'Kirsty!' Lisa called from behind her. 'You *don't* hate me! We're Best Friends Forever!'

But Kirsty, shocked, pained, full of rage, kept running and didn't look back.

It was raining hard by the time she got home. Mud had oozed into her school shoes. It clung to her insteps and between her toes and she'd run so hard that her sides were aching – a cruel, crushing pain like a too-tight corset. In the walkway to her back door, she paused, bent over, bracing herself against the pebbledash, and retched. Mum was sure to ask questions, and it would be awful.

Fortunately for Kirsty, Sarah was too preoccupied to notice the state she was in. Baby Vicky (still a baby at three) had been a nightmare all day, the washing machine was still playing up, and she was still waiting, with a wailing Vicky clamped under one arm, for The Man to arrive to fix it. With every passing minute, she made mental leaps back and forth from distrust that The Man could fix the washing machine, to outright rage at his future failure. She was so distracted that she didn't ask why Kirsty was so late, or notice how muddy her clothes were.

Kirsty had her bath, scrubbed herself, washed her hair three times and lay for a long time in her bed reading old Enid Blyton books until she felt better. Then she watched *The Secret Garden* while eating a salad cream sandwich. Later, as she was helping Mum load the (apparently fixed) washing machine, the phone rang. It was Denise, Lisa's mum, which was strange, because Sarah and Denise didn't really know each other well, and Denise didn't even have a phone. She must be calling from a phone box or a neighbour's house.

'No, Kirsty got back here at normal time,' Mum was saying, twisting the phone cord around one thin wrist, looking anxiously at the stuttering washing machine. 'Maybe she's at Bryan's place? Kirsty? Did Lisa say anything about going to Bryan's?'

'No,' Kirsty told her truthfully.

'And she walked back with you, didn't she? Through Marne Way?'

'Yes,' Kirsty lied.

'Kids,' Sarah said into the receiver. 'They don't think, do they? She's probably at Bryan's, isn't she? I bet you she'll be there. All right. All right. Bye-bye.'

It was two days later, on Sunday, and they were halfway through dinner when Denise called again, and Kirsty could tell from Mum's face, from how hard her hand gripped the receiver, how her throat flushed red as if it was draining all the blood out of her face, that something was wrong. Lisa hadn't come home all weekend. She wasn't at her dad's and Bryan hadn't seen her. Denise was at the police station now. Could she talk to Kirsty?

Gingerly, Kirsty took the phone from Mum. Denise's voice sounded far away, as if she was at the end of a draughty tunnel. It felt strange to talk to Lisa's mum on the phone, because she'd barely spoken to Lisa's mum in person. Kirsty very rarely went round to their house, and when she did Denise was almost always at work, and Stuart, Lisa's stepdad, would be the person who let them in and then leave them to do whatever they wanted. There was something a bit frightening about that lack of supervision; maybe it was that that had led to Kirsty half-believing all those wild tales about the Omani lodgers…

Denise's voice was whispery, hoarse, as if she'd been shouting. 'You don't know where she is, do you, love?'

'No,' Kirsty answered truthfully. 'I last saw her in the park.'

'The park?' Mum broke in. 'What were you doing in the park? You're not *meant* to go through the park! I *told* you…'

Kirsty kept her eyes closed, but tears still spilled. 'I'm sorry, Mum.'

Denise again: 'Where were you in the park? Kirsty? Tell me, no, listen, don't tell me, tell…' She took her mouth from the receiver. 'What's your name again? Shay? Detective Shay. Talk to him, will you? Tell him everything?'

The policeman was on the phone now. He asked to speak to her mum. Mum listened to him, her mouth set in a tight line, and when she put the phone down, she lit a cigarette, something she rarely did in front of the children.

'You've got to go to the police station now. They'll come and get you.'

They'd come and get her? Kirsty had read the phrase 'frozen with fear' before and always thought it was a bit silly. Now though, that's exactly what she was.

'Are they going to arrest me?' she managed.

'What? God no!' Mum said. 'No, they just want to ask you about the park. What were you doing walking through the park anyway? I told you never to walk through the park.'

'It was only this once,' Kirsty lied.

'Why though? Was it Lisa's idea?'

Kirsty nodded. 'Yes.' It was the truth.

'And why didn't she walk home with you?'

'She said she had a date.' This was the truth too – Lisa had said that, but it was a lie. It had to be, hadn't it? Kirsty's armpits began to trickle. Her chest shuddered.

Mum looked very serious. She pulled Kirsty closer, leaned into her face. 'What did you say?'

'She said she had a date,' Kirsty whispered, 'but I don't think it was true.'

'A date? Like meeting a boy?'

Kirsty nodded.

'Shit.' Mum never swore in front of the kids either, normally. Her face was pale.

'I'm sorry—'

'Never mind that, Kirsty. Are you sure about this? If you are you've got to tell the police, OK? Who was the boy she was meeting?' Mum asked urgently.

'I don't know. She said she was going to marry Tokki? One of the lodgers? But then she said it was a lie and then she said it wasn't and—'

'Jesus Christ, Kirsty! Why didn't you tell me this before?' Mum shouted. Baby Vicky, startled, began to wail. 'This man? Tony?'

'Tokki. He's from Oman—'

'Tokki. Tell the police all about him, all right? Everything she said, tell them!' She was dialling Dad on the phone now, Dad who lived with his new girlfriend on the other side of town; Dad who they rarely saw any more, who Sarah only referred to as 'That waste of space'. Now she was telling him he had to come over right now and take care of the baby… 'I don't *care*, Dave, you've got to have her. Why? Because I've got to go to the police with Kirsty, that's why!'

Later, Dad and baby Vicky stood at the window, watching as Kirsty and Mum climbed into the police car.

'Nice trip! Nice trip!' the baby bellowed, and hit at the window with one sticky fist.

CHAPTER FIVE

Nowadays, a ten-year-old girl would be questioned with their parent, or an appropriate adult. Nowadays, a child would be spoken to in a more informal setting, perhaps with a female officer, but this was 1985, there were no local female officers, and no-one thought to talk to Kirsty in her own home. In the brightly lit reception area, Detective Shay – a large, ruddy man – took her away. He explained to Mum that it would all be fine – 'Just a few questions' – and he smiled, gaze drifting down from Mum towards Kirsty, and almost, almost focusing on her face, but not quite. Mum didn't ask to go with her. In the bright light, under the vague gaze of Detective Shay, her mum seemed to shrink. There was something awful about that – Mum was tough, no-nonsense, she didn't-suffer-fools-gladly and gave-as-good-as-she-got, and here was some man treating her as if she was semi-invisible, as if she already had no say over Kirsty, no power at all. Mum hesitated, smiled, patted Kirsty on the head like a puppy and told her to be a good girl and she'd be waiting out here for her, OK?

Kirsty felt panic well up in her then, and she grabbed at her hand, not wanting to let go and trying not to cry.

'I'm not that bad, am I?' Detective Shay said. 'I'm not that big and scary, am I? Eh? Look, look!' He pushed up Kirsty's chin, and did something inexpert with his face – pushing his nose to make it look as if it had made his tongue stick out, pulling one ear lobe to make the tongue go away. He must think she was a baby. Again his eyes didn't focus on her. It was as if he was watching himself on a TV screen just over her head.

So she dimly registered Mum's little hand squeeze, a squeeze that told her to go with the nice man and not to worry. Then she let her go, walked back to the hard benches.

'I'll be waiting here for you, all right?' And she gave a little wave as Kirsty was led behind the big scarred desk, through some heavy doors, and away into the bowels of the building.

The corridor leading to the interview room smelled of faint bleach and fainter urine. They turned into a small room, painted sickly green, and on the scarred table was a telephone and a big tape recorder – both hearing-aid brown. The scratchy, hessian texture of the too-large chair dimpled her skin all the way through her leggings and her toes didn't reach the floor. This made her feel silly, shy, impossibly young. The big tape recorder hissed loud as a collapsing tyre in the silence. The policeman said something then, it sounded prepared, officious, and full of words that Kirsty didn't really understand, but when he asked if she understood, she nodded.

'Can you speak for the tape, Kirsty?'

She nodded again, blushed, whispered, 'Yes.'

'And can you keep your voice up?'

'Yes?'

And so it began.

*

It was the hiss of the machine that did it. Every time she left a silence, the noise seemed to grow. It embarrassed her – she could imagine the empty gaps on the tape, gaps she was expected to fill with FACTS. She imagined how stupid and brainless she must sound. She imagined all the policemen sitting together, listening to it, shaking their heads at how inarticulate she was. One would ask, 'Does she have Something Wrong Her?' And if they thought she did, then that would give them a reason to send her away from Mum, maybe to a Home for the Handicapped.

'Just tell me about Lisa. Kirsty?'

And so she began to talk. She talked and talked and *talked* about anything and everything to fill the silence. She told Detective Shay about how Lisa wanted to be an air hostess and that she'd swum with dolphins in Majorca even though there weren't any dolphins in Majorca, but Lisa said they must have got lost because they were definitely dolphins because she rode on their backs. But maybe she didn't even go to Majorca anyway. She told him about how desperately Lisa had wanted to be Mary in the school play but Louise Langhorne was picked instead and Lisa cried all afternoon. She told him that Lisa said her house was haunted, because once Bryan had seen a long white hand push itself under the toilet door when he was having a poo. She told them that they were going to live together all their lives and always be best friends and live next door to each other when they were old ladies, and have dogs and... finally, she was stopped.

'Tell me about the park. She was meeting her boyfriend, you said.'

'She said she had a date,' Kirsty whispered. 'I thought she was lying. I got angry with her. We—'

'Who was she meeting? The name?' A touch of impatience.

'I don't know.'

'You do, Kirsty.' He put his glasses on and read something off a sheet of paper. 'Toqueer Al-Balushi?'

'I don't know who that is,' she told him truthfully.

'Tokki. That's what he calls himself. You know him?'

'Yes,' she whispered.

'Toqueer Al-Balushi. Mohammed Oman.' He threw the names down like heavy weights. The tape hissed like a threatening snake. Kirsty felt her heart stutter. 'Do you know them?' Kirsty shook her head. 'You have to speak for the tape, Kirsty.'

'No.'

'But you've met them?'

'No?'

'No?'

'They came to Harvest Festival,' she muttered.

'They came to your school?' He sounded surprised. 'Did the teachers know?'

'I don't know. I don't think so. I mean, they saw them but I don't think they asked why they were there or anything.'

'Tell me about them. Tell me about them and Lisa.'

'I don't want to,' she whispered.

'Why not?'

'I don't want to get Lisa into trouble.'

'Why would talking about them get Lisa into trouble?'

'I don't know.'

'I think you do know.'

'What?'

'Is she with one of them? Kirsty? Has she gone off with one of them? Tokki? Was she meeting him when she disappeared? I know she was, because that's what you told Mrs Cook, wasn't it?'

'I said she was meeting her boyfriend. I didn't say it was Tokki though. And I think maybe she was making it all up anyway—'

'Did you see him in the park?'

'No.'

'Are you sure?'

'Yes.'

His eyebrows raised, his back stiffened. She'd disappointed him. She'd said the wrong thing.

'Well, we'll come back to that. Kirsty, I want you to tell me about Tokki, about what Lisa told you about him. You've got to tell me everything, without being silly about it, or I won't be able to help, OK?'

And so she started telling him what they wanted to know. She stopped prefacing things with 'She was making it up' or 'She was lying' because that's not what they wanted to hear. They wanted to hear everything Lisa had said and hinted at, about the engagement, about being princesses, about S.E.X. Kirsty told them everything, things she didn't understand, things she only half remembered, things she only thought she remembered after the questions made it clear what they wanted her to remember. It all poured into the tape recorder and when the press got hold of some of the things she'd supposedly said, they made headlines.

Tragic Tot Told 'You're My Wife', Given Booze

Missing Girl Shared BED with 'Prince'
Lisa Cook 'Watched Video Nasties with Lodger'

Detective Shay told her that she was being a Good Friend by Telling the Truth. He kept lollies in his desk drawer and gave them as rewards whenever she told him something he said was Useful, and Kirsty wanted to be Useful. *You want her to come home, don't you?* Of course she wanted Lisa to come home. But every day Mum walked her to school with Baby Vicky in the pushchair, kissed her goodbye, and watched anxiously as Kirsty walked stiff-legged into the playground where the other kids stayed in distant eddies and stared at her. Her classmates kept a distance that they probably believed was respectful, but instead made her feel infected, alien, and so very lonely. She couldn't wait to see Mum and Baby Vicky waiting at the gates every day at home time – couldn't wait to feel Vicky's sticky hand on her face, see Mum's kind smile. They were the only people who wanted to be close to her, it seemed.

'They'll find her,' Mum said. 'They'll find her and everything will be all right.'

'Will it?'

'I promise it will. I'll make sure it is.'

She believed her. Mum could do anything. All they had to do was find Lisa, and everything would be all right. As soon as Lisa was back, everything would be back to normal.

*

A week later the news said that Lisa's coat had been found. The man on the TV said it was by the canal.

'They searched that canal though,' Mum muttered to herself. 'How'd they miss it?'

'Her coat?' Kirsty felt excited. If they'd found her coat then they'd found Lisa; she kept the notebook with the details of 'Angels Times Two' in her pocket, and there was no way she'd be careless enough to lose that. 'Is she back home?'

And Mum had looked pitying, infinitely sad. 'Not yet, love,' she said.

That week was the last time Kirsty sat in that now familiar room, facing the hissing brown tape recorder. Detective Shay was there along with another man who told her he was Detective Chief Inspector Lepp. They smiled but there were no lollipops, and their attention strayed to the door, to the notes handed in after a respectful knock at the door. These notes commanded the same interest that Kirsty used to. There was a commotion outside. A crowd. It sounded like market day, or a small crowd watching fireworks, except there were no oohs and ahhs. Another note, and one of the detectives turned off the tape recorder and they left the room without telling her why. When they came back they were wearing expressions of grim cheer, while outside, the crowd noise had coalesced into coherence, chants, shouting and Kirsty heard someone say the c-word… the *bad* c-word. Her face flushed with embarrassment but neither detective seemed to have noticed. They muttered something to each other, turned to her. Detective Lepp put one hand near to the tape recorder, but didn't turn it on.

'We've got him,' he told her.

'Who?'

'Toqueer.' His smile widened and Kirsty wished it hadn't because his teeth were awful, big and long and brown as a rotten apple. 'You don't have to be scared of him any more.'

'I'm not scared of him,' Kirsty whispered.

'You don't have to be scared any more, because we've got him.' He went on smoothly, 'But we can only keep him here, and keep you *safe*, if you do the right thing and tell us when you saw him in the park, where he was, what he said, if anything? You're going to do the right thing by your friend, OK?'

'I didn't see him at the park though.'

He looked annoyed. 'You did. You told us so.'

'Did I?'

'Yes.' His face was grim. 'The date? You told us she was meeting him. Now's not the time to start playing with us.' His teeth were out again, but not in a smile, more of a grimace. 'Think of your friend, Kirsty. Think of her and tell us what we need to know.'

He paused, fished in his pocket, found a pack of lollies. 'I know you're scared – here, have this, it's the last one!' He smiled. She smiled back, took the sweet. 'You're a good girl, Kirsty. You just have to do this one last thing and then everyone will know how useful you've been. OK?'

'OK.' Kirsty felt dazed at his sudden gentleness.

'Now, don't eat that lolly until afterwards, I don't want you crunching all the way through the interview!' His face told her that he was making a joke. She made her face respond in kind.

'Good girl. Right, here we go,' he said then, and pressed record.

*

DCI Lepp: Was there anyone else in the park? A man?

KC: Yes.

DCI Lepp: And what colour skin did the man have?

KC: Dark.

DCI Lepp: And did you recognise him?

KC: I don't know. I think so.

DCI Lepp: And who was he, do you think?

KC: Tokki.

DCI Lepp: Toqueer Al-Balushi?

KC (crying): Yes.

DCI Lepp: And where did you see him standing?

KC: By the gate?

DCI Lepp: The gates of the park? The main gates on Queen Street or…

KC: The little gate, by Kwik Save.

DCI Lepp: And did Lisa see him?

KC: I'm not sure.

DCI Lepp: Think hard, Kirsty. She was meeting her boyfriend, you told us that, so did she see him? Walk over to him?

KC I think she did.

DCI Lepp: You think, or you know?

KC: Yes, she did.

DDCI Lepp: Do you know what time it was when you saw him?

KC: No.

DDCI Lepp: You'd been in the park for a while, so what time was it, do you think? About five?

KC: I don't know.

DCI Lepp: Because there are two young ladies who say they saw you and Lisa in the park at four forty-five, and they saw Tokki at the little gate a few minutes later. Do you remember those young ladies? They remember you.

KC: What?

DCI Lepp: They saw you both, and then they passed Tokki just before the Kwik Save gate. They saw him go into the park. Did you see them?

KC: Yes.

DCI Lepp: Do you think you left Lisa at about five?

KC I think so.

DCI Lepp: We need you to be sure on this, Kirsty.

KC: Yes, five, because I heard the clock strike.

DCI Lepp: So if you said you saw him at five, and you know it was five because the clock struck. Kirsty? You have to speak up for the tape? Here, blow your nose. Better? Do you need to take a break? No? OK – so you saw Toqueer Al-Balushi in the park sometime between four forty-five and five. You saw Lisa approach him. Then you left, yes?

KC (crying): Yes.

DCI Lepp: And why did you leave?

KC: I was scared. I was cold and scared and I wanted to go home. I want to go home now. Can I go home now?

Kirsty couldn't remember seeing any girls in the park, but after a while she started to think that maybe she *could*. Both detectives were very very concerned that she remember, and so she (almost) did. And if those big girls saw Tokki in the park, then he *must* have been there, he had to have been. And so, he was – logic dictated it. Both the big girls and the police thought it, and they would know, wouldn't they? And if they had Tokki, they had Lisa! Maybe they'd eloped or something, but surely she'd be back at school tomorrow, or certainly by next week, and they'd be best friends again, and Angels Times Two would still happen, and…

'Can I go home now?' she asked again.

Detective Lepp turned off the tape recorder. Then he laughed as if she'd made a deliberate joke. 'Yes, you can go home now.'

'And when can I see Lisa? Is she here or is she at home?'

Both men's faces closed. They didn't answer, and she thought she'd said something wrong. When she was handed over to Mum in reception they asked for a quiet word. Kirsty saw them in the corner, watched Mum's shoulders stiffen, then nod rapidly, jerkily. When she turned she kept her head down. She was crying, Kirsty could tell. They left through the back entrance ('Why the back entrance?' 'Because there's a crowd out front.' 'Why?' No answer) and got into a waiting taxi. Mum held her hand very tight all the way home, and didn't speak, so after a while neither did Kirsty.

At home the silence carried on. Kirsty began to feel that she'd committed some terrible error that she couldn't yet fathom, but asking about it would only make it worse, and so she allowed herself to be bathed, dressed in fleecy pyjamas and tucked into bed, just like a baby, and she returned Mum's long, tight hug and said goodnight, thinking that maybe tomorrow she'd understand what she'd done wrong.

CHAPTER SIX

Kirsty woke confused. The room was too light, it was late – it was ten o'clock in the morning! She'd be late for school! Baby Vicky was on the landing, her face pressed up against the bars of the stair gate.

'Mum sad.' She grinned.

And Kirsty could hear Mum crying now, all the way from the living room. She managed to open the gate and escort Baby Vicky down the stairs, place her on her rocking horse and then hovered in the doorway, staring miserably at Mum until she was noticed, wordlessly beckoned over and again given that tight, almost suffocating hug.

'You all right, my darling?' Mum choked.

'What's happened? Why aren't I at school?'

'He just confessed.' Mum took a long, shuddery breath, moved away slightly, wiped her eyes on her sleeve. 'They just called me.'

Things went very still then. Who had confessed? And what exactly did 'confessed' mean? Was it a sickness?

'What? Who?'

'That bastard lodger of theirs. The police just called me.' She wiped her face and took Baby Vicky into the kitchen, put her in her high chair in front of the telly. Back in the living room she closed the door, sat next to Kirsty, took her hand. 'He won't tell them what he did with her,' she said softly, but with anger. 'That's what they said. He's playing about with them.'

'Playing?' An absurd, almost funny picture entered Kirsty's mind of Tokki and Lisa playing jump-rope in the park. She giggled, a slightly hysterical yip of a sound, and her heart pounded, her face flushed.

'But where's Lisa been then? Is she going to school today?'

Mum kept her face still, as if she was angry. 'No.'

A pause. 'Where is she then?'

'She's dead. He killed her.'

Sarah never forgave herself for the bald, brutal way she'd broken the news. She was angry, scared, bitter, in shock, but that shouldn't have mattered; the only thing that should have mattered was Kirsty. And when Kirsty began to scream, and later lay, rigid and blank, still in her pyjamas, Sarah – too late – hugged and kissed and cajoled her daughter, all the while knowing that she had made a terrible thing worse.

Kirsty herself didn't remember much of the next few days. Her only recollections were vague, dream-like montages of fear and tears and sudden, frozen calm. She seemed to be the small, dead star around which chaos orbited: Mum talking talking talking, alternately chatting about nothing and obsessing on the one thing that mattered: thank god it wasn't you! And it *could* have been you, that's what I keep thinking, it could have been *you*! Did he do anything to you, anything? Even a little kiss… or… anything? Dad walking from room to room, arms hanging uselessly, eyes reddened. The phone calling calling calling. The curtains drawn all day. She was brave. She was so brave, they kept saying that. It was all down to her that Tokki had been arrested! It was all down to her being brave and telling the truth and… This last was the only thing that eventually got through, pierced the numbness. Kirsty tried to remember what a good thing she'd done. She tried to feel brave. She told herself that the worst was over. Mum told her that. The police had told her that. And adults always told the truth.

*

Tokki had been found sleeping rough behind King's Cross station. Word spread quickly enough that a joyful crowd was already waiting at the police station, keeping their spirits up by jeering at every vehicle they saw pulling into the car park, just in case Tokki was in it. When he finally did arrive, the police were thoughtful enough to draw the crowd's attention by putting a pillowcase over his head, and their joy deepened as they screamed, pushed, spat. A couple of little girls were hoisted onto their parents' shoulders. One of them – a blonde cherub who couldn't be older than four – had been coached by her dad to shout at his command, and as Tokki was led to the door, her little piping lisp rose high and sweet over the shouts. 'Go back to the jungle!' and everyone laughed, pinched her cheeks, called her a little madam – 'Out of the mouths of babes, eh?' – while her dad flushed with pride.

That was the commotion Kirsty heard while she was being questioned by Detective Lepp, Tokki was being led to his holding cell just as Kirsty was being shown the back door. They were only metres apart.

And he did confess to the murder, right away – or so they thought. He was contrite, tearful, he begged forgiveness. He hadn't meant to make a mistake and he shouldn't have run. It was only when he registered the number of questions they seemed to be asking about his landlady's little girl that he stopped apologising and merely smiled politely, uncomprehendingly. Because nobody thought to arrange for a translator, they reached an impasse; the police thought he was being obstinate, playing with them, refusing to tell them what he'd done with her. Tokki, mired in confusion, waited for more clues. What did this girl have to do with an expired student visa?

When a classmate had told him that the police were looking for him, he assumed it was because he hadn't updated his visa. He made his way to London with a view to going back home to his mum in

Oman – and that was as far as his plan went. He had no money, and a shaky understanding of English. When he was eventually found, scared, hungry, sleep-deprived, he was relieved, so happy to be out of the cold that he went willingly with the police, eager to make amends for 'the bad thing' he did. In the station he'd nodded through the interview, said sorry, even cried, asked for absolution, but of course, he had no idea what he was really admitting to. It was only, finally, when they showed him a picture of his landlady's little girl, said the word 'DEAD', that he realised just how bad things were, but of course by that time he'd already said he was 'very bad man' that he 'make mistake' that he 'deserve the bad' and by then it was too late. He stopped speaking altogether then, sat silent and shaking, only offering a nervous, terrified smile that quickly made its way into the headlines as 'The Smirk of a Killer!' Once, on the way back from questioning, an impatient, disgusted constable hit him hard on the back of the neck with his truncheon, telling him he'd better start talking about that poor lass he killed, and Tokki swung one ineffectual punch back, which proved what everyone knew already: he was dangerous. A man with no limits.

*

Nobody could have predicted how big this story would become, what it tapped into and just how much people wanted to *talk*. This was a small city in a disregarded area; the industry that had once underpinned it, that had swelled it to city size in the first place, was in its death throes, and bringing everything down with it. The Victorian terraces, built to house workers for factories that no longer existed, stood in decaying rows like bad teeth, and relatively recently built estates like Beacon Hill, which had been optimistically designed to accommodate yet more workers, were now merely slums in the making. When the core of the community was ripped out, bad things filled the gap. Most of them were depressingly ordinary outrages – rapes, burglary, the odd spot of arson, all the old favourites – and this city had more than its fair share of them, but now it also had something special – it had a straightforward Good vs Evil Child Murder, and it had an energising effect on the locals. Because the murderer wasn't One of Them, it was an easy case to follow and wallow in with no grey areas, no room for doubt. Even before he'd been found and arrested, the public's mind was made up: Toqueer Al-Balushi was a killer. Even the fact that there was no body was OK; he'd crack eventually and tell the police where he'd put her. No-one doubted that. In the meantime they could undo their moral buckles and let all those luxurious prejudices flop out… They weren't *racialist* but that college was an accident waiting to happen… never wanted to mix, never *wanted* to fit in, and *I swear to god I saw one of them eating a baked potato with his hands! I smelled curry on my* Woman's Own*!*

It was exciting that this worst nightmare came true. It was exciting to talk to journalists, exciting to see your street on the news, to peer over the sober shoulders of reporters and wave at the camera. It was exciting to know that you lived somewhere where things still happened, and this excitement ran through the city like electricity through a corpse, until everything was permitted, anything could be said, anyone could be listened to.

Throughout all this, Kirsty was supposed to be kept safe. Mum told her she'd be safe and her name was meant to be a secret. The *fact* of her was meant to be a secret, but secrets can't be kept in a place like that, not when the sudden light of publicity turned on its glare, and stayed long enough to burn. As soon as the neighbours saw the police car outside her house, they jumped to conclusions… What if that little girl had done something? They watched her walk out of the front door, only just visible between uniformed bulk, and thought, 'What does she know?' They watched her mother following behind, head down as if ashamed, and wondered what *she* knew. Someone swore they'd seen handcuffs on Sarah's wrists! And calls were made – to sons and daughters who'd moved away, to old friends, distant family… 'Whatever's happening you're not getting the full story from the papers, I'll tell you *that*… that girl knows *something*…' and soon Kirsty's name was an airborne virus, and after Tokki was arrested, all bets were off. Kirsty was the last person to see Lisa alive, and there were plenty of reporters who wanted to know everything about her – sudden, interested strangers who scribbled shorthand in notebooks and asked just the right questions to get just the right story.

The police failed to protect Kirsty, not from malice but from ineptitude; they were simply out of their depth.

But that's an explanation, not an excuse.

*

Bryan became the first stop for national journalists. Loquacious, energetic, angry, he would talk to and at anyone, he enjoyed posing for pictures and had no scruples about spilling family secrets. It was Bryan who gave them family photos, and let them into Denise's home while she was out, allowing them to take photos of Lisa's bedroom, Tokki and Mohammed's room ('Only One Thin Wall Between Tragic Tot and Killer!'). They took pictures of Lisa's Care Bear collection, her never-used roller skates in the wardrobe, the small, lipsticked kisses smeared around a picture of George Michael she'd cut out from *Look-in* magazine, and all on the promise of fifty quid. Bryan – for a while – was perfect source material.

Bryan outlived his usefulness quite quickly though. He gave away everything too soon and exhausted his small value. That first fifty pounds was all he made, but rather than get angry at the journalists, he turned his bewildered rage on Kirsty. That girl, she was hiding something! *She* was the one who got Lisa into this, ask her, *ask* her! Perhaps it was an attempt to stay relevant, part of the story, or maybe that was crediting him with more cunning than he had. Either way, the press did indeed turn from Bryan to Kirsty, and this made him madder still, in both senses of the word.

The press were nice about Kirsty at first. The received wisdom was that she, too, must have been sexually abused. She should be respected, cared for, given time. One 'expert' from the *News of the World* 'reached out' to her and her family, saying that the paper would pay for counselling. Sarah – mindful of the police's guidance – didn't respond to that or to any requests for interviews, but this silence was interpreted as coldness, as arrogance. This family weren't grateful enough! What were they hiding? The public deserved to know! Kirsty went from victim to assumed perpetrator in a series of editorial meetings on Fleet Street… It no longer mattered that she was as much a child as the missing girl. Being dead afforded you a respect that being alive, and stubbornly silent, didn't.

Thanks to Bryan, they knew where she lived and they thought they knew just what to ask her – *Kirsty, why didn't you tell anyone about the abuse? Kirsty? Did she cry when she told you? Kirsty? Kirsty! We deserve to know!* And Kirsty would keep her head down, shield her face, not say a word as she struggled out of the front door. They were outside the school holding pictures, shouting, *Is this the coat Lisa was wearing when she was killed?* Waving a photo of them both, arms around each other, dressed for last year's school disco. *Was it this coat, Kirsty? Was she wearing a coat, Kirsty? Was she wearing any knickers, Kirsty? Why won't you talk, Kirsty? It doesn't make you look like a good friend if you don't talk, Kirsty! Don't you even care?*

The teachers tried to break it up, failed. The local police were stretched too thin. Parents complained and Miss Farnell called Kirsty and her mum into her office to say that maybe she should stay at home for the next few weeks? All this, it was disruptive for the other pupils, surely she could understand? And so Kirsty lost the only respite she'd had. They were outside the house and the neighbours complained, shouted. The shouting proved to the journalists that Kirsty lived in a 'violent area' ('As if it is!' Sarah said. 'We own our houses round here! If you want violence, go to Beacon Hill!') while the neighbours blamed Sarah and Kirsty for the intrusion, even while they made mugs of tea for the journalists and let them use their toilets.

All they could do was endure it. Kirsty couldn't leave the house and neither could Mum. She did her practical best, mixing and matching metaphors with increasing desperation: 'We'll just hunker down and weather the storm.' 'It'll all be water under the bridge by tomorrow.' 'Today's newspapers are tomorrow's chip wrappers. And next year it'll be forgotten.' Like most promises made by anxious parents to frightened children, it almost, but never fully, came true; Kirsty never, ever, truly recovered. She'd been pushed off the main road of her life, thrown into some muddy, interminable lay-by, she'd lost momentum, she was too injured. At the time though, she nodded when her Mum told her that nothing lasts forever… 'Give it a month, a few months, a year…', 'You won't always feel like this; time is kind; time is the best healer.' Tomorrow Kirsty would wake up and Lisa would be the second thing she thought of; another day she would be the third or fourth thing. And one, magical, mystical day, What Happened to Lisa simply wouldn't pop up at all, and Kirsty would know she was healed. 'It will happen, my love. I promise.'

Kirsty believed it. She was young enough to still believe then.

CHAPTER SEVEN

Toqueer Al-Balushi was charged with the murder of Lisa Jade Cook, to which he pleaded not guilty, but seeing as he'd already confessed, that made no difference at all. The police let it be known that they now suspected him to be involved in the murder of another little girl – Tracy Spellar – in a neighbouring county a year earlier. Her body *had* been found, cut in two neat slices and buried by the railway lines. The police pressed him to confess and fully expected him to do so, but he never did and he rescinded his confession to Lisa's murder.

Of course, Mohammed, who had also been targeted by the press in those early days, had the presence of mind to distance himself as far as he could from his friend. Tokki was merely an acquaintance, they weren't in the same class at Marlborough House and didn't see much of each other because, unlike Tokki, Mohammed was a Good Muslim, a Sunni who attended prayers daily and volunteered at a local youth group. He made sure to mention that he had been at the house every minute of that fateful weekend, even forgoing prayers, in order to support Denise – a good woman, his English mother. Just before he left the country, he gave one grave interview to the *Mirror* which appeared under the headline 'Beatings, Torture "Normal" in Child Killer's Secretive "Cult" claims classmate!' – in which he threw Tokki even further under the bus. 'He is Ibadi Muslim. They are different. They do things which we true Muslims could not abide. I am glad he has confessed and I hope he has asked forgiveness from Allah also.'

Tokki's confession and Mohammed's careful approaches to the press should have made Denise's life a little better, but they didn't. Ever since she'd had a phone line installed – the police told her to do it so they could get in touch with her 'if anything happened' – it rang endlessly and was rarely the police, but strangers who hated her, who hissed at her. Notes were shoved under her door. Twice someone posted shit through the letterbox and once someone set fire to the backyard. 'Nigger Lover' was spray-painted on the side of the house and both her dogs disappeared and were found later in the scrubland outside Beacon Hill, mutilated, their collars placed neatly next to their little corpses, the address still visible on the blood-flecked ID disc. Denise was spat at in the street, followed by cars. It seemed that people hated her more than they hated the man who'd killed her daughter. She'd let him in, after all, taken his money, let him do god knows what to her little girl.

It was another violent attack that seemed to have put an end to Denise's torture. In June, Marlborough House was firebombed, the remaining international students fled, and the place burned solidly for two hours before the fire service ambled up. Each day, as the bricks cooled and the scorched grass powdered, the calls, the notes, the threats lessened, and eventually ceased. Like a cast of some Pompeiian corpse, the blackened hulk of the building crouched on the edge of Beacon Hill, and over the years it crumbled, but remained. Much like Denise herself. Kirsty wasn't so lucky.

Long after the press had abandoned the town, Bryan trailed her, suddenly popping up from behind bushes, lurching out from alleyways to scream, and shout, and chase her. Sometimes he just stared. Stared and spat obliquely at her, never hitting her, but making sure he made her flinch. A few times he'd thrown rocks – sharp, flinty rocks, as big as a bird's egg – and he was a good aim. One of them smashed her forehead open and she'd stumbled home, blind with blood, claiming to have fallen. Mum didn't ask her any questions, just drove her to casualty, where she was stitched up and told to be more careful. She still had a scar.

Kirsty couldn't fathom this hatred. She'd never met him before. All she knew about him was that he got into fights and Denise had thrown him out as soon as he turned sixteen, and since then he'd lived in a squat near the station. He had a shaved head, wore Doc Martens and hung about with skinheads in the park, drinking Special Brew. Bryan had attended the same primary school as his sister, and he still hung over the place like smog. Tales were told about how he'd thrown a chair at Mr Wolverson, and how he'd nailed a dead frog to the bonnet of Miss Farnell's car (it was rumoured that she was French, and that was enough for Bryan). Once he called Mrs Butler a rotten old bitch. The tables were still scarred with his vividly misspelled graffiti. Bryan got his first professional tattoo at thirteen – a smudgy British Bulldog wearing boxing gloves. It joined the rest of his clumsy body art – an ear crookedly pierced with a darning needle, a couple of scratchy swastikas on his hands. But that's all he was – a vaguely thrilling myth, a 'Bad Lot'.

When Bryan wasn't torturing Kirsty, he was outside Denise's house. She still didn't let him in, so he'd position himself on the opposite side of the street and rant, throwing rocks and cans at her front door, screaming, wheedling, or merely staring at the curtained windows in silence. Before long he took his show on the road so the whole town had a front-row seat… he was in the park, in the pubs, in the streets, dashing about in a crook-backed speed-walk, rage seeming to pump out in his wake like a hateful exhaust pipe.

People complained about him – not only Denise's neighbours, but shopkeepers tired of his disruptive antics taking away trade. The police would arrive then and tell him to move it, but they didn't arrest him. There was a tacit feeling that Bryan – though undeniably a terrible human being – had been further unhinged by loss. Lisa's murder was his get-out-of-jail-free card, and he should be put up with. Even Sarah seemed to agree: 'Not the sharpest tool in the box. Never has been. You've got to feel sorry for him really. After what happened. He'll calm down eventually.' But Kirsty knew different. She knew Bryan was mad. Not angry-mad, but crazy-mad, and where adults saw a wounded animal that would heal, Kirsty saw dangerous insanity that could never heal. Children understand the madness of other children, they know that it's untethered from life experience, common sense, and the only thing on your side was their deficiencies – their lack of care and attention to propriety, their lack of subtlety. These were the things that attracted the censure of adults, and that censure was the only thing that would stop them killing you.

Bryan carried on haunting her. When she went to secondary school, the phantom of his hate, along with the uneasy interest of her new classmates, changed her from a normal little girl to a frightened, dark-faced ghost. She had no friends and she didn't want any either... look what happened to her last friend. Sometimes she couldn't get out of bed, couldn't face going to school and could she stay at home and look after Baby Vicky, please? But Baby Vicky would be going to school soon. Time was moving on, things were changing. The only thing that wasn't changing was Kirsty.

Later, she could see an ironic corollary between herself and Bryan: they were both, in their own ways, trapped by what had happened, like a bug in hardening sap. At least Kirsty eventually left town. Over the next few years, Bryan watched as his compatriots moved on, grew up, matured, while he stayed exactly the same. After a while he was only able to command the attention and respect of those far younger and arguably even stupider than him, but even these cronies, too, outgrew him. Not a month went by without him appearing in the court section of the local paper, but his crimes crossed the line of pathos from violence to necessity. Shoplifting alcohol and ready-made sandwiches from Tesco Metro, aggressive begging, non-payment of court fines.

Kirsty didn't witness this latter first-hand though. By the summer of 1986, Sarah had spent more than a year watching her daughter getting stripped to the bone by gossips, conspiracy theorists and aggressive well-wishers, grimly waiting for it to pass, but now she'd had enough. She made the decision to move, move far away. It would be Kirsty's best chance to get over 'that business'. It was only much later, when Kirsty was an adult herself, that she fully fathomed how hard this must have been; Sarah had left her own settled life in a city she herself was born in, to give Kirsty this chance. However meagre the support she received from her ex-husband was, it was still *something*, and Sarah had nothing to go to – no family, no friends, no job, but she refused to let any of that faze her; Kirsty had to be Safe. End of story.

'And you can still see your dad in the holidays. Hop on the train? It'll be exciting!'

And that did happen, once or twice, before Dad receded too, consumed by his own – new – family who didn't welcome Kirsty and weren't shy about letting her know. Sarah tried hard to hide the angry phone calls during which she remonstrated with him, shed angry tears, until finally Kirsty told her not to bother any more. 'You're the only parent I need, Mum; I don't even know him.' It was designed to make Sarah happy, but it was also true. Sarah was big and brave enough to – almost – fill any shadowy gap.

Down south, Kirsty's accent caused giggles, so she learned to change it, lengthen her vowels and use different slang. She made some friends, called herself Kirsten. Baby Vicky became Victoria, Mum could answer the phone without fear, and there were no more notes. Life was better, it became, often, good. But despite all this, Kirsty never felt fully safe again. She was still trapped, partially living in the past, in the shadows of half memory.

One day, when she was about fourteen, she was suffering through an especially dull school assembly led by the local vicar, when one phrase wiggled out of his pious drone and into her mind: *The truth will set you free.* This pairing of truth and freedom was something she'd never thought of before; after all, experience had taught her that truth was cloudy, frightening, slippery, something that adults were better stewards of than children. Now though, the older she got, the more doubts she had… The way she thought about it now, it was obvious that the police had been under pressure to get an arrest, and they'd known who they *wanted* to arrest, they just needed a reason. Kirsty had provided the reason and had been coached and cajoled into strengthening their case. After Tokki retracted his confession it had become clear that everything was precariously based on what Kirsty had told them which was based in turn on what Lisa had told her – these breathless tales of stolen kisses and forbidden love, of princesses and jewels, had been translated as grooming, as abuse. But that didn't mean it was true, did it? Why would Lisa being engaged to Tokki be true, when the swimming with dolphins and the uncle with a private plane wasn't? How could the police happily consign some things into a bin marked 'Fantasy' while others – equally bizarre – were treated as absolute truth? Adults in authority were fallible, it seemed. But what if they were worse than fallible? What if they were corrupt?

There was another side to the case that so far she'd never seen. Tokki was black and foreign and Muslim. In a city that was predominantly white, English and (arguably) Christian, he, and all the other students from Marlborough House, stuck out. Looking back, there had been no black kids in Kirsty's school, no black teachers, and before she'd had that brief, strangled conversation with the lodgers, she'd never spoken to anyone of colour in her life. Outside of Lenny Henry and Floella Benjamin there weren't even any black faces on TV. For the first time Kirsty started to see the whole thing through the prism of race. How much of Lisa's fascination with the lodgers had been based on their novelty, and how much of the things she'd said about them had come entirely from her imagination and half-heard comments about Lusty Africans? How much of the hysteria surrounding the case had come from the same thing? She remembered the little blonde girl shouting, 'Go back to the jungle, you baboon!' At the time it had been the word 'cunt' that had shocked her; the racism had slid by almost unnoticed. That was the way things were in that time and place. Had the police ever seriously thought of finding and charging anyone else? The town had its fair share of violent men, but had the police asked her any questions at all that hadn't centred on Tokki? And where did that leave her? Even though she'd left that stagnant gene pool of a place, she'd never, ever questioned its narrative. And that made her culpable. Worse, it made her responsible.

So she started trawling through the detritus of her memory like a clear-eyed detective searching for the little shards of truth, hoping to catch enough to put them together like a shattered mirror, do what the police should have done and, in the process, free herself from guilt. She began keeping a case file.

Using the cumbersome microfiche machine in the library, she went through old newspaper reports on the case, copied everything as it was written and glued her notes neatly in a scrapbook. She photocopied maps of the area, of the park, the canal, Beacon Hill estate. She took the very few photographs she still had of herself and Lisa, covered them carefully with sticky plastic, and pinned them onto the pages, like frail moths. Eventually the scrapbook became so large and unwieldy that it had to be reorganised, then split into two, then three, then four. Later still she kept her notes on floppy disk and now, after more than twenty years, these voluminous files were all stored on a cloud… suitable for something dead and gone that still hovered over her and wasn't going anywhere.

CHAPTER EIGHT

In June 1986, Tokki made his first suicide attempt by taking apart a toilet cistern, sharpening the siphon lever into a crude knife and jabbing it into his neck. The wound was superficial, but it led to headlines, an enquiry into prison safety and, inevitably, an upsurge in public interest into the Lisa Cook case. That same week, the two girls who'd claimed that they saw Tokki in the park when Lisa disappeared now said they weren't sure they'd seen him after all. Maybe it was another black man? Or maybe not even a black man at all?

The following March, Tokki mounted his first appeal, which failed. Then, a few years later, also in March, Lisa's father died – 'of a broken heart!' screamed the *Sun* – though actually of alcohol-induced liver disease that pre-dated Lisa's disappearance. Her stepfather, Stuart, who had been more of a father to her than him, died only two years later, leaving Denise alone.

A decade later, there was that mini-series based on the case. Bryan told the papers he'd sue the production company over the depiction of his sister ('They made her out to be a slut!') and Tokki ('He was portrayed like an African saint when we all know he's a paedophile and a murderer. It's PC gone mad!') but predictably his threat went nowhere. Later still, when DNA analysis became more reliable, Tokki was definitely ruled out as a suspect in the murder of Tracy Spellar, the girl by the railway tracks, and his legal team pushed again for the Lisa Cook case to be reopened. The request was refused, but now, with the advent of the internet, the case was starting to be discussed and picked over by the public again. In this pre-social-media universe, the Lisa Cook case lurked first on Area 51 in Geocities, along with alien sightings and Bigfoot cover-ups; it popped up on ghoulish AltaVista searches, on primitive blogs – one of which, much later, became DarkHearts.com, a site that Kirsty, like many others, became obsessed with. They wanted to get to the truth, and so did she. But what she hadn't been prepared for was just how much of her life was on there, some of which she'd never seen before.

There she was in her pretty pink coat, leaving the police station – in the picture the coat was grey, smeared with thumbprints of over-handling. Who had cut this picture out of the paper, and kept it close enough to handle this frequently? Who had thought this picture was important enough to share with the world now? Here she was getting in the van on the day they finally moved away – it must have been taken with a long lens from across the street. Had one of the neighbours taken it, hoping to sell it? Old Mr Hyde? The Johnsons who used to give her sweets at Christmas? There was a photo of her outside the house Down South. She was in her new school uniform, nervously squint-smiling at the camera. Who could have sold that picture but Dad? She almost called him, before remembering that she didn't have his new number. There she was with Lisa on their joint eighth birthday party, arm in arm, standing on tiptoes as if they were ballerinas. There they were up a tree – blurred in dungarees, half hidden in the leaves. When was this? Where was this? Bryan must have sold these. It seemed that Dark Hearts owned pieces of her she never knew she'd had. She wanted them back.

Her research wasn't nostalgic, it was painful, even masochistic. Lee told her it wasn't good for her, he'd been saying that from the very first time they met, and he was right. Lee was always looking out for her. He was the best thing that had ever happened to her. Thank god for Lee.

*

They had met nearly ten years ago at some godawful party Victoria (who now insisted on being called Vic) had thrown to celebrate… celebrate what? It could have been anything – a stair carpet, a new coat, the apocalypse… Vic, in those days, threw a party on any pretext, and they were always messy affairs. Without fail, there would be flaming sambuca shots, knots of sweaty fools, giggling over their NutraSweet-cut cocaine in the toilet, and by the early hours the bath would be splattered with vomit, the floor would be littered with broken glass, possibly a broken bone or two. These parties were devilish! Oh, they were messy/crazy/not-to-be-missed, and Kirsty hated them. She only went along because – well, she had to, didn't she? She had her role to play, Vic needed keeping an eye on… Mum had made her promise.

Both sisters lived in London by then. Kirsty was working at Lambeth Social Services in Child Protection and Vic had followed her to the city, beginning a hospitality course at Metropolitan University, only to drop out halfway through the first year. Now she worked as an estate agent in property management, but had her eye on moving to sales. She wanted to snag one of those Mini Coopers they gave to top sellers. She'd already snagged someone else's husband – a peaceable, pliable stockbroker called Ollie, who doted on her as if she was some rare, exotic pet.

Sarah doted on her too. Perhaps because she'd been so small when all 'that business' had happened, Vic was untainted with pain. Sarah could look at Vic and know she had no hard, ill-judged words to regret, nothing to look back on and think, 'That's where I failed.' And so Vic inhabited the one sentimental spot in Sarah's no-nonsense, practical mind, and she had to be swaddled at all times. When Vic moved to London, Sarah told Kirsty often to 'Make sure she's not too daft. Make sure she eats, keep an eye on her, will you?' Sarah must have been ill by then, but it wasn't her nature to talk about her fears or feelings to doctors or daughters.

Kirsty only found out about the cancer when it was terminal, after Vic had married Ollie, and Sarah no longer needed to worry about her. In those earlier days though, Kirsty took her promise seriously. She made sure to meet Vic for drinks, first with her gaggle of student friends, and later with her ghastly colleagues from the estate agency, who were all blonde, all called silly things like Allegra, Clarissa or Thea, all conspicuously richer and more sophisticated than Vic. She had answered the phone at two a.m. and spent hours talking her drunken sister out of calling her latest ex (they all had silly names too: Harrison, Taylor, Tobias). She went to Vic's parties, put in her hour or two of subtle supervision, and left before the glass started breaking.

Kirsty arrived at the party expecting exposed wires and rubble, or at least a bit of 1970s linoleum, but it was already fairly immaculate with big blank windows, shiny wood floors. Very grown-up. There were fewer trust-fund Clarissas there, more normal people, old enough to worry about keeping the babysitter up if they stayed too long. Ollie's influence, she presumed. Vic herself was all kitsch suburban chic – decked out in an unfamiliar vintage dress, with a nipped-in waist and lace Peter Pan collar. Still, after a while, once the drink started flowing, she shook off a lot of that poise, and soon she was wheeling out the sambuca and pushing back the furniture so she could execute a clumsy forward-roll just like the old days. The music was turned up. Vic announced a dance-off in the hall, started organising teams. Usually that would be Kirsty's cue to slip away, but it was only ten o'clock, and Vic would see her trying to leave. There was only one logical thing to do, and that was to hunker down in the kitchen, avoid the carnage that way.

Kirsty managed to edge into the kitchen, silently shutting the door behind her, then let out a long sigh and kicked her shoes off. The clunk of heels was loud on new tile, and a man, half hidden in the alcove beside the fridge, gasped and spun round, clutching his chest.

'Jesus!'

'Sorry,' Kirsty muttered, irritated that there was someone else already in her bolthole, already bored with the possibility of having to have another trite, distasteful conversation. ('Child Protection? Oh my god, how depressing! What's the worst thing you've seen?')

'Christ, I thought I was safe!' The man closed the fridge door with one hip, and passed her a beer. 'Has the dancing started?'

'No, not yet.'

'Well, I'm not risking it. I'm staying here.' The man crossed to the door, opened it a crack, peered out, closed it again. 'Jesus. It'll end up like one of those Oh So Crazy parties. "Yay! Look, I'm young again!"' He waved both large, finely shaped hands in the air, his mouth open in idiot delight.

'Like in one of those Brat Pack movies – the eighties ones,' Kirsty agreed.

'Yes!' The man pointed to her with his bottle. 'They're horrible, those films, aren't they? They're a middle-aged man's idea of a crazy party with crazy teenagers. Telly through the window, like that. If we're lucky someone'll try to *breakdance* and break a fucking hip.'

'You have high expectations of this party, I can tell.' Kirsty smiled. He wasn't like most of Vic's party guests; he was funny, confident enough in himself that he didn't care about seeming eccentric, handsome enough to get away with it. 'Wait for the flaming shots.'

'Flaming shots! Of course there'll be flaming shots! That train's never late,' the man replied. They exchanged lugubrious grins. 'I'm Lee.'

'Kirsty.' They clinked bottles. 'So how do you know Vic?'

'I *don't* know Vic. I know *Ollie*. I've worked on a few of his properties – joinery, bit of painting and decorating, stuff like that, and lately I've done a bit more bespoke stuff…' Lee placed one finger on his cheek in exaggerated thought. 'Perhaps I'm part of his divorce settlement? Anyway, I'm apparently his cut-out-and-keep working-class pal. I think he wants to improve my prospects. Called me last week, said he'd bought a new place and maybe I could take a look. I got here tonight, and there's some girl he's lined up for me to meet.'

'What was she like?'

Lee frowned. 'Young. Loud. Called something stupid like Dementia or Chlamydia.' He shook his head. 'Nope.'

'Is she still out there?'

'As far as I know. I palmed her off on some chinless wonder and came to hide in here. I reckon if I give it another half hour I'm free.' He drained his beer, opened another. 'Why the hell are *you* here anyway? You seem better than this.'

'Family duty. Vic's my sister.'

Lee's face dropped. 'Shit. Shit, I'm sorry.'

'It's all right. I came to terms with it years ago.'

'No, I mean I'm sorry for slagging off her boyfriend and all that…'

Kirsty smiled widely. 'If you get me another beer I'll keep my mouth shut. And I won't deliver you to the tender mercies of your young, loud date.'

'I doubt my young, loud date is tender or merciful. Here.' He passed her an open bottle, pointed at the door, his mouth tugged down in amusement. '*Your* sister? Really?'

'Afraid so.'

'Well.' Lee shut the door, frowned humorously. 'She's very… lively.'

'She's the "crazy" one,' Kirsty replied. 'I'm the dull, older one.'

Lee gazed at her, very seriously. 'I wouldn't say that.'

A sudden shyness struck Kirsty then. She gazed at the bright floor tiles, feeling a happy blush spread across her cheeks. From the hallway came a crash, the sound of rolling bottles, and a collective, excited 'OHHHHH!'

'Woman down!' someone shouted gleefully. 'Vic! Legend!'

Kirsty groaned. 'That's my cue.' She walked into the hall to see her sister pinned to the carpet by one of the heavy gilt mirrors that had fallen from the wall.

Vic struggled like an upturned insect and giggled weakly. 'My head hurts,' she said.

There was nobody in the hall Kirsty recognised, they all looked young – like teenagers – and they all thought Vic – or the spectacle of Vic – was hilarious. They stood around smirking as Kirsty struggled to lever the mirror up. Then Lee was there, silently taking it from her, leaning it carefully against the wall while Kirsty picked the glass out of her sister's hair.

'What'd you do?'

'Handstand. She was doing a handstand!' a giggling girl said. 'Legend! Lady? You're a fucking *legend*!'

'Don't put your hands on the floor, there's glass all over it!' Kirsty told Vic. 'Where's the Hoover?'

'*Where's the Hooooover?*' mimicked Vic. 'Where's the *Hooooover?*'

'She's a legend,' another girl told her. There was a note of 'don't spoil the fun' aggression in her voice. 'She's all right.'

The girl was very young; a teenager – sixteen or seventeen, or maybe fourteen or fifteen behind the skilful make-up. What was *she* doing here? What were the equally young strangers doing here? Their sly little faces shone with gleeful excitement. Vic must seem impossibly old to them, and her antics as darkly funny as those of a senile relative, while poor Vic obviously felt like she was still one of them.

'Yeah.' Vic scrambled up from the floor, tossed her head, shaking an inch-long splinter of glass from her hair. 'I'm all right.'

'See?' The girl was a smug echo. 'She's all right.'

'You've cut yourself,' Kirsty told her. 'Look, your leg.'

Vic twisted to look at the thin trickle of blood running down her calf. 'Can't see anything.'

'Let me clean it up.'

'Oh SHUT *UP!*' Vic shouted then, with that sudden, drunken hate born of embarrassment. 'Shut *up*, will you, I'm *FINE.*' And she limped towards the living room, leaving little bloody heel prints on the floorboards.

'She's a fucking legend, your sister,' the giggling girl confided again. 'Isn't she? My mum *hates* her.'

'What?'

'My mum? We live in the flat above? *Hates* her!'

Jesus… Vic was reduced to inviting random teenage neighbours? How much did she not want to grow up? Kirsty closed her eyes, feeling all of her thirty-one years, and Vic's twenty-four combined.

Then she felt a hand on her elbow. Lee was looking at her with amused sympathy. 'As my old nan used to say, "Once the blood flows, the party's peaked." Fancy a drink? The pub at the end of the street is OK, I think?'

'I should stay, for Vic,' she said.

'Haven't you heard? Vic's a fucking legend. She's FINE.' Lee smiled. 'Anyway, she's Ollie's responsibility now. Come on. Let's go and get a drink.'

Kirsty nodded gratefully, grabbed her coat from the bedroom – the bed thankfully not groaning with sexual coupling, the room occupied only with one weary-looking man texting his wife – and together they slipped out into the quiet street. Away from the pulse of music, the shrieks of the guests, and all that determined fun, Kirsty felt her shoulders relax, and her arms, loose, dangled by her sides.

'Thank god,' she murmured to herself.

'D'you remember *Lethal Weapon*?' Lee asked her. 'And Danny Glover? Whenever he escaped from some hostage situation or whatever, he'd always say—'

'"I'm too old for this shit,"' Kirsty finished.

'Well,' Lee nodded behind them, 'I'm too old for that shit.' Then smiled and touched her wrist gently. 'Thanks for walking my elderly ass out of that place.'

'You're not elderly.'

'I feel it. I've reached the stage when I ask for the music to be turned down in pubs. Speaking of which…' He opened the door to the quiet bar, and steered her towards a booth. 'What'll you have?'

*

The night they met was actually two nights and two days. For the first time ever, Kirsty called in sick to work so she could stay in bed with Lee, cook with Lee, laugh with Lee and have more sex than she'd had in the last five years. She'd never met anyone like him. They drank red wine and talked and she told him more than she'd ever told anyone else about her family, about school, about Lisa and the police and the hate driving them away. Curiously, Lee, whose dad had been in the army, had lived in the same city at the same time, but he was older – five years older – and so they'd never met. There was something comforting in this idea, that they might have passed each other on the street, caught each other's eye maybe, and now, all these years later…

He remembered the Lisa Cook case, the media scrum, Marlborough House being burned down.

'It's a bad town. Of all the places we lived, that was the only one I hated,' he told her.

'D'you remember Bryan? Lisa's brother? He gave me a hard time.' She tried to keep it matter-of-fact. 'He seemed to blame me for everything. It was him that gave me this scar.' She pushed her hair away from her temple to show him the white, twisted line that ran from her hairline to the corner of her left eye. 'That's why I still have a fringe like a kid.'

'I like your fringe.' Lee stroked the scar. 'But I hate that this happened to you.'

'Oh, it wasn't just that. He'd follow me, chase me, spit at me. He threw things at the house and… it was awful.' She found that she was crying.

Lee held her hand tight, and he didn't speak, and his body was hard, and when she looked at him his face was set in painful indignation.

'Why would he do that?' he said.

'He was nuts. And he blamed me for leaving her in the park.'

He shook his head. 'What, you would have been nine? How was this your fault?'

'I was ten.'

'Ten! Well, that makes all the difference! Of course it was your fault!' He reached for a cigarette, smoked in hard little sucks and blew out the smoke with a kind of rage that she didn't understand but felt obscurely guilty about. 'What a nasty little bastard he was.'

'Did you know him? He was pretty famous around town.'

Lee said nothing.

'I'm sorry to bring it up. It's a depressing subject, and—' Kirsty began.

Lee picked up his drink. 'You don't have to do that, you know. You don't have to apologise.'

'Yeah, but—'

'I'm a big boy, I can handle depressing subjects.'

'I know. I didn't mean… I wasn't criticising you…'

He took her hand. 'OK, here's… I want to say something. And it… it might not be *good* and it might be the stupidest thing I *could* say, but…'

Kirsty closed her eyes as if waiting for a blow. *Here it comes*, she thought. *Here come the questions… Why did you leave her… Why didn't you tell your mum? I bet you didn't really see Tokki in the park, did you?* But he hesitated for such a long time that she opened her eyes again. His face was so pained, so... so *sad*. He looked close to tears.

'Lee? Are you OK? Lee?' She took his hand. His skin was warm.

Just then, the landlord came over, nodding apologetically at the cigarette.

'Shit, this smoking ban. I always forget... I'll just nip outside to finish it, is that alright?' He'd already put on his coat.

Left alone for those few minutes, Kirsty reflected on the horrible start she'd made with such a nice man. Dumping all this on him right away... no wonder he wanted a break from her so soon. He might not even come back. But he did, and as soon as he sat back down, she apologised again.

He swallowed, moved his head just a little, as if shaking off a cloud of small flies. 'You have nothing to apologise for.'

'I don't advertise it. I don't even mention it, normally.'

'But why did you with me?' Lee asked.

'I don't know. I felt safe, I suppose.'

Lee took a deep breath, let it out slowly, nodded to himself and pressed her hand. 'Good. I'm glad you do, and, Kirsty? You have every right to talk about it but none of this was your fault, yeah? And if I can help, I'd like to. You won't be burdening me, nothing like that. I want to help you.'

His eyes, hazel, serious, were so beautiful. His brown skin, the web of small lines that fanned out from his eyes when he smiled. The smooth forehead behind which his sharp, courageous mind never slept. She loved him. She loved him right then and there, and knew she always would.

From the very start, Lee possessed that righteous indignation, that defensive anger that Kirsty had never been able to find in herself. Lee was a godsend.

CHAPTER NINE

'You want to get hold and hang on tight to that one,' Sarah told her. 'Not many like him.'

'I know. I don't deserve him.'

'Oh you do. You're a good catch. Good head on your shoulders, always have.' She coughed, a long, strangled hack. Kirsty massaged her back until the fit was over and Sarah looked at her tissue judiciously. 'No blood.'

'Well you're getting better, that's why.'

Sarah smiled crookedly. 'Maybe you are daft after all.'

'The doctor's not said anything about you being worse—'

'That doctor wouldn't say shit if he had a mouthful.' In her last illness, Sarah had embraced swearing with the zeal of a religious convert. 'I've got cancer, Kirsty. That train only goes one way.'

'I wish you wouldn't talk that way.'

'I know I can with you and you won't have hysterics. You can take it, not like Vicky. She's not practical like you are. When I go, you'll carry on looking out for her, won't you?'

'Oh, Mum, you're not going anywhere—'

'She's with Ollie now, and that's all right, but I can't help thinking that he's left one wife and that sets a precedent as far as I'm concerned. Keep an eye on her. Promise.'

'Promise.'

'And Lee? Lee! I know you're outside the door listening so just come in.' Sarah held out one hand, pale and fluttering as a moth's wing.

'I wasn't listening.' He took her hand, sat down by the bed. 'I was just giving you some time.'

'Aye, well, there's not much of that left.'

'Mum, don't—'

'Shhh!' Sarah said sharply. 'Lee knows what I'm on about. He's not full of shit, he knows I'm on my way out. Now listen.' She turned to Lee, all the light of her fading life blazing through those hard, blue eyes. Lee kept her gaze. They looked very seriously at each other. 'I'm giving Kirsty to you. She's the best thing I ever made. She's the best thing anyone ever made, I reckon. But she doesn't think so. She's broken up inside and I can't fix her because maybe I was one of the ones that broke her in the first place. But *you* can. That's your job. That's what I want you to do.' She gripped his hand very hard then, hard enough that his knuckles went white. 'Will you do this for me?'

'I will,' Lee said solemnly and Sarah gave the smallest, briskest of nods, and let go of his hand. Kirsty watched the blood flow ruddily back into the white.

'All right. Now, go home now. Both of you, you look tired. Lee? Take her to the cinema or something? Have a nice evening.' Sarah waved them both off. She was tired now. 'See you tomorrow.'

Lee had tears in his eyes as they walked down the hospice corridor. Kirsty half expected, half wanted him to say something facetious – something about Sarah having a good grip maybe, but he didn't, and neither did she. When they were back in the car he said, almost to himself, 'I'm glad she trusts me with you.'

'Why wouldn't she?'

But Lee didn't answer.

At the funeral a month later, Kirsty thought back to that exchange. *Was she really broken? Was she something that could be bestowed, like a gift or a curse?* It made her feel uneasy, bitter, and guilty for being both those things, and grateful for Lee for taking her on, damaged as she was. She looked at Lee through her own dry, cried-out eyes as he helped the undertaker's men lift the coffin, and she made him a silent promise. *I'll fix myself. I'll get to the bottom of what happened to Lisa and then I'll be free. I won't be your burden any more.*

*

But when she showed some of her research to Lee, he didn't like it.

'How is this helping?'

'It's seeing if I can get to the truth—'

He frowned. 'I don't get it. Why do you need this?'

'I—'

'I mean, how can going over the same ground again and again help you get over it?'

'It's not about getting over it though, it's about finding out what really happened! Every month more stuff comes to light, like here, look.' She pointed at a post in Dark Hearts. 'This is about some boys in the park – they were there a lot that spring apparently, people remember them and there's even this picture, look,' someone had posted a picture of the youth club, some grainy figures hanging around the open door, 'somebody, sometime, will come forward, maybe one of these boys, and maybe they saw something and maybe—'

'That's a whole lot of maybes.'

'Yes, but the whole thing is based on maybes, that's the problem!' Kirsty felt energised, excited to share. 'And look, someone who was at Marlborough House at the same time says he saw Tokki going into the prayer room that day at four thirty.'

Lee peered at the screen. 'It says "an anonymous source said they saw a man who *may* have been Toqueer Al-Balushi entering the prayer room at *around* four thirty".' He looked up. 'That's not definite at all.'

'Well, it's something to research, isn't it?' Kirsty felt thwarted, annoyed. 'The police won't do it, so—'

'So you're going to track down this "anonymous source", are you? How?'

'I'm not. But someone else might, there are loads of people interested in this case, Lee! There are loads of people who think Tokki didn't do it, and there are loads of inconsistencies. Look.' She clicked on a file marked 'Evidence'. 'Here, Lisa's coat was found a week after she went missing, but it was near the canal, not where I left her. And how did the police miss it for an entire week?'

'They were incompetent, that's why.'

'Well what about those girls? Here…' She opened another file, this one named 'Witnesses', and read aloud: '"The teenage girls say they saw Al-Balushi approaching Lisa Cook in the park at approximately four forty-five p.m." That's from 1985. I never saw any girls! I know I told the police I did, but they pressured me until I…but I *know* I didn't see them! And, look, in 1987 they both say they made it up.'

'Well, that happens. Kids make things up for attention.'

'No, but listen to this – this is new: "One of the girls who falsely claimed she saw Al-Balushi in the park now says she was told to lie."' Kirsty looked at Lee. The feverish zeal that always took over when she opened her files was impossible to hide. Plus it felt good! It felt good to share it with someone. 'Why would someone tell her to lie? Maybe they pressured her, like they did with me?'

'Who told her to lie? The police?'

'Well, it doesn't say. But—'

'Why wouldn't she say? Why tease people after all these years? Sounds like another attention-seeker to me.' Lee's face was closed. His arms were crossed. 'You can't believe everything you read—'

'I'm *not* believing everything I read!' Kirsty shouted. 'I'm asking questions, that's all. What's wrong with that?' They were dangerously close to rowing now. 'People are covering things *up*, Lee! Someone who might be innocent is in prison and—'

'And these are the people you're entrusting with digging up the truth, yeah? These are the intrepid internet sleuths who are going to free an innocent man?' Lee snatched the mouse and went back to Dark Hearts. 'Look.' He pointed to an image of herself, a school photo from when she was ten. A prolific poster named ARKane had labelled it 'LIL KIRSTY IS NOT SO INNOCENT'. 'These people are proper dicks, Kirsty. They're not interested in the truth, they're just interested in spinning out a story. And you're *part* of that story, you're like the meat in their sandwich. How can going back again and again, revisiting the whole thing, reading all this crap about yourself, help you?'

'You said I should talk about it,' Kirsty said in a small voice.

'I didn't say you should obsess about it though.'

'I want to remember, that's all. I want to remember exactly what happened, and if I do that, then…'

Lee's voice softened. 'Baby, what? What will happen then? With the best will in the world, your friend will still be dead, you'll still have gone through hell. Nothing will change, there's not like a magic key you're going to find and bang! You're made whole again. And memory doesn't work that way anyway. The further away you get from something, the hazier it gets, that's just the way it goes. All you're doing is remembering how you once remembered remembering something.' He smiled quizzically. 'And then you're down the rabbit hole, aren't you?' He nodded at the computer. 'Along with all those trolls.'

'But people *do* remember things years later. Repressed memories? Hypnosis can bring them out.'

'Oh, come on. You know as well as I do that's nuts. Hypnosis? You can make anyone think *anything* under hypnosis. People think they're bloody *chickens* under hypnosis. Wait—' He frowned. 'You're not messing around with that sort of stuff, are you?'

'Hypnosis? No.'

Lee's face was drawn, and his eyes were grave. 'Because that can really fuck a person up, Kirsty.'

'I'm not.'

He paused for a long time. Then went over to the computer, slammed the lid shut. 'I don't want you to look at this stuff again. I don't want you to, OK?'

She reached for humour. 'You're forbidding me? How are things in the 1800s, Lee?'

'I mean it. Stop it. For me.'

'It's not that easy though...'

'It's easy if you try,' he muttered.

'I *do* try.'

'No.' He shook his head grimly. 'You want to wallow in it, that's what I think.'

'That's not fair.' Kirsty felt sharp tears. The clean, sharp outlines of his face blurred. 'That's not *fair*.'

'It *is* fair. It's just not what you want to hear. Get rid of this crap, OK? No more.'

Lee and Kirsty didn't argue often, and the arguments they had never lasted long. This one, so early in their relationship and ostensibly over within half an hour, was the worst because it changed their relationship forever, setting it on a fault line of lies: Kirsty not only didn't erase the files, she added to them. Behind Lee's back, she spent the next ten years collecting every YouTube clip, every Reddit thread, and every passing mention of the case in any media. Her mind yammered at her: *Get ahead of the story and you can control the story; capture everything and lock it up; keep the Bad Thing in the cage, and kill it with its own poison.*

She was in control, or so she believed, for a long time.

And then, she wasn't.

CHAPTER TEN

'I'm *pregnant*!' Vic screamed over the phone.

'Oh my god.' Kirsty sat down too quickly on a kitchen chair. She felt as if she'd been punched.

'Three months! Nearly to the *day*. Ollie's mum *swears* it's a boy from how sick I am, but I really *really* feel like she's a girl? I don't know why – it's just a weird feeling I have. Like, a real intuition. You know I get those.'

'Ollie's parents know?' Kirsty heard her voice, faint, thin, as if it was coming from a cheap speaker.

'Well, god, yes! Right from the start. They're lovely, they're so *involved*. They wanted to see the test itself but I told them I'd thrown it away because, you know, it's all covered in wee.'

The words, still thin but quavering, fell out of Kirsty's mouth before she had a chance to think. 'You told them before you told me?'

There was a pause. 'Well, *yes*? They live round the corner, practically.' Vic and Ollie had recently moved north to Marsden, a chichi village some ten miles outside Vic and Kirsty's home town. They'd bought a huge doer-upper of a house (*Two buildings and a barn*, as Vic always reminded her) that they were converting into one ugly vanity project. 'I mean, how could I not tell them? They're family?' She gave a little incredulous I-can't-believe-you're-being-this-rude giggle.

'*I'm* your family! I'm your *sister*!'

Another pause. Then Vic said, with injured dignity, 'I couldn't though, could I? Not until I knew I was... you know, *OK*. Most miscarriages happen in the first trimester—'

'I know that,' Kirsty said frostily.

'And I *know* you know that, that's why I wasn't going to tell you right away. To spare your feelings, after – you know… your… *problems*.' The pause she left after 'problems' was filled with hurt. 'I was just being sensitive!'

*

Kirsty's problems. Never her and Lee's problems, but always Kirsty's. Everyone saw it that way, everyone except Lee, who was scrupulous to reassure her that it would happen one day. Some couples don't get pregnant for years, and then it just happens; some people are pregnant and don't know – the tests are wrong… you hear about that all the time.

'What, the "I Thought I Needed a Poo and Instead I Had a Baby!" stories in *Take a Break*?' Kirsty could still smile about it in the early years.

'I saw one the other day: "My Hangover from Hell Was Twins!"'

'"Gluten Intolerance or Pregnancy?"'

'"Ten Tell-Tale Signs Your IBS Is Really Your Baby."'

'That's not a real one! Come on, is it?' Kirsty said.

Lee nodded solemnly. '"Local Woman Discovers One Weird Trick—"'

'"To Never Get Pregnant,"' Kirsty finished bitterly.

Every time Lee sat beside her, took the negative test from her hand, and snapped it in half with one brisk gesture. Every time he told her, 'It will happen. It will.'

But it didn't.

They were both tested and they were both fertile. It made no sense. They should try to relax, up their vitamins, keep an ovulation calendar. Lee even stopped smoking. But nothing changed. Every period felt like a little death with no coffin, and they were both so hyperaware of the other's sadness that they couldn't share their own. The rueful jokes stopped, silly baby-name discussions ('Herod! Clytemnestra!') ended, and when Lee started smoking again, Kirsty said nothing and neither did he.

And now, here was Vic, seven years her junior and pregnant without a hitch. Kirsty tried so hard not to cry on the phone, and when she failed, she managed to pass off the tears as tears of joy. Vic was mollified, and they parted friends, but as soon as she put the phone down she collapsed. Lee found her curled up on the bed an hour later, rigid as a mummy, wet eyes wide. He lay down with her silently, and they clung to each other like wreckage, not saying a word.

After a while she told him she couldn't carry on working in Child Protection. She couldn't carry on seeing these awful, damaged, wilfully shit parents, pumping out kid after kid, with no thought or care or…

'I've had enough.'

'OK.'

'Just… I don't know. I'll retrain? Or go into Adult Services?'

'Whatever you need to do, love.' Lee stroked her hair. 'Whatever makes things easier.'

Like always, love for Lee rose up, washed away the scum of numb depression, and if she was strong, he was strong. That was the way it was with them. They had each other's back, and they always would. Thank god for Lee.

*

Vic's pregnancy was not straightforward. There were sudden spikes in blood pressure, bleeding. The childless, mannish midwife told them, with sad delight, that the baby was small, that Vic would have to be monitored and looked after. Vic promptly prescribed herself bed rest for the remaining five months, and suddenly realised how much she needed her sister, her one living relative!

'What about Ollie's parents? I thought they were really involved?' Kirsty couldn't resist asking.

Vic's reply was both pathetic and heartening. 'They're *old* though, and they do my head in. Please, Kirsty? You're the only one I trust to get me through this. You're so calm and practical and *fun*. Ollie's great but he's so… he tries so hard to be careful that he ends up *fussing* and if you're not working at the moment…?'

'I can't just leave Lee though.' It wasn't just that.

'Well, what if we find more work for Lee? He's already going to be doing the staircase.'

This was true. Ollie had brought Lee in to build the new staircases complete with clever, hidden shelving units, and Vic also had her heart set on a bespoke shoe cupboard. ('If I hear her use the words "girly", "sparkly" or say anything about *Sex and The City*, I'm walking off the job,' Lee told Kirsty.)

'What if we find more stuff for him to do? That means you'll see more of him if you stay here, won't you?'

And so Kirsty agreed. They could do with the money now she'd resigned, and, secretly, she was flattered to be asked. It made sense, it would be nice. Family time. Lee, however, wasn't convinced. He didn't want Kirsty anywhere near 'That Place'. It wasn't good for her, what with all those memories, all that horror, but Kirsty told him that she was hardly going to go back there and socialise with anyone, was she? She didn't know anyone there anyway – after all, she left when she was eleven. No, she'd just stay with Vic – a safe ten miles away from the city – until the baby came, that's all. It would be nice.

And it was nice. Vic, chastened by illness, was good company. They watched movies together, they went through pictures of Sarah, of themselves when they were small, deciding on which to get framed, talking about where they should hang. When she didn't have an audience, Vic was actually a lot of fun. She dropped the ditsy persona and showed a sly observant humour that Kirsty hadn't suspected she had; Ollie's octogenarian parents were a lot more entertaining after they'd left and Vic was imitating them for Kirsty's amusement. She even poked gentle fun at herself… A long-time devotee of what she called 'the spiritual', Vic spent her days in bed hoovering up books on astrology, near-death experiences, past lives; she would sometimes read out passages to Kirsty, who'd roll her eyes and smirk.

'Typical Aquarius!' Vic said, poking Kirsty playfully.

'I'm not Aquarius though. I'm Pisces, aren't I?'

'That's just what a typical Capricorn *would* say.'

Vic, bed-bound, ordered mood lamps and chakra-bonded pyramids and intuition oil ('I'll use it in labour'), and in all this she was indulgently encouraged by Ollie. For fifteen years he'd lived with his ex-wife in blameless, dour domesticity, until this young woman – this impossibly flighty, attractive girl – had made him want more, and now that he had her, he was determined to take her every whim seriously.

Vic's beliefs, omnivorous and facile as they were, had honest, serious roots. She missed Sarah. Maybe Mum was still here, watching over them? What if their palms, their auras, their pasts and futures could tell them that? What if the baby itself was in some part a link with Sarah; what if she contained in herself a spark of her grandmother? It was this deeply felt love that allowed Kirsty to respect her beliefs, and, if not altogether share them, at least see how they could be a comfort to those left behind. Kirsty missed Sarah terribly too, and now, with the baby coming, it seemed doubly cruel that she wasn't there. Some of the books Vic pressed onto Kirsty were even quite useful (not that she'd ever admit that to Lee, who maintained his scornful mistrust of 'woo-woo' in all its forms). *The Power of Now*, for example, had a lot in common with those books on mindfulness Kirsty had at home; she recognised a lot of herself between the pages of *The Awakened Empath*. If Vic wanted to take it one step further and pay to get her chakras balanced, her aura read, and her future spelled out by tarot cards, what was the harm if it brought down her blood pressure, helped her carry the baby to full term? And maybe there was some, tiny, element of truth in the whole thing?

'It's so nice, you being here,' Vic told her. 'It's like we're proper sisters again, isn't it? Like when we moved and we had to share a room, remember? I had bad dreams and you'd give me a cuddle, remember?'

Kirsty didn't remember that. It seemed like a conflation of her own life and Vic's dewy-eyed recollection of some idealised sisterhood. As far as she remembered, it was Kirsty who'd had nightmares, not Vic; Kirsty who'd crawl into her sister's bed, pulling her sleeping body in close so she could hear her breathing, feel her heartbeat, using Vic's life to chase away the dead girl she dreamed of. But it might have happened the way Vic said too – she was so sure of it, and it was a nice memory to have, even if it was, possibly, false.

'I do remember that.'

'It was nice, wasn't it?'

'It was.'

'I read something the other day – listen.' She opened a book named *Spiritual Sisters: A Lifetime Odyssey*: '"Sisters carry their mothers within them, just as they were carried in their mother womb. While some see life as unspooling in a straight line, the Spiritual Woman knows, deep in her womb, that there is no past and no future, just a continuous circle of love passed from mother to mother."'

She snapped the book shut. 'Isn't that lovely?'

'Mmmm.'

'And, you know what? The further I get along with the pregnancy? The more I feel Mum here, don't you? I really, really feel her here!' She was weeping a little now. 'And you do, too, don't you?' Vic had lost weight recently, her face was drawn, her eyes ringed with brown. She was thin as a stick until the belly, swelling grotesquely below her flat breasts. It was as if the baby was sucking the life out of her. 'Do you think she's proud of me?'

'Of course she is!' Kirsty said warmly. 'We all are!'

'I'm scared I won't be good at it, you know, being a mum. I won't know what to do… You're better than me at that stuff, you're practical. Like Mum.'

'Vic, you're going to be all right. You are. I'm sure every mother goes through this – the doubt and the fear and all that – but you can do this.'

'Will you stay for a while after the baby comes? I mean, there's loads of room, and Lee can stay too, of course.' Vic stared at her piteously with those huge, tired eyes. 'Please? At least think about it?'

Kirsty decided to sidestep answering for the moment. 'What does it say in the baby books about this? Feeling scared?'

'Oh. The baby books are stupid,' Vic said petulantly. 'It's all routine, routine, routine, like the army of something. It's all about the *baby*, nothing about the mother. There's nothing about self-care.'

'Are there any prenatal groups you could join or something?'

Vic rolled her eyes in disappointment. 'How can I when I'm stuck here?'

'Internet groups then? Support groups?'

'I want to be a *person*! Not just a pregnant lady,' Vic answered grumpily. 'You don't know what it's *like*!'

Kirsty nodded. She didn't. She wished she did.

'And it's not the same as family, is it? I mean, in the olden days, all the generations would live together, like a commune, and they'd all

look after each other's kids and, like, learn from each other and…'
She squeezed Kirsty's hand. 'Just think about it?'

'What would Ollie say to that?' asked Kirsty with a smile,
playing for time.

'Oh.' Vic made a dismissive movement with one thin hand.
'He'll do whatever I tell him to do.'

*

By the last trimester, Vic deemed herself well enough to leave the
house. She spent most of her time having her chakras balanced,
going to reiki and homeopathy consultations and hypnobirthing
sessions. She saw palmists, crystal healers and, latterly, a tarot card
reader. It was this last that brought Angela Bright into both their
lives.

CHAPTER ELEVEN

'I met this wonderful lady!' Vic was sitting up. 'There was this flyer? At hypnobirthing? Tarot readings. Well, I know it's a bit old school, tarot, but it made me think that I really ought to have one for the new baby? So I called and I met this *adorable* old lady. Like something out of a fairy tale! Anyway, I met her and she gave me the most lovely reading – look! I made notes!'

Kirsty had time to glance at a page of Vic's cramped, childish handwriting, covering half a side of A4 before it was pulled away again.

'Anyway, she thinks, like we do, that a baby is really the child of all the women in the family, so she asked questions about me, and you, and even Mum…'

'What kind of things did you tell her?' Kirsty asked doubtfully.

'Nothing personal!' Vic told her. 'It was for the baby, not for *you. God.* Anyway, then I asked her loads of questions too and it turned out that her daughter is a psychic – a really, really successful one too – in America. Read this.' Vic pushed the iPad into Kirsty's hands. 'Click here.'

Born in Ireland (the Emerald Isle), Angela Bright comes from a long, distinguished line of mediums, all the way back to medieval times. She accepted her gift at four years old, when her sister Lily, who had passed over years before, became her teacher and guide to Spirit.

For more than a decade, Angela has been using her gift to deliver healing to the world. She was one of the world-renowned mediums appearing regularly on TLC's *The Bridge to Beyond*. Angela tours nationally as well as lending her talents to Hollywood moguls, and stars of screen and TV alike.

She can be contacted for individual readings, remote reading and house cleansings.

A studio portrait of Angela showed a woman in her mid-thirties, slim, with a no-nonsense dark blonde bob and a pair of soulful eyes and a sad smile.

'OK, guess what?' Vic was fizzing with excitement.

'What?' Kirsty was nervous.

'She's coming here! Angela Bright!'

'All the way from the Emerald Isle?'

Vic ignored her. 'You've got to see this!' she said and she tapped on the YouTube link below, a montage of Angela's appearances on *The Bridge to Beyond*, which seemed to be some kind of psychic detective tag-team affair.

On camera Angela Bright came across as a kind of psychic Mary Poppins, brisk, yes, but partial to holding hands and murmuring endearments in a slightly overdone accent that couldn't be firmly placed as belonging to anywhere in the UK. 'I need you to help me understand' was one of her catchphrases, and, unlike the two other mediums, she wasn't given to double-takes and humorous banter with visiting spirits. Angela didn't play to camera; whether striding through a misty graveyard in Yonkers, or staying the night at a haunted motel in Maine, she took it very seriously, gave it her all, and seemed to suffer for it. The body of the little boy was not found, but an exhausted Angela told his parents 'he had found peace'. The noisy spirit upsetting guests in a country hotel was quelled with kindness, as Angela listened to something in the silence, rocked, cried, before telling the owners that the place was now Clean. 'This spirit was strong, and yes, she was angry, but it all came from pain. There was a loss of a baby, perhaps in that room itself, and she couldn't move on. She just wanted someone to hear her.' Angela's eyes were watering while the background music swelled to a soupy sadness. 'So many women were left alone, left friendless. That pain doesn't go away. Not without help.' Kirsty was slightly ashamed to notice that she, too, had tears in her eyes.

'See? I told you!' Vic crowed. 'She's amazing, isn't she? And it's all about *women*, you know, finding *peace*. Look at this one!'

This clip was longer – a solo live appearance. Angela's tiny, tidy figure was dwarfed by her own face on the big screens flanking the stage. Every gesture she made was considered, deliberate. She gave the impression of someone determined to eke out their energy, determined to make it to the end, no matter how it tired her. And it did tire her, you could tell. By the middle of the show, her magnified face, creased with the effort of helping, understanding, seemed to have aged ten years, her carefully arranged hair drooped, her shoulders stooped with fatigue, but still she carried on. There was a boy who needed to come through: a boy killed in Vietnam at nineteen, desperate, *desperate* to tell his mother that in the afterlife he had all his limbs – 'And he's showing me a…? In England we'd call it a rugby ball, but, no, he's shaking his head at me now. It's a football? Can you understand this? An *American* football? And he says – and he's smiling at you, he's shining all his love on you at this moment – he says he's with The Team. He made The Team… Can you understand this?' A long-dead daughter insisted she talk to – 'A lady with a name beginning with T? T or J? Yes, is that you, my love? And what's the name? Teri? I wonder why I'm seeing a J… your husband was John? That explains it. Teri, I have your daughter here. Chatterbox, isn't she? She wants you to heal. She's telling me… Can you understand this… She's telling me now that, whatever happened between you two, she's saying she takes responsibility. She's saying it wasn't your fault, you need to live *your* life now. Is that something you can understand?' The woman flung her arms around Angela Bright, sobbing, sobbing in gratitude.

There was a lot of that kind of stuff. Angela Bright seemed to specialise in bringing sons and daughters back to tell their families they bore them no ill will. '...and she's nodding towards a... What is that? A camera? A camera film? There are some pictures of her, that you haven't wanted to frame and put on the wall because it's too painful, but she's telling me now, she's saying, *Do it, Mum.* She's saying to me now that she's always with you, folding you in her arms, and she says that the pictures can be a... link? Between you two now that she's passed. A bridge. And I can feel such love from her. Can you? Can you feel the love?'

The audience were mostly women, mostly in middle age. When they stood to hear their message, they were all of a type, built from their sensible shoes up in a series of quivering tiers, like large, stacked cakes. They had salt and pepper hair, bifocals, and fleeces. Some gripped their walkers with palsied hands. Some had faces weakened, marred or drooped by illness, but they were all perfectly normal women you could pass on the street and never look twice at. None of them looked credulous, none of them looked insane. The exit interviews were sober, thankful, quite a few said that Angela Bright was the first psychic they'd seen, and she'd single-handedly allayed any doubts.

'I felt my sister in the room, I knew she was speaking to me, through Angela,' said one woman. 'Only my sister could know what she told me. How do I feel? I feel like I can get on with the rest of my life now.' Everyone was there to feel better, and by the end of the event, they did.

Everyone apparently but Angela Bright herself. In an interview shot backstage she explained that her gift took the form of feeling as well as seeing visions, and as a result, she both witnessed and felt the pain and the suffering of those passed, those speaking through her. 'Sometimes at the end of a large demonstration, I can barely stand up.'

'How do you manage it?' asked the person with the camera.

'I'm not sure I *do*,' Angela answered, after a hesitation. 'But I have no choice. I can't turn it on and off, and in a big room there's so many energies flowing into me… it can be overwhelming.'

'Do you ever take time off? Recharge?'

Angela lifted tired eyebrows. 'Sometimes I ask the spirits to… dial it down a little,' she admitted. 'And, bless them, they *do*, or they try to anyway. Sometimes Lily – my guide – will step in and ask them to wait. But in a funny way, I don't think I have the right to relax. This gift was given to me for a reason, and the people I help are more important than any aches and pains I might suffer. It's important. *They're* important, so if I can help, I will.'

And there the clip ended in a swift dissolve.

'I *so* want to get a private session with her.' Vic was gently massaging her stomach, her eyes still fixed to the screen. 'Maybe we should get one together?'

'What does Ollie think?' Kirsty asked. She didn't know what else to say.

'Oh, he won't think at all. After all, I'm the one having the baby, aren't I? I'm the one who'll be doing all the work, won't I?'

'I'll help, you know that.'

'But you're going to leave,' Vic said in a small voice.

'I'll stay after the baby comes, for a bit. I promise.'

'How long is "a bit"? We're the only family we've got, aren't we? It's not like Dad's any use.'

'You've told him about the baby though?'

'I emailed him, but he never got back to me. That's what I mean, Kirsty! This is *it*, we're family and I don't want us to be apart. I want the baby to have her Auntie Kirsty nearby!'

It was a sentiment calculated to go straight to Kirsty's heart and lodge there like a tick. The two of them were a meagre family at best, but maybe with the baby, and with Ollie and Lee buttressing them? Maybe they could fashion a real unit.

Vic pressed her advantage. Her eyes misty, she clutched Kirsty's hand and said, 'You know those big Mediterranean-type extended families? I always wanted that, didn't you? Aunts and uncles and cousins and… we could have that, Kirsty, couldn't we? If you stayed here? Lived close? And think how happy that would have made Mum! And it's not like you're going to ever afford a place in London, is it? Ollie says the prices here are insane compared to London – you and Lee could get a detached place here for the price of a two-bedroom flat there, and…'

Before Kirsty knew it, she'd agreed to think about it, and, inevitably, Vic took this tentative assent and turned it into future fact. She announced the good news as soon as Ollie and Lee walked through the door.

*

'What?' Lee asked when they were alone. 'You told her we'd do *what?*'

'Stay,' Kirsty mumbled.

'What are you, out of your mind?' He took the dish towel out of her hand. 'Stop that, will you, sit down!' He steered her into the island, made her sit down on one of the fearsomely expensive, insultingly uncomfortable stools. 'Talk to me!'

'She's lonely, Lee. She's my sister and I'm the only family she's got. What am I meant to do, just bugger off as soon as she's had the baby?'

Lee gave an exaggerated nod. 'Yes!'

'Look, I'm not even working, and you could work from anywhere really – within reason, I mean. And it's not like we like the London flat, is it? If we moved further up north we could afford to buy somewhere maybe.'

'What, here? I hate villages. You hate villages!'

'Well maybe not here. Maybe in the city, or closer—'

'No,' he said simply.

'What d'you mean, no? Why no?'

'Why yes?'

'Because it's… home—'

'It's not! You left when you were a kid and you never went back! It's a bad place where bad things happen, and I'm not going to let you go back there.'

'You're not going to *let* me?'

'That came out wrong. What I meant was – you're being manipulated. Vic'll play the good sister for a while and then get bored and then where will you be? Stuck living in that shithole? Come on!'

'She won't! I want to be near my family, I want to be useful.'

'But that's another thing, the being useful thing.' Lee took her hand. 'Vic did perfectly well without you before and she will do after the baby. You're an adult, yes, but so's she, and she also is a very rich adult with a husband she can twist around her finger whenever she wants. You want us to move up here, but what happens when Vic decides she doesn't want you any more? She's like that, you know she is. She's… careless about you.'

'But these last few months she's really changed, Lee. Look, I'm under no illusions about her. I know she's spoiled and silly sometimes. I know she's a bit of a drama queen, but being pregnant has changed her, it really has. And I want to be closer to her, that's all. I could make the move to Adult Services better here than there, too.'

'What, you've already looked into that?' Lee asked.

'A bit.' This was a lie. She hadn't at all. But there were three large hospitals in the city, so there was bound to be some jobs going in one of them. 'I want to get out of London. You do jobs all over the place anyway, and the only thing keeping us there was my job, and I don't have that any more.'

'I'm not moving there,' Lee said sullenly.

'No, and I wouldn't expect you to. I don't want to either, but maybe we could base ourselves outside somewhere. A town? Come on, Lee…'

In the end, over the next few weeks, a compromise was arrived at. Kirsty would stay with Vic after the baby came, but for no longer than a few months, and they would only move when and if she got a job and Lee could be certain of steady work away from London. If both those criteria were met, then they'd look to buy somewhere, but not in Marsden, and not in 'that shithole'. It was a fair deal, and one that Kirsty broke almost immediately when she got a job the following month.

'Adult Social Services, hospital-based, designing care plans for the elderly once they leave hospital. It's perfect, Lee! I mean, I couldn't turn it down, could I? What if nothing else showed up?'

Lee didn't say anything.

'Of course, I'd have to move further into the city. Commuting from here is crippling, Ollie says…'

'How much further?' Lee asked.

'Just off the motorway?' Kirsty hedged.

'What does that mean? Just off the motorway? Which hospital is it?'

'Queens?'

'The one in the centre?'

'Centre-ish.' Kirsty felt a tiny swell of panic just then, like an internal warning – *why* had she done this? Jumped on the first job she saw, broken the pact with Lee, headed straight back to the city that had done its best to destroy her, the place that still haunted her; why? The feeling was so strong that she only just managed to rationalise it away – she was Supporting Her Sister. She was

Thinking About Her Career. She Wanted to Get on the Housing Ladder. 'I found a nice flat, by the cathedral?'

'Well, that's nice, isn't it?' Lee mumbled. His face was as scrupulously blank as an egg.

'Not that I'll be there long, just until Vic has the baby and you sort out work, and then we can buy somewhere.' It sounded bright, positive, well thought out, and if she'd been talking to anyone else, she'd have believed the words coming out of her mouth. But faced with Lee's grim scepticism, she faltered. 'Lee? It's a stop-gap, that's all, until we get a place of our own.'

Lee lit a cigarette ruminatively. He wasn't allowed to smoke in Vic and Ollie's house, but Kirsty wasn't about to remind him of that. Instead she waited, half hoping he'd capitulate, half hoping something else… that he'd do what he'd threatened to do at the start and forbid her to move; that he'd threaten to leave her; that he'd do anything except do what she asked. Then she could go to Vic and say, quite truthfully, that Lee had put his foot down and they were moving back to London. Suddenly, autonomy seemed like the last thing she needed.

But none of that happened. All Lee said was, 'I hope you know what you're doing.'

'I do,' Kirsty told him eagerly. She didn't.

Lee finished his cigarette then, and wordlessly went to bed. Kirsty stayed in the kitchen, cleaning the already clean surfaces, and again she felt that little psychic tug. It had happened more and more lately, the dizzying sense of being pulled into an unfolding past, helplessly catapulted back, back… Rain, mixed with hail, clattered against the window.

'Lisa?' Had she said that out loud? Why? She shivered, closed her eyes, told herself to stop being silly. Then she ran, like a scared child, up to the room she and Lee were sleeping in – the room that would become the nursery. Lee was asleep, and his broad, warm back was comforting, familiar, adult. *I'm a grown-up now*, she thought. *I'm a grown-up and I have nothing to fear.*

But that night she had a dream; the first of many telling her that the opposite was true.

CHAPTER TWELVE

She and Lisa were playing in the middle of the street – a wide expanse of empty road, seemingly floating in space. There were no trees, no houses, and the road went on and on forever, bubbling out into a heat haze north and south. Kirsty couldn't see who was holding the ropes, but they moved quickly with an even, robotic speed. She'd been jumping for a long time and she was tired, but she couldn't stop because Lisa wouldn't let her.

'Down in the valley where the green grass grows, sat pretty *Lisa*, pretty as a rose, she sang and she sang and she sang so sweet, and along came *Tokki* and kissed her on the cheek.'

Kirsty looked up. The sky had darkened. 'It's going to rain.'

'Keep skipping!' Lisa told her. 'Keep skipping or I'll die!'

But Kirsty hesitated, misjudged her jump. The ropes twisted around her ankles. She fell on the ground but the ropes carried on moving, hissing through the darkening air, hitting her, whipping her back, her face, and Lisa, still chanting, was far away now, until soon, Kirsty couldn't hear her over the sound of the ropes and the rain.

*

She woke, with a start, sweaty. Lee wasn't there, and for a moment she didn't know where she was – this room, this little pink box, felt like Lisa's room. Kirsty looked around, expecting to see those Pierrot prints, the lipstick stains around George Michael, as well as Lisa herself, sleeping soundly in her pink, ruffled bed, clasping a Care Bear. This strange merging of time didn't leave her quickly either. In the bathroom she was surprised to see the pale moon of her own haggard adult face, and not the plump, pink-cheeked, nervous face of the child she once was. On the stairs there was a smell, ersatz orange and grease, like the chapstick Lisa used to smear on her lips in wintertime. It wasn't until Kirsty padded into the kitchen, saw all those gadgets that didn't exist in 1985, and made a pot of coffee, that things began to feel normal again.

From upstairs came Vic's thin, excited wail. Kirsty bounded back up the stairs, burst into her sister's room. Vic was sitting up in bed, the iPad on her lap. She was smiling like a child at Christmas.

'She's *coming*!'

'The baby?'

'No! Angela Bright! The psychic? She's coming from America and she's agreed to carry on cleansing the house and—'

'Cleansing the house?'

'Well, she's been doing it remotely, from LA,' Vic told her as if it made sense. 'But she says if her schedule allows, she'll finish it in person! Oh my god, Kirsty!' She looked as if she was about to cry. She hadn't looked this happy at her own wedding. 'She's coming here! Maybe! Maybe she'll give me a personal reading?'

'I thought her mother had already done that, though – given you a personal reading?'

'Oh yes, but she's not a professional, like Angela is.' The lovely old lady had served her purpose, it seemed, and Vic had a brand new hero. And one with a TV show, to boot.

And Kirsty felt a premonition of darkness, vague, far, but tumbling towards them like a cyclone. That feeling stayed with her all day. In fact, it never left her again.

*

Lee had been right all along. Once the baby arrived (not the envisioned girl, but a large, red, squalling boy they named – inevitably

– Milo) and Vic had recovered enough of her figure to feel happy leaving the house, Kirsty found herself surplus to requirements. Vic threw herself into baby signing, baby yoga, exercise classes, and something hellishly winsome called TumbleTots. The sisterly closeness they'd enjoyed didn't entirely dissipate, but Kirsty had to work harder for it, and this she did by Being Useful. It was Kirsty who persuaded Vic that vaccinations wouldn't give Milo autism. It was Kirsty who reassured Vic that Milo was absolutely normal, even if all the other babies at music appreciation class smiled when they heard Mozart and Milo cried instead. She would come away from these encounters feeling tired, but vindicated: she was Needed; she was Family. She'd made the Right Decision to come back.

But, increasingly, there were days when she wasn't needed, evenings when Vic relied on her NCT family for calming instruction rather than childless Kirsty, and on those days Kirsty had no option but to throw herself into work, arriving early, leaving late so she didn't have to face long evenings alone in the lonely flat above the florist's that she'd kept bare-walled, deliberately un-lived-in. Every night she'd call Lee, and if it went to voicemail, she'd leave a rambling, humorous message, all about work, about the single strange man who lived in the flat above, alone but for his dog and his frequent gentleman callers (Lee had privately dubbed him Dennis Nilsen). If he picked up, they'd probably talk about the weekend, about how she was owed some TOIL and maybe they could do something special on Monday if he could take the day off… but phone calls have to end and what could she do after that? Sleep? Sleep was increasingly elusive now, and her dreams didn't feel like dreams somehow, but urgent, cryptic messages she couldn't fully fathom. Lisa, the park, the rain, and guilt. That was what she dreamed of, and that was why she dreaded sleeping.

*

Peg Leaves had been admitted to hospital three weeks before, after suffering a stroke that she defiantly smoked her way through, only relinquishing her Rothman Royals when she couldn't jam them into her drooping mouth any more. She'd refused to let her family call an ambulance, and instead lay, grim and stoical, in the back of her great nephew's Transit van, surrounded by a pack of panicked, suspicious relatives who stormed into the hospital demanding that Someone Help Peg Now!

Peg Leaves lived – inevitably – at the Beacon Hill estate. She was a legend, a landmark. She and her large, fluctuating family had great (and misplaced) faith in their Rights as Taxpayers – ironic given that very few members of this murky clan had ever held down a legal, taxable job. They Called a Spade a Spade and Minded Their Own Business and Looked After Their Own, but they couldn't survive without Peg, and they knew it. Peg was the one who possessed enough social savvy to heal rifts with the neighbours, bend recalcitrant head teachers to her will, stave off the bailiffs for another week or so. Peg was the receptacle of family lore, tradition, the font of all memory and wisdom. Her face was a relief map of a hard and humorous life, her hair still dyed a defiant yellow, and on each finger a ring or two dug down deep into the flesh. She was indestructible. But she wasn't looking indestructible any more… Years of bad food, smoking and almost professional indolence had left her with diabetes, blood clots, swollen legs, and locked, painful joints, all of which she'd done nothing about because she didn't like doctors. None of them did, the entire Leaves family distrusted hospitals on general principle, but this time they had to go against their nature and relinquish Peg to the tender mercies of the NHS, which they did with truculence and bad grace, assuming that she'd be fine in a day or two. The hospital might have Peg now, they told each other, but they weren't going to keep her. As soon as they could they'd pull her from the mouth of the State and bring her back home where she belonged.

But Peg was sicker than they'd thought, and scared too. Her fear scared the family further, and they coalesced into a small, charging army, fearless and savage, with Mona – Peg's daughter – leading the charge. When the hospital told Mona that Peg was too sick to go home, Mona hissed, spat, cajoled and whined until the whole family were threatened with being barred from visiting altogether. They retreated, but since then, the family's relative quiet had been unnerving. The general suspicion in the hospital was that the family would try to sneak Peg out of the door, regardless of how ill she was, setting the scene for a pitched battle with wider Social Services – a siege of the sort the whole clan enjoyed, and the hospital couldn't afford to fight. Their only gambit was Kirsty; she seemed to have the ability to calm any situation down. She was their master negotiator in situations like this, their trump card.

Peg let it be known from the start that she liked Kirsty, going so far as to say that she 'had a good head on her shoulders' and this, for the rest of the clan, was tantamount to a papal blessing. Thanks to Kirsty's hard work, Mona was beginning to accept that there was no way Peg could go home without proper support. Then the consultant met with the family and erased all that careful work with one breezy command: the house had to be inspected, Mona must install handles on the walls, a commode and bed downstairs, and work out some way of getting a wheelchair in and out of the front door, and to do that, she had to let people in. Strangers. Officials. This was the sticking point for Mona. Her world was her family, and everyone outside the family was not to be trusted. She wanted Respect. Her mum deserved Dignity. The consultant doctor pointed out that there wasn't a great deal of dignity in not being able to walk, defecate or eat without help, and this had landed very badly with Mona, who backtracked to her earlier threats to get Peg out by force. The consultant unhelpfully countered with references to police injunctions, and Mona hit the roof.

They called Kirsty back in immediately.

*

Peg Leaves was the kind of woman Kirsty enjoyed. Like Sarah, Peg was a strong, no-nonsense lady with a foul mouth and a froggy, self-deprecating laugh. She was also, once she was forced into it, a realist. She knew she couldn't leave hospital yet. It was her daughter, that was all.

'She's forty years old and she can't do without her mum. Daft cow, in't she?' The stroke had muddied her voice, thickened her tongue.

'How can we make her understand?' Kirsty asked. 'You're going to need a lot of help, and she obviously wants to do it, but I'm not sure if she understands—'

'That she's going to have to wipe my arse?' Peg smirked. 'No. She's not good at that. Four kids she's had and I did most of the nappies.'

'It's the house too, though. Where is it you live again?' Kirsty felt her old accent slip back. 'Victory Road?'

'Yeah, Beacon Hill,' Peg affirmed.

'Would it help if I went over there to see her?'

'She won't let you in. I'll talk to her.' Peg looked tired now. She tried too hard to seem well. Kirsty patted her hand, and was about to leave when Peg suddenly opened her eyes wide. 'I know your face,' she muttered.

Oh god, was she having another stroke?

'Yes, I'm your social worker, Peg. We meet every day—'

Peg's tired eyes expressed irritation. 'No. No, I'm not daft, I know that. I mean, I know your face from before. Can't place it though.' Her dim eyes searched her face, her mouth puckered. 'You're… Denise's girl?' A dim, frightened confusion ripped over her face. 'No. No you can't be, she's dead, isn't she? Isn't she?'

'Yes,' Kirsty managed. 'But I knew Lisa. Maybe that's why you remember me.'

'That poor little cow. Nearly thirty years now,' Peg murmured. 'Did you know Lisa?'

Peg blinked slowly. 'Not many people I don't know.'

'Who do you think killed her?' The words were out of Kirsty's mouth before she knew it. They shocked her. It hadn't even been on her mind to ask that question.

Peg turned shrewd eyes on her. 'So you don't think it was the coloured feller either?'

'I don't know,' Kirsty said, ignoring the 'coloured feller' remark.

Peg's eyes were closing. 'Thirty years. Lot of stuff comes out after thirty years, doesn't it? It all comes out.' And then she was asleep.

*

A text from Vic.

> *Reminder to RSVP to our Housewarming! This Saturday from 3, little kids welcome, big kids: Put on Your Dancing Shoes!!*

This was followed by another, not from a mailing list.

> *Hun BIG surprise @ party! Angela (B) is in UK!!!!!! & has DEFINITELY agreed to come & do cleansing ceremony (2 houses + barn = sooooo many unhappy spirits). SO excited can you come early to help set up?*

This Saturday. This Saturday would be the thirtieth anniversary of Lisa's disappearance. Strange that that hadn't registered before… strange that it did now. Kirsty felt suddenly very tired, bone tired, as Sarah used to say. She knew she should text back immediately or Vic would be put out. She knew she should make absolutely sure that Lee was going to come, otherwise the party would be unbearable. She didn't do either of those things though. Instead she felt her fingers stretch to her keyboard, tap with a sure touch, as if autonomous.

Lisa Cook anniversary. Click.

The first thing she saw was Bryan.

Click.

CHAPTER THIRTEEN

THREE DECADES ON

Who killed Lisa Cook? We look at the murder mystery that shocked Britain on the thirtieth anniversary of the little girl's disappearance.

THREE decades after schoolgirl Lisa Cook went missing, lawyers for her killer are calling for the case to be reopened.

**Suspect 'made false confession'.
Body never found. Investigation 'flawed'.**

On 29th March 1985, the bright ten-year-old's life changed forever as she walked home from school.

Toqueer Mohammed Al-Balushi, an Omani student who lodged with Lisa's family, soon confessed to her murder, but experts say the evidence is sketchy, the investigation was flawed, and Al-Balushi's confession was coerced.

Over the decades, armchair sleuths have picked over the case, but have continued to draw blanks. Now, Toqueer Mohammed Al-Balushi's legal team have demanded that the case be reopened, claiming that Lisa's killer may still be at large.

Life without Lisa: Legacy of a child murder

Bryan Cook's features soften when he looks at the two photos he carries with him everywhere.

'I look at Lisa, and I look at my daughter,' he says, 'and in her I see the woman Lisa might have become.' He pauses, to wipe his eyes. 'And she's so much like Lisa. Same blue eyes, same feisty temper. It's almost as if God gave us a little bit of her back to us.'

That day, little Lisa Cook left school at the usual time. She never arrived home. Bryan, then sixteen, and living away from the family, didn't know his sister was missing until the next day.

'I came over on Saturday morning to help my stepfather, Stuart, pack the car for a car boot sale. When I got there, he asked if I'd brought Lisa with me.' Bryan shakes his head at the memory. 'Apparently she'd told them she was going to stay at mine and they'd believed her. When I told them I hadn't seen her, we all began to panic.'

Bryan's final memory of his sister is of her on the morning she disappeared.

'I used to live near the school, and I saw her hanging around the gate with her friends in the morning, talking about the school disco. She wanted to go, but she didn't have the outfit she wanted. She asked me if I'd talk Mum round into buying it for her. I remember I teased her, saying she could sell off some of her Care Bears if she wanted money that badly, and she got really angry with me!' His eyes twinkle again, with fond sadness. 'That was Lisa, she wanted to be a grown-up even though she was still a kid.'

Bryan, together with his mother Denise, and Stuart Brammer – her second husband – went searching for Lisa around their estate.

'In those days nobody had a mobile phone. Mum didn't even have a landline, so even if we'd had their numbers, we couldn't call around Lisa's friends to see if she was with any of them. All we could do was look for her.'

As darkness fell they were joined by neighbours, friends and eventually the police. Frantically they searched back alleys, garages and sheds.

'I shouted myself hoarse,' Bryan remembers of that first night. 'When we had to stop the search, I went back to the house with Mum, and she was absolutely hysterical. She held one of Lisa's dolls and kept saying, "She's never going to come home, is she?" and I tried to reassure her, but somehow, then, I knew that what she was saying was true.'

In the chaos and emotion of that night, no-one noticed that there was one other person missing from the Cook household. Two young students from Oman – Mohammed Oman and Toqueer Mohammed Al-Balushi, known to the family as Mo and Tokki – had recently begun lodging with the family, taking Bryan's old bedroom. Mohammed Oman was present and helped with the search, but Al-Balushi claimed to have stayed on at Marlborough House – the English school both attended – to worship privately in the prayer room. He never came back to the home.

At the mention of Al-Balushi, Bryan's face darkens. 'I never liked him,' he admits. 'As soon as I met him, I had a bad feeling about him. Mohammed would smile, look you in the eyes at least, but the other one seemed very stand-offish. I remember he said he couldn't use the same bathroom as a woman, so he had to shower at the sports centre in town. I asked Mum why he took the room knowing that there were two females living in the house, and she told me that they wanted to live with a family, because they were so far from home.'

Still though, Denise Cook refused to believe that Al-Balushi might have something to do with her daughter's disappearance. 'She told me that he called her "Mum",' Bryan says grimly. 'She treated them like her own sons. There was no way she'd ever suspect either one of them.'

But Bryan did. Frustrated with the search, he spoke to Lisa's friend, Kirsty Cooper. What she told him was shocking.

Bryan's voice throbs with pain. 'Tokki had been abusing Lisa. He told her they were married, and Lisa believed him. She thought she was grown up, but she was just a little girl. She thought what he was doing was normal. As soon as I heard what had been happening, I went straight to the police.'

Nevertheless, it was another full twenty-four hours before Kirsty Cooper was interviewed. Does Bryan still bear the police a grudge?

'I do,' he whispers. 'It was nearly forty-eight hours after Lisa disappeared before they got round to talking to the last person to see her – Kirsty. If they'd spoken to her sooner, she could have told them about the abuse, and maybe Lisa would still be with us. Maybe Kirsty knew more than she told them, too. I tried my best, but I was sixteen years old, and doing their job for them. And, because I was a bit of a tearaway in those days, they didn't take me seriously. They left it too long – by the time they spoke to her, Tokki was long gone.'

Al-Balushi was found days later in London city centre, by a member of the public who recognised his face from the news. 'Even then it was an ordinary person like you or me that found him, not the police, even though they're trained to!' Bryan says.

Despite confessing to the murder of the little girl, Al-Balushi later claimed that he didn't understand the questions, and believed he was arrested for a minor visa violation.

'As soon as he was caught he tried to wiggle out of it.' Bryan's eyes blaze with anger. 'It didn't work, but he's still sitting pretty in prison, he gets his halal meals specially made for him. He won't even tell us where he put my sister's body, so she can have a decent Christian burial. We're left in limbo. Where's the respect?'

Shortly before his death in 1990, Lisa's estranged father Pete told the *Daily Mail* that he felt unable to properly grieve for his daughter, since her body has never been found. Does Bryan feel the same way?

He nods. 'It's hard to grieve because even now, there's a tiny little bit of me that hopes she's alive somewhere. Dad died hoping that we were going to find out what actually happened to Lisa and to rule out once and for all that she is alive somewhere. He even asked to visit Tokki in prison to see if he'd tell him the truth face to face, but Tokki refused to meet with him,' claims Bryan.

And Denise?

Bryan's voice is husky with pride. 'Mum is a trooper. She's very strong, very private, and she'll never let anyone see her fall.' Once more he fingers Lisa's photograph. 'And, like me, she won't give up on the truth.'

Timeline of Lisa's disappearance
29th March 1985

Lisa Cook doesn't come home from school. Her family and neighbours search the area, but the police don't launch an investigation for another **two** days.

31st March 1985

Kirsty Cooper is questioned at the police station, with no parent present. In a series of taped interviews she tells officers that Lisa had 'married' Al-Balushi in a 'special ceremony' and was going to live in Oman and be a princess.

Police visit the Cook family home to speak to Al-Balushi, but are told he left the home on Friday morning and hasn't been seen since. The police put out an appeal to find him.

3rd April 1984

Kirsty Cooper's name is leaked to the local press. Police deny that she is being questioned, but put a police guard outside her house, leading to a media circus. An unnamed source gives the press details of Kirsty's evidence. Kirsty claims that Lisa suffered sexual abuse at the hands of Al-Balushi, and that she herself was being 'groomed' by his friend and fellow lodger Mohammed Oman. She further claims that both men visited the girls' school on at least one occasion.

7th April 1985

Toqueer Mohammed Al-Balushi is found 'in a distressed state' at King's Cross station. A member of the public takes him to the police station. Al-Balushi is questioned by police, with no legal representation and no translator. Six hours later he confesses to Lisa's murder, but claims to have forgotten where her body is.

9th April 1985

Al-Balushi takes back his confessions and denies murder.

30th June 1985

The language school attended by Al-Balushi and Oman is gutted by fire. Two teachers and fourteen students are treated for burns and smoke inhalation. The fire is judged to have been a deliberate arson attack.

29th March 1995

As the investigation fails to bring up any credible leads, Lisa Cook is officially declared dead.

Kirsty looked at Bryan's mournful face staring out of the screen. She wouldn't have recognised him... the years hadn't been kind.

The Bryan she remembered was scrawny, sharp-featured, and his eyes peered bright and stupid from sunken pools of sleepless brown. This Bryan's face was two faces; the first lost in a nimbus of fat, the second falling in tallow-like wattles into a slovenly neck. His eyes were still the same though – watchful within worn sockets, but that gleam of evil animal intelligence wasn't there any more.

He was still a liar, though. He hadn't come to talk to her the day Lisa disappeared. Even if he'd tried to, there was no way on earth her mum would have let him in the house – Bryan's notoriety was such that even adults knew his reputation. Now, here he was trying to get some kind of credit for telling the police about Tokki, when he'd done nothing; nothing at all apart from making a bad situation even worse.

And that stuff about Denise? There was a chance that she'd forgiven him… maybe even let him back into her life, but the Denise Kirsty knew would never have supported him selling his story to the papers that way. Denise was private, dignified and stoical. Bryan was the exact opposite.

Kirsty shut down her computer, took a few moments to blink away the after-image of Bryan's stupid, pompous face. Then she texted Vic back. Of course she'd come early to help! Looking forward to it!

One of those things was true.

CHAPTER FOURTEEN

It was the hottest March on record. That's what Ollie told everyone as he swung around with prosecco. 'Since records began!' Vic had tasked him with maintaining a strict orbit around the guests outside, and his sweaty face was getting more and more mottled as he leaned in with drinks. 'Hot enough for you?'

The garden was packed because, so far, nobody had been allowed into the house. There was a gazebo set up in the garden; next to the trampoline already crowded with children, parents on the patio peered like meerkats at every shriek, and, seeing that it wasn't their child, turned away again, with their raised glasses.

'Who do the kids belong to?' Kirsty asked.

'Oh, some are from the NCT group, some are from baby massage, some are from TumbleTots,' Vic answered casually. 'Lovely bunch of girls, I couldn't have got through the first few months without them. Could I? Could I, Milo?' Milo wobbled and drooled on her hip, either dozing or succumbing to sunstroke. He had the same, dropsical look as Ollie. 'Actually, can you take him? He looks like he needs some Auntie Kirsty time! Don't you? You *do*!'

Of late this was Kirsty's role – the childless, doe-eyed aunt who could be relied on to do the heavy work. And Milo was undeniably heavy. It was strange how Vic didn't need help setting up, help choosing the music or help with the food – she'd hired caterers, for god's sake. She only needed someone to handle the baby so she wouldn't get vomit on her new dress.

So many babies and so many women with babies that she didn't want to meet but had to. Vic steered her around by her elbow, introduced her to everyone, passing her around like a bowl of nuts. *My sister, Kirsten. I've told you all about her. Yes, that's the one! That's her. God, I couldn't do what you do! Social work! It's a vocation though, isn't it?*

Vic had taken to saying this a lot. As if being a social worker was somehow both exotic and illustrative of Great Maturity. Kirsty caught sight of Lee at the buffet, comfortable in his un-sweaty T-shirt, back straight, sipping a beer while some banker type was holding forth about… what? It sounded like reputations? Regulations? And Lee was nodding, wearing that little smile that others read as polite and interested, but Kirsty knew was ever so slightly ironic. When they were alone she knew that Lee would ditch the irony and gleefully tell her all about the conversation, imitating the man's meant-to-be-noticed asides about bonuses, huge deals lost and won, promotions… and all in that silly voice (posh Scots. Who knew that was even a thing?).

The general absurdity of his surroundings seemed to have perked Lee up. He was of the opinion that people should make the best of things… he didn't want to be at his horrible sister-in-law's horrible party, but he was, so he may as well have some fun. At the beginning of the day, Vic had introduced him to a group of guests as 'My amazing brother-in-law, he makes bespoke furnishings – look at these beautiful units? That was Lee,' and Lee countered with 'All chipboard and superglue. Lucky if they'll last six months.' Later, when Vic told them that, yes, Ollie was thinking of extending his portfolio into property development, Lee added cheerfully, 'He has his eye on hoarder houses and crime scenes. There's a lot of adult nappies and blood, but it's all finders keepers. If you're lucky you get to keep the war medals.' He smiled joyfully as Vic paled, her jaw tightening in fury. She made no more introductions. Maybe

Kirsty should do that; embarrass Vic into leaving her alone, stop throwing her at more and more smug mums…

Sensing Kirsty's eyes on him, Lee smiled, beckoned her over. 'Kirsty, this is Alistair. He's in murders and executions.'

'Mergers and acquisitions,' Alastair said after a baffled pause.

'Oh, OK. That makes more sense,' Lee said smoothly.

Just then, Vic tapped her glass with a spoon to get everyone's attention. She stood, slim and glowing on the new decking. She was excited.

'I'd like to thank you all for being part of this special day.' She gazed at the guests with prosecco-dimmed eyes. 'As you know, Ollie and I have been working *so* hard on the house. Not one house, either, because this was originally *two* homes and a small *barn*! So as you can imagine, the amount of work it's taken to get the place *live*able, I felt like we were caught in an endless episode of *Grand Designs*!' There was an appreciative ripple of laughter, a sympathetic wave. Alastair called out, 'We've all been there!'

'Anyway, after a year of *hard* work, *no* sleep and *hundreds* of trips to B&Q, we got here. We finally made it!' She waved her hand. 'And I'm so glad you're here to help us celebrate!' A man at the back gave a little cheer. 'But, before I show you around the house, can I ask two things? One, *no shoes* please. Two – as some of you know, I have a spiritual side, so I wanted to make absolutely sure that not only are *we* ready to move into the house, but that the *house* welcomes *us*.' She laughed. 'I can see a few eye-rolls, a few anxious looks, but you know I'm a bit crazy!' Again that little ripple of indulgent laughter. 'I'm the wacky sister. Aren't I, Kirsten?'

'Mmm,' Kirsty managed.

'You see, I still embarrass her!' Victoria blinked slowly, lovingly. 'Anyway, I've arranged for a very special ritual. A house cleansing. We wanted to build a bridge—'

'That's more your line, isn't it, Lee?' Alastair put in.

Lee answered with a cock of his beer bottle. 'It is, but after the cabinets they couldn't afford me.'

'—between ourselves and the past, to ensure *unity*. A *peaceful* house.' Milo chose that moment to throw up on the decking. There were a few stifled giggles. For a second, Kirsty saw Vic's face ripple with fear – she looked vulnerable, then, frightened, much as she had during all those months of bed rest. A flush spread up her neck, as it always did when she was nervous or excited. Today meant so much to her, it was practically existential. Kirsty felt a wave of fierce protection flow from her to her sister; she caught her eye, nodded encouragingly. It seemed to give Vic the strength to finish her prepared speech.

'*Any*way. I'd like to introduce you all to a very special woman, who, for the last week, has been spiritually cleansing our home remotely from California, and through fate.' Vic's fingers made little speech marks in the air. 'Her schedule allowed her to join us this evening for the final ritual.' Vic gave a little pause. 'I'd like to introduce to you: Angela Bright.'

She swayed ever so slightly on her heels, surveyed the crowd, assessing the impact of her news. It wasn't the greatest of impacts, to tell the truth. There were some nods, and one woman held one soft palm over her mouth in what might be excited shock, but could also easily be amusement. Mostly, people carried on looking at each other with a kind of guarded expectancy, hoping for someone to break ranks and take the lead. Kirsty realised that nobody knew who Angela Bright was. She might be famous in America, but here she was nobody. Someone whispered, 'Who?' Kirsty busied herself with Milo, so as not to witness any more of her sister's embarrassment. Lee wore an expression of happy expectation.

Vic turned to the house. 'Angela?' Her neck glowed. Her taut skin stretched over her all-too-prominent jaw. Angela didn't appear. 'Can you join us out here?' Vic's voice was strained now.

'D'you mean *here,* here, or "here", as in "here in spirit"? Is this a seance?' Lee put in cheerfully.

'Leave it, Lee,' Kirsty hissed at him under her breath.

Vic smiled tightly again. 'She was finishing the sage-burning in the conservatory. That's at the very back of the house, so a long way away. She probably just hasn't heard… Oh, wait, yes, here she is now! Angela Bright!' and she led a polite scatter of applause as a woman appeared, stepping gingerly from the house to the garden. She had the same smooth ash-blonde hair, the same gym-toned arms, the same tanned skin as Vic, although Angela Bright's looked distinctly genuine, while Vic's was sprayed on at The Tanning Shop every two weeks. She wore a simple black shift dress and there was nothing witchy-looking about her. She could have been a newsreader. Or a senior civil servant.

'Hi, everybody. My name's Angela Bright—'

Kirsty felt Lee behind her. 'What's her name again? Someone really should tell us her name.' He poked one finger into her ribs, and she could feel his chest trembling with suppressed laughter. That made Kirsty laugh too, she managed to turn it into a cough.

'I am a psychic medium. I've had the gift all my life—'

'Like herpes,' Lee whispered.

'The past is all around us. I think of it as a stain that just won't shift, a mark on the fabric of time.'

Lee poked Kirsty's ribs again. She stamped on his foot. Milo hiccupped.

'Things can get trapped, like insects in amber. They've died, but they don't know how to move on—'

'So it's house cleaning *and* fumigation she does?' Lee whispered.

'Shhh! Don't, you'll set me off!' Kirsty giggled.

'Would you sit in someone else's dirty bathwater?' Angela Bright was saying. 'No? Well, that's what we're doing every time we move into a house – we're sitting in years, *centuries* of dirty bathwater—'

'So she deals with water damage as well?' Lee whispered. 'It's an all-round service, isn't it?'

'Please!' moaned Kirsty.

'Emotions are energies, and energy does not die. There's not a scientist in the world that would disagree with me on that. And what we find when a building is renovated, or altered, is that these emotions are stirred up again – replayed, so to speak.'

'Science!' Lee whispered. 'She's a *scientist*!'

'I know there are sceptics out there.' Angela Bright looked directly at Kirsty and Lee. 'And that's as it should be.' Her lips smiled. 'It's very wise to… question things. But we all know that there are things out there that – so far – defy explanation. I believe that at some point, hopefully in our lifetimes—'

'Or our next lifetime maybe?' Lee muttered.

'These things will be not only accepted, but explained, and the gift I've been given can be used to help, not just individual clients but all mankind.'

'That's quite a remit there,' Lee whispered.

'Stop it, you're being rude now!' Kirsty whispered back.

'Can I ask if you do readings?' one of Vic's friends was asking. She had her hand in the air as if asking a teacher.

'I… *do*,' Angela Bright told her. 'But, apart from being here tonight, I'm taking a short break from face-to-face readings. But I can be contacted via my website and I can do remote viewings via email.' Her tight little smile flashed on, off. She turned briskly to Vic. 'Shall we?'

'Of course, but can I say that we're very lucky to have Angela's *mother* here as well! She's a wonderful tarot card reader, and perhaps, if you're very lucky, she may agree to doing some readings later? Sylvia?'

Kirsty noticed Angela Bright's jaw tightening, her eyes suddenly hard. One foot tapped on the decking. 'She's tired.'

'Oh, she's not, is she? Too tired?' Vic was impervious to Angela's obvious anger. 'Sylvia? Can you… *There* she is!'

Vic pulled a frail-looking older woman from the crowd. A rather wonderful-looking woman with a soft halo of white hair, like a dandelion dock, mischievous blue eyes, a shy smile.

'If you visit Angela's website…' Vic inclined her head to the awkward-looking younger woman, 'you'll see that she's descended from psychics, and Sylvia herself is also very *powerful* in her own way. Aren't you?' She twinkled at the old lady, who merely inclined her head, smiled meaninglessly.

Angela Bright whispered something to Vic then. 'Ah, yes, Angela's right to… nudge me. All right then, it's time now to enter the house, please, everyone. And can we follow Angela rather than just running about the place? That way she can… talk you through everything…'

After the guests had taken off their shoes, they were all led through the house (*Two houses! And a barn!*) by Angela Bright who took her time describing the energies she'd found in each room, and the methods she'd used to tame them. Vic chimed in about the renovation and furnishings, and where everything had to be placed according the different energies, and it took such a long time that even Lee's humour was tested. He peeled off from the tour and sought sanctuary in the kitchen. Kirsty found him picking at the weird halloumi skewers no-one wanted, and listening to Ollie who had also somehow managed to escape. Ollie was now more than partially in his cups. All that drink-serving and 'Hot enough for you?'s had taken their toll; now he wanted to talk.

'She has some kind of show in the States. One of those medium shows. Victoria saw her on the TV when she was pregnant with Milo? And she had to have all that bed rest? What was the show called? Something about angels…'

'*Touched by an Angel?*'

'No. God, what was it?'

'*Charlie's Angels*?' Lee was trying to hide his smile now.

'Or maybe not angels, maybe bridges? Bridge something…'

'*Over the River Kwai*?'

'No.'

'*Painting the Forth Bridge*? *With Angels*?'

'There you are,' Kirsty interrupted. She flashed a stern look at Lee, and a slightly weary, mothering one at Ollie. He had that doddery, broken-veined look of a man who should have switched to water a few hours ago. 'Everyone's in the sitting room now.'

'Which sitting room?' Ollie asked.

Kirsty saw Lee raise his eyebrows behind his back and mouth, 'Which sitting room…'

'The… I don't know. The one with the red sofa?'

'Ah. Why there? The other sitting room's much larger.'

'Angela says that that room is the nexus of the house,' Kirsty told him, as if it was a perfectly reasonable explanation. 'So she's doing a positive energy ritual there.'

'Is she on overtime then?' Lee put in. 'You need to watch that, Ollie. I've heard that positive energy rituals can run into serious money. Negative energy… it's like damp. You never get it first time.'

Oliver summoned sudden gravitas. His rheumy gaze met Lee's sorrowfully. 'You're being facetious.'

Lee's smile faltered. 'I'm just having a laugh, Ollie—'

'You think the whole thing is silly,' Ollie went on, 'and it may be. But I love Victoria, and this is something that's very important to her. She's found this whole process very, very difficult. All those months of not being able to move in case she lost the baby, followed by months and *months* of hard work on this house, when she still wasn't a hundred per cent. The isolation, having to do everything for Milo with no help.'

Kirsty opened her mouth, closed it.

'She wasn't alone though.' Lee's voice was serious. 'She had Kirsty the whole time.'

Ollie made a vague dismissive gesture with his hands. 'Yes, but it's not the same thing, is it?'

'The same thing as what, exactly?' Lee seldom allowed people to rile him, but he was getting riled now.

'Lee…' Kirsty said.

Ollie didn't notice though. 'I'm tremendously proud of what she's done, and how she's coped. And if some of the ways she's coped seem a little wacky to *you*, I'd like to ask you to keep it to yourself. It's… it's not *polite*.'

'Polite?' Lee said seriously.

'You may think it's all hokum, and I'm inclined to agree with you, but Angela helped Victoria through a particularly hard time, and I'm grateful to her for that, and Victoria was so happy to have her here. She's been so worried about the whole thing, you know, wanting everything to be perfect.'

'Of course,' Kirsty mumbled. She didn't want to look at Lee. If she did he might go for Ollie right there.

'Well, you know your sister. She's a giver. She doesn't like to worry people. She's like a swan – all beauty up top and pedalling like mad below the water. There's been a lot of strain. She was so scared that we'd never have children – naturally, I mean – and she worried that fertility problems might run in the family.' Kirsty managed a nod. 'But she didn't want to talk to you about it, burden you with it. And so I think Angela became that *rock* for her. And when she happened to be in the country it made sense to invite her over tonight as a guest of honour, introduce her to Milo. She's planning on asking Angela to be his godmother.'

'Oh.' Kirsty could feel Lee behind her, feel him place one soothing hand on the small of her back.

'Yes, so it means so much… so *much* to her, this night.' Oliver's eyes glistened with ginny emotion.

'Huh.'

'Sorry to have been so sharp with you, Lee.'

Lee was about to answer when the door opened and Vic poked her harassed but happy face into the kitchen. 'Ollie! Fireworks! Now? Please?'

'Ah, yes! Lee? Would you like to light the touchpaper?'

'No, I'll pass,' Lee replied. 'You're better at things like that.'

'Well I don't care who does it, but it has to be *now*,' Vic snapped. 'I promised the neighbours that the fireworks would definitely be over by seven. They have two very anxious poodles.'

'Right-o!' Ollie fairly scampered out of the kitchen. Vic closed the door behind them; she could be heard giving him painstaking instructions on the order she wanted the fireworks to be lit. 'We have to end with the hearts. The *hearts*!'

Kirsty and Lee stayed in the kitchen, which now throbbed with quiet. Kirsty poured herself a glass of wine, held it in one trembling hand. Lee finished his beer, rolled the bottle to and fro over the marble-topped island. From outside a tiny fizz of a rocket was politely applauded.

'I fucking hate your family sometimes,' Lee said quietly.

'I know. I do too.'

'Were they just *born* that way?'

'Well, Vic was. I can't be held responsible for Ollie though.'

'I just don't… I know I went too far, took the piss too much, he called me on it and I apologised.'

'You didn't really apologise though,' Kirsty put in.

'Well, why the fuck should I? I was only joking. He knew that.' He wrinkled his brow. 'And then he turns around and says all *that*—'

'I know.'

'"Fertility problems running in the family". Fuck's sake.'

'I know,' Kirsty said quietly.

'And poor Vic with no support, no friends, just a sister who gave up everything to move in with her, wait on her hand and foot—'

'But I don't think he meant to—'

'It'd be better if he *did*.' Lee's voice throbbed with anger, with near tears. 'If he was *trying* to hurt you it'd hurt less.'

'Oh, I'm all right.'

'Yes, you fucking well are. Come here.' He pulled her into a hug. His arms were roped tight with muscle, his face warm, and his breath, when he spoke, tickled her ear. 'You're worth a million of him. Him and your sister combined. And it's going to happen. The baby. It will happen.'

Kirsty stiffened, gave a sad laugh, tried to pull away. 'Well, let's not go there.'

'Oh love, we're *already* there.' He pulled her closer. 'We're there together. We'll get through it together too, not guided by Angela what's-her-name. Lansbury? Merkel?'

'Angela Rippon, I think.' Kirsty smiled.

'Angela Rip-Off.'

There was a loud explosion in the garden, a shriek from the crowd.

'Sorry about that!' Oliver could be heard. 'That one went off at a funny angle, didn't it? How about we all stay a little further back...?'

Kirsty put her finger in the air. 'Angela's Ashes?'

'And we have a winner!'

They laughed together, clasped together. Outside, the fireworks fizzed.

'Kirsten? Kirsten, come here! Come here you! I want to introduce you properly!'

Victoria swayed a little by the patio doors. Standing beside her was Angela Bright, a vague, foxed expression on her face, a glass of very flat prosecco pinched between lean fingers. Kirsty noticed that she was still wearing *her* shoes while everyone else shuffled around in their bare feet. Had she just refused to? Or was Vic too in awe of the woman to ask her?

'Angela – this is my sister. My only sibling!' She let dewy eyes rest on Kirsty's features just for a minute. 'I always have to explain that, because we look nothing alike, do we?'

Angela Bright shifted her weight from one hip to the other and smiled in a non-committal way. Then she slightly inclined her head, her lips almost forming words, but not quite, and fixed her gaze on something just slightly above Kirsty's head.

'Kirsten is my older sister. Older by – seven years, is it? God. She was like a second mother to me when we were growing up, weren't you, Kirsty?'

Vic must be pretty drunk to slip up and call her Kirsty. She hadn't done that for years, she thought it sounded common.

'She used to dress me up like a little doll, curl my hair, push me about in my pram, d'you remember?'

'Vaguely.' Kirsty smiled tightly. She was absolutely sure that had never happened. 'How long are you in the UK, Angela?'

Angela Bright's eyes drifted down, focusing on something apparently fascinating on the wainscoting. 'Not long.'

'And you live in America? How long have you been living over there?' Kirsty asked.

'I've been based in California for the last five years. But I also have a home in Lily Dale.' She left a pause that Vic scrambled to fill.

'Lily Dale is like Mecca for mediums, isn't it, Angela?'

Angela nodded slightly, her eyes pained. 'It's a spiritualist community in upstate New York. I'm fortunate enough to be one of the registered mediums there.'

'I'm desperate to go,' Vic told the room. '*Desperate!*'

Kirsty coughed. 'And where are you from originally?'

'I *told* you! Angela was born in Ireland but she was brought up near where we used to live!' Victoria said brightly.

Angela looked a little bit alarmed. 'I haven't lived here for a long time,' she muttered, and her neck flushed with heat, just like Vic's. It spread warm fingers into her hollow cheeks, and a nervous smile twitched at the corners of her lips, as if snagged by some invisible thread.

'It must be nice to see your mother. Hard living on the other side of the world from her,' Kirsty said. It was an anodyne statement, but it seemed to rattle Angela. The neck flush deepened.

'My uncle died,' she said eventually. 'That's why I'm here. The estate needs to be… dealt with.'

'Oh, I'm so sorry!' Victoria wailed. 'I had no idea!'

'Yes. Well. It happens,' Angela said shortly.

There was another pause. For a psychic medium, Angela Bright was incredibly inept at putting people at their ease. She was so different in person to how she'd seemed in all those YouTube clips Vic had shown her. A frigid aura seemed to engulf her, keeping people from getting too close. Kirsty almost felt sorry for Vic – she must have entertained all sorts of best friend fantasies about this woman, and now, here she was, about as warm as a carved idol.

'It was nice to meet you anyway.'

Angela Bright inclined her head, blinked at the carpet, and Kirsty was about to move away when Vic called Lee over. Her voice sounded slightly desperate.

'This is my marvellous brother-in law. Lee? Come and meet Angela.'

Lee grinned with slightly insulting enjoyment. 'I've never met a psychic before,' he told her. 'What's my aura? It feels reddish. Am I right?'

'I rarely read auras,' Angela murmured.

'I often think that we all have a little bit of psychic ability. Don't you? Kirsty?' The desperation was back in Vic's voice.

'Um. Yes? Maybe. I mean—'

'Great Aunt Tess used to read tea leaves.' Victoria nodded proudly. 'And Granny Cooper she was always seeing things – ghosts and… and… *things*.'

'I remember her *saying* she saw things, but I don't know if it's true,' Kirsty said. 'I think she was just a bit gaga—'

'No! No, she *did*. And I'm sure there was another aunt who read cards, and…' *Poor Vic. So anxious to be different, so terrified of not fitting in.* 'And speaking of cards, your mother's been doing a splendid job. Out in the gazebo?'

'She's doing what?' Angela's voice had just a trace of the local accent. It almost made her seem human. 'Where is she?'

'Outside? In the gazebo? A few friends asked her to read their cards and she's been out there for quite a while now…'

Suddenly Angela stalked out of the room, into the garden. Vic and Kirsty could see her marching over to the gazebo.

'Kirsty, go and see what's happening, will you?' Vic hissed. 'Go and see why she's upset.'

And so Kirsty dutifully did just that. She wandered into the now mercifully chilly garden to find Angela Bright hovering at the edge of a crowd of wavering women, all with their heads inclined, gentle smiles on their faces, listening to Sylvia talk self-effacingly about tarot.

'I'm nothing compared to Angela, of course. She's… oh, she was always so *talented*! Me, I tend to just use the cards, but Angela, oh my lord, she was so *intuitive*! And she worked so *hard* too – that's the thing, you can't just rely on talent, you have to practise. It's like being a tennis player, I suppose, or an athlete – not that I'd know anything about athletics! With my osteoporosis I'd snap like a twig if I tried anything… a headstand even.' She rolled her eyes drolly and got an appreciative chuckle back. 'No, as soon as Angela came into her gifts she was determined. Just absolutely single-minded. That's why she had to go to America, of course, because that's where the money is—'

'Mum?' Angela broke in.

'Yes, darling? I didn't see you there! Just singing your praises, don't get embarrassed—'

'I need your help with something.'

'What? What with?'

'Just something to do with the cleansing. Please?' Angela put out one impatient hand, like a mother with a dawdling child.

Sylvia got up with visible effort, nodded goodbye to her audience, and followed her daughter back into the bright house, a pace or two behind. They didn't speak.

The women made general huffing, assessing sounds that could be translated as *What a lovely old woman*, and *What's the daughter's problem?* Kirsty wondered that herself.

Despite the furnishings, the rugs, the cushions, the house was too big to feel homely, and the acoustics were strange. It reminded her of somewhere but the full memory was just out of reach… Some sounds carried from the furthest ends of the place, while others stopped dead, as if blocked by invisible barriers. Maybe Vic was right. Maybe the house (*Two houses! And a barn!*) *was* haunted in some way. Despite being only a room away from the garden, the noise of the party didn't reach Kirsty, yet from much further away, upstairs in fact, she could hear definite murmurings. As she crept up the stairs (telling herself that she was just trying to find the toilet, that was all) she recognised Angela's voice, speaking, presumably, to her mother. They were both sitting in Milo's room.

'—here?'

'Well, why shouldn't I? I was invited too.'

'It's my job.' Angela sounded sullen.

'And I was helping you. I was talking all about you, and how wonderful you are! Surely you can't hate me for that?' Sylvia sounded close to tears. 'I'm *proud* of you! And now you can see how much interest there is here, you could come home, couldn't you? Live with me?'

'I'm not staying, Mum, you know that.'

'Didn't think you'd go back,' Sylvia replied after a mournful pause. 'I thought, after Mervyn, you'd stay a while… It's lonely there by myself and I can't get around as well as I could.'

'That's why you need a smaller place. You said you—'

'I just need a bit of help where I am, that's all. If you came back, even for a bit—'

'I'm not coming back though!' Angela almost shouted. 'It's not happening, OK?'

'OK,' Sylvia answered softly. 'I don't want to upset you. I'd never want that.'

'Then why—' The door to the stairs opened, and the noise from the crowd downstairs drowned out the rest of the sentence. Then the bedroom door opened too, and Kirsty ducked into the room next door (a magnolia box earmarked as a meditation room). She didn't want to encounter Angela Bright on the stairs, and she wished she'd never overheard this strange and pitiful conversation. She heard Angela's light tread on the stairs, then the living room door closing, then a sob from the room next door.

Sylvia was sitting on the rocking chair by Milo's cot, dabbing her eyes with a handkerchief. She started when she saw Kirsty in the doorway, and hurriedly put on a smile.

'Allergies,' she said.

Kirsty smiled sympathetically. 'Can I get you some water? Or…'

'No, no. I tell you what you can do, though, you can help winch me out of this chair!' Her face had almost recovered. Those blue, blue eyes were poking fun at herself as the tears dried. 'I'm getting to the age when I can't get up under my own steam.'

'Do you need help down the stairs?' Kirsty had her by one elbow now. She weighed nothing. She could have picked her up and carried her like a doll.

'I will, yes. God, I tell you, it's funny – getting old. You never think it's going to happen, and then, suddenly…' Her face creased with pain. 'Can we just stay here for a minute? Let me get my breath before tackling the stairs.' She leaned against the wall and took a few deep breaths. 'She was right. I shouldn't have come,' she muttered to herself. Then she smiled. 'That's another thing, you talk to yourself when you start getting old. I have some good chats with myself! You must think I'm dotty.'

Kirsty shook her head, smiled. 'I don't think you're dotty.'

'Work with dotty people, do you? Used to it?'

'I'm a social worker at the hospital, so yes I *do* and I *am*, but I still don't think you're dotty. Ready to go downstairs now?'

Sylvia nodded. They ambled gently down the stairs, arm in arm, and when Kirsty opened the door at the bottom, a sudden wave of noise hit them both. This house was genuinely unsettling. Upstairs they could have been two people alone on an island, and down here…

'There you are!' Vic was looking more than a little pink around the eyes. Her wine glass wavered. 'Lee's been looking for you! And Sylvia? Angela needs you.'

She took Sylvia's other arm, and led them both over to a long, low, blue sofa, where Angela was sitting, back ramrod straight, expression-less face set, ignoring the increasingly timorous conversation around her. When she saw Sylvia she frowned, but when she saw Kirsty, her face went through a strange kaleidoscopic ripple of different emotions, each too brief to grasp. As if being propelled by an unseen force, she moved towards her, took her hand, which Kirsty, though startled, didn't think to pull away. From behind her she felt people staring.

Angela Bright closed her eyes, opened them, she looked directly at Kirsty. Blue eyes on brown.

'You've lost someone,' she said. 'Someone is missing.'

'What? What d'you mean?'

'What?' Vic echoed. 'Angela, are you seeing something? Can you *see* something? In Kirsten?'

Angela put two fingers to her brow, closed her eyes and frowned. 'I have such a feeling of loss. Loss, and fear and… guilt? Does this make sense?' Her eyes met Kirsty's again, and they were pleading. Now, for the first time, she resembled the woman on the YouTube clips. 'You think you're to blame. Can you understand this?'

'I think you should stop there,' Lee said firmly, moving to Kirsty's side. 'Stop that now.'

Angela Bright didn't stop, she didn't even hear him. 'You're missing someone. A girl. She's coming though. You'll see her soon.' For the first time that evening, Angela's face, filled with fractious emotions, with the stuttering need to transmit knowledge, looked like the face of a real person. The smooth, pale skin around each eye was pulled taut, and out of her too-young sockets shone old, old eyes. 'You're going to see her soon.'

'She's been trying for a baby,' Vic put in. 'Is it that you see? It *is*, isn't it?'

'That's enough now.' Lee was more forceful now. 'Stop.' He took Kirsty's hand. 'Let's go.'

But still the medium ignored him and grabbed Kirsty's wrist with one sudden movement. Her grip was strong… strong enough to check Lee. 'Do you know who she is?'

'Yes,' Kirsty found herself whispering. 'Yes.'

The medium's fingers dug into her wrist painfully, and Kirsty, hypnotised, stared at her face, as the medium's eyes rolled back in her head, her grip tightened further.

She whispered, 'You have to prepare. If you do, and you're careful, she'll appear. You won't have to wait much longer.'

Dimly, Kirsty registered Lee's alarmed anger, Victoria's tipsy concern, but she couldn't move her eyes from Angela Bright. She felt the words burrow down into her brain like a tick.

'She'll appear. You won't have to wait much longer.'

'What for?' she murmured back.

The medium replied, 'You've been expecting her for a long time. And soon you'll see her.'

Then, the medium's grip loosened and fell – the next day, Kirsty would see four digit-sized bruises circling her wrist – and the moment was over and the outside world came rushing into the strange, sudden vacuum. She stood, dazed. Vic gave her water, Lee was talking, Lee was upset, and Kirsty wanted to tell him to calm down, but she didn't. Instead she walked back upstairs to Victoria's needlessly large en-suite, where she sat on the toilet seat and started to cry.

A minute later there was a knock on the door. Kirsty hurriedly turned on a gushing tap, patted her eyes, grimaced at her stricken reflection.

'Just a minute.'

'It's me.'

'Lee? Wait a minute…' She unlocked the door. 'I just needed a bit of a break.'

'Vic's outdone herself tonight, eh?' Lee was grim. He closed the door behind him and perched on the side of the bath. The beer bottle quivered in his hand. 'She should write a book. *How to Make Your Sister Feel Like Shit in Twelve Easy Steps.*'

'It wasn't her fault. She didn't make Angela say all that.'

Lee took out a cigarette, lit it, blew deliberate smoke at the carefully laundered and softened Egyptian cotton towels arranged ever-so-carefully on the heated rack. 'I don't know how she manages it. It's a gift.'

'It wasn't her fault. Put the fag out, will you? She'll go mad if she knows you've been smoking in the house.'

'That's my intention, my love. To drive her mad.' Lee squinted through smoke, smiled crookedly. 'It's the only weapon I have. It's my superpower.'

'How is she?'

'Vic? Fine. Not up here. Why would she be up here? With the sister who ran off in tears?'

'Lee…'

He shook his head. 'Just what the hell was all that about anyway? Why would Vic *tell* her anything about it?'

'Maybe she didn't.'

'Well how else would what's-her-face know?'

Kirsty turned over limp arms in her lap, her palms falling open. 'I don't know. Maybe it wasn't anything about getting pregnant.'

There was a silence. 'What was it about then, do you think?'

'Lisa? Maybe it was about that.'

'Why though? Why would Vic even mention what… happened back then? I doubt she even thinks about it. It's not directly about her, so there's no way she'd mention it.'

'Maybe Angela Bright is the real deal?' Kirsty managed to smile. 'Maybe she saw into my soul.'

'Bollocks,' Lee said shortly. He ditched the cigarette into the toilet. It fizzed there like a tiny firework. 'Have you been thinking about it much?' he asked eventually. 'About the Lisa thing?'

'Not so much,' Kirsty lied.

'And you haven't been going on any of those nut-job conspiracy sites, have you?'

'No.'

'Well that's something.' Lee lit another cigarette. 'It's old news now.'

'It's the anniversary today.'

'Shit, love, why didn't you tell me?' Lee put one hot, firm hand on her shoulder. 'Let's go. Let's go home.'

'We can't. We're meant to be staying the night, she has a whole breakfast arranged for tomorrow, and I'm meant to help her with it—'

'Oh, fuck her. Let Witchy McWitchface help her. We're leaving. We'll go back to your little pied-à-terre.'

'We've both been drinking so we can't drive, and it'd cost a fortune to get a cab all that way—'

'Kirsty, at this stage of the game, I'd pay a couple of grand just to avoid anything else your sister might throw at you.'

'It wasn't her fault—'

'Will you stop saying that?' Lee's voice was suddenly furious, hoarse. 'Will you stop saying she doesn't mean it! She might not plan, me*ticu*lously, how she's going to make you feel like shit at any given moment, but she *always* manages it by default. It's like an instinct. It's her one talent, apart from annoying the shit out of any right-thinking person. When are you going to wise up about her, Kirsty? How much time do you have to spend crying in bathrooms about your sister before you start protecting yourself?'

'Don't shout at me.'

'Well, I'm frustrated. I'm…' He lit another cigarette. 'I don't want to see you hurt, that's all.'

There was a knock on the door, and someone turned the handle, once, twice, jiggling it in impatience. A fruity-sounding woman coughed, tapped on the door again. 'Is there anyone in there?'

'No,' Lee answered. 'Nobody.'

There was an indignant pause. 'Because you've been in there rather a long time, and people do need to…'

'To what?' Lee asked.

Kirsty began to smile despite herself. 'Lee, stop it now.'

'To *use* the *toilet*,' came the icy reply.

'Let me get rid of this rat first,' Lee called. 'Shouldn't be too long now, I've nearly forced it down the U-bend.'

'*Rat?*

'Oh yeah. Old house. Old *houses*, I should say, because this was *two* houses and a *barn* originally, wasn't it? And where there's barns, there's always rats. Big, sturdy ones that bite your arse soon as you sit down on the loo. They wait under the rim.'

Lee grinned at Kirsty, who was now shaking with silent laughter.

'The lady of the house brought me in specially to deal with it. I came by the tradesman's entrance at the back, so none of the party guests would see me. Don't let on, will you?'

There was a confused shuffling sound from outside. Kirsty bit her lips to keep from laughing, while Lee pumped the toilet flush, squeaked, flushed again. 'Get down there, you bastard!'

'Oh my god!' came the voice from outside.

'It's putting up a bit of a fight, this one!' Lee called over the sound of the flush. 'I might need to brain it with a spanner if it carries on like this.'

That did it. They heard the woman trot down the stairs; Kirsty let out a bark of laughter.

'And there's worse where that came from,' Lee told her. 'One more conversation with one more fat golfer and I won't be responsible for my actions.' He took one of her hands. 'Let's just go back to yours, drink that nice bottle of wine I decided not to bring after all, and fuck like rabbits, what d'you say?'

'Vic'll be upset.'

'I doubt it. She's bulletproof. You're not though. Come on.'

They tiptoed down the stairs, past the kitchen, and out through the front door. Lee doubled back to retrieve another bottle of wine and came back laughing. 'Some woman in there's going on and on about rats. Scandalised. Quick, let's get out quick.'

They ran down the drive, giggling, out into the night.

CHAPTER FIFTEEN

That night, Kirsty dreamed. She dreamed that they were by the canal, she and Lisa, and the strange low limelight of a coming storm touched their hair a brassy gold. Kirsty couldn't see Lisa's face very well, just her smile, and her smile was so happy, guileless. When they held hands, the snake ring felt hot against her palm, its red eyes little pinpricks of fire.

Lisa said, 'Let me teach you,' and squeezed her hand hard, and Kirsty, suddenly, didn't want to be taught. She tried to tug her hand away. The dark water shifted like something alive. Lisa's smile began to fade.

'I don't want to go without you. Please?'

But even as she begged she was backing away towards the water which seemed to reach up to embrace her. She slid into it like tar until only her hand stayed visible – the forefinger extended, pointing to the surreal sky, and the snake's eyes shone before one fell out and dripped down Lisa's palm like blood.

Kirsty woke sweating, crying, and Lee – good, kind Lee – cursed Vic and her stupid party and that bastard psychic. 'You'll be all right, love. You'll be all right, I'll make sure you are, OK? OK? You're safe, you're safe.'

*

But she wasn't safe. On Monday she got the first note, shoved under her office door, printed – incongruously – in some childish font.

You shouldn't have come back

She should have thrown it away; crumpled it up and thrown it in the bin. She could have taken it to the police? But even now, Kirsty shrank from the idea of doing that. What if they shepherded her back into that same little room, had her hunch over the same hearing-aid-brown tape recorder… And what could she say anyway? Where was the threat? And so she didn't do anything. She smoothed it out, put it in an envelope, kept it in her desk drawer.

The next day there was another.

There's no place for you here

And two days after that, a third.

Whatever you think you know, you don't

She almost told Lee. She almost asked estates if they had CCTV footage of the corridor. But in the end they went into the envelope too. There was a dark familiarity to this feeling – she was under siege, under threat. But this time she wasn't going to buckle. This time she wouldn't run. This time she'd exercise some control over the situation herself.

*

The Peg Leaves situation was still stalled. Mona – after a fractious conversation with one of Kirsty's colleagues at Social Services – had shut down negotiations completely, and once again, Kirsty was wheeled out to repair the damage. Since Mona refused to come to the hospital, Kirsty went to see her; for the first time in decades, she found herself in the Beacon Hill estate.

In a strange way it was a welcome trip. For the last month or so, Kirsty had lived alongside her past, feeling it encroach on her while she stayed frozen, unprotesting. Being back in Beacon

Hill felt as if she was showing some mettle, proving that the past couldn't break her. Still, her hands were sweaty on the steering wheel, a tension headache throbbed at her temples. She imagined how Lee would react if he knew where she was right now and decided not to tell him.

She drove past houses that, flimsy when first built, were now dilapidated, the mish-mash of flats on the estate's outer edge sometimes boarded up, sometimes decorated with St George's flags, Christmas lights that had never been taken down. One house in the middle of a row was completely burnt out, police tape still fluttering from the stump of a gatepost.

The visit to Mona was, predictably, a non-starter. Either she wasn't in or she was pretending to be out. Kirsty had expected this, and so she brought out her previously prepared note – handwritten, a careful paragraph of respectful fealty to Peg, and sorrowful reiteration of what might happen if Mona didn't co-operate. On the way back, she decided, almost on a whim, to call on Denise. Over the years, they had kept touch with each other, Kirsty sending her a Christmas card every year, to which Denise always responded with a brief letter at New Year. That she hadn't been to see her in all the time she'd been back seemed, suddenly, a cruel oversight that she had to make up for right now.

The house, she noticed with a shiver, was exactly the same. The same mottled crazy paving, the same PVC door, the same doorbell chime – 'Why do birds suddenly appear', off-key. And Denise was the same – a solid oblong of a woman with a wood-carved face still topped with improbably auburn hair, stiff as wire. She smiled, flashing new dentures.

'It's nice to see you, Kirsty. Heard you were back.' Her voice was strong, clear, with a slight clotted whisper running through it like a seam.

'Word gets around, eh?'

'It always has, and it always will. Mona told me. Saw her a few weeks back, asked about Peg, she mentioned you then. Come in. Have a cup of tea.'

'I'm so sorry I haven't been to see you sooner; I—'

Denise made a dismissive gesture with one liver-spotted hand. 'Stop. Get yourself inside. It's starting to rain.'

The house seemed smaller, barer, but it was obvious that Denise didn't live alone. There were three half-drunk cups of tea on the table, and as they passed the closed living room door, Kirsty heard a TV, and every now and again a short, sharp laugh like a nasty cough.

'I am sorry though, that I haven't been before. It's taken me a while to get settled. Thanks.'

Denise paced a mug of murky tea before her. Kirsty took a small sip, tried not to grimace. The milk was sour.

'Married?'

'Yes!'

'Kids?'

'No.'

'Well, they're more trouble than they're worth,' Denise said kindly. 'What are you doing with yourself at Queens then?'

'Social work. Care plans for the elderly, that kind of thing.'

Denise raised her eyebrows. 'Well you've got your work cut out with Peg then.'

Kirsty inclined her head, smiled. 'You're not wrong.'

'What'd you come back here for? You were in London, weren't you?'

'Well, it's a good job,' Kirsty said lamely. 'And, you know. There's no place like home.'

Denise made a noise, wheezy as a dying washing machine, slightly menacing. It took Kirsty a moment to realise it was a laugh.

'You're too young to be so daft. It's bad, this place, and you know it. It's bad to most of us, but worse to you.'

'You're still here though?'

'I've got no choice, love. Remember Bryan? He's here. Got a little girl of his own now. Can't move away from family, can you?'

'Bryan lives here? With you?' That nasty laugh from the living room seemed more sinister now. What if Bryan was just there, within a few feet of her? What if he was standing behind her now? Her spine seemed to fuse together.

Denise shook her head. 'I'm old and daft but not that daft. No, he doesn't live here. He's calmed down a bit, but still… You look pale. He's not been hassling you, has he? Bryan? Like he used to? He can get… This time of year brings out the worst in him. If he's calling you or sending letters, just tell me and I'll make him stop.'

'Does he do that? Send letters?' Kirsty asked eagerly.

'Only to newspapers, as far as I know. Why? *Have* you been getting… anything? I'll have a word with him if… threats? Is that what you mean?'

'Not threats. Just notes. And you? Are you getting any… threats, or—'

'Threats? No. Not any more. All I get now are calls from the papers every March, or when he tries an appeal, the odd letter from the bleeding-heart brigade… "This innocent man has suffered enough." It's funny, isn't it? You're left alone for three hundred and sixty-four days and on the three hundred and sixty-fifth, that's when you get remembered. As if that's the one day you need someone telling you what a bloody awful mother you are.'

'How's Bryan?'

Denise made a harrumph sound. 'Bryan is Bryan. You saw that interview in the *Mail*?'

'Yes.'

'Aye, well.' Denise paused. Kirsty could hear the little wheeze in her throat, a desperate appeal for nicotine. Her dry fingers found a cigarette packet. The click and fizz of a cigarette being lit was loud in the quiet. 'You know how much they paid him for it? Two hundred quid.' Denise laughed. 'He said they might want one with me. Said it'd be a grand and we could share it. I said, "What do I need with five hundred quid?" and you know what he said? He said, "No, you'd get two hundred and I'd keep the rest because I did all the work!"'

'Jesus, Denise. I'm sorry.'

'Oh, don't be. It's funny is what it is.'

'Did he tell you beforehand, that he was doing this interview?'

'Kirsty, what people don't tell me would fill Wembley Arena. Things just happen and I'm the last to know. Like this judicial review? Did they tell you about that?'

'What?'

'He's looking for a judicial review.' Denise never said the name Tokki or Toqueer. He was always 'He' or 'that bastard'. She let out her breath in one smoky rasp. 'It's the same thing as before, but this time he's got a team of people, they say.' Denise began to chuckle. 'A team. Like it's the Premier League for bastards. Papers called. I just said no comment, like I always do. That gets to them. They want me to cry and all that. Make a statement. Well, they can whistle for it.'

'I'm sorry, Denise.'

'Well, it's not your fault.'

'It's not fair on you though,' Kirsty murmured.

'It's not, no,' Denise said shortly. 'But it's nothing new either. Anyway, how's Vicky?'

'She moved to Marsden last year—'

'Marsden? She's not short of a bob or two then, is she?'

'Married well. And had a baby, so I wanted to move closer to her, so, here I am.'

'You wanted to move, and here "you" are?' Denise smiled. 'What about your other half?'

'He's got to finish a few things before he can move up here properly.'

Denise just nodded. Her eyes were hooded. Finally she said, 'It's not good to be here alone, Kirsty. This place won't be kind to you.'

'I'm not alone. I won't be for long anyway, Lee will be moving up soon. And I get to look after my nephew, spend time with my sister. Keep her on the straight and narrow. She's away with the fairies.' She laughed nervously. Why was she nervous anyway? 'At her house-warming the other day she had some psychic there. To bless the house.'

'What?' Denise's voice fractured into a catarrhy laugh. 'She's got more money than sense, that girl!'

'That's what Lee says too. He was really pissed off about it.'

'Why's that then?'

'Oh, she – the medium woman – she upset me a bit. She didn't mean to, but she said some stuff and—'

Denise hesitated. 'What about? Lisa?'

Kirsty was startled. 'I don't know. Lee thought so, and he gets protective of me, and, well, he doesn't like all that psychic stuff.'

'I used to get them all the time,' Denise said after a pause. 'Psychics. They always want to tell me something about her. After… what happened, they called a lot, sent me letters. Wanting to help, they said. Stuart always got rid of them.'

'What kind of things were they saying then?'

'They said they had a message from her, that they could help find her. All that.'

'And now? Do they call you now?'

'Aye. Not so much, but sometimes. Around this time, you know.' Denise spoke guardedly. Kirsty couldn't gauge if she wanted to shut the conversation down or wanted to be asked more.

'Have any of them… said anything you believe?'

Denise left a long pause. 'I'm not sure. It's… sometimes they say things that are spot on, you know? And then you think, oh well, they've just read the papers, that's all. But sometimes they say something and you think… bloody hell, how'd you know that? And I don't think they're bad people. I think they believe it, some of them anyway. And they want to help, give me some comfort. I don't know. I can't get angry with someone wanting to do that.' Denise lit another cigarette. 'And who knows? There might be something in it.' Again, that meditative silence, pregnant, cagey.

'Has anyone… told you something you believe?' Kirsty found herself asking.

Denise left a long silence. 'There's this woman, I've known her for donkey's years. Lives just over the way there.' She waved vaguely upwards. 'She's… said things that have made me think maybe there's something in it. She does my cards every now and then. It might be all rubbish or it might not, but at the end of the day what's the harm if it makes a person feel better?' Denise sounded a little defensive now, and Kirsty went straight into mollification mode.

'I think you're right. They can't all be bad, psychics. I mean, if they're… helping?'

'If it's someone you trust,' Denise said carefully. 'That's the thing, you've got to trust them. They have to be a good person.' She looked up, squinted humorously. 'Don't worry, I've still got most of my marbles.'

Kirsty smiled back. 'You're as tough as old boots,' she said.

'I am. And so're *you*. There's a lot of bad things about this town, but the upside is it makes you tough. What happened to you? It's made you tough. You've just got to believe it, that's all.' She patted the table briskly, got up slowly. 'Anyway, I've got to get on with tea. Alex and Tom…' She waved vaguely in the direction of the sound of the TV.

'Alex and Tom?'

'Alexsei and… what's the other one? Tomash or something. I call them Alex and Tom. Polish. Lodgers.'

'You… you still take in lodgers then?'

'I'd be left high and dry if I didn't.' Denise was all efficiency now, clattering plates out of cupboards, opening tins of murky-looking meat. 'And it's company. It's quiet living alone.'

'Mind if I use the loo?'

'Aye, you know the way.' One finger pointed towards the stairs. In her distraction and sudden activity, Denise seemed to have shed years. Kirsty too, heading up those familiar stairs, felt younger with each step, until, by the landing, she could have been ten years old again.

There was Lisa's room. There was Tokki and Mohammed's room. Or was it Alex and Tom's room now? She pushed open the door, peered into a room coarsened by Polish cigarettes and aftershave. Then she opened the door to Lisa's room, and for one strange moment it was dingy pink-and-white, the rumpled bed heaped with Care Bears, the kiss-practice George Michael picture still Sellotaped next to the smeary mirror, and Lisa herself was there too, just out of sight for sure, but surely there, smelling of orange chapstick and indifferently brushed teeth. But that only lasted for a second. The room was merely a mirror image of the room next door – a cramped, male, space. An adult space. Suddenly it felt wrong, so wrong, unfathomably wrong. How could Denise have done this?

How could she have given over Lisa's old room to another lodger – and a male lodger at that…? How could she have moved on? Kirsty backed away and went to the toilet, tried to calm down. What had she done with Lisa's clothes, her Care Bears, her silly little Pierrot pictures? Were they rotted to mulch in landfill? Burned? It seemed insane that a mother could do that, just erase all memories of a dead child.

'But what do I know about being a mother?' she told herself out loud. Perhaps she was being unreasonable. She'd unwittingly spun a Miss Havisham-type fantasy around Denise…

A Denise that stayed in her house, where all those bad things happened, where her daughter was groomed, abused. That had to be unhinged, surely? Why should Denise be trapped living entirely in the past, guilty, bitter, dead inside? And she had to make money, didn't she? Why not take in lodgers? Kirsty looked at herself in the mirror; the same mirror she and Lisa had once covered with toothpaste when they were five, the same mirror they'd practised pouting in when they were ten. She looked at her own, peevish face. *Be honest with yourself, Kirsty; you don't want Denise to be OK because that makes you NOT being OK even worse.* If Denise didn't feel guilt about letting out her dead daughter's room, then why did Kirsty feel so crushingly guilty? How did Denise manage so well?

Perhaps it was the woman who did her cards. Perhaps that's what helped her move on? *After all, what's the harm if it makes you feel better?* She patted her face with water, took a few deep breaths, and walked down the stairs again, past the still shut living room door, back into the kitchen, where Denise was listening to talk radio and clattering pots.

'That lady who does your cards? Would she see me?'

'Don't see why not,' Denise told her. 'She lives over the way, you could pop in on your way back.'

'No. I mean, I'm a stranger. I don't want to just ambush her. Maybe if you give me her number?'

And Denise did just that, her no-nonsense cursive covering the back of a shopping list.

Sylvia McKnight 706546

'Wait, is she an older lady? White hair?'

'She's younger than me!' Denise answered. 'But yeah, it sounds like her. Why?'

'I think I met her the other night, at Vic's! It was her daughter that was doing that ceremony thing! That's... so weird!'

'Not that weird,' Denise told her. 'The older you get the more you see things like that. Call it coincidence if you want, but still... Anyway, yes that's her. Must be. What was the daughter called?'

'Angela Bright.'

Denise smirked. It was impossible to fathom what the smirk meant. 'That's what she's calling herself now, is it? Used to be Mary, or something like that. What's she doing back here?'

'She told me she'd come back to sort out her uncle's estate.'

Denise snorted. 'Estate? Makes it sound like the National Trust! It's more like Soweto where they live. *Estate*, ye gods. You'll be able to see it if you take the long way back to town – trailers, car yard. She lives there, Sylvia does; as for what's-her-name, Mary or *Angela* or whatever, she upped sticks years ago. Left Sylvia struggling too, apparently. Sylvia's hardly got a pot to piss in now.'

'She... Angela, I mean, she did seem... They didn't look like they had the best relationship.'

'No. Though to hear Sylvia talk you'd think she was a saint. Some mums are like that, aren't they though? Can't see their kids for what they are. But don't tell Peg I said that, 'cause she likes the girl.'

'Peg knows Angela Bright?'

'Peg knows everyone. No, I think Mary, or whatever her name is, is Peg's niece? Something like that. Alex! Tom! Dinner!'

Kirsty knew that was her cue to leave.

She put Sylvia McKnight's phone number in her pocket, and she did take the long way back to work, but the haze across the flat, murky fields obscured most of the estate. All she could discern were some long, low trailer-type buildings, some heaped scrap metal. It made her sad to think of such a sweet old lady living somewhere that dismal. But at least she had somewhere to live. What plans did her daughter have for her after selling the land? From what she'd overheard at Vic's party, it didn't sound as if she'd be staying with her daughter in America any time soon. Perhaps Kirsty would call up Sylvia, ask for a reading? It wouldn't feel a peculiar, now that they'd already met and Denise had vouched for her. And maybe there was something in it? If it helped, what was the harm? Also, the old lady must be lonely, out there on that wind-lashed land all by herself… Kirsty slowed down, almost swung the car over to the side of the road with a view to walking over there now. Then she thought better of it. Work beckoned. And Sylvia McKnight wasn't going anywhere.

CHAPTER SIXTEEN

Back at the hospital, Kirsty threw herself into Peg's after-care plan: even though everything still depended on Mona, and Mona wasn't playing ball, Kirsty still believed that if she reworded and rehearsed the pitch, Mona would see sense. But by six she was ready to give up; her office was stuffy, the plan becoming unwieldy, unworkable because she was trying to please everyone and the harsh strip light hurt her eyes and tightened her skin. She was just shutting down her computer when the ward sister knocked on her door.

'There's a lady – a friend of Mrs Leaves? She wants a word with her social worker – can I send her to you?'

'I'm about to leave. But, sure. OK. What's it about?'

'Won't tell me. I'll just go and get her.'

The ward sister came back a few minutes later. 'OK, she's being a bit mysterious now. She says she doesn't want to come to your office, but in the cafe?'

'Why?' Kirsty asked tiredly, irritably.

'She says she wants to help. Something to do with… you know… the whole family. Being difficult? She says she has an idea.'

Well, she might be worth listening to. Anything, *anything* that might break the Peg Leaves impasse would be useful.

And so Kirsty made her way to the incongruously named Spice of Life cafe in reception, looking out for a woman built on the same towering frame as the Leaveses. What she saw wasn't like that at all. The only person in the Spice of Life was a small-boned, fragile-looking old lady, with a halo of white hair and blue, blue eyes.

Sylvia McKnight.

It was such a shock that Kirsty actually froze a few paces away and watched the woman sit, vague, troubled, looking tenderly at anyone passing who might, conceivably, be a social worker.

'Mrs McKnight?' She watched the vagueness clear, and something like delighted gratitude flooding in its stead.

'How strange! I was *hoping* it would be you!' the woman said.

'Families,' Sylvia said. They were sitting in the corner of the cafe, nursing tea. The steam rose between them, a gauzy screen. 'They're difficult, aren't they? But they're all you have.' She smiled. 'I'm too sentimental, that's what my daughter says. She's right too, I *am*, but if you *can* help you *should* help. I've always thought that.'

Kirsty shook her head.

'I'm confusing you. I'm sorry. What it is, why I'm here, I'm Peg's sister-in-law? Well, ex-sister-in-law since my brother recently passed away. And they weren't married. And they hadn't lived with each other in ever so long. But still. Family.'

'How can I help?'

'I wondered if we could have a chat about what happens after she leaves? The reason I'm asking is that Mona – you know Mona? She's my late brother's daughter? – yes, well they all want her back home, of course they do, but my worry is that they don't really understand what a big job it's going to be. Looking after someone who's… poorly. I've just gone through that myself with Mervyn. I just want to make sure that Peg won't be sent home too early, and just forgotten about. I don't mean by *you*, but by the system…? You read about things like that all the time, don't you?'

'You don't have to worry about that, Mrs McKnight, we have a care plan—'

'And I bet Mona's doing everything she can to ruin it,' Sylvia said with a sad smile. 'Oh, don't get me wrong, I know why she'd do that. She's afraid. She... she's still a child, Mona, in some ways. She's scared that Peg's getting older, she doesn't want to see that she's not as strong as she was, and she can't face the idea that, someday, she'll lose her. So she's digging her heels in. That's what's happening, isn't it? I know you can't talk about cases, but that's how it is, isn't it?'

Kirsty slightly inclined her head.

'Right, well, here's how I might be able to help: I've got this big house, and I'd like to help her now. It's only right, isn't it? Maybe she could come and stay at my house? Peg and Mona? I wouldn't mind having Social Services come in, and I'll make any changes needed to help her get around? And my daughter, Marie? You met her, didn't you? I'm sure she'd help while she's here...' Her voice trailed away just a little, doubtfully. 'Do you think that would work?'

'Marie? I thought she was called—'

'Angela? Yes, she is. Sorry.' Sylvia peered at her, smiled. 'Don't worry, I'm not senile! She is called Angela. Now. It's more of a professional name. But she was born Marie. I just... forget sometimes. Drives her mad!' She took a sip of tea. 'Now, how about this idea?'

It was an intriguing idea... semi-ridiculous, but deeply meant. There was no way it could happen. Kirsty played for time a little though, not wanting to disappoint such a kind-hearted woman, and – she realised this suddenly – not wanting to end the conversation either.

'What does the family think about all this?'

The woman's face seemed to fold in on itself. The eyes softened, the mouth pursed.

'I've been a coward about that. I should've spoken to Mona, but she's... she's a tough nut to crack. Well, you know all about that, don't you? Her and Mervyn never saw eye to eye and so I think I might have got tarred with the same brush; she's always a bit rude to me, and I'm a little bit afraid of her! Isn't that silly? I've known her since she was a baby, but still. That's why I wanted to talk to the hospital first. I'm a bit embarrassed now, wasting your time like this.'

'You're not wasting my time!' Kirsty told her warmly. She wanted to tell her not to take it personally, that Mona was rude to everyone, but then Sylvia probably already knew that…

Mrs McKnight smiled. 'You're very polite. Anyway, how's your sister? And that lovely baby of hers?'

And so they chatted. Just light conversation, tentatively appraising each other. Kirsty asked about Angela, and Sylvia beamed with pride as she talked about her career in America.

'I've seen pictures of the house – lovely it is! And a pool! But they have the weather for it there, don't they? She goes to all these parties and premieres and I don't know what else! Far cry from here, eh?' Sylvia gestured at the walking wounded in reception, the dark, smelly forecourt, the whole gritty city beyond.

'Is she staying with you at the moment then?'

'Me? No!' Sylvia was surprised, as if staying with your lonely, isolated mother was something bizarre. 'No, she needs her home comforts. And my place, well, it's still very ramshackle. Draughty, you know. The generator goes quite often. But obviously I'll sort all that out if Peg comes to stay,' Sylvia said stoutly.

'It should be a comfortable place for you too, shouldn't it? You mentioned having osteoporosis?'

Sylvia pushed one thin hand through the air, dismissive, humorous gesture. 'Oh don't worry about me! I've been fine up to now, after all. If you gave me double glazing and proper heating and all that I wouldn't know what to do with myself!'

Kirsty remembered how much pain she'd been in at the party, how desolate and depressing her home had seemed from the side of the road. Sylvia's idea of fine was different to most people's, it seemed, especially her daughter's. Kirsty tried to imagine the manicured, poised Angela Bright in Beacon Hill. She couldn't.

Eventually though, their conversation dried up a little, and when the lugubrious manager of the Spice of Life skirted around them for the third time, they took the hint and got up to leave. Standing upright, Kirsty could see that Sylvia had lost even more weight since the party. She was now almost pitifully thin; tiny wrists swam in the sleeves of her cheerful yellow cardigan, and her twig-like calves tapered even further to impossibly slim ankles – so slim that at first it seemed that she was wearing oversized men's boots, but which were in fact completely normal ladies' brogues. Then, suddenly, the old woman's face turned the sick cream of parchment, her eyes, filled with what looked like agony, fixed on Kirsty's. She wobbled on her heels, caught the edge of the table, sat back down again.

'Mrs McKnight? Are you OK?'

'Little bit dizzy, that's all.' The woman laughed self-deprecatingly. 'Got up too fast.'

'Stay here. Let me get you some water.'

The woman put one hand up – *I'm fine*, the gesture said – but she made no attempt to get back up. Her colour had returned to her cheeks a little though, and her gaze was less ghastly, though more confused. She looked like someone waking up from a trance. She drank her water with little, bird-like sips.

'Are you feeling any better?' Kirsty asked anxiously.

'I am, thank you.'

'And did you drive here, or get a taxi, or…?'

'I walked. That's probably what happened. I overdid it. It's a long trek, but I like to walk, and I never thought anything of a few miles' hike when I was younger. That's the thing, your body gets old, but it doesn't tell your mind. So you end up doing silly things like this, worrying people. Anyway, I'm fit as a flea, now! Thanks again for looking after me!' She got up with difficulty.

'You're not walking home?' Kirsty cried.

The woman took out an impossibly old mobile phone. 'Well, I could call a taxi. I think there's a number in somewhere? I put it in, but I'm terrible with technology. And taxis don't like going to where I live.'

Kirsty hesitated. 'Well look, I'm on my way home. Perhaps I could give you a lift?'

The woman shook her head firmly. 'No. You get yourself home. I'll be fine.'

'I'd feel a lot better if I dropped you back. It's no trouble.' Kirsty was firmer now too.

'It's way on the other side of town though, Beacon Hill?' she inclined her head apologetically. 'If it's too out of the way—'

'No. No it's not out of my way. Not really. Please, let me do this.'

The geography of Beacon Hill seemed to change in the dark. The place had swollen, spread like a stain, and Mrs McKnight's directions added to the sense of disorientation; lefts and rights were taken seemingly at random. They drove past the burnt-out house Kirsty had seen earlier.

'Terrible business that,' Sylvia said. 'Arson, they say. It was in the papers a few years back – one or two kiddies killed, parents. My late brother knew the family.'

'He did?'

'Oh yes. He was on the news and everything. The whole family, and the dogs, burnt up like that. Terrible. I think it was that that made him sick. They said it was cancer, but I'm sure the shock didn't help.'

'I used to know a family here too. When I was little. Denise Cook? I think you know her too?'

'Oh lord, Denise! Oh, did you know little Lisa? God love her! That was a terrible business.'

'It was,' Kirsty managed. She missed the turning and shot out towards the motorway. 'Oh god, sorry! Sorry, I'll need to turn around.'

'No, it's my fault. Nattering on about that horrible business. Must've brought up some bad memories for you, I'm sorry.' They were silent for a time. 'Do you have any children yourself?'

'No.'

'Oh well, you're young yet.' Sylvia's voice was warm in the dark. 'It will happen.'

I'm not that young, Kirsty thought.

Soon they were driving over unpaved land, a spur of packed earth which petered out into scrubland.

'Here.' Sylvia pointed at some rusted cars, scattered like forgotten toys. 'Stop here. It's a mess, isn't it? Mervyn – my late brother – he ran his business from here. Scrap metal, he had a repair shop, but to be honest, he just collected more than he sold, bless him. He was one of those people that can't let things go, you know the type. Everything had a use, he thought. Here it is.' The woman pointed at a long, low sprawling structure a good twenty yards away. A dim light showed pinkly through curtains.

'It looks like there's someone in?'

'No,' the woman said. 'I leave the light on all the time. It's silly, but it makes me feel a bit safer. Since I've been alone, you know. And it's more cheerful.'

'Right, well let me make sure you get in safely.'

'No! No, I'll be fine, you've done enough.' She was unbuckling her seatbelt, opening the door.

'Please, let me get you inside at least!' Kirsty held out one stiff arm out for support.

The woman almost recoiled. 'I've not Hoovered for a few days,' she said. 'It's a bit of a muddle.'

This sudden, prickly character shift was something Kirsty had seen a lot of since working with the elderly. It was as if they sud-

denly ran out of trust, but it always came down to fear. Told by
the TV for so many years that Strangers Couldn't Be Trusted, that
they would rob you, humiliate you, murder you, older women
were caught in a trap of loneliness – desperate for human contact,
garrulous, clingy, yet also, suddenly, cautious. Kirsty saw all this
and her heart cleaved with empathy. She responded, as always,
with self-deprecation.

'Well, it can't be worse than my place. But if you'd prefer me
not to come in, then I understand.'

After a moment, the woman put out one hand, allowed herself
to be helped out of the car. 'I didn't mean to be rude.'

'You weren't rude!' Kirsty said warmly. Sylvia was so slight,
cupping her elbow was like handling a hummingbird. 'I'd be the
same. Stranger danger.'

'Oh, you're not a stranger! I already feel like we're fast friends.
It's just that it gets… hard, that's all. To keep things shipshape.
When you're getting on a bit. And Mervyn left things in such a
mess. I've made a start sorting things out, but…'

'Please don't worry. Let's just get you inside.' Inwardly, Kirsty
prepared herself for the worst: dozens of cats, piles of newspapers,
overflowing toilets and reeking adult nappies, but when the door
was opened, she saw none of that. The kitchen was… lovely, like
something from a fairy tale, low-ceilinged, cosy and warm. The
faded linoleum tiles on the floor, the mellow gold of the kitchen
table glowed. Kirsty breathed in the mingled smell of furniture
polish, of baking, of the beautiful bunch of fresh pink roses
placed proudly in a cut-glass vase. Mrs McKnight seemed to take
strength from the atmosphere too; as soon as the door was closed,
she stood straighter, her movements were quicker, more assured.
She insisted that Kirsty stay for a cup of tea, steered her to one of
the two chairs at the kitchen table, next to the roses. They still had
the card attached:

If Angela Bright had l(
living on this piece of wi
Something about this w
her face, looked at her sh

'Mothers and daught(
led to think that they sh
true. When I had Marie
In those days that was ol(
And I wanted a child so
it never happened. Ever)

The shock of that ph
almost made Kirsty cry.
the steam would accoun

'And then, when she
was musing. 'I tell you,
and I believe it now. An(
for that long, when you'
long, and then it happe1
about anything to…'

'Make it stay.'

'Yes. Make it stay. E>

'So…'

'So I… I haven't be(
that she had the gift, a1
I didn't train her as I sh
poor. Mervyn was alwa)
but they only made us p
with an old fogey like n
had… problems.'

'What problems?'

'Problems I'd caused
both. He was such a ho

While on the path of knowledge, God provides us with teachers, I give thanks for Angels on Earth – Angels like you, Sylvia!

'Beautiful flowers,' Kirsty murmured.

'Aren't they though? And it was so kind.' The woman gazed at the card. 'Lovely. Now, tea. Do you take sugar?'

'No, thanks. Is this a… client?' Was that the right word? It sounded faintly sex worker-ish…

Sylvia McKnight smiled. 'Oh, I don't have clients. That sounds very organised and professional. I just have people I try to help.'

'Sorry, I meant people who pay for readings? Is that what they're called, readings?'

'Oh, I don't charge.' Sylvia handed her a mug of tea. 'I have no business charging money for what I do. That'd be wrong. And anyway,' her smile now was sad, 'if you bring money into something it changes things, doesn't it? It stops being a favour and becomes a service and if it's a *service* and they don't hear what they *want* to hear, well, before you know it things can get nasty. Judging and gossip and…'

'I know what you mean,' Kirsty replied after a pause.

'I thought you might.' Mrs McKnight laid a curious emphasis on the words.

'So what kind of things do you advise on then?'

'Oh lord! Problems don't change, it always boils down to loneliness… people are lonely at work, in their marriages or because they're not married. People are lonely because they're trapped, or they have no anchors, or they're shy and give too much, or they're shy and are too scared to give. It's the one thing we all have in common, isn't it, loneliness? What I do is tap into the cause. It's hard, isn't it, to admit that something's lacking in your life? But when you *do*, you can do something about it.'

'I suppose so.' Kirsty felt something inside her stiffen, raise its head in instinctive alarm. 'Anyway, I'd better get going.'

'Of course.' Mrs Mcl
rassed you.'

'No, you haven't.'

The woman held up
ity. 'I have. And I'm so
lord, there's a lot of aw
things like the cards to
the most vulnerable of
awful to think about. I
internet and all those
She shook her head. 'T
can't bear the idea of be
it's never seemed right
I really believe that.'

'What about your da
money from it, doesn't s
see the woman unsettle

'She does,' Sylvia sai
In both senses of the w

'But how does that s
incisive questions. Kirs
a work context and th
prevarications and apol
Sylvia McKnight? She
just waited for a reply..
this, to be curious and i
inside her loosen, som

Sylvia pursed her lip
She paused, looked at I
I'm her mother, not he
only my opinion after
doing so well – lovely

liveable space here. The rest of the house – it's clean, but cluttered. Marie couldn't really have friends over, even if… anyway.' Her tone changed abruptly. 'That's all water under the bridge now, isn't it? She's done very well for herself and the older you get, the more you realise that your values are just that, *your* values, and they may be wrong. Or outdated. Marie, sorry, *Angela*, has made a better stab at her life than I did at mine, so maybe it's me in the wrong, not her. She's helped more people in her career than I have, after all. Not that I had a career, I was a full-time mother, but still… And if she gets paid for it, well, the money's good, isn't it? I know that now.' She gave a little laugh, halfway between self-deprecation and woeful humour.

'I'm prying,' Kirsty said softly. 'I'm sorry.'

Sylvia reached out one hand, patted Kirsty's arm. 'You aren't! I'm just rattling on. I seem to have lost the knack of talking normally to people! No small talk!' She twinkled at Kirsty. 'I was never very good at small talk!'

'Me neither.'

'Rubbish! I saw you at that party! You were quite the belle of the ball, chatting away very comfortably with everyone!'

Kirsty frowned. 'I doubt it.'

'No, you were, you *were* or I wouldn't say it! You know just what to say to people to put them at their ease, I watched you. And you're lovely with kiddies, a real natural. The baby, Milo? He adores you!'

Kirsty thought of Milo's red little face, alternately red with rage or blank as an unstruck coin. 'Really?'

'Really. And then you were so kind to me. Helping me down the stairs like that, so sweet, so attentive.'

'And then I made a bit of a fool of myself. Crying like that,' Kirsty muttered, thinking about Angela Bright's sudden clutch, her large, blue eyes, the sudden sense that they were no longer in this over-decorated show home, but instead outside, by the canal, in the mist. 'I embarrassed Vic. I must have embarrassed Angela too.'

'Angela's bombproof,' Sylvia said flatly and her face was closed up tight. 'Don't worry about her.'

'And then we – me and Lee, my husband – we just left. That was rude too. Don't you think so? Lee just wanted to get out of there, he was upset...' Kirsty didn't know why she was saying this, but as she did she looked at Sylvia, hungry for approval.

Sylvia hesitated. 'Your husband... he was protecting you, maybe? Obviously you were in pain. And so he defended you. Maybe he was a little aggressive about it...'

'D'you think he was aggressive?'

'No. No, I used the wrong word.' Sylvia, her face lowered, seemed to be grimacing. 'Maybe I should have said "forceful". He... he did what he thought was right.'

'He was worried about me. He can be a bit overprotective, I suppose.'

'Well, you know, we all need protection, don't we?' Sylvia said kindly. 'Especially when you're lost, you're not appreciated. Especially when you give and give and give when you should hold back a bit.' She picked up her mug with both hands, raising it to her mouth like a child. Her eyes were now suddenly very tired. 'I know something about that.' There was a pause.

'I should let you get some rest.' Kirsty got up from her chair. The kitchen felt very still now, pregnant, like the air before a storm. 'Can I get you anything before I leave?'

'I'm fine. I'll be fine.' The woman's smile was slow, weary, complicated. 'You take care of your*self*.'

'I can't really help with Peg – I mean, I don't think Peg would be able to stay here, lovely though the offer is. She'll have mobility issues and things that—'

'Oh no, don't worry. Now I think about it more it was a silly idea. I just...' Sylvia spread her hands on the table top, '... wanted to help. But sometimes you can't, can you? But thanks for humouring me. And for getting this old crock back home in one piece!'

Kirsty realised that she didn't want to leave without… without what? Making amends? Learning more? No; without a route back. She took out her card.

'In the meantime, take this and maybe I'll see you at the hospital – visiting Peg, I mean.'

'Yes, that would be lovely. Not that I get there often. I prefer to visit when the family aren't all there. They're a bit much, aren't they?'

'They are a bit. Can I…?' Kirsty shook her head bashfully. 'Never mind.'

'No, what?'

'Can I maybe come over for a visit again? Just to see how you're doing and—'

'I'd love that.' Sylvia's voice trembled and bloomed with warmth. She got up slowly and walked over. 'And do you mind if I give you a hug?' Despite her small frame, Sylvia's arms were strong. 'You're a lovely woman, Kirsty,' she whispered into her hair.

'Oh, I don't know about that.'

'Well, *I* do.' She gave one more, almost painful squeeze, stepped back. 'And every time you doubt yourself, just think about how you helped this silly old bat get home in one piece and give yourself a pat on the back. Whenever you think you're a bad person, remember what I said, promise?'

'Promise.'

Sylvia stayed in the bright slit of the doorway while she got back into the car, and as she drove back towards Beacon Hill, Kirsty watched her waving, waving in the rear-view mirror, until she was only a splinter of light in the dark, obscured but not extinguished. All throughout the drive home, Kirsty felt all the usual complex, contradictory emotions roiling and fighting in her mind for precedence, but something had changed: the fear, the guilt, the sadness crashed like waves, dissipating into harmless foam, against something new, a solid, implacable sea wall of calm. For the first time in years, there was something new, fresh, at last.

CHAPTER SEVENTEEN

Kirsty got into the habit of popping in to see Sylvia once or twice a week after work. She was always alone, and there was never a hint that Angela had been to visit.

'I'm worried I'm keeping you from your husband,' Sylvia told her after a few visits. They were sitting, as usual, in the kitchen. Sylvia had made a ginger cake, warm and dense with spice. 'Let me give you some of this to take back for him.'

'We… we live apart at the moment,' Kirsty told her.

'Oh!' Sylvia looked pained. 'Oh, I'm so sorry! I thought there were *problems*, but—'

'No, not like that!' Kirsty said hastily. 'It's just timing – I started the job before he could finish *his* jobs. He'll move up here soon, and then we'll buy. This is just temporary.'

Sylvia nodded seriously. 'Good. It's not good to be alone.'

'It's not… but what did you mean, problems?'

'What? Oh nothing. Nothing. I must have just been picking up on, well, you feeling a bit lonely, that's all. I mean, why else would you waste your time coming to see an old bat like me?'

'I *like* you, that's why. And it's nice to meet someone *good*. Coming back here wasn't easy.'

'So why did you come back?' Sylvia's eyes were sharp through the tea steam.

'Well, Vic? Milo… I wanted to help out there. And then I got my job of course.'

'Do you see a lot of your sister?'

'N-no. Not *as* much. She's busy, you know, with the baby and the house.'

'And the job, it must be a promotion or something? To leave London and move back here, I mean?'

'N-no. More of a sideways move, I'd say.' There was a pause. Outside, the sunflowers in Sylvia's front yard shifted in the wind, rattled like snakes. 'I'm not entirely sure why I came back, to tell the truth,' she admitted, with a self-conscious laugh.

Sylvia opened her mouth as if to speak, shut it, opened it again. 'I can read your cards? If you think it might help?'

Kirsty had never had her cards read before. All she knew about it were the horror stories, the obvious scams and cold reading. But Sylvia noticed, smiled, patted her hand.

'Don't worry. You don't have to believe in it or follow the advice or anything like that. See it more as a way of concentrating your mind on the things that really matter at the moment.'

'Do I have to ask a question?'

'You can if you want, but if you do just ask it in your head. I don't need to know it. Want to get started? Yes? Just hold the deck. Don't shuffle them or worry about anything. Just think of your question, if you have one. It shouldn't be a question with a "Yes" or "No" answer – more an "If I do this, what might happen" question, or a "What is influencing me at the moment that I haven't understood yet" type question. OK?'

'Will it tell me anything really bad?' Kirsty asked.

'No, it's not like that. It might tell you bad things that have happened or tell you that if you carry on the way you're going bad things might happen, but that's why we do the cards – to forestall events or encourage us on. It's just a bit of a cheat sheet into the future, that's all. I'll talk you through it, don't worry.'

Sylvia gestured for the cards back, closed her eyes for a moment, and began laying them out.

'The first card represents where you are right now. It's the Ten of Swords.' Mrs McKnight's voice was soft in the dim room, softer than the sound of her pencil on paper, as she made notes on the spread. 'You feel alone, almost betrayed. Unsupported. And the card crossing is the King of Swords.' She looked up. 'This is a court card – they generally represent a person in your life. This is a man in a position of power over you. He is just, but inflexible. Someone you've relied upon to believe in you, but there's a rift – a disagreement. This has left you feeling... *betrayed*, almost. Can you understand this? Don't tell me why, just nod yes or stay silent.'

Kirsty nodded. Mrs McKnight went back to the cards.

'The past. The High Priestess. You've been experiencing heightened psychic awareness lately – maybe over the last few months. Maybe you dream and the dreams come true? Or maybe you want to go deeper into things – open your mind to other realms. But this man...' she pointed at the King of Swords, 'has stopped you from really digging into that. He feels threatened by that.' She frowned, shook her head. 'I don't know why. The King of Swords is not normally an angry person – he's all about reality and rules and the way things should be, yes? But here he's... furious. Hiding it, but furious. Scared maybe?'

Her hands hovered over the cards. 'I feel it's linked to this – this card is the heart of the spread. Even if it doesn't make sense to you right away, the card in this position tells you what to look for – it's the key to the code if you like – the past. And it's the Two of Swords.' She let out the air in her cheeks in one solemn puff, looked up. 'Guilt. Fear. This is someone who's buried their head in the sand for years, someone who's tried to run away but can't escape.'

'Is it a man or a woman?'

'It's not a court card. This is an emotion, attached to the querent. I think it's you. And it's linked directly to this: the near future card is the Ten of Wands.' Mrs McKnight looked up, smiled sadly. 'You're seeking forgiveness. You want to put down your burden. The running away hasn't worked, you've nowhere else to run. You need closure.'

'Yes,' Kirsty whispered.

'This…' She pointed at the cards running vertically on the right of the cross. 'This tells you what to do from now on, how to get through this.'

'Is it good?'

'No questions. Not yet,' Mrs McKnight told her. 'Your power card is Death. You want to let go of harmful influences. You want to transform yourself. This turmoil will end – it's already ending – but there will be sacrifice. There always has to be, if you want to move on. Something has to die to make way for something to live.' Mrs McKnight looked up again, her tired, kind face creased with concern. 'Are you all right, darling? Do you want me to stop?'

'No. No, it's all right.'

'But here,' warm, gentle excitement filled Mrs McKnight's voice, 'here are the influences around you – it might be people, or it might not. It could be a past influence that's trying to come back, to help. It's the Six of Cups; one of my favourite cards! Traditionally they're the cards of friendship, and this is about children, childhood innocence. A reunion. This card tells me that you're being guided and protected. Perhaps you'll meet someone here, an old friend? Perhaps they know you're here already, but they're just waiting for you to make the first move?'

'And they're good?'

'This person loves you. Always has. Let me look at the way they intersect with the last two – your hopes and fears and… Ah! The Empress. A mother figure, kind and compassionate. A wise counsel. She protects you and loves you, no matter what. She's on your side, come what may. Then, the last card – the outcome: the Three of Cups! Oh, this couldn't be better! I want you to look at this card now, come, come over here!'

Three women held aloft three golden cups against an impossibly blue, cloudless sky. One had her back partially turned, but the other two faced outwards, smiling.

'Collaborations. Women helping each other. Emotional support, respect and joy! It's as if there's a silent partner here – look at the woman with her back turned – it's her that keeps the circle together.'

'Lisa?'

'Don't tell me anything!' Sylvia told her. 'Now, three is a powerful number. Think about it – Christians have the Trinity, in Buddhism there are the Three Jewels. Hindus have the Trivedi. Wicca has the Triple Goddess. A structure with three sides is the most stable – think of the pyramids. The number three crops up everywhere: three's a charm; three wise men; three of a kind. This card tells you to rely on your intuitions, to believe in yourself. It tells you that you aren't alone any more, that you're part of something bigger now. It tells you that you're starting on the right path and you should carry on. You can put right what's been wrong.'

*

'She's just such a lovely woman, Lee! So kind and independent and… you wouldn't believe that that Angela woman is her daughter!' Lee made no reply. She could hear the window open, close quickly. He'd be throwing a cigarette out of the window, trundling around the M25, heading home. *His* home. A sudden flash of irritation ran through her. 'Are you listening?'

'Yes, I'm listening. She's a nice old lady. You told me about her last week, and the week before.'

'She's more than a nice old lady,' Kirsty told him sulkily. 'She's more of a friend. I want you to meet her properly—'

'Why? So I can cross her palm with silver?'

'Why've you got to say things like that? She's a really nice woman, Lee. She *is*. And she's *lonely*, and—'

'Yeah, *why* is she lonely? If she's this lovely old lady made of rainbows and sunshine, why isn't her own daughter living with her?'

'But that's *why* she's lonely, can't you see? I think she was looking forward to Angela coming back but then she's hardly seen anything of her.'

'You're not her daughter, Kirsty.'

'No. But I'm lonely too!' The words were out of her mouth before she knew it, and they were angry, jagged. She imagined them tumbling through space, into his ears, stunning him into understanding. 'We're in the same boat, me and Sylvia, aren't we? We're both living alone not because we want to, but because we're waiting to be... You *told* me you'd move up as soon as you could and we'd start looking for a house—'

'And I haven't finished all my jobs yet.'

'But you could have done by now! You didn't have to take that one on in Stevenage, did you?'

'No. But it'll be fifteen grand by the time I finish, could I afford to turn my nose up at that? You're not being practical, Kirsty.'

'Maybe not, but you promised. When I moved here you promised—'

'That's the thing, Kirsty, *you* moved.' His voice was flattened with logic, rigid with fact. 'It wasn't *me*, was it? Who left who?'

'We agreed!'

'You can only agree if there's been a discussion, Kirsty, and I don't remember much of a discussion. The way I remember it is that you just flat out told me that you were moving back – *temporarily* – to help Vic... and how's *that* worked out, by the way? Then you say we're moving to the shithole you escaped thirty years ago, where we know no-one, and you get a job and a flat and I just had to accept it.' His control was beginning to crack.

'Don't shout at me.'

'I'm not shouting!' Lee shouted. 'But you tell me you're lonely as if that's my fault. D'you think I'm not lonely? Why the hell d'you think I've been taking on all these jobs? I'm working on four hours of sleep a night because I don't want to come back, alone, to an empty flat and stare at the walls and wonder where the fuck my wife went!'

'Lee—'

'And now you've met some old witch in the woods who tells you nice things, and I have to be interested and happy for you and… well I'm *not*. I don't *like* the idea of her and didn't like her daughter either, and I don't like your sister and her fat Tory fool of a husband and I fucking *hate* where you're from, OK? Happy now?'

There was a long pause. She could hear in the background that familiar confusion of music… bits of ragga, bits of reggae, along with the long, mournful bellow of someone selling mangos. He must be nearly home now. He must be stop-start-stopping down Peckham Rye, past Khan's Bargains, past the furniture shop where everything was clumsily fashioned into the shape of jungle animals. She had a sudden, almost physical yearning to be there too, her hand on his knee, listening to the radio, the sun on their faces. When she opened her eyes, focused on the grimy walls of her flat, the silence from the street outside, she discovered, with no surprise, that she was crying.

'No. I'm not happy,' she managed.

'Neither am *I*!' Lee said warmly. 'Can we just stop this? Can you just come *home*, Kirsty? Please?'

Her phone buzzed with an incoming call. Vic. 'I've got to take this call, sorry.'

'Fine.' All the heat had drained from his voice. The anger too. He was controlled again, blithe.

'I'll call you—' she began, but he'd already hung up.

They made up later. They always made up. Lee said he'd make time to spend a weekend together soon – maybe look at a few houses? It was quite a concession, and it made her happy. But the fissure didn't completely close. Lee wasn't normally an angry person. *He's all about reality and rules and the way things should be… But here he's… furious. Scared maybe?*

CHAPTER EIGHTEEN

Five days later Kirsty got a call.

'Not sure I'm doing this right. Technology,' Sylvia McKnight's voice whispered on voicemail. 'Can you pop over? There's something I need to talk to you about.'

Kirsty called back but there was no answer. Called again, the same thing. Outside, a blustery, mean wind burrowed up sleeves, down collars and plastered damp trousers to frozen legs. The streets were empty. Everyone was inside, the curtains drawn against the weather. Kirsty imagined the old lady alone in her draughty, ramshackle house, frightened. She'd sounded frightened, embarrassed by the fear, but frightened nonetheless, and she'd called Kirsty, not her own daughter. That decided it. Within a few minutes Kirsty was in the car, heading to Beacon Hill.

Now that the nights were lighter, the depressed chaos the woman was forced to live with was even more apparent: tarpaulin flapped over rusted cars with weeds growing between the wheels, through the bonnets and boots, and half-frozen/half-rotted rubbish dotted the mud – crisp packets, cigarette packets, and things so long rotted they could have once been anything. Mervyn must really have been a hoarder extraordinaire. A needlessly large BMW was parked in the middle of the detritus, new and shiny.

When Kirsty knocked on the door, it was opened by Angela Bright. Her thin face froze, and she braced both toned arms against the rotting door frame to keep Kirsty on the doorstep.

'Can I help you?'

'I came to see Sylvia.'

Angela still didn't move. 'We're kind of in the middle of something here.' The woman was rude, strangely, defensively rude, her body a hostile barrier. It was hard to believe she could be related to Sylvia.

'I need to come in,' Kirsty told her, in a rare show of defiance.

From behind Angela, Sylvia's voice wavered, 'Let her in, Marie. Just let her in, will you?'

'Don't call me that!' Angela hissed. She still didn't move. 'We're busy. You should leave now.'

'Let her in. We've finished for now. *We* can talk again tomorrow, OK? *Angela?*' There was a little bit of steel in Sylvia's voice now too. Angela let one tight arm drop, then she retreated, gathered her coat from the kitchen chair.

'I need them back soon though,' she told her mother.

Sylvia made a tired, vague gesture. 'Can we talk about it tomorrow?'

Angela paused, seemed about to say something but changed her mind. On her way out she gave Kirsty the briefest of glances. Kirsty and Sylvia stayed silent until they heard the BMW's motor start and purr off into Beacon Hill.

'I'm sorry you had to see that,' Sylvia said. They'd decamped to the adjoining room – a clean but cluttered space strangely at odds with the carefully organised kitchen. Kirsty sat on a low, shawl-covered sofa, while Sylvia poured chai tea and set it on a scuffed coffee table. 'She… she likes things done and dusted, that's all. Me, I like to take my time over things. Especially important things.' She sat down on a wicker peacock chair.

'Was it about the estate?'

Sylvia bent to put her tea on the floor. The wicker groaned. 'Yes.'

'She wants to sell it then.'

Sylvia frowned. 'No, that's the strange thing. She wants it kept as it is.'

'What?'

'She can do what she likes, legally. Mervyn left everything to Mar— *Angela.*'

'So you'll stay here?' There was something immensely comforting in knowing that Sylvia would always be here – twinkling in her bright kitchen like a good deed in a bad world. 'That's not bad, though, is it? Maybe you can do what you planned and clear the place up? Get a new generator.'

'No, that's the thing.' Sylvia looked at Kirsty with strained bafflement. 'She wants it kept just as it is. I'm not allowed to change anything – not even clean the yard up, or get proper heating or, anything.' She shook her head. 'I wasn't expecting that. Kirsty, she says she doesn't want it touched. She says,' her eyes were wide with slow shock, 'she says I'll have to leave.'

'What? She can't do that?'

'She can though. It's her property! She said I should go into sheltered accommodation, but it wouldn't be here. Maybe twenty miles away or so? Kirsty, I've lived here nearly all my life!'

'But why wouldn't Angela let you stay in your own house if she's not going to knock it down, or sell the land?'

'Well, I want to know that too. She could level this place, build a lovely house here for me, sell the rest of the land and make a fortune; not that she needs the money, but still. Or she could sell everything and I could have a bungalow in town somewhere – I wouldn't mind that, I told her I wouldn't mind that, but she wasn't having any of it.'

'Why? This is insane, Sylvia!'

'I don't know. I don't know what's in her mind,' Sylvia replied carefully. 'All I know is that she's set on it, and when she gets set on something, she doesn't budge until she gets her own way.' She shrugged.

'That's really not fair!'

Sylvia left a long pause before replying. 'Well, maybe not. But you can't choose your family, can you? And we all need family.'

'Even if your family don't want you?'

'Especially if they don't,' Sylvia murmured. 'After all, if they're not nice to you, you feel like you have to earn their love. That's the only way you can feel you deserve it.' She frowned at her lap, then looked up, and her eyes were very bright, very blue. 'You know something about that, I bet? After all, you came back to help your sister.'

'Yes,' Kirsty said after a pause. 'And that didn't work out the way I'd hoped.'

'But… was it the only reason you came back?'

'What do you mean?'

'I'm not sure.' Sylvia's eyes blinked anxiously, then back to her lap. 'That's why I called you. I didn't think for a minute you'd end up seeing all this soap opera with me and Marie, I called you before she arrived. There's something I don't understand, and I wondered if we put our heads together…' She sat on the wide-backed chair like a little doll, her mouth pursed, her eyes serious, as if she was listening to something deep inside herself. 'I don't want you to think I'm going dotty. Unless I *am*, in which case, please tell me and I can get myself carted away.' She gave a little cheeky smile. 'Come to think of it, if I *do* get carted away, at least I'll have a roof over my head.'

'Do you have a solicitor, Sylvia? I can help—'

Sylvia put up one hand. 'No, that's a side show. I want to talk about you, not…' She got up. 'Wait there. I need to go and find something. It's upstairs so I might be a while.'

'Can I help?'

'Yes. You can stay down here and make another pot of tea? The leaves are on the kitchen table and keep an eye on it while it brews, will you? About five or ten minutes? I think we're going to need a good strong cuppa once I show you what I'm talking about.'

She was longer than ten minutes, and Kirsty was about to venture further in the house to find her, when she reappeared holding a small pile of newspaper clippings.

'This is what I called about. I came across these today; god knows why I didn't find them before. Sit down.' She put the papers down on the table. 'This is your last chance to bail out.'

Kirsty sat down, smiled. 'I'm in it for the long haul, Sylvia.'

'You say that,' Sylvia was serious, 'but I won't blame you if you want to stop coming over. I won't blame you if you think I'm dotty, or... I just don't want you to think badly of me? There are some things I keep to myself, not to be secretive but to protect people I love. Some of these things are...'

Kirsty leaned forward, took one thin, trembling hand. 'Sylvia, we're friends. We're good friends. Whatever you say or show me won't change that, OK?'

Sylvia looked at her with heartbreakingly gentle eyes. 'I hope that's true, I really do.' She blinked, withdrew her hand. 'Here it is. I don't only read the cards. Sometimes I dream things and I jot them down when I wake up. Other times I just let the words flow through me. Automatic writing, it used to be called. It's me writing, but *not* me at the same time. I always know I'm writing, even if I don't know what I'm writing, and I always keep them in a file to look at them later to see if anything... important came up, a message from... oh I'll just say it! A message from the other side. I don't blame you if you think I'm... but these...' she cast a quizzical look at the papers '...I don't remember writing any of this at all! It's in my handwriting, but I don't recognise the words. I have the strangest feeling that it wasn't written for me to interpret, but for you. It's about *you*, I'm positive! Here.'

And she handed Kirsty the first quivering paper.

KC KC KC KC. As the initials went on, the writing grew harder; in some places the pen had been ground into the paper, enough to rip it. Then, light as a feather brush, was written, *LJC LJC LJC.* The letters were packed close, interlocked.

Mrs McKnight wordlessly handed her another sheet, this one from a page of the local paper dated a week ago. It was decorated with the same initials, and more... *OLD FRIEND IS KEY* was written in block capitals, the 'friend' lightly crossed through. *ANGEL* headed another long chain of words, written round and round an advert for a care home. *KIRSTY TAKE CARE TAKE CARE TAKE CARE BOYS IN THE PARK ARE A BAD LOT TAKE CARE.*

'Am I right?' Sylvia asked. 'Is it a message to you?'

Kirsty heard her own voice as if it was coming from a long way away. 'Lisa.'

'Lisa Cook?'

Kirsty closed her eyes and nodded.

Sylvia took the paper back and nodded briefly, grimly, to herself. 'That's what I thought. There are... more? I don't want to overload you, darling. Look, let's forget about it. Let's just—'

'No. No let me see.' Kirsty reached for another sheet, this one a page from the *Daily Mail*, and not just any page, the first page of Bryan's interview. On his forehead was drawn what seemed to be two reversed curly brackets, followed by a crooked little duckling, but Kirsty knew what they really were: two kissing faces and a number 2.

Angels Times Two.

'When did you write this?' she asked hollowly.

'I don't know. But the date on the paper? It's before we met. Do you know that man? You do, don't you?' Sylvia asked. 'Kirsty, what's this about?'

'Lisa. It's about Lisa,' Kirsty whispered. 'That's her brother.'

'Oh my lord, it is! That's Bryan! God, I wouldn't have known him, but then I haven't seen him since he was a nipper! But why would she… why would she be trying to communicate with you via me? Why not just to you? Unless she has been? Dreams?'

'Yes, I've been having dreams. How did you know?'

'Because, look here – look how hard the pencil dug in.' Sylvia pointed to Lisa's initials. 'There's force there. She wants to make you notice her, so she won't just be trying one thing,' she told her. 'What happens in your dreams?'

'I don't understand them. We're playing in the street, or we're in the park, and she tells me to look for something, or says I need to learn something. She… tells me to find her.'

'Does she say where she is?'

'No. Never.'

'Are you sure? Sometimes you have to interpret things – does she mention a… street? Or a hiding place?'

'No.'

Sylvia shook her head. 'I don't know why she hasn't done that yet, then. But it will get clearer, I feel it. Take notes of your dreams, any strange coincidences, anything out of the ordinary, write them down and bring them to me and maybe, if we put our heads together, we'll… work things out.' Her face was tired, grim, determined. 'We'll do this together.'

CHAPTER NINETEEN

A week later, Kirsty had a visitor at work.

'I promise I won't take up too much of your time, I'm just here to have a bit of a chat and see Peg – oh, look, isn't this a lovely office? How grand to have your own office!'

'You look very nice. Posh!'

Sylvia batted her eyelids, mock-pouted. 'I'm meeting a gentleman for lunch,' she said.

'Oh, who?'

'It's nothing like that, I'm just teasing. It's a solicitor – Marie's solicitor. *Angela's*, I should say, she hates it when I get her name wrong. I have to sign some papers.' Sylvia's smile was fading. 'Something about the land. It must be.'

'Don't sign anything!' Kirsty told her immediately. 'Ask for copies and take them home to look at, but don't sign anything. Maybe I can get someone to take a look at them for you—'

'You're very kind. But this isn't your battle, darling. Not that it's a *battle* anyway. Keep your strength for when Peg's family descend on you later.'

'What?'

'Oh yes, it's one of her granddaughter's birthdays, and they're all coming over. That's why I came early, because well, you know what they can be like when they're all together.' Sylvia gave a wry smile. 'I wanted to avoid the crush.' She turned, reached into her bag. 'Also, I wondered if you'd had any thoughts about things, dreams… or anything else?'

The 'anything else' was loaded.

'Not dreams, but…' Kirsty reached into her desk drawer, 'I should have told you about this earlier maybe. I've been getting these.' She handed her the envelope of notes. 'Nothing in the last week or so, but…'

Sylvia read them, frowned. 'What do they mean?'

'I don't know. I don't know why anyone would want to… warn me, or threaten me, or anything like that.'

'"Whatever you think you know, you don't",' Sylvia read aloud. She had paled, aged. 'What can that mean?'

'I don't know. Unless…do you think it might be something to do with Lisa?' Kirsty cocked her head towards the door. 'What's that?'

It sounded as if a pack of excitable animals were running down the corridor. Mona's voice rose above, like a fairground caller: 'Mum! Mum! Look who's come!'

Kirsty groaned, left Sylvia in the office and made her way to the ward to find Peg Leaves' bed obscured by visitors; there had to be ten people there at least. A crumpled helium balloon had been tied to the bedside table, and Kirsty heard the faint but unmistakable sound of a can of lager being opened. Woeful Mrs Footitt in the bed opposite turned mournful eyes on her.

'It's not even visiting hours, is it? Listen to them all effing and blinding.' She spoke in a loud voice, designed to be overheard, and it had the predictable effect on Mona. Kirsty watched her turn, her eyes narrowed, her mouth open, about to sling some sharp comment, but when she saw Kirsty, she shut her mouth with a snap and even managed a smile. She nudged the man next to her who hurriedly hid his can of lager, nudging the man next to him to do the same. It was funny really; this clan, this scourge of the county, abashed as teenagers caught drinking in the park. They moved apart for her, making a narrow channel leading to Peg, yellow and supine, and Peg held out her hand, gave Kirsty's a gentle squeeze.

'Watch,' she wheezed. 'She's going to tell you all to fuck off home.'

Kirsty smiled. 'As if I'd use language like that, Peg.'

Peg rasped a little laugh. 'You would. You *would*. I bet when you get out of here you'd make a whore blush.' This, from Peg, was a high compliment. Kirsty felt the guests' respect rise with their mirth.

Then, suddenly, the laughter stopped and Mona stiffened. In fact, the whole family stilled, as if through some tribal telepathy. The atmosphere itself seemed to pause.

Sylvia was standing beside Kirsty now. 'How are you feeling, Peg?' she asked gently. 'You look better!'

'Sylvia.' It was a statement rather than a greeting.

'You look much better! Stronger. I bet it won't be long before you get home.' Sylvia's voice was high as a girl's; wounded, trying not to appear so.

'How've you been then?' Peg was evasive. 'Not seen much of you. Saw Marie the other day. She's visited a fair few times, hasn't she, Mona?'

'Mmm. Been to the house too. Helped out,' Mona said levelly, and Kirsty was surprised that the unbending, sober Angela would have voluntarily entered Mona's lair, let alone helped with the housework.

'I would've done myself, but I've had a lot to do. Since the funeral. You know,' Sylvia replied with subtle dignity. There was a strange silence.

'I sent flowers,' Peg said eventually.

'Yes. They were lovely. Thank you.'

'By rights some of Mervyn's stuff should come to us. Laini, and the other kids,' Mona put in. 'They're his grandkids after all.'

'Well, that's not down to me,' Sylvia told her. 'He left everything to Marie – *Angela*, as she likes to be called now.'

'Called her Marie the other day and she was all right.' Peg smiled mirthlessly.

'Well, she always liked you, Peg,' Sylvia answered drily. 'Perhaps that's why she let you get away with it.'

'She's always been a good one, has Marie. Always. Good head on her shoulders.' Peg paused then, a little insultingly, as if daring Sylvia to contradict her. Sylvia didn't, and the conversation, never fully alive, died right there. The clan had coalesced into one cold barrier, waiting for Sylvia to leave, which, wisely, she did. She caught Kirsty's eye as she turned, gave a tiny shrug of brave good humour. The family waited in insulting silence until her footsteps had died away, before ratcheting up their noise level, and within a few seconds, all trace of their strange sinister hate had gone.

'Laini! *Laini!* Put that bloody phone down and give your nana a kiss! Not long now! Back at home soon, eh? When do they say? When'll you be back? Put the phone *down*! When then? Today? You look all right enough to go home today? I can call Ryan for the van.'

Peg was chuckling amidst the fervour, looking better than she had done in weeks. She held Mona's hand, wagged her finger at one of the men, blew a kiss to Laini, patted the bed next to her. 'Kirsty? Tell them when I can go home, will you?'

'If you carry on doing this well, you'll be able to go home soon.' Kirsty had rehearsed this exchange all morning. Lead with the positive, speak primarily to Peg.

'When though?' Mona asked. 'Now?'

'No, not now.'

'Fuck's sake, you *said*—'

Kirsty spoke again to Peg. 'Nobody wants you here longer than you need to be.' That was very true. 'And you're making great progress.' This was less true.

'She'd get better quicker at home,' Mona muttered.

'You know what, you're right, Mona.' Mona was the type to respond well to slightly exaggerated respect, and be secretly impressed that anyone would dare use her first name. 'Studies *show* that you're absolutely right. Patients recover far better at home with their families than being stuck in hospitals.'

'That's what I've been *saying*. That's what I've been *saying* all *along*,' Mona muttered, pleased.

'And you've been right to say that all along,' Kirsty told her. 'All we need to do is make sure Peg's on a level where I can convince the consultant that *when* she goes home, she'll carry *on* getting well. You know what consultants are like. So we need to make sure the house is set up—'

'But—' Mona began.

'She's right. You know she's right,' Peg put in. The colour had left her cheeks. Her grasp on Mona's hand had slackened.

'Get all the handles in place, and make all the other... adjustments.' Kirsty guessed that talking about commodes, rubber sheets and bed baths wasn't the best way to go right now, but by dropping it in that Mona hadn't done any preparation at all, she also knew that the wider family would start putting pressure on her now to do just that. Wider society had no power over families like this; censure had to come from within.

'It's Laini's birthday.' Mona pointed at the pubescent girl stabbing at an iPhone. 'We wanted Peg back for that. Laini had her heart set on it, didn't you? Laini?'

A lesser social worker would have simply reiterated her terms: *Peg is staying until you get out your power tools; deal with it.* Kirsty was better than that though. She widened her eyes, wrinkled her brow, spoke directly to the girl.

'Oh, I'm sorry, Laini. Happy birthday! Is Peg your gran, then?'

The girl bobbed her head, her eyes not straying from the screen.

'Put that fucking thing down or you'll get a slap!' hissed Mona. Laini, unfazed, sighed, put the phone in her pocket, turned hazy, insolent eyes on Kirsty.

'I'm so sorry you couldn't celebrate at home, I really am. But what a lovely granddaughter to have – not many would come to visit their gran in hospital on their… what is it? Your sixteenth birthday?'

She guessed that Laini would enjoy being 'mistaken' for being older. Sure enough, the girl cracked a small, distracted smile and her blue eyes focused just a little.

'Eleven,' she muttered.

'You look a lot older than eleven,' Kirsty said truthfully. Then she made a vague hand gesture to include the rest of the unnamed crowd. 'I tell you, not many families would have been this patient. I know it hasn't been easy, doing without Peg.'

'Six weeks now!' put in Mona plaintively. 'And it was only meant to be a week!'

Nobody had ever said that Peg would be hospitalised for a week. No-one. Mona had just pulled this grievance out of the air.

'I know, and I really feel for you all… Look, I shouldn't say this, because it's… I don't know… unprofessional…' Kirsty kept her voice low, looked seriously at the floor; she knew that appearing to break the rules and give away secrets worked very well with people like Mona, and sure enough, sullen interest was already showing on her face. 'But you're lucky she's here. Not all hospitals go the extra mile like this. Some of them – and I'm not naming any names – just want to get patients out of the door as soon as they can. Especially older patients with complex needs…'

'Kilton?' Mona put in eagerly. 'Or King's Med? I've heard bad things about King's Med. Heard they covered up stuff there – drips full of shit and body parts left in cupboards—'

Kirsty kept her voice low, confiding. 'Let's just say *I* wouldn't want to work in any other place. So I know it's hard, and I really feel for you, especially you, Laini, what with your birthday and all—'

'Oh, she's all right. She doesn't care about anything but that bloody phone, do you? Put the phone down! We're having a nice time with Nana!' Mona snatched the phone from her. One of her nails snagged the girl's hand. Laini howled and the men snickered. One of them pressed Kirsty to have a sip of lager. She knew then that she'd won them all over.

'Thanks, but no. And if the staff see you drinking, they may limit visits to Peg,' she told him. 'I really don't want that to happen.'

'She's right,' Peg managed. Her eyes were closed, her breath laboured, and that yellow tinge to her skin had deepened. 'Chuck it all down the sink. And take the empties with you.'

'Mum—'

'Mona! Leave it! Do what she says now!' Peg raised her voice and, like a cloud of summer flies, the family quickly and quietly packed up and moved out en masse, leaving only the bobbing balloon. With her guests gone, Peg was able to register Mrs Footitt's outrage, which she did with the last of her strength. 'And you can fuck off an' all,' she managed, but it was a whisper. It barely moved beyond the end of the bed.

Out in the corridor, Mona was waiting. A red-faced, phoneless Laini simmered with ostentatious rage, one hand gingerly cradling the other.

'You're not full of shit, are you?' Mona asked as soon as she saw Kirsty. 'She's going to be all right, isn't she?'

'Peg's a strong woman,' Kirsty replied diplomatically.

Mona nodded. Her lips tightened and Kirsty thought for a horrible moment that she was going to cry. Seeing someone like Mona showing any human emotion outside of anger or truculence was always unsettling.

'Mum.' Laini had sidled up closer, tugged at Mona's hoodie pocket, sagging with the confiscated phone. 'C'mon.'

Mona spun around and spoke sharply. 'You're not getting it back. Not today.' When she turned back to Kirsty, her threatened tears had receded. 'So a few more days and she'll be home, yeah?'

'Well that's really up to you now, Mona.' Kirsty pressed her advantage.

'*Mum!*'

Mona slapped Laini's hand away. Her daughter responded with well-practised melodrama.

'You opened the *cut*!' Laini shoved her injured index finger in Kirsty's face. 'Should I see a doctor? Is it broken? It's broken. I bet you it's broken! Last year? I broke my arm? And this hurts the same. This hurts *worse*! And my dad *gave* me that phone! For my *birthday*! It's *my* phone!'

Guilt and belligerence battled on Mona's face. 'Oh for fuck's sake, let me look at it.' She jerked the child's hand upwards. 'It's not broken. Barely a scratch. And you never broke your arm! When did you break your arm? Here. Here, take the thing if it'll shut you up!'

And Laini grabbed the phone, immediately forgot about her finger and retreated to the ward exit, frowning at the screen.

'Diva,' Mona said to Kirsty. 'She's such a liar, that one, I tell you.'

'"She lies like a rug",' Kirsty said softly to herself.

Mona's face softened with genuine humour. 'She *does*! See?' She called, 'Laini? She thinks you're a diva too! We all know what you're like!'

Mona was already moving towards the exit. Back in the ward Peg was asleep. And Sylvia? Probably already sitting in front of some smug solicitor being diddled out of her house. The poor woman. Doubly cursed – related to the worst family in the county, and simultaneously rejected by them. What was wrong with people?

CHAPTER TWENTY

Later that day, Kirsty saw a ghost. A ghoul from her childhood. She watched as it stepped out of the lift, passing close enough to brush her sleeve, and headed straight for Peg's recumbent figure, already shouting in a hoarse, familiar voice.

Bryan looked as if he'd stepped from the page of his interview in the *Daily Mail*; he was even wearing the same clothes. He seemed shorter than she remembered him being, but then she'd been a child when she last saw him – bellowing in the back of a police van sometime in 1985 – but he still crackled with that crazed energy, he still had that ungainly kink in his spine, that little, aggressive hunch. He barrelled straight down the middle of the corridor, droopy face set, pursued by two porters and the ward sister.

'Where is she? Where is she then?' His voice hadn't changed much either – still that peevish whine that years of smoking hadn't touched. 'I know she's here 'cause she told me, and I've got my lawyer on speed dial!' He turned around in a wavering circle. He seemed lost, bewildered by the number of wards and his dim eyes blinked stupidly. It would have been comical if it had been anyone else.

Kirsty sped up, managed to get in front of him. She, the ward sister and the porter blocked his way. 'You can't be here now, it's not visiting hours.'

He turned his rheumy eyes on Kirsty, and, amazingly, looked away again with no recognition.

A dull, animal rage was beginning to flare in those empty, doll-like eyes. 'You can't stop me from seeing my daughter! I've got my lawyer on speed dial!' Sour waves of old lager flowed from his mouth, his skin, his clothes.

'Your daughter's not here,' the ward sister told him. 'This is a geriatric ward.'

'Her arm's broke, she said! She's here!'

'There. Is. No. Girl. Here,' the sister told him again, in a voice that would make any raging beast quail, and this was the wrong tack to take with Bryan: like a lot of men with almost no impulse control, he was unfailingly enraged by women in authority. Kirsty could see the situation getting out of hand fast, and the last thing she or the hospital needed was an angry Bryan circling the building like a shark.

'I've got rights!' bleated Bryan.

It was strange, seeing him now, how unafraid she was. He was just a sad little man, out of shape, peevish, petulant; nothing to be scared of. There was something almost delicious about seeing him in this state. He had no power over her. He couldn't frighten her. She wanted to prolong this epiphany.

'Let me handle this,' she murmured to the ward sister.

'No,' the sister replied. 'I'll call security.'

'He's going to calm down, aren't you, Bryan?'

The use of his name confused him, short-circuited his anger. 'How'd you know my name?' he asked dully.

Kirsty took a deep breath. She might as well tell him. If he went crazy, like in the old days, there were witnesses, people who would step in to help her.

'I knew you when I was small. Kirsty. I knew Lisa.'

Now recognition filled his rheumy eyes, and, incredibly, he smiled. He smiled as if they were old friends, as if this was a social event.

'Oh! Look at you! Kirsty!'

Kirsty registered the wide-eyed amusement of the ward sister, knew that this would go down as yet another of Kirsty Cooper's

Little Workplace Miracles. She ushered him away to the lifts – mindful that there was CCTV in them, in case Bryan got nasty. But at each floor Bryan recovered his loquacity and not his anger. All the way through the casualty waiting rooms and to the Spice of Life, Bryan kept up his plaintive, practically verbless monologue:

'I do my best, anything she wants I… Calls? Calls! Night and day. Used to. Got her that phone. Special, well you do, don't you? Kids? Ninety quid at CeX and why? Can't call her own dad? Hurt she was, crying, help, well of course. Who wouldn't? Not me! Yes, milk, three sugars. Kirsty? You a nurse then?'

'Not a nurse, no,' Kirsty told him. 'A social worker.'

Bryan's small eyes seemed to retreat even further into his skin, and he sat like a big, broken doll, staring at his hand lying loosely on the table top.

'Why's she need a social worker?' he asked eventually. 'Everything she wants I get her? Mona's got that prevention order out on me but—'

'Wait, what?' Kirsty frowned, blinked. 'You know Mona?'

'My ex. It's her birthday. Laini's. My daughter. She called me. Said she'd bust her arm or something. And, yeah, there's this order out on me, but I had to come, didn't I? Had to? Not fair to get the social workers on me, is it? Just being a father? I mean—'

'I'm not Mona's social worker. Or Laini's,' Kirsty said sharply. 'I didn't even know you were related to them.'

'Huh!' Bryan was all smiles again. 'Reunion then? Old friends then? Funny coincidence, isn't it?'

Kirsty stared at him. He really didn't seem to remember the torture he'd put her through. He really did seem to believe that they were old friends, that they were friends still.

An old friend. An old friend is the key.

Kirsty closed her eyes for just a moment, but in that moment, the world spun. Her thoughts flurried and settled like snow in a paperweight. *Of course. Of course.*

Kirsty take care take care take care.

Bryan was talking now, and quickly, as if to make up for all that silence before. 'They put words in your mouth. The papers. They… it's all fake news. Like the stuff I said about you? I never said that, hand on heart I never. I never said you knew anything about… or… or that you *lied* or anything—'

'I don't remember the article saying that.' Kirsty, strangely, felt like laughing. This was typical, vintage Bryan – furious, needless denials that only served to incriminate himself further. It was like that time he strenuously denied robbing the corner shop before anyone knew it'd been robbed. Except the old Bryan would have punctuated his denials with violence, whereas this Bryan was just a soft lump of pathos, wiped clean, apparently, of complex memories. 'It said that the police should have spoken to me earlier, that's all.'

Bryan nodded vigorously. 'That's right! You're right! They should've. But newspapers don't print the truth, do they? You should call them – put the record straight. Compensation.'

Kirsty opened her mouth, was about to remind him that that was exactly what the article *had* said, but decided against it. Bryan, it appeared, was still a master of circular logic, but at least he did it with a smile nowadays.

'You see he's appealing? Again? That bastard?'

'I know.'

'He comes back here, I'll have his balls.'

'He's not likely to come back here.'

'Oman should have him. He'd probably get beheaded out there. That's what they do out there. I've seen it on YouTube.' Bryan sighed heavily. 'Justice. And I'm here? Birthday? Then I get this call: "Dad, Dad! My arm's bust, come and get me!" Well, what am I supposed to do? Let her die? By… by the side of the road?'

Quite how Bryan had lurched from Tokki to Laini's mythical broken arm to a dead body by the side of the road was beyond Kirsty.

'Her arm wasn't broken. She wasn't even hurt, don't worry. She scratched her finger, that's all,' Kirsty told him. 'She's probably at home now.'

'Can't go there. Order out on me. Had to come here. Got her a present, too. Look…'

Bryan dug around in his pocket, brought out a small box. 'Look.' An oily, smug smile seeped onto his face. 'Sterling silver ring, that is. One of a kind. Girls like jewellery, don't they?'

One of a kind. It was probably from Argos.

'They do, yes.'

'Look!' Bryan was opening the box now, with blunt, dirty fingers. Kirsty realised she was bracing herself for the phrase, 'It's got real rubies for eyes!'

Kirsty take care take care take care.

Nestling in velveteen, held in place by plastic, was a ring fashioned into the shape of… a fairy. Not a snake! Thank god, it wasn't a snake! But the relief was short-lived.

Bryan was still talking. 'Specially made. Angel. Like her. She's my angel.'

'What? What did you say?' All the tensions came back like a scummy tide. 'Angel?'

'When she was little? I used to say that her auntie Lisa was an angel in heaven watching over her, and that *she* was— you all right?'

'I… I probably need to eat something, that's all. I didn't realise Laini was… that you and Mona were…'

'We're not.' Bryan looked peevish. 'Worst mistake I ever made, getting with Mona, I tell you, she's… and Mum? Mum's on Mona's side, that's all. Women. Thick as thieves.' Bryan's face was now

covered with a sheen of sweat. 'And now she's got the Poles in…
Can't even go home to my old mum, given away my room!'

You're forty-six, for god's sake, thought Kirsty.

'Still, it's company for her,' she said.

'Well, they're hard-working, the Poles,' Bryan said with great largesse.
'Got nothing against the Poles. It's the niggers you've got to watch.'

'Bryan—'

'I'm just saying what everyone thinks.'

'Everyone doesn't think that, Bryan.'

Bryan fairly beamed with dim smugness. 'You're a good lass,
Kirsty. Always were. But you're too PC. You know what they're
like – you of all people should know. Muslims. It's in their blood.'

Kirsty began to feel a little bit sick. Talking – or rather listening – to Bryan was better than being threatened by him, but it was
still like swimming in a canal of pus.

'I've got to get back to work now, Bryan. It… it was nice to
see you again.'

'Nicetoseeyoutoo,' Bryan told her. 'Stayintouch? Goforabeer?'

He was patting down his pockets for a cigarette, glancing at the
door, rising from his chair.

'Don't leave your ring!' Kirsty gestured to the open box. She
didn't want to touch it. Neither, apparently, did Bryan. He leaned
against the table.

'Favour?'

'What?'

'The ring? Give it to her? Mona's got this prevention order out
on me. Can't breach it. Just slip it to her? Laini? When she comes
to see her nana?'

'I can't do that, Bryan. I really can't get involved in that.'

'Favour? Old friend?'

She almost laughed. Old friend? Bryan's memory was a miracle
of selectivity.

'I could lose my job if I did that, Bryan.'

And so he swept it up and shoved it back into his pocket, nodded to her and walked towards the doors, back slightly bent, neck extended, a toothless old shark swimming against shoals of passing patients.

An old friend is the key.

CHAPTER TWENTY-ONE

Kirsty made sure she was safely in her office before she let herself start shaking. Sweat poured down her sides and her cheeks pulsed with heat. She could almost feel Lisa in her small office, almost smell that long-forgotten familiar scent of orange lip balm, apple shampoo, sugary dirt. She was here, she was here and she was telling her something... Lisa wanted her here, had brought her here. This child, thirty years dead, needed her.

Her gaze fell on the notes, and her shock began to fade, turned into a kind of fury. All these years, she'd run. All these years she'd resisted Lisa's call because she was afraid, because people had made her afraid. She was afraid for her own sanity, her own equilibrium. Bryan had made her scared of her own home town, Vic had made her scared of being superfluous, Lee had made her scared of her own past, and now this person – whoever it was – was trying to scare her into running away again.

She looked at the notes with a sneer. They were no longer threatening but spiteful, desperate. You shouldn't have come back. Really? Well I am back, and I'm staying. You can't make me run away again. I'm not a little girl any more.

'They're scared of me,' Kirsty said to herself. 'Whoever's sending these notes, they're scared of *me*.' And she felt an unfamiliar pride then, a pride with its roots in revenge. If they were scared of her now, they'd be terrified soon, because she was going to find out what happened to Lisa.

'The truth will set me free,' she muttered to herself, and shoved the notes back into her desk drawer. Then she set her out-of-office message, quickly gathered her bag and coat. She would go and see Sylvia. Between them they'd work out what to do next. She made her way back down to the main exit, so preoccupied that she didn't notice Lee, walking towards her through reception, cradling a huge bunch of flowers. He had to grab her arm as she passed.

'What're you doing here?' she asked dazedly.

'Well, I was going to meet my girlfriend, but then I thought, "Why not visit the old ball and chain?" We had a date, remember?' He thrust the flowers at her. '*Flores para los muertos.*'

'Jesus, Lee, you're in a hospital! Don't be tasteless.'

Lee looked around. 'I don't see many Spanish speakers. Or Tennessee Williams fans. But, OK, yes, point taken.' He peered at her. 'You all right? You look terrible.'

'Thanks. Yes. Hard day.' Kirsty nodded at the flowers. 'Where'd you get them?'

'Oh, they were tied to a lamp-post by the motorway and I thought, "I'll have them."' He winced. 'OK, even I know that was dark.'

'Let me get you out of here before you get lynched. Can you take them though? I've got my hands full here.' Kirsty hitched her bag up on her shoulder, took his arm.

'You're sure you're OK?'

For a moment she considered telling him about Bryan, about the notes, about Lisa getting closer. Then she came to her senses.

'Just a hard day, that's all.' There was no way she could call Sylvia now, no way they could talk over what had just happened… For the first time in her life, Kirsty wished Lee wasn't with her. 'Where'd you park?'

'Slow down, will you!' Lee grabbed her arm now. 'You look like you're fleeing a burning building. What's up?'

'Nothing. I'm just… I just want to get out of here. Where's the car?'

'The *van*, my lady. I drove straight up from sunny Stevenage. I'm parked just up there.'

They turned the corner towards the street, and there, just over the road, was Bryan, lurching out of a pub, heading unsteadily to the cashpoint next door.

'Shit. Turn round!' Kirsty hissed at Lee.

'What?' Lee was too loud. 'Why?'

'Just turn round!'

But Bryan had already seen them. He lurched forward, into the road. A car had to stop, the driver screamed at him; Bryan ignored it all with the serenity of a mad monarch.

'There she is!' he called, grinning.

'Hey, Bryan,' Kirsty said through tight lips, and turned her back, tugging at a suddenly immobile Lee, but Bryan wasn't to be shaken off so easily. He hurried along, caught up with them.

'Called her? Tried to? Can't even give her a present.' Bryan was lachrymose. 'Terrible, that. Isn't it? To use the child against the father? As a weapon? Not a crime is it? See my little girl?'

Kirsty turned. 'Go home, Bryan,' she told him severely. 'You're going to get yourself into trouble. Mona's probably coming back for visiting and if she sees you—'

'Give her the ring though, Kirsty? Come on? Present…'

'No, Bryan.' Kirsty reached behind her for Lee's arm; she could do with a bit of back-up now, but he wasn't there any more, he was a few metres away, lingering at a bus stop, almost as if he was trying to merge with the crowd. Of all the times to hang back! She made an irritable gesture at him, watched him walk, slowly, his face averted, back towards her. Bryan also watched him, with increasing joy.

'You're that Lee kid! We used to knock about, didn't we?'

'No,' Lee told him, and instantly, Kirsty knew he was lying. 'No, sorry, mate.'

Bryan snapped his fingers. 'No, it's *you*! You used to come round to ours, remember? '84? '85? With that other lad, what's-his-name... Dale? Remember?' He pushed his face closer, a repellent ripple spreading over his face, like a cousin to a smile. 'What happened to Dale then? He's still knocking about here?'

Kirsty stared at Lee. Dale Bradley had been best man at their wedding, he'd known Lee since he was small – their fathers served in the same army unit together, For three years they'd lived on the same barracks, gone to the same school. Dale was the first of Lee's friends Kirsty had ever met; ten years ago, they'd gone to his son's christening, and Lee had been a pallbearer at Dale's funeral the year after that. And Bryan had known Dale, and knew Lee? Lee had had some connection – tenuous though it might be – to Lisa? To her own past?

'Sorry, mate,' Lee said again, and his own smile was ghastly now too. 'You've got the wrong person, mate.'

'No. I'm good with names. And faces,' Bryan was saying happily. 'I've got that kind of memory. I've been tested.' He punched Lee's shoulder gently. 'How're you *doing*?'

Finally, Lee shook off his torpor, took Kirsty's arm and fairly dragged her away. Behind them Bryan bellowed, 'Mate? *Mate!*' until he was drowned out by an ambulance siren.

Kirsty and Lee drove back to her flat in silence. The grind and squeak of the old tumblers in the lock as she put in her key and turned seemed very loud and the unstirred air smelled dusty. Lee sat down heavily on one of the stiff little Ikea chairs left by the previous tenant and sighed. An ambulance drove past, and Kirsty could hear the metal shutters of the florist's below being pulled down.

'How long are you going to keep this up?' she asked eventually.

'I... have no plans.' Lee looked miserably at his loosely folded hands.

'I've *told* you about Bryan! I told you what he used to do to me! I don't understand how—'

'I don't know what to tell you.'

'How about the truth, or do I have to go to Bryan for that? You *knew* him? You *and* Dale knew him? And you didn't think to tell me? In all these years? Did you just *forget*? Or—'

'Of course I didn't forget. I never forgot. Kirsty, it was… the longer it went on the harder it was to… come clean.'

'You were *friends* with him! With Bryan!'

'I was never "friends" with him—'

'With the bastard who used to follow me, and spit at me, and blame me for what happened to Lisa? —'

'I wanted to!' Lee's face was frozen into rivulets of pain. 'We'd only just met, you told me about all of that stuff right at the beginning, when we were in that pub, remember? I wanted to tell you and I almost *did,* and then I went outside, called Dale, and he made me see that that'd be the worst thing I could do. I mean, what was I supposed to tell you? Oh yeah, funny story, I knocked around with the bloke who scared the shit out of you? A bloke who was a nut-job *Nazi* by the way? Dale said you'd walk out on me right there if I said anything; and he was right, wasn't he? Would you have gone out with me again if I'd come clean?'

Kirsty wasn't listening though. Her mind, leagues ahead of her sense, was already into conspiracy territory.

'Now I understand. Whenever I tried to talk about it, or do some research about what really happened, you'd shut me down, you'd say I had to move on, stop dwelling on it, but it wasn't because of *me*, caring about *me*, it was because you were worried I'd find out! That was it, wasn't it? Were you in the park that day too? You and Bryan and *Dale* and… did you see Lisa? Did you?'

Even in her rage there was a large part of her that wanted Lee to keep on denying things, push back… She wanted him to do what he'd always done and convince her that she was wrong and he was right. There was safety in that, comfort.

But he didn't. Instead he bowed his head, looked at the carpet. His brown, strong hands dangled from his knees.

'I wasn't. But I don't expect you to believe me. Not the mood you're in now,' he muttered.

'"The mood I'm in"?'

'I'm sorry. I'm… I'm just in a bit of shock, that's all. Give me a minute.'

'What, now I'm supposed to feel sorry for you?'

'No. I don't think you should feel sorry for me,' he looked up and his eyes were old. 'But I *do* think that if you'd calm down and *listen*—'

'Don't do that! Don't do that patronising "calm down little lady" thing.'

He dropped his gaze again. 'I didn't think I was,' he said flatly.

There was a long silence. Lee dug out a crushed packet of cigarettes from his pocket, put one bent cylinder in his mouth, lit it with shaking hands.

'What about Dale?' Kirsty's voice was calmer now. 'How did you get him not to tell me anything?'

'I didn't have to. His dad was stationed in Germany just before it all happened. He didn't know anything about it. Then my dad was stationed in Aldershot – we left in June – and that was the last time I saw Bryan. I didn't even remember him very well, and we *weren't* friends. I'd just turned fifteen then, Kirsty, I moved around so much, went to so many different schools; I'd get bullied unless I made sure I wasn't, and how I made sure I wasn't was to gravitate to the bullies, copy them, get under their wing a bit, you know. Bryan was just *that*… I was a little kid, I had the wrong accent, but I knew that if Bryan liked me I'd be left alone. Plus he could always get hold of cigarettes and lager.' He laughed shortly.

'It's not funny,' Kirsty told him.

'It's not, no. It's pathetic, is what it is. But, listen, didn't you do stupid things when you were a teenager?'

'Not like this. And not things I'd lie about.'

'I didn't think I had a choice! Look at it from my point of view, OK? I meet you, and you're fucking *amazing*; you're what I've been waiting for. Then you tell me all about this horrible experience you had when you were a kid, and I put two and two together and remember maybe knowing someone who made your life a misery. So, I call Dale, I'm seeing this girl, I love her to bits, and it's really serious, what would you do? He said I should just keep it to myself, why upset you for no reason? What are the odds on meeting the perfect person in the first place, you know? Why fuck it up because of one weird coincidence that didn't mean anything?'

'So us meeting, that was a coincidence then?'

'No, Kirsty, it was a plan. I deliberately worked for Ollie, so I could wait till his marriage broke up and get myself invited to his future wife's godawful party, so I could hopefully chat up her sister, thereby keeping quiet about who I knew when I was fifteen. Come on, that's insane. Listen, please?'

He leaned forward, his eyes pleading. 'Kirsty, I made a mistake. I was trying to protect you in a really badly thought-out way. I can see that now, but it's not a hanging offence, is it? Come on!'

'If you barely knew Bryan, why did you run away from him today? And why did he recognise you straight away? He didn't recognise *me* straight away, and I really did know him for years, but you? Bingo! "Hi, Lee!"'

Lee opened his palms, all weary confusion. 'I don't know why he recognised me. I wish to fuck he *hadn't*.'

They were silent again for a long time.

'I'm taking a shower,' Kirsty said eventually.

'Do you want me to order food?'

'I don't care,' she told him. His stricken face pained her, so much so that she could feel herself wavering, giving up. But she made herself resist, turned, locked herself in the little bathroom. As the water pounded her mind yammered: *Boys in the park are a bad lot. Boys in the park are a bad lot. Boys…*

Three things in one day: An old 'friend'. The angel ring. Lee being one of the Bad Lot Boys in the park. The more Kirsty thought about it, the more woozy she felt, and the more she wished she could speak to Sylvia – the only other person on earth who would understand how she felt and help her figure out what to do.

When she got out of the shower, pink and wrapped in towels, Lee was still sitting at the table, but instead of wearing the abject expression he had before, he was now red with rage. He held her phone in his hands.

'You've got a message from your guru,' he said.

'What?'

'"*I'm worried about you. Someone close isn't being fair.*"' His voice was a nasty, mincing parody of a nosy old lady. '"*They're lying and will still lie. Any word from L?*"' He held the phone in one hand, the other curling into a fist on the table top. 'What's that mean?'

'Give me that!'

'Who's L? It's me, isn't it?'

'No.'

'Of course it's me,' Lee said slowly, quietly. 'What other L would it be? What's she been saying about me?'

'It's… all this, Lee, it's difficult to explain. It's…' She closed her eyes, heard his chair scraping closer to hers. The tension in the room dropped, was still dropping. 'It's Lisa. L is Lisa. Sylvia says she's in contact.'

Lee paused, looked at her. 'Fuck *off.*'

'But that's got nothing to do with anything, anyway. You're just trying to change the subject!'

'So what else has she been – sorry *Lisa* – been telling you about me?'

'Nothing about you. Why? What're you scared of?'

'Honestly? You losing your fucking *mind* is what I'm scared of!'

'It's not a difficult question, Lee!'

'No. No, it's not a difficult question. Difficult is being briefly acquainted with some wanker decades ago – that's *impossible* to understand.'

Kirsty took a deep breath; decided to ask a question that only a few hours ago would have seemed insane.

'Do you know what happened to Lisa? Tell me the truth.'

She sounded quite calm.

Lee flinched as if he'd been slapped. 'What did you just say to me?'

'Lisa.' Her calm was cracking now. 'I think you know something about what happened. I think you were in the park that day and you saw her and—'

Lee got up then, and walked straight out of the door. She could hear his footsteps on the worn stair carpet and they were slow, dragging, as if he was injured, and still Kirsty sat, as if frozen, on her chair, hearing him climb into the van, close the rattling door, start the engine. She began to thaw only as she heard him drive away. When she made it to the window, she saw that he'd taken the discarded bouquet Kirsty had left on the passenger seat and tossed it onto the street. Some scattered flowers were already being nosed into the drain by a stray dog. The sky, grey, threatened rain.

CHAPTER TWENTY-TWO

Kirsty had spent her entire life avoiding conflict; now she was the source of conflict – or if not the source, the person who made sure it escalated. She cried, now, for many reasons: shock at her own audacity, at Lee's betrayal, at being faced with the ogre from her childhood. And this shock was sharpened by doubt in herself – had she been fair? Was Lee squirming under pressure or genuinely, crushingly contrite? Was his anger justified, or was it merely deflection? Had he run like a caught coward, or had he fled under friendly fire? And Bryan… him showing up, a 'friend' who was not a friend, the ring for his daughter in the shape of an angel… The fact that Bryan was connected to the Leaveses, that he was thrown in Kirsty's path like that. Perhaps (surely!) this was merely evidence that she was back dealing with a small underclass in a small city. This wasn't like London: this was a place where everyone knew everyone else, no-one left, and all families, at some point, had a common ancestor. Looking at it like that, it would be more surprising if Bryan *hadn't* had a kid with Mona. And the ring? Well, it was just a ring, a cheap bit of ugly tat, that's all. A snake or an angel, it was just a ring. The Argos catalogue was full of them…

And so she called Lee, but he didn't answer the phone. She left three voicemails before he turned it off. He'd never *ever* turned his phone off before. She didn't know what that meant. Pain? Anger? Cowardice? Guilt? It was all so cripplingly confusing that she cried like a child. When Sylvia called her at eight, she was still crying.

*

'Poor man,' Sylvia murmured. 'I mean, poor *you*, but, oh, he must feel terrible. So guilty.'

Kirsty's voice was a cracked whisper. 'I handled it really *really* badly.'

'Well, yes and no. I can understand why you… It's none of my business but… Well, he *did* lie, didn't he? And for – how long have you been together?'

'Nearly ten years.'

'But, now I'm thinking of it, he didn't *lie* so much as not tell the whole truth. There is a difference, I think. Don't be too hard on him, Kirsty! He's a *man* and men are like that. They don't like to be challenged. I could see that in him when I first met you at that party – he's *forceful*, yes, but it's all to protect you, isn't it?'

'But that's the thing, Sylvia, this wasn't to protect me, it was to protect himself.'

Sylvia hesitated. 'Yes. Yes, I can see your point.'

'And he only got angry when he read your message. Before that it was me that was angry and as soon as he read your text he just turned it all around and suddenly he was the victim—'

'He read your private message?' Sylvia was shocked.

'Yes!' Something about Sylvia's disapproval kick-started Kirsty's own righteous indignation. 'That's not right, is it? I mean, I have every right to be angry about that, don't I?'

'You certainly do,' Sylvia replied warmly.

'He has a… problem with psychics and mediums—'

'Why?' Sylvia asked. 'I mean, I could tell, of course. At the party he made that quite clear. I felt sorry for Marie, having to ignore him. But, do you know *why* he hates me?'

'He doesn't *hate* you, he doesn't really *know* you. I'm sure if he did he'd think the world of you. It's psychics and fortune tellers and all that he hates. He thinks they're all charlatans.'

'Oh lord, I've caused so much trouble,' Sylvia whispered. 'I'm so, so sorry! I should've kept my mouth shut, minded my own business.'

'It's not your fault. He just needs to calm down.'

'And, does it take him a while to calm down?' Sylvia asked after a pause.

'He doesn't get angry often, but when he does it takes him a long time, yes. But this was different. I've never seen him like this before.'

'Mmmm,' Sylvia said, after another delicate pause.

'What? What do you think about it?'

'What I think is neither here nor there,' she said stoutly. 'It's what you think that matters.'

'I'll give him an hour and try again,' Kirsty said miserably.

'Well – and this is none of my business, so please tell me to keep my nose out – but, well, *he* stormed out, didn't he? *He* kept the truth from you for all these years, didn't he?'

'Well…'

'And so why is it *you* who's trying to smooth everything over? It seems to *me*… no. No, it's none of my business.'

'Tell me.'

'Well, do you remember your cards? The Ten of Swords had you feeling betrayed and unsupported? And crossing that was the King of Swords? Do you remember what that card means?'

'Someone who is all about reality and rules and the way things should be?'

'Exactly! And if you remember, the rest of the spread pointed to that man being frightened or something being discovered, willing to lash out about it.'

'Well that happened, didn't it? I found out he knew Bryan and now he's ashamed and…'

'Ye-es. That's a part of it, for sure. But something tells me that that's not all of it. That spread – it's stuck in my mind – it was so *vivid…* that spread went deep. Do you remember the last card? The Three of Cups?'

'And I thought that meant Lisa…'

'And I think that too. But not just her. You and me also.' Sylvia paused. 'Sometimes the cards reveal their meaning over weeks, over months. They're tricky that way, but they always tell the truth, however much you might not want to hear it. They're... merciless. But if you're strong and take what they're saying on board, they never steer you wrong.'

'I've never seen that side of Lee,' Kirsty said, almost to herself. 'Never. It was scary. It came out of nowhere.'

'Nothing comes out of nowhere,' Sylvia told her. 'Take care of yourself. Write down your dreams, look out for clues. Something is coming to a head, I can feel it. You can too, can't you?'

'Yes,' Kirsty answered. 'Yes I can.'

*

Two days later she received another note at work, but this time it wasn't shoved under her door. This time it was in an envelope, neatly Sellotaped at eye level.

Everything that is happening and everything that will happen is because of you. You cause trouble wherever you go. Bad lot.

After reading this, Kirsty stayed sitting, her head on her desk for some minutes, trying to take deep breaths. She tried to summon up the strength she'd had before during the epiphany in her office. She tried to make herself believe that the person sending the notes was scared of her, desperate. They had to be, didn't they, if they were trying this hard to make her leave?

But, oh! She wanted to leave now! She wished to god she'd never come back now! If she hadn't come back, she would never have known that Lee was a liar, she wouldn't be alone.

It was true. She did cause trouble, this was all happening because of her. She'd discovered things she'd never wanted to discover, unearthed secrets she'd rather never have known. Her marriage was in limbo, her sense of self was fractured. And she'd done this all herself by coming back here and stirring up the past like a wasps' nest.

The sound of her phone made her jump. *Sylvia.* Kirsty felt a welcome wave of safety.

'I was just thinking about you. I had a feeling you might need a chat?'

'Oh my god, Sylvia, you have no idea!'

'Did… call…' Sylvia's voice wavered in and out, crackling like an old record. 'After…?'

'I can't hear you very well, the signal's—'

'… awful after… can't help… my fault…'

'What? Sylvia, you're breaking up—'

'I…' in and out, like a ghost, 'strange… note…'

'Note?' Her heart quickened. 'What note? Where?'

'Under my door… came in the night.'

'What did it say?'

'*Whatever you think you—*'

'*—know you don't,*' Kirsty chimed in.

'Same thing?' Sylvia's voice was as wavering as the connection. 'What does it… I don't know… mean… you?'

'I can't hear you. I'll come over after work if that's all right? We can talk about it?'

Sylvia's voice throbbed with relief. '… like that… scared.'

Then the phone cut out.

*

The note and the knowledge that Sylvia, too, had received a note from what must be the same person thrummed through Kirsty's body like caffeine, and her mind was split in two all day – half of her roamed the humid, soupy wards and negotiated the crowded sick and their

sick-looking relatives swelling the corridors, with a brisk pace. She
rap-rapped on doors, nodded, took notes with a brisk efficiency
that smacked of central casting. The morning held meetings with a
psychiatric nurse with halitosis; an abrupt accountant on the autistic
spectrum who needed painstaking guidance on how to care for his
dementia-ridden mother; and something her jolly, over-medicated
line manager had dubbed a 'file cleanse' ('best-practice-overview-
sort-the-wheat-from-the-chaff'). All the while the other half of her
mind ran along feverish lines to the same fixed points: Sylvia, Lisa
and, between them, some hidden, buried truth, and this dispelled the
self-doubt she'd felt in the morning. The truth, she knew for certain,
was within her grasp, being pushed closer and closer by Lisa herself.

She skipped lunch and opted for caffeine pills washed down with
more coffee from the Spice of Life. It tasted like iron filings. Time
sped, she was efficiency itself, and she was walking purposefully
down a busy corridor when she collided with a woman who was
just leaving the lift and dropped her phone. It broke into three
neat pieces.

'Shit!' Kirsty – un-caffeinated, well-rested, less-distracted Kirsty
– would have apologised. This Kirsty merely barked, 'Can you find
the battery? It went over there somewhere?'

The woman stayed still, making no attempt to help or move on.

'Give me a hand?' Kirsty complained.

'No.' The voice – cold, imperious – was familiar. Angela Bright.
Kirsty stood up then. They faced each other like warring cats.

'Angela,' Kirsty managed eventually. 'Kirsty. We met at—'

'I know where we met.' Angela, not smiling, had her feet planted
wide, as if to bar Kirsty's escape.

'Are you here to see Peg? She's asleep just now and it's not visiting
hours yet—'

Angela Bright raised her head, as if sniffing the air. Her lips
smiled. 'Why don't I buy you a coffee?'

'I really don't have time.'

'I insist.'

'You insist?'

'I think we should talk.'

'What about?'

'About my mother. About Sylvia. You've been calling and going over to the house a lot.' She spoke slowly, looking Kirsty straight in the eyes.

'Yes. She's a very interesting woman.'

'And why are you interested in her?'

Kirsty felt her heart rate rise further. Angela Bright was obviously spoiling for a fight.

'Why wouldn't I be interested in her?'

'I want you to stop going to see her, calling her, everything.'

And Kirsty, jittery, over-caffeinated, full of adrenaline, laughed. It was like something out of a soap opera – *Kirsten and Angela clash! Catfight ensues!* And for once, she didn't want to defuse the situation; for once she didn't want to cave, exercise diplomacy or politeness. She wanted to see just what would happen if she stepped out of role; no longer the grown-up in the room, but the provocateur.

'Have *you* been to see her recently? She talks a lot about you… she's told me a *lot* of things about you.'

Angela's face rippled with disgust. When she answered, her carefully modulated voice was ever so slightly polluted with a hint of the local accent – like gravel at the bottom of a clear-running stream.

'You don't know anything about me.' She took a step forward and Kirsty felt that thrilled boldness recede just a little bit, letting old, fearful Kirsty step forward once again. 'Whatever you *think* you know—'

'*You don't.*' Kirsty's eyes widened.

'That's right. You got it.' Angela smiled nastily.

'Now I get it.' Kirsty's voice was soft, wondering.

'Get what?' Angela's voice dropped further and the accent dropped with it, right into the gutter. 'You don't know anything. And whatever *she's* told you about me, it won't be true, let me tell you that.' She added, whispering, 'She's... she's old. She doesn't know what she's saying half the time.'

'I think she does. I *know* she does. Why're you scared of me?'

By now they were inches apart, oblivious to their surroundings. A long moment passed before either of them noticed the ward sister, flanked by a lugubrious porter, standing there demanding to know what was going on. In the corridor behind her the curious faces of patients and staff bobbed like pale balloons.

Angela took a step back. So did Kirsty. Reality rushed into the vacuum between them. Kirsty, feeling her hands shake as if she'd just put down a heavy weight, put them in her pockets.

Angela Bright smiled professionally. 'Just a misunderstanding,' she said, her voice once again a fluid, mid-Atlantic drawl. 'I got out at the wrong floor. This lady was explaining that this ward was closed to visitors, that's all.'

'Kirsty?' the ward sister asked doubtfully.

'Yes,' Kirsty made herself say. 'That was it. Just a misunderstanding.'

'What ward do you need?' the sister asked dubiously, but Angela had already turned and was striding back to the lifts, entering, pushing the down button with one thin finger. As the doors closed and their eyes met, Angela smiled blandly at the sister, waited until she departed, then dropped the smile, stared with sullen hatred at Kirsty.

'Stay away if you know what's good for you,' she said and that accent was back, a local snarl, straight out of Beacon Hill estate.

The doors closed.

CHAPTER TWENTY-THREE

Sylvia McKnight's house was as warm and womb-like as ever. The comforting smell of chamomile tea wafted up from the little teapot. The two women had been silent for some time.

'I'm sorry, Sylvia. But, it had to have been her sending the notes. After she came to see me today and after the things she said, who else could it be?'

'She… she wouldn't have meant any harm.' Sylvia was looking at her own nervous hands, as if begging them to believe her. 'Marie… she's… Sometimes she doesn't understand what she's doing, that's all.'

'Sylvia, why are you doing this? I know she's your daughter and you love her, but come on, this is… nuts. She's trying to scare both of us, and why? Is it just that she's jealous? Because we're close, and you and her…'

Sylvia smiled bleakly at her hands. 'Jealous? Oh no. No, she won't be jealous of you. She's not built that way.' One finger unfurled, tapped the table. 'I've never understood Marie. She's not like other people.' A vague, sinister phrase. 'In all these years I've been too much of a coward to think about… what she's really like, let alone talk to her about it. I've always been afraid that if I did, people would realise it's all my fault.'

'You can talk to me!' Kirsty said warmly. She touched one cold hand, dry and hard as petrified wood. 'You know you can! And I'm not going to think it's your fault, am I?'

'You might when I tell you.' She sighed, shuddered, sat a bit taller, and Kirsty watched grim acceptance creep onto her face. 'I've always been afraid.'

'Of what? Sylvia, you have to tell me. Please?' Kirsty held her hand. 'I won't judge, I just want to understand. And, whatever it is, well, we'll face it together.'

'It's a long story.'

'Well, they're the best kind.' Kirsty smiled.

'Not this one. This one doesn't have a happy ending. But it has to be told.' Sylvia nodded to herself. 'It's time. It's time I was brave.'

'I always wanted to be a mother,' Sylvia began. 'There were years and years of disappointment, before I finally managed to get pregnant. I knew from the start that she was a girl, I knew from the start that she was Marie. It was as if she told me herself. Marie-Belle McKnight. I wanted to make her life perfect. I wanted to give her something most children never have, that *I* never had – absolute security, absolute faith in herself, and *privacy*. When I was little there were too many of us in one small house… no books, no music and it was all noise. I had to go to the outhouse in the yard to be on my own, and even there I wasn't really alone – I could still hear them. I had to go back. I wanted Marie to have the opposite. We lived in the country.'

'In Ireland?'

'Yes. Galway. And we had horses, we grew our own vegetables, fruit. Like people on a desert island. It was our own world.'

'It sounds idyllic.'

'*I* thought it was. Oh we had so much fun!' Her face creased fondly at the memory. 'We cooked and we went on long walks and climbed trees and took day trips to the sea side and we *drew*… it was a lovely time. Then it all changed.'

'How?'

'I thought it'd be good for her to see a big city – somewhere foreign, but not foreign if you know what I mean. We'd been reading that poem – "They're Changing Guard at Buckingham Palace".'

'"Christopher Robin went down with Alice",' quoted Kirsty with a smile.

'That's the one. Marie loved it! So as a special surprise I arranged to go to London for the weekend: see the changing of the guard, the Tower of London, all the sights. Well, she was excited – looking back, maybe a little too excited. As soon as we arrived she got upset. Overwhelmed. There were too many people, there was too much to see, and she just shrank down into herself. Couldn't talk, barely looked anyone in the face and when she did she'd cry. I had all these activities planned, but it was a torture for her. I thought it was just shyness – after all, I'd kept her away from the world, and now, suddenly, I take her to a city like London, with all those millions of people and all that noise. I mean, no wonder she... I told her, look, let's just go home, but she told me no. She wanted to go to the British Museum and see the mummies. She was set on that. So, the next day that's what we did, and she seemed all right, quiet, but all right. Then, suddenly, she was gone! I searched for her like a mad thing, running, shouting for her... You don't understand panic until you lose your child, that *fear*! It turns you into an animal almost! Anyway, an American family found her eventually. She'd crammed herself between these two cabinets and hidden right back by the wall. She'd only been a few feet away from me the whole time and she'd never said a word! And when they got her out she didn't speak to me, or talk, or... Then the mother? Of this American family? She took me aside and said that crowded places like the museum weren't the best place for a child with autism. Well, I was offended! I said that she didn't have anything wrong with her, that she was just shy and they should keep their opinions to themselves! I grabbed Marie's hand and we marched out of the place, her screaming her head off and me just mortified.'

'*Is* she autistic?'

Sylvia shook her head. 'When we got back home I went to the library to do a bit of research. I thought maybe there was something in it… maybe it wasn't just shyness, or isolation, maybe there was a real problem? I wanted to understand, you see. I wanted to know what I'd done wrong and how I could fix it. Nothing in the books rang true though.'

'So what had happened in the museum to upset her like that?'

'She told me that one of the mummies had started speaking to her. And she couldn't understand them and she couldn't understand why no-one else could hear them. She said she spoke back and people gave her funny looks and so she got scared and hid. I told her that none of this was real and she just had a big imagination and she calmed down. As soon as we were back at home, as soon as we were on the train back home actually, she was normal again – happy, smiley. I asked her what had happened to make her feel so sad and shy *before* the museum and she said she could see what people were thinking, feel all their emotions rushing into her, and it had all been too much for her. Well, I knew that feeling. I'd had the gift all my life, and I remember how hard it was when I was little, too. Oh, I could've kicked myself for not seeing it before! I was *relieved*, Kirsty. This meant I could help her, because I knew what she was going through. But… '

'What?'

'I started to tell her that I understood, that I'd been the same way, and my mother before me, that it was something the McKnight women had, that it was a talent, a gift, and I could help her. I wish someone had said that to me when I was five, I'll tell you that. But she… she didn't like what I was saying. She said, "I'm not like you or anyone."'

'Woah.'

'Yes. She sounded so adult, so sure of herself. She said she didn't need training, and started showing me the things she could already do – she knew who was calling before I picked up the phone. She could find things I'd hidden or lost. After that she changed. I'd go to hug her and she'd pull away. She didn't like me reading her stories, teaching her her ABC. She never let me teach her anything ever again apart from tarot. It takes people a lifetime to master tarot, all the combinations, the spreads; it took Marie about ten days. I've never seen anything like it…' Sylvia looked up, gazed gravely at Kirsty. 'I know this must sound made up, but it's all true. All of it. She was gifted in a way that was beyond me. So I did what any decent mother would do; I tried to get her as much support as possible to help those gifts along.'

'Where? Where did you go?'

'Well, I didn't know where to start! I thought maybe the doctors could test her, but then I remembered the woman in the museum and thought they might just say she had some syndrome and medicate her. Then I called up Mensa and they sent a test, but she wasn't that sort of gifted. Then I saw an advert in the library – the Society for Psychical Research were giving a talk about their work with ghosts, that sort of thing. And I thought that they, of all people, might listen to me without thinking I was mad. So, we went along and that's where we met the Star Child people.'

'"Star Child"?' Kirsty almost sniggered.

'It sounds silly and *I* thought it sounded silly at the time, but remember, Kirsty, I was desperate. By this point she was hurting herself, screaming, crying, or just shutting down completely and not saying a word. What was I meant to do? My child needed help and thirty-odd years ago there wasn't the internet to help you find out about things, make contact with people. Star Child, for me, seemed heaven sent.'

'Who were they?'

'They were a new organisation and they were deliberately pig-gybacking on ghost talks, medium shows and things like that, to meet people like me. They were very open about it and what they said made real sense: some children are different, they're more than intuitive, they're gifted and so they have to be taught and cared for in a different way. This was exactly what I'd been looking for! After the first meeting we went home and cried, it was such a relief to be told that there was a place for her in the world. We got more involved in the group and Marie made friends with the children – her first real friends. And *I* met people too, which meant that for the first time in years *I* could talk about *my* gifts without people thinking I was mad. Loneliness is a funny thing. Sometimes you don't know you're lonely until you stop being lonely. That's what it was like for me anyway. I'd given my all to motherhood, for all those years it was just me and her, and now I was meeting other mothers, being part of a community. It was… it was lovely. And then it stopped being lovely.'

'How?'

Sylvia frowned. 'You know if you put a frog in boiling water it'll jump straight out? But if you put it in cold water and gradually bring it to the boil, the frog will stay there until it dies? It won't register any danger. Star Child was like that. The first few months were all about support, praising the kids' talents, learning to deal with anxiety, things like that. Then it changed, but so gradually that I couldn't be sure if what was happening was real, or I was making too much of it, or…'

'But what changed?'

'Well, from the start we were told that kids like ours weren't just gifted, but specially gifted, important to the future of the planet. They were old souls who operated on a different level to the rest of us. We'd all lived before, but Star Children had total recall of every past life, and had consciously returned to earth to change it, and we should let them lead. That's why they could be a handful sometimes, they weren't being trusted to take the lead, and they resented it. I know it sounds... I *know* what you're thinking, but remember, this was very gradual. They made you feel as if you were discovering it all yourself, or rather, you were being *trusted* with this knowledge because you were special yourself. They wouldn't just dump the information on you like that, they'd lead into it, saying things like, "We understand this sounds crazy, but..." and "We don't blame you if you want to leave us right now, plenty have when they couldn't take the truth." They took you aside and told you privately, saying that it would be best not to tell any other parents because they weren't quite as open as you were.'

'Sounds like a cult,' Kirsty managed.

Sylvia nodded. 'Yes. It was. They had that covered too though. They'd kind of poke fun at the fear of cults. One of the things they said in meetings was that if a "cult" has over a thousand members, they call it a religion, if it's over two thousand it's a political party, and anything above that means it's normal life. Democracy could be defined as a cult. And we'd laugh, nod. It made sense. And, after all, we were all there because we knew our children *were* different, special. Some parents were scared of their own kids, others' marriages had broken up... The things normal kids responded to – mainstream education, reward charts, sleep routines – simply didn't apply to ours and we knew that but didn't know why. Some of us had spent years resisting doctors trying to medicate them out of their gifts. We didn't trust the system. Now, here was Star Child telling us that we were right all along and together we would change the world. It was irresistible. And of course they weren't just saying that to the parents, they were saying that to the kids as well. So if parents started having second thoughts and stopped going to the meetings—'

'Their kid would kick up a fuss about it,' Kirsty finished.

'Exactly.' She shook her head. 'I stayed longer than I should.' She winced. 'I knew on some level that something was off, but I didn't *want* to know: Marie was so happy and it was so lovely to meet people again, be out in the world again. I kept taking her to the training sessions. They told me she was immensely talented, but she'd do even better if I wasn't in the room with her – it was all about vibrations and focus and…' she pushed one tired hand through her hair, 'and every time I went to pick her up, she was so *happy*! It made me realise how unhappy she'd been before. Lonely, just like me. Kirsty, she *glowed*! She stood tall, she ate well, she slept well, she woke up energised. She hugged me again. It was miraculous! I saw that she'd changed, and that they were changing her, but it was for the better. I thought it was for the better anyway. Then she started going to a few weekend retreats, and, no, I wasn't allowed to go. When she came back from these retreats she was just a little bit different, just a little bit less herself, and she didn't want to tell me what she'd done, or how she felt, or…'

'What did you do?'

'At the next meeting I stayed behind to ask some questions. Well, they tried to give me the brush-off, but I – and I was very polite about it – I wanted to know details; just ordinary things like how many children were on the same retreat, what activities they did, that kind of thing. I know, I know it sounds insane now, that I sent her off in the first place without knowing these things, but it was a different time then – parents were more trusting of authority, more intimidated by people in charge.'

'What did they tell you?'

'Nothing,' Sylvia answered flatly. 'They told me nothing. Just that it was "child-led activities", which could have meant anything. I asked if I could become more involved in the group, maybe go along to the next retreat as a helper, but they said no to that too. I wasn't qualified enough, they said.'

'How could you not be qualified? You were her mum.'

'I know! I said that too, and oh, they didn't like that. Not one little bit. Oh they smiled, said they'd put me on the list for volunteers and showed me the door. She was meant to be going away that next weekend, but we got a letter saying it was cancelled – no explanation. Then at the next meeting, one of the other mothers told me that her boy had gone.'

'So they lied about it being cancelled?'

'They did. Marie was confused. She kept asking me why she didn't go, maybe it was because she wasn't special any more... so I asked. They said it had been an administrative error, and she was down for the next retreat – four days, this one was. And when she came back, she was... different. Very distant with me.'

'Why? What did she say?'

'Nothing at first. She was angry with me for asking... almost violent. It was like we'd stepped back in time; she didn't eat, wouldn't talk, stayed in her room ripping off the wallpaper – she ripped it all off one wall. Finally she told me what it was about. At the retreat there was a session about "Tick" people and "Cross" people. Tick people were positive, good influences, and Cross people were bad people – stupid people. They had to make a personal list of both types. Then they were told to pass their lists around to see if the rest of the group agreed with them. Well, when she got her list back, everyone had said that my name shouldn't be on the Tick list, because I wasn't positive enough. Well, you can imagine, Marie was really upset! She was confused, and hurt, and... and *alone*. Imagine it, alone with all these people saying her own mother was a bad person! A *stupid* person that didn't love them. She couldn't call me, she couldn't come home...'

'That's awful! No wonder she was upset!'

Sylvia nodded. 'It *was* awful. It was indefensible. But they didn't stop there, the Cross and Tick exercise happened on the first day of the retreat. She had another three there for them to work on her, and that's what they did. From what I know about the group now, and piecing together things Marie told me, what they did to her was standard operating procedure; they want to control the kids and the best way to do that is control the parents. If they can't control the parents, if the parents ask questions – like I did – they turn the kid against them, in the hope that the parent will see sense and come back on board. So they made a fuss of her, everyone in the group gave her a hug, the leader told her it wasn't her fault, or my fault. She was told that I used to be a "Tick" person, and I could be again, so long as I stopped being jealous of her talents. That's the way they put it – jealous. And that was what she'd had to listen to for four days: how ordinary and small, and *jealous* I was. Jealous! Of my own daughter!' There was a bitterness in Sylvia's voice now, a quiet rage. 'Well, they didn't get their wish. We never went back. I had to keep her in her room for a week. I had to put a lock on the door to stop her trying to get out. She tried climbing out of the window, but I caught her. And all the while I'm getting calls from Star Child, visits from them.'

'And, how was it? How was Marie then?'

'She had nightmares. She missed them, she missed her friends. I put her in school here, thinking she'd make more friends, but she didn't. Not really. The thing is, I went into Star Child because she was different, she was psychic, and after Star Child, she was *still* different, still psychic. That hadn't changed. She changed though.'

'How? How did she change?'

Sylvia's head was bowed, she spoke to the twisted fingers on her lap. 'She became cruel. She threw stones at cats, ran dogs into the road. She'd started at school that September and I thought that might help, but it made things worse. She said things that made other kids cry. She knew just what to say. She knew just what it was that would hurt the most. I seemed to spend my life in that head teacher's office, making excuses, making amends, and Marie would say the right things – you know, promise not to do it again – but she always did. She thought she could do anything, that she had the right to do anything. That's what Star Child had done to her.'

'How has she managed to hide it? I've seen clips of her show and she's so different on TV to how she is in life.'

'She learned how to act. As she got older she spent a lot of time with Peg and her family, and I think she saw how *they* were, you know, they take no prisoners, always in trouble. Well, I think she saw them and realised that she had to learn to look more normal, she had to make people like her or she'd end up staying here for the rest of her life, like them. And she was always ambitious, she liked money, nice things, nice clothes. I think she taught herself to fit in, you know? And it's worked out well for her, hasn't it?'

'But if she likes money so much, why won't she sell the land and buy you somewhere more comfortable? Why has she been here so long? She must be losing money hand over fist while she's here.'

Sylvia looked as if she was about to speak, but stayed silent.

'Why is she sending us these notes? Why did she threaten me today? Why doesn't she want us to be friends?'

'I think she's scared,' Sylvia said after a pause.

'What of though?'

'You,' Sylvia said softly.

'Me? How could she be scared of me?'

Sylvia took a deep breath, let it out through pursed lips. 'I think it not you, but something you know. *That's* what she's scared of.'

'What?'

'I'm not sure, but she's been scared since that party at your sister's house. Before that she was like she always is – cool, very measured, you know. But as soon as she saw you, she changed. Later that night when we were alone, she was livid, absolutely *livid*, saying you being there was a set-up, that she never would have come if she'd known the client was your sister, and god knows what else. I didn't know what she was on about and I don't know now... I've tried since to hang back, weather the storm, and it did seem to blow over a bit until she saw you a few weeks ago, when you came over to visit, remember? You met each other here? Well, she called me later that night and was wild... She was saying things she hadn't said since she was little, and she seemed convinced that I was in some sort of conspiracy with you. That's when I began to worry.'

'What does she think I know?' Kirsty was perplexed. 'Is it something about Lisa? It must be, mustn't it?'

Sylvia shook her head. 'I don't know.' But her eyes were down, and her body shrieked evasion.

'I think you do,' Kirsty whispered.

Sylvia's phone pinged in her pocket, and when she saw the name her mouth tightened. 'That's Marie now. She's coming over. You'd better leave.'

'What does she think I know?'

'You have to leave. If you don't she'll... I don't know *what* she'll do. I'll... I'll try to find out what's going on in her head and I'll call you. Wait for my call and don't call me in case she's here, all right? That will just make things worse. Look, she's coming now and she's only been at Mona's so she'll be here any minute! You really have to leave!'

'Will you call me?'

'Yes! I promise! Now, get yourself gone, all right? And be careful, please!'

On the drive through Beacon Hill, Kirsty passed Marie's big, sleek BMW. Its headlights swept and dazzled her as it sped by, smooth as a shark through dark water.

CHAPTER TWENTY-FOUR

Sylvia didn't call though. Instead Kirsty received a gnomic note at work the next morning.

Mrs Mackie (?) called apologies call back no message

Kirsty read it, peered questioningly at the receptionist, read it again. 'Did you take the message?'

'Nah. I found it when I came on shift.'

'So who took it? Becky? Corrine? The one with the glasses?'

The receptionist looked tiredly at her. 'I'm a temp. We all are mostly. It's not like we know each other.' He seemed wearily amused at Kirsty's assumption of work camaraderie. 'It was here, that's all I know, and you're the only Kirsten we've got on staff.'

'When did she call?'

The receptionist rolled his eyes irritably. 'How am I meant to know that? Could've been any time. Could've been last night even.'

Kirsty managed to swallow her sudden flash of pure hate, managed to nod, to turn and walk slowly to her office, the pink note quivering in her hand, its exact meaning horribly opaque. No message? But there was a message – call me back was the message. Wasn't it? Or was she saying she'd call Kirsty back? That's if it was from Sylvia at all – maybe there was a Mrs Mackie looking for her, who knew? No. No, it had to be Sylvia, and the fact that she'd called the hospital was telling, sinister – why not call her mobile? Perhaps the muddled meaning was less due to the receptionist's sloppy note-taking, and more down to Sylvia's panic – a garbled warning; a request for help.

The more she studied the note, written in the crabbed hand of a stranger, the more powerfully she felt that Sylvia was in great trouble. She called, but there was no answer, just automated voicemail. She called again, the same. She tried to tell herself to calm down, that nothing was wrong, that she was tired, stressed, overwrought… *You have a full day of work, lots to do, deal with this afterwards.* She was telling herself this even as she was heading to the door.

She left the car by the lock-up garages near Beacon Hill and cautiously walked the rough track leading to the house. It was the first time she'd been there in full daylight, the first time she could see just how much rubbish there was on the track, and how, closer to the house, the wind moved like a live thing over the vague, humped shapes of cars, over rusting axles, rotting timber, sinuously draped tarps… it moved and whispered, both beckoning and warning. A group of brown sunflowers thumped their heads, rattling with dead seeds, against the kitchen window.

Trembling like a child, Kirsty made herself knock on the door, made herself call, 'Sylvia? Are you there? Are you OK? It's Kirsty.'

No answer.

She couldn't peer through the window because the curtains were drawn, so she squatted down on the sagging boards of the porch and opened the letterbox. One chair was pulled away from the table, left at an angle as if someone had leapt from it quickly, and on the floor – what were they? Papers? Cards? A vase of flowers had been upended, the water pooled into milky murk on the polished table top. There was no way Sylvia would leave her house in this kind of mess.

Her heart now slapping in her chest, the coppery taste of adrenaline in her throat, Kirsty stalked the perimeter of the house, reaching a side door, where, half stuck in the mud, its screen smashed, was Sylvia's phone. With stiff fingers Kirsty picked it up. Stuck into the mud in the hollow the phone had made – too eccentric and too neatly placed to be accidental – were two tarot cards: The Empress, one enigmatic eye gazing through the mud, pinned under the King of Swords. Sylvia had left her a clue, a message. Sylvia herself was The Empress, the mother figure, the all-knowing, benevolent guide. And the King of Swords? A man who was all about reality and rules and the way things should be… a man who was now challenged, frightened and furious. Lee.

Then she heard the sound.

A snap, or a click. Something being opened, or shut, and it was coming from the stubby, shaded woods beyond. She wasn't alone here… someone else was there, maybe waiting, watching, weighing up their own options. Adrenaline surged and froze, and Kirsty's every sense became suddenly, quiveringly alert. She could wait or she could run back to the car, strap herself in and get the hell out of there. Her car was only a few hundred yards away, but a few hundred yards of open, flat land where she'd be horribly, vulnerably visible. But what choice did she have? Hugging close to the side of the house, she edged back towards the front again, pushing her way through the nasty, hairy sunflower stalks, her feet crunching on dead seeds. From here, she could see the snout of her car poking out from the line of garages. She took a deep breath, and was about to dash towards it, when she heard another sound from the woods – the release catch of a car door. Whoever it was in the woods was waiting too. She half heard/half imagined footsteps over leaves, over frozen mud and pushed herself further into the sunflower patch, feeling the ground dip at her heels, the warped boards at the base of the house bowed in enough to give her a little more shelter. She waited for what seemed like hours, barely breathing, the rubbish collecting around her ankles, hearing only the wind, until, with terrifying suddenness,

Sylvia's phone rang – a shrill peal like an alarm. Loud enough for the person in the woods to hear it, loud enough for the residents in Beacon Hill to hear it! Kirsty fumbled with the thing, cutting her palm on the shattered screen, and managed to turn it off, but following like an aftershock was another sound – the slam of a car door, the gunning of an engine, coming from the scrubland, and it was coming closer, lumbering like a beast through undergrowth, straight towards the house, straight towards *her*. If she stayed where she was, she'd be seen, perhaps even hit. She had a sudden, clear understanding that whoever it was behind the wheel of that car had hurt Sylvia and would hurt her too if she let them.

Still gripping the phone – hard enough that later she found three needle-like shards of the broken screen embedded in her palm – she kicked at the rotten boards, feeling them bend and splinter, felt her heels slip backwards into a crawl space that had been carved out between the kitchen floor and the bare earth. With great difficulty, Kirsty shuffled backwards into the hole, tasting sour soil and feeling the rough ceiling scrape her scalp, snagging her hair, tearing some out at the roots. Her face was pressed into the ground, breathing was difficult. Outside, the car was circling the house in a long, slow orbit, as if the driver was teasing her, tormenting her.

With great difficulty, Kirsty managed to turn over. Now that she lay flat, breathing was easier, but the stench was even worse: there were a fair few animal carcasses by the smell of it… rats, probably. A nest of dead rats rotting on top of one another, and… *Stop! Stop that! You'll make yourself panic, you'll make yourself scream!*

She lay in this grave-like space, soundlessly crying with fear, trying not to breathe too deeply, trying to reserve as much of the foul but breathable air as she could. There was nothing to do but wait. Wait and try to stay sane.

The car still circled the house, slower, slower, until finally it drove away. Kirsty allowed herself to relax just a little, but she stayed where she was, just in case. Sure enough the car returned about ten minutes later as if the driver had been trying to flush her out. It parked right in front of the house, only a few feet away from where Kirsty was hiding.

She heard the door open, heard footsteps, too slow and softly deliberate to betray any clue of gender, of mood or intent. Footsteps crunched softly on leaves, then creaked with sudden, shattering volume on the stairs just above her head. Whoever it was was trying to open the front door, rattling the handle angrily. The boards above Kirsty groaned. She heard the familiar sound of a cigarette being lit, the click of the lighter, the fizz of the paper. Then Lee's voice, 'I know you're there!'

Kirsty felt one tear seeping from her now tightly shut eyes. It merged with the trickle of blood from her scalp and ran into the stinking earth with the blood from her palms.

'Leave her alone. Leave *us* alone! Hey!' He pounded on the door with such force that the boards above Kirsty's head shook. Little puffs of dust fell into her wet eyes. 'Whatever you think you know about me, you fucking well *don't*, all right?' He hammered at the door again 'You don't know *anything* and if you start filling her head with all this…*shit*, I'll…' He gave one, final, kick at the door. The wood just above Kirsty's left eye splintered. She could see dim, dirty light through the gap.

The boards shifted and groaned again, as he turned, walked slowly down the steps. She heard footsteps receding, a car door opening and slamming shut, the faint jangle of keys. The motor started and the car drove away – neither slow nor fast – and kept driving. Still, she made sure to stay hidden for the next hour or so and when she finally emerged, turning over and shuffling out like a bear, the light was painful and her damp, numb legs refused to support her; she tumbled over like a new-born foal and lay for long minutes in the dirt until the sensation stole back into her legs with a prickly, vicious electric that made her cry out. Lee's half-smoked cigarette lay just beside one cut palm.

Lee must have been the person in the woods, the one in the car. It was Lee who had forced her to hide under the house, Lee who hated Sylvia enough to threaten her. Sylvia knew what he was really like, knew long before Kirsty, and had left the tarot card as a warning to her. But where was Sylvia? Had she run, or had she been taken?

CHAPTER TWENTY-FIVE

She drove home, almost catatonic, and arrived back at the flat with no memory of having driven at all. The unforgiving bathroom light showed that something under the house had left a hessian-like print on her cheek, along with a smudge of something oily and brown. A nasty, smoky stench rose when she shook her hair loose with smarting palms, and beneath that, from her very skin, something more fetid, rotting and dark.

She spent half an hour pulling out tiny strips of glass from her palm with tweezers. The shower uncovered lots of other little smarting wounds and sudden vulnerabilities. When she washed her hair some of it came out at the roots.

She emerged cleaner, but no longer herself. The face in the mirror was now strangely child-like; eyes wide, mouth a vulnerable bud. Her hair fell on her forehead in wayward little curls like wood shavings.

'I don't know what to do,' Kirsty whispered to herself. 'Tell me what to do, Lisa. Just tell me what to do because I'm lost and it's dark and I'm scared. Tell me what to do, please? Should I call the police? Should I go back there? Help me. What do you want me to do?'

*

Lisa was skipping. They both were. It was one of those complicated games with two ropes and an ever-changing chant that girls seemed to know in their bones. The ropes, as always, moved quickly with an even, robotic speed.

Lisa was chanting. 'Pol*ice*man, pol*ice*man, do your duty. Here comes Kirsty and she's such a *cu*tie!' They faced each other, pink-faced, happy and breathless. '"She can JUMP, she can TWIST. But I bet she can't do THIS!"' Lisa executed a neat backflip.

'How'd you learn *that*?' Kirsty was impressed. 'That's ace!'

'That's for me to know and you to find out!' Lisa replied smartly. She started a new chant. 'Down in the park where the green grass grows, sat little *Lisa*, pretty as a rose, she sang and she danced and she danced so sweet, along came a little girl and kissed her on the cheek.'

Kirsty looked up. The sky had darkened. 'It's going to rain.'

'Shame shame double shame.' Lisa had her eyes shut tight.

'Lisa?'

'We don't know her real name. Join *in*!'

'I don't know this one.' Kirsty wasn't jumping any longer, and she had to duck away from the swinging ropes, which were cutting through the air with a nasty mechanical swish. 'Do one I know!'

'You do know it. I taught it you,' Lisa called, and she was further away now, moving swiftly, as if on a hidden conveyor. She was nearly at the end of the street, but the street didn't have an end… '*Made* a *mistake,* stay *awake.*"

'Wait!' Kirsty was shouting. 'Don't leave me, it's dark! Lisa!'

Lisa was now just a pastel smudge caught in the threshing ropes. 'You left *me*,' she shouted. 'You *left* me.'

'I'm sorry! Lisa! Tell me where you are… Tell me where you are and I'll find you, I promise!'

'Those lads,' she called back in a sing-song voice. 'They hang around the park, you know where! Stay awake, I'm not too far to find!'

'Who hurt you?' Lisa was far away now, a shimmer. 'Lisa?'

'Wake *up*,' Lisa called back. 'Wake *up*!'

*

And Kirsty did wake, stiff and bruised, still wrapped in a towel, at first not recognising where she was. The sunlight slanted through the thin blinds and she was curled up tight as a foetus on the little sofa. She didn't remember even lying down, let alone sleeping, and her head and face felt huge, swollen, her palms smarted. When she sat up the room swam for a moment before settling into a stable image. Her phone lay before her on the cheap coffee table – bristling with messages. A text from Lee:

Can we talk?

Then another.

I miss you, I'm sorry.

This is the man who lied to me for years. This is the man who I heard threatening an old lady while I cowered under a house next to dead things. This is a man I no longer trust. That's not the man I know. That's not… that's not a safe person.

A voicemail from Vic: 'Are you all right? Angela said she'd seen you at the hospital and you were acting strangely? And I called Lee and he says you had a row? What's going on? Call me? I'll be at baby signing and then going for drinks with the NCT girls but I'll have my phone… It's not *like* you to be… Angela says you were aggressive, and that's not *you*, Kirsty! And Lee is in bits… Just, call me, OK?'

It is me, though, Kirsty thought. *It's me now, now I know how much I've been lied to, how much I've been manipulated.* She texted back:

You can tell Lee to stop dragging you into things. He knows what he's done. This is my business not yours! And tell Angela that I know all about her too!

Never in her life had Kirsty sent a text like this. Rarely did she give in to righteous indignation let alone reach the vertiginous heights of rage. She felt the same strange joy of going rogue that she'd felt when she confronted Angela at the hospital. But this time it was tripled: this time she was facing down Angela, Lee and her sister. They all thought she could be used, lied to, threatened and they were all wrong. It had taken her a while, but finally she was seeing things for what they were.

Just then her phone rang. A number rather than a name. A man's voice, unfamiliar, local and harassed-sounding, standing on a crowded street.

'I'm with your mother?' he told her.

'What?'

'She had a bit of a fall, but she's all right, and...' His voice faded as he spoke to someone. 'You want to? Yes?' Then back to full volume. 'I'll just put her on now.'

'Hello there, darling.' Sylvia sounded tired, but strong. 'Can you come and pick me up? Twisted my ankle.'

'Sure... not... casualty?' the man was saying, and Sylvia told him, *No, nothing like that, just need my daughter.*

'Oh thank god! What happened to you?' Kirsty asked, through tears. 'I'll come now, where are you?'

'I'm just sitting by the war memorial. On Parliament Street? Just under the angel.'

'I'll be ten minutes.'

CHAPTER TWENTY-SIX

Sylvia was standing, wavering, next to the war memorial, a large canvas bag slung awkwardly over one shoulder. A distracted man was by her side, earnestly scanning the traffic. When Kirsty arrived, he helped Sylvia into the front seat of the car with a certain guilty eagerness – it was his lunch hour, and he was already late back to the office.

'She was lying down...' he said.

'I tripped,' Sylvia said. 'Loose brick.'

'And she says she's all right, but maybe she should go to casualty?' The man added this sotto voce, as if Sylvia couldn't hear him. 'Best not to take chances when you're getting on a bit, eh?'

'I'm a clumsy old bat, aren't I?' Sylvia twinkled. 'Thanks for staying with me!' The man raised one cheerful hand, and sped back to work.

Once they were driving, Sylvia was able to let her energies sag, ditch the self-deprecating smile and the I'm-a-silly-old-woman jokes she'd used on her rescuer. Kirsty could see just how exhausted and frightened she was. She'd never looked so old, so frail.

'I knew you'd come. I knew.'

'Of course I'd come. What happened? I went to the house—'

'Did you see the things I left? The phone? And—'

'And the tarot cards! Yes, yes!'

Sylvia's face relaxed a little. 'I knew you would. I thought when I was doing it, I thought that of all the people in the world who'd look and understand, it'd be you. And I was right, thank god!'

'He called me your daughter, that man?'

Sylvia eyed her affectionately. 'I knew he'd think it was funny, an old crock like me being friends with a young girl. Anyway, it feels like you are my daughter. It feels like you're the daughter....' She trailed off, winced in pain.

What happened, Sylvia? Shall I take you to the hospital? The police?'

Sylvia closed her eyes. They sank into bruised-looking sockets, her lips tightened, her clasped hands were still. She could have been carved from wax. The only thing that hinted at life were two tears that ran from the corners of both closed eyes.

'I'm calling the police now!' Kirsty told her.

Sylvia opened her eyes. 'No! No, don't do that, that would make everything worse. Even worse. When were you there?'

'At your house? This morning at about ten.'

'Did you see anyone there?'

'Someone was in a car. I had to hide from them.'

'Who was it in the car?'

'I don't know.'

Sylvia's astute eyes gleamed. 'I think you do.'

'Lee.'

She sighed, wiped away her tears.

'Take me to your house. Take me there and I'll tell you everything.'

Back in the flat, Sylvia sat on the sofa and wincingly allowed Kirsty to remove her shoe and gently manipulate her hurt ankle, which thankfully wasn't swollen or bruised.

'Did you really hurt it tripping over a brick?'

'I tripped over something. But not a brick, I don't think, and not in town.' Sylvia put a cushion behind her back, and sighed.

'Your husband. He's a dangerous man. He came yesterday. He tried to force his way into the house and when I tried to call you he smashed the phone out of my hand. I managed to make it to the front door, into the car yard, and into the woods. He hunted for me, but I know those woods like the back of my hand, so he never found me. When I was sure he'd gone, I left the cards with the phone in case you came round. I needed to warn you in a way only you'd understand.' Her brows contracted with sorrow. 'I'm sorry to have to tell you this. But thank god you're free of him!'

'This happened last night?' Kirsty asked.

'You know what he's like,' Sylvia told her softly. 'You said yourself that he tried to run you down.' Her blue eyes were wide with sorrow.

'I didn't say he tried to run me down.' Kirsty said. 'He drove at the house. At least I think it was him, but it might not have been—'

'Oh love,' Sylvia murmured sorrowfully 'Just listen to yourself. You know what you saw, you know what he's like. He did the same to me, didn't he? I turned my ankle running into the woods in the dark because he was after me! You don't have to lie to me about it.'

'I'm not—'

'Kirsty.' There was a tired authority in Sylvia's voice. 'We have to look at things as they are, not as how we want them to be. No matter how painful. You know that. And god knows I know that now, too.'

Time stuttered, stopped. Kirsty found herself sitting on the floor while her mind yammered, *Not Lee, not Lee, please not Lee! I thought I could take it but I can't, not Lee, please? If he could do that, he could do—*

'He's capable of anything.' Sylvia closed her eyes then. Her lips pressed into a line. She nodded to herself. 'You knew that already, I think.'

'I *don't*.' Kirsty's voice rose. She half stood. 'I *don't* though!"

'Sit down! Sit *down*, darling! I shouldn't have... I should have been more careful about what I said, that's all. Sit down please? And can you take my hand again? Give me a bit of courage. You're not the only one who's been… wilfully blind about things. I understand it, I've *lived* it; longer than you have, too.'

'What do you mean?'

Sylvia looked wearily at her own shaking hands. 'I should've talked to you about it earlier, but I swear I didn't know for sure until last night.'

'Didn't know what for sure?'

Sylvia's eyes flickered. She gave a little groan, then: 'Do you have any paracetamol? And maybe a drop of whisky for courage? I've been a coward for so long. But don't hate me!'

'I couldn't hate you!'

'You might after this. God knows I hate myself.' Sylvia took a deep, shuddering breath. 'I lied to you. I let you believe that I didn't know any more about Lisa than what was in the papers, but of course I do and I did then.' She let one tear run down her cheek. 'I remember I expected her to contact me somehow. I knew she was dead – I mean from the other side. I expected it like when you expect the phone to ring, you know it's going to ring, and then it does.' She stopped. 'The longer I waited the more I put it down to the fact that she'd passed so soon. Sometimes they're weak at the start. It's as if they're not dead, but dying still… They need someone to tell them what to do – especially kiddies, they're used to Mum telling them what to do, where to go, aren't they? But she didn't come through and I felt so bad about that because I wanted to help. I knew Denise, not well, but still I knew her, and Lisa was a local girl. I wanted to help so badly. I thought maybe I was wrong, and she wasn't dead, and that's why I couldn't hear her.'

Sylvia sighed. 'Then, when that man confessed, she *did* come through, and she was so *vivid*, she was determined to be heard. I thought she was trapped between worlds, confused like so many of them are, but it wasn't that. She wasn't confused, she was refusing to go, and that's what she's still doing. She wouldn't shift until I understood exactly what she was saying. But – god forgive me – I blocked her. I didn't want to know. I tried as hard as I could *not* to understand what she was telling me because it was just too *awful* to bear.' One tear fell on their clasped hands. Then another. 'Then I met you. She brought us together and now she's trying everything she can to… she can't wait any more, she's chivvying us along with dreams and coincidences and everything else, and I can't put her off any longer. No matter how painful things are, it's not fair to her or you. I have to face them.'

'What do you mean?'

Mrs McKnight paused. 'Have you ever met a bad child? Not naughty, or disturbed, but *bad*?'

'Evil?'

Sylvia winced. 'It exists, you know.'

'Lisa wasn't like that. She was *silly*, she told lies, but there wasn't any harm in her, she was just—'

A spasm of anxiety ripped over Sylvia's face. 'I'm not talking about Lisa.' Her whole self seemed to turn inward, as if she was having a quick, urgent conversation with herself. She gave a tiny nod, pulled up one sleeve to show a nasty-looking reddish bruise spanning her wrist. Then she guided Kirsty's hand to the back of her head, where a lump the size of a heaped tablespoon was hidden beneath her hair.

'Who did this to you?'

'The person who killed Lisa.'

Kirsty's eyes widened. 'Who?'

'Marie,' Sylvia said. 'She's not… she's not good. She never was. I can see that now.'

CHAPTER TWENTY-SEVEN

Sylvia's hand holding the whisky glass trembled. She took a sip, grimaced, took another sip. 'I told you some of the story. Star Child. How she became cruel; how she thought she could do anything, that she had the *right* to do anything she wanted because she was special. But even that would have been… I could have *coped* with that, I could have helped her change, I know it. But then she… All these years I've tried not to believe it, but I can't fool myself any more.' She looked up, openly weeping now. 'She did this awful thing!'

'But how?' Kirsty whispered. 'She was just a child—'

'I don't know for sure. Maybe she had help – there were some boys in the park that day. She talked about them a lot, you know, afterwards.'

'Was Lee one of them? Was he there?' Kirsty managed.

'I'm not sure.' Sylvia looked up, her eyes red. 'You hate me for saying that, don't you? But I'm *not* sure! I wish I was.'

'Where's the proof?'

'She was in the park that day. My late brother, Mervyn, he used to run a youth club; it was one of his schemes that started well but ran out of steam. He wanted it to be a boxing gym – imagine! He encouraged boys – boys who were bored, with nothing to do and might get themselves into trouble if they started hanging around with the wrong people – he encouraged them to get into sports. He was good that way. Anyway, on that day he arrived early, earlier than normal, and he took Marie with him. She was bored now, and she wasn't in school then – they didn't want her going any more because she was so disruptive. They couldn't expel her, but they made it very clear that they didn't want her any more, so what could I do? I took her out and started to homeschool her. That day I was at the library, looking for textbooks and things. I asked Mervyn to keep an eye on her, but he didn't. Not a close enough eye anyway. She was nagging him, having tantrums, and eventually he told her to play outside. There was a girl out there you see, an older girl, and he thought she could play with her.'

'And the older girl was Lisa?'

'And it was Lisa, yes. Then some boys turned up, and Mervyn noticed that they were chatting up the girl, Lisa, and he noticed that they were drinking and letting her drink too. So he put a stop to that, or he thought he had anyway. After a while he opened the club up properly, but no-one was there – the boys and Lisa had left, and Marie wasn't there either.'

'Where'd they go?'

Sylvia shook her head. 'We never found out. Mervyn started to panic then, he couldn't find Marie anywhere. With the canal being so close, you can imagine what he thought. It was an hour before he found her. She was by the canal, in the bushes by the bridge. He thought she was having a wee or something. Anyway, he told her off, shut up the club and brought her home.'

'That doesn't mean anything though,' Kirsty managed.

'No. And if it was just that I wouldn't have worried. But there were her clothes, her coat was stained down the front. Mervyn thought it was mud, and some of it was, but I knew it wasn't just that. I knew there was blood there too. And there was some in her hair too.' Sylvia's voice shook. She took a sip of whisky, paused, took another. 'And her nails were torn. It looked like she'd been in a fight. I asked her, I asked if anyone had hurt her, if the big boys had hurt her. You can imagine what I thought, can't you? But she just laughed and said no. I put her in the bath and her legs were all bruised – are you sure nobody hurt you? *No, no Mummy, nothing like that.*' She put her glass down again. 'She said, "It wasn't me, it was the big girl who got hurt."'

'Oh Jesus,' moaned Kirsty.

'So I said, "What big girl?" and she said, "You'll see her on the TV soon." Well, I kept asking her things and she kept answering them, but she wasn't answering them if you know what I mean? It was like she was teasing me. I'd go, "Who hurt the big girl?" and she'd say, "Who?" but with a smile, you know, and then turn around and say, "No-one did, I made it up." I kept asking her over and over and she'd just ignore me, or look all innocent or – and this was the worst – *laugh* at me.

'Then, a few days later, it was on the news. She loved that. That's when I got scared. I took her to the youth club. I had this idea that she'd tell me more if we were there, maybe she'd remember more, or feel like telling me more… I remember she started talking about a treasure hunt, she wanted to take me on a treasure hunt. So she led me to the canal, under the bridge, and then she points up to the bank and says, "There." "There what?" I said. "That's where the treasure is," she told me, proud as punch. "I put it there." So I went and looked and there was a coat. Well, I'd watched the news and I knew what the police were looking for. So I asked her, very gently, very carefully, "How did you know the big girl's coat was there? Was it a feeling you had, or did you dream it?"'

'And what did she say?'

'She laughed at me. I got angry then, I said, "Did you put it there?" and she laughed again and said, "I didn't say *I* put it there, I just said it was there. You found it. Maybe you put it there." Like it was a game.' Sylvia closed her eyes. 'I should have asked her then, did you do anything to that girl? Did you see anyone do anything to her? But I didn't.' She opened her eyes again. 'I didn't because I was *scared* to. That's the truth. I thought, I'm here, now, by the canal and it's dark and there's no-one here and... something might happen to *me*!'

She looked at Kirsty with naked, guilty appeal. 'I have to tell the truth, that's what I thought! I got away from there quickly. The next day I went to the police, said I'd just happened to see it.'

'You were the —'

'"Anonymous Passer-by"? Yes.'

'But why did the police believe you? I mean, that canal bank had already been searched.'

'You met them, didn't you?' There was an edge of amused contempt in Sylvia's voice now. 'They weren't the brightest colours in the paintbox, were they?' Her face became serious again 'Anyway, afterwards I went home and had a few drinks to steady my nerves but I ended up getting drunk for the first and last time of my life. I needed to forget what I knew, I wanted to wake up the next day and have it all blurry in my mind, like it was a dream. And it almost worked. After they had the coat and they caught that lodger, I thought it was all over with, and I convinced myself that Marie had nothing to do with any of it. That she'd just heard news reports and was letting her imagination run away with her. Or maybe she had known the coat was there but that was because of her gift.' She shuddered to herself and closed her eyes once more.

'Did Marie ever mention it again?'

'No. And for a month or so everything was OK, she let me start teaching her, she seemed to have decided to be nice again, gentle. I thought she was over it – whatever it was that made her so... cruel sometimes. I thought I had my little girl back.' She smiled sadly. 'It didn't last, of course, but I put any suspicion I had to the back of my mind. Even when that man took back his confession, and the witnesses, the girls? When they said they'd lied, even then I didn't let my mind go anywhere near thinking...'

'What changed?'

'After Mervyn died, just when Marie had come back, I was sorting through things, and I found a loose floorboard in her old room. I angled it up, and I found Marie's old jewellery box from when she was little. This was one of the things in it.' She brought something out of her bag. 'You'll probably recognise it.'

The notebook was covered with a thin patina of dried mould, and the pages gave off a smell, an ancient reek of decay and damp. The edges were mottled and waved, but the writing was still clear. The pictures were still clear.

Angels Times Two
WE like BOYS and FASHION and HAVING FUN!!!!

There was the logo – more hesitant and childish than it seemed at the time. Here was the list of practice interview questions that Lisa had culled from old copies of *Smash Hits*: 'We should learn them so we know what to say.'

Q: If you were an animal what animal would you be?
A: A cat cos they are beutiful and elegent and mysterius
OR!
A dog – playful and loyl and cuddly

Q: Whats your favourite make-up tip?
A: BLOT YOUR LIPSTICK
OR
By good quality make-up

Kirsty had had a problem with that one, she remembered, and so she'd aped something she'd once heard an Avon lady say. It never occurred to her that Lisa had probably done the same thing.

There were more questions, more silly doodles, and then (and this was what caused Kirsty, finally, to let the book fall, close her own eyes with a moan) a strip from a photo booth. Two weeks before Lisa had disappeared, they'd pooled their ten-pence pieces and gone to the passport photo booth at the Co-op. There they'd arranged themselves, giggling and awkward, one buttock each on the little twirly stool: *One Two Three CUTE. One Two Three CRAZY! One Two Three HAPPY! One Two Three SEXY!* And in that last black and white square they were so, so young, so ignorant, their 'sexy' faces more redolent of nausea, eyes narrowed, necks contorted. *Bless them*, she thought. Bless *us.* Lisa had written on the back:

Best Friends 4 EVA!!!!

'She must have taken it from Lisa's pocket. Before she dumped the coat,' Kirsty whispered.

'I found it just after your sister's party. I put it back where it was, but since then, since I started believing that she might really have hurt that poor little girl, I hid it somewhere else. There's… there's more things in it.'

'What things?'

'There's… oh this is awful! There's some hair. It looks as if it's been torn out from the scalp.'

'Jesus!'

'And some other things… a lipstick?'

'Lip balm? Orange lip balm?'

'Yes! Like… keepsakes. Treasures. God forgive me, I didn't have the heart to look through it all. I hid it somewhere else thinking I'd give it to you, to the police. But then, when Marie came over—'

'When did she come over?'

'Last night. After Lee left I managed to get back to the house and I called her from there. I – stupid of me I know – but I thought she'd help me, take me away somewhere safer. But it didn't happen that way.'

'What happened?'

'She came over right away, and she was angry. She was really angry. I hadn't seen her like that since she was small. Lee had gone back to your sister's house, he's been telling her that you're delusional, that you're obsessed with digging into what happened to Lisa again. Your sister must have told Marie, and that panicked her. She's… ill. She's like she used to be. She wanted the box and when I said I didn't know anything about a box, that maybe Mervyn had thrown it away, or moved it, that made her more upset. So… she did what she used to do.' Sylvia gestured at her injured arm, her bruised scalp.

'How did you get away?'

'I did what *I* always did, I played along. I said sorry and I pretended to look for it. We searched all over the place until she eventually began to trust me a bit, and then I told her to come back this evening. I said we'd start going through the workshop, the cars, everything. When she left, I waited for an hour and I left. I walked all night. I thought about going to see you at the hospital, but I worried that Peg might see me and she'd tell Marie. They're close, those two, and she must have told Peg so many bad things about me over the years; the whole family hate me now. I didn't want to put you in danger, so I… I just kept going. Then that nice man found me and called you.'

'We have to call the police.'

Sylvia nodded grimly. 'I know. And I nearly did last night, but then I realised that we need the box.'

'Why?'

Uncharacteristic irritation distorted Sylvia's face. 'Think about it, Kirsty! The box has hair in it, lip balm in it; they didn't have DNA analysis and all that back then, but they do now, don't they? If we have the box, we have more proof. You know as well as I do that they won't believe me, or you, not on our word alone! Since when would the police believe one old lady and a disturbed woman about something like this?'

Kirsty's semi-hypnotised gaze cleared just slightly. 'What d'you mean, "disturbed woman"?'

'I mean that Marie's awfully convincing. She'll have told your sister you're crazy, Lee will have too. She'll have used your argument with Lee as proof and she'll make sure we'll be written off as cranks and nothing will happen, you know this!'

'Vic wouldn't do that, though. She wouldn't believe someone saying that about me.'

'Wouldn't she?' Sylvia looked at her with pitying shrewdness. 'I met her, remember? I saw how much she was under Marie's thumb then, and imagine how it must be now, months later? No, believe me, Marie thinks you're out to get her, so she'll be doubly out to get you. You need to go and get the box.'

'What? No! That's dangerous! What if she's there?'

'She's *not* there. I made *sure* she's not there.'

'Where is she—'

'Listen to me, Kirsty.' There was a hard urgency in Sylvia's voice now, a grim rebuke. 'This isn't a request, it's what has to happen, OK? She did something to Lisa, and that won't be the only bad thing she's done, will it? Some poor man is rotting in prison because of what she did, and what you told them. I've done my bit, now it's time for you to do yours! This has to happen. *Lisa* wants this to happen. You know that.'

'Yes,' Kirsty murmured.

'You've *always* known that, haven't you? Deep down?'

'Yes,' Kirsty whispered again.

Sylvia's voice softened. 'You're a good girl.'

'Am I?'

'Yes. And here's your chance to put everything right. Now, listen closely and I'll tell you where to find it.'

CHAPTER TWENTY-EIGHT

The house, under its awning of grey clouds, looked very different from the rear. Sylvia had specifically told her to hide her car in the overgrown scrubland at the back so it wouldn't be seen by anyone approaching from Beacon Hill. The front of the place was, as ever, a bit scruffy, littered, but elevated by that oblong of welcoming light from the kitchen; the back of the house was a disaster zone. A row of small, mean windows showed that the rooms were filled with garbage – it pressed against the panes, even bursting through at odd intervals. Some of the broken windows were covered with cardboard taped down with electrical tape; some remained broken. Kirsty had seen hoarder houses before, and Sylvia had said on that first day that she had trouble keeping on top of things, but this was… different. These rooms spoke of a deliberately wanton, almost aggressive chaos, and Kirsty realised she was afraid of going inside, not because of Angela, not because of the box and what its contents would reveal, but because the house itself felt… *insane*. That was the word for it. Insane.

She told herself to stop being so stupid, to stop letting her imagination run away from her. She told herself that this had been Mervyn's house, that he had been the hoarder, and she willed herself to feel familiar pity for Sylvia, having to endure living in such a place. It worked enough for her to get through the back door and into a thin, fetid-smelling channel that led, according to Sylvia, to the 'back stairs'. Even though the room was small, only two or three metres in length, it took her twenty minutes to navigate the newspapers piled up in ancient rows, and topped with books, the broken chairs, the bags of clothes and stained duvets and mouldy plastic flowers, all covered in cobwebs. Each column teetered as she squeezed past, releasing little puffs of noxious dust that made her splutter. The floor itself was a trodden-down path of cardboard and discarded food, all condensed into slippery rot. Things were moving, too, sinuous things that weaved in and out the tiny free spaces. Rats? Probably.

The stairs, when she finally got to them, were also unsettling. They didn't belong in this house. They wouldn't belong in any house, as far as Kirsty could see. They were curved into a steep spiral, stately, like the grand staircase from a country home, or a movie set – Dracula's house maybe – and made of some dark, gloomy wood that still shone, despite the pockmarks and the moss. Kirsty saw that it wasn't fixed to the floor and was only attached to the wall with a few cheap-looking brackets. She placed one tentative foot on the first step, and the whole staircase wobbled alarmingly. Surely Sylvia didn't mean her to use this staircase? She peered up into the gloom; maybe the top half was more secure? She hoped so. Each cautious step she took caused the stairs to tremble, the brackets squeaked and sighed but after a nerve-racking five minutes, she finally made it to the top, and stood on the L-shaped landing. 'You'll find the key in the bathroom,' Sylvia had told her, 'in the cistern, wrapped in cling film.'

The bathroom was large and cold. The bottom of the bath was stained brown, like the toilet, like the linoleum. Kirsty shivered, opened the cistern, dislodging the calcified remains of long-dead spiders and, wincingly, peered into the water. There the key was, nestling at the bottom of the murky water.

'Turn left at the end of the corridor,' Sylvia had told her. 'The door's marked "Lily". The lock might be stiff, so take this.' She had given her a long knife with a bent tip. 'I use this to jimmy the lock, it's the only thing that works. When you're inside the room, look behind the wardrobe. There's a hole in the wall and the box is in there.'

'Nearly there. Nearly there now,' Kirsty whispered to herself as she dug into the wet cling film with cold fingers, and slid the key into the door, turned it forcefully, prepared to use the knife if the lock stuck.

But the lock didn't stick. The door wasn't locked at all.

The force she used swung her inwards and she stumbled, fell, landed painfully on her knees, and hit her head on something hard and metal. Dazedly she saw that she was at the foot of an old-fashioned camp bed in a child's room, that the knife with the bent tip was still in her hand and she could feel that someone was behind her. She turned clumsily and instinctively lashed out with the knife, heard a sharp gasp, jabbed the knife again, and again she heard a gasp, and saw something drop and tip. The lid opened and a ballerina twirled to 'A Dream Is a Wish Your Heart Makes'.

Kirsty had time to see one thin, brown hand, a flash of dark blonde hair, before some unknown instinct told her to grab the box, get back on her feet and charge back to the still open door. She got as far as the staircase before she was tackled from behind and taken down and she watched, helplessly, as the knife skittered behind her and the music box slithered out of her hand, down the stairs, landing with a dull slap on the filthy floor below.

Both women scrambled up, but Kirsty was quicker. She launched herself onto the top step of the rickety stairs, pulled herself upright by the bannister, and felt the whole thing lurch to the right. Both brackets were pulling themselves out of the cheap plasterboard wall, and the whole thing was twisting, groaning, about to fall. Kirsty tried hard to outrun the collapse, but suddenly it gave way with one violent crack. The whole thing now hung from one remaining bracket, and Kirsty was trapped, her feet dangling into the blackness of the lower floor, her forearm clamped in something, she couldn't see what for the dust. Her body twirled, swung, her head slammed painfully into plasterboard, and she tried desperately to twist her arm out of its clamp – better to fall than to be left with Marie! Better to break her leg than never get out alive. She struggled; she struggled harder to free herself, twisting painfully, peering through the blood running into one eye, to see what was trapping her and how she could get loose.

Angela Bright was lying on the landing, two feet above her, with both strong, thin hands clamped around Kirsty's wrist. The tendons stood out on her neck.

'Don't let yourself drop! Please!' she said. 'Hang onto me!'

'No!' Kirsty struggled, kicked.

'Please!' Angela pleaded. 'You'll get hurt! Please! Let me help you!' And just then the remaining bracket gave way. The whole staircase collapsed with a groan, like a dying dinosaur, and with almost superhuman strength, Angela Bright pulled Kirsty, no longer kicking, upwards. Back onto the landing, where they lay together, choking on the cloud of fetid dust rising from the lower floor.

CHAPTER TWENTY-NINE

'Yes. Why, why did you help me?' Kirsty asked dazedly.

'You were falling,' Angela answered. 'I had to.'

Angela rolled away then, grabbed Kirsty's knife on what remained of the ragged landing, one hand behind her back. 'I've got this, now. Just in case you try to hurt me.'

'I didn't bring it to hurt you!'

'Oh, c'mon.' The local accent was back. 'I know why you're here. You were going to hurt Mum, or me.'

'What? No! I love Sylvia!'

'If you love her so much, why've you been sending her those notes? Why've you've been frightening her, showing up at the house? Why did you sneak in through the back with a bloody knife?' Angela sounded so much like Mona now, it was incredible. 'She's told me all about it. No matter what her faults are, Kirsty, she's an old woman now. It's me you want, so deal with me, not with her.'

'Wait, what? What are you talking about?' Kirsty asked breathlessly. She shuffled herself into a more upright position. Angela's hand was shaking, and her eyes were fearful. This wasn't the Angela she'd met or the Marie she'd been told to expect. 'I haven't sent any—'

'No – no, don't come closer.' Angela's voice was loud, panicked.

'It's *you* who's been threatening *me*! Threatening *us*, I should say – me and Sylvia!' Kirsty's voice rose now too. 'She's scared of *you*, not me! She's told me all about it, and she knows I'm here. She *sent* me here! And if anything happens to me, if she doesn't hear from me soon, she'll call the police.'

Angela froze. 'What are you saying to me?'

'If I don't get back to her she'll call the police and—'

'She *sent* you here?'

'Yes, why—'

'And *why* did she send you here? To find something?' The knife dropped a little bit. 'Something in a hole behind the wardrobe, was it?'

'I won't tell you.'

'To find a box.' Angela was speaking to softly now, almost to herself. 'And what did she tell you was in the box?' Kirsty stayed stubbornly silent. Angela took her phone from her pocket then, and Kirsty watched her take a few deep breaths and put the thing on loudspeaker. Sylvia answered immediately. She'd been waiting for the call.

'Where've *you* been then?' Sylvia's voice was peevish, petulant, not at all the voice that Kirsty had become so familiar with. The accent was thicker, coarser, it was the voice of a disagreeable old woman, a Peg without a heart. 'How long does it take you to do one simple thing? I—'

'Tell me where it is again? Lily's room?' Angela was speaking with her eyes on Kirsty. Tears were forming but her voice was remarkable steady.

'*Yes*, Lily's room. It's in that box, the one you used to have, that ballerina thing, in the hole behind the wardrobe. Are you up there now?'

'Nearly.'

'Well, be careful. Don't use that back staircase, it's a death trap. Use the front one, OK?'

'Why would I use the back one?' Angela was still looking directly at Kirsty. 'Like you say, it's a death trap.'

'*I* don't know. Knowing you, you'd forget that and do it anyway. You're good at forgetting things, aren't you?' A nasty, clotted chuckle came from the phone. 'You can forget anything if you put your mind to it.'

'Well, you always put me right, don't you, Mum?' Angela blinked slowly. One tear rolled down her cheek.

'I do. Got to, haven't I? Now, if you see that Kirsty woman—'

'Why would I see her?'

'Just let me finish, will you? I don't think you *will*, but just in case you *do*, well, remember that this is *your* house. And she's a trespasser? You have every right to… you know. You've got that knife, haven't you?'

'Yes. I have the knife.'

'Good girl.' Sylvia sounded mollified now, honeyed. 'Anyway, nearly over now. Nearly over, darling, isn't it?'

'Yes,' Angela managed, the tears streaming now.

'And that'll be the end of the whole thing, won't it?'

'Yes.'

'Bye then. Call me later.'

'Bye, Mum.'

CHAPTER THIRTY

Angela was exhausted. She propped herself up on arms so thin they looked snappable. It was difficult to believe that only moments before she'd hauled Kirsty to safety.

'Did you hurt your head?' she asked dully, without looking. 'Here.' Angela ripped off a piece of her own expensive shirt and passed it over. 'Press down hard. It might need stitching. You should get yourself to hospital if you don't want a scar.' She sounded not unlike Denise, or Peg for that matter – the same seen-it-all-before brusqueness. Familiar, almost comforting. Before she knew it, Kirsty was saying thank you.

Angela threw the knife over the side of the landing. It hit something with a tinny clang. Then, suddenly, she was sobbing loud as a child, her hands lying uselessly in her lap.

'You heard what she said, didn't you?' she managed after a while. 'You're a trespasser. She wants you dead for trespassing. I'm not going to do anything. She gave me a knife too, but I dropped it when you rushed into the room.' Angela's voice was hoarse. 'I wasn't going to use it. I don't have it in me to do anything like that.'

Kirsty said nothing. Huge portions of her brain felt frozen. Her phone rang and she didn't even hear it.

Angela was looking at her with wet eyes filled weary empathy. 'Answer it. It'll be her. Answer it, she'll get mad if you don't. Put it on speaker, let's see what she'll say to *you*, shall we?' She gave a sad little smile as the tears started, silently, once more.

Kirsty pressed the speaker button. 'Hi.'

'Oh, darling, I've been so worried!' This Sylvia's voice throbbed with love, anxiety, and relief. 'Are you at the house now? Did you find the box?'

'I…'

Angela shook her head in an emphatic '*no*'.

'I haven't found it yet,' Kirsty said.

'Why not?' Sudden impatience, wheezy petulance. 'Why *not*? You have to soon, darling, because I just spoke to Marie and she's… she's very angry, she scared me. She says she's going down there in the next hour, so please, get it, all right? I'd hate you to be there when she is, you don't know how violent she can be! Do you remember where it is you have to look?'

'In the room marked "Lily".' Kirsty watched Marie mouth along with the words. 'In the hole behind the wardrobe.'

'That's right. And remember to go up the back stairs.'

'Yes. OK.' Now Kirsty felt like crying.

'Darling?' Sylvia's voice was cracked with concern. 'I know it's hard, but it's nearly over now. Isn't it?'

'Yes.'

'And, I hate to say this, but if you have to defend yourself, in any way – she's dangerous, after all. And you have that knife, don't you?'

'Yes.'

'Good. Good. Kirsty?'

'Yes?'

'Do you remember what I told the man? The man who helped me in town?'

Kirsty closed her eyes. 'You told him I was your daughter.'

'And it's true. I couldn't ask for a better daughter, a better *companion*… oh, I'm being silly, crying like an old woman! But you know I mean it, don't you? Don't you?'

'Yes,' Kirsty whispered.

'All right then, call me as soon as you can and stay safe, darling.'

'I will.'

Kirsty put the phone down then, and she too started to cry. She felt Angela's small, warm hand on hers. From somewhere below them, a rat squeaked, a trash tower tumbled. It was Angela who spoke first.

'It's funny that I never questioned why she was giving me a knife to find a box behind a wardrobe. She said it was to make the hole bigger if I needed to, but why not a hammer? Why would I have to make the hole bigger anyway? But I just didn't think to question her. Why did you need a knife?'

'In case the lock didn't work. She said it jammed sometimes.' Kirsty spoke in a bloodless monotone.

'Why a knife? Why not a screwdriver?'

'I don't know. I didn't think.'

'That's what she does,' Angela said softly. 'She brings you along with her, doesn't she? And you never think to ask questions along the way, and before you know it...' She gave a shuddering sigh. 'You're doing exactly what she wanted you to do. I can't blame you – you came into this cold. Me, I should have known better.' She gestured to the knife that Kirsty still held. 'She must have told you all sorts of things about me; I don't blame you for being scared. She's told me terrible things about you. I was scared too.'

'What about me?'

'Lies.' Angela gestured at the two phones. 'You heard it. Let me ask you this, how did she get you here today?'

'She said I had to come here and find a box before you did.'

'She told me the same thing. What was in the box?'

'A box of... evidence.'

'She told me the same thing.' Angela smiled crookedly. 'D'you want to know what was in that box? I opened it just as you came into the room. Nothing. Nothing at all. It was just a way of getting us both here, getting us in the same place. Are you all right? You look awful.'

'I feel awful.'

'I bet.' She got up with a groan, then said, 'I'm going downstairs. I'm going to sit in the kitchen – it's the only cleanish place in this dump – and I'm going to have a drink. God, I'm tired.' She turned. 'Aren't you tired? Yes? Come on then, come with me. Ask me anything you want. Let's get this shit-show over with.'

CHAPTER THIRTY-ONE

And so Angela led the way through a series of cluttered rooms, to the front staircase, built firmly of ugly concrete out of the floor itself, leading straight into a long, low room like a bunker, another fetid space with slimy floors. This led to another room – or possibly a hallway, it was difficult to know, packed with mouldering bin bags filled with clothes, then another, then another, until finally they found themselves in the small room adjoining the kitchen, where the detritus from the rest of the house stopped dead at the door, like an attested lava flow.

'She always kept these two rooms clean,' Angela explained. 'These were the rooms people saw, you see. I bet you never saw the state of the rest of the place, did you?'

'No,' Kirsty admitted, grimacing as Angela, grunting, managed to heave the door shut behind them.

'I didn't think so. It would ruin the effect a bit, wouldn't it? The cottage in the woods with the smiling old lady is a nice image, and it doesn't go well with rat droppings and rot, does it? Oh stop it,' she noticed Kirsty's pursed mouth, 'I'm only telling the truth, aren't I?'

'She's let it go a little, but then she's old, and it's a big place and—'

Angela shook her head. 'She really got in amongst you, didn't she? Even after what you just heard her say, you still… It's always been like this. Trust me. I grew up here, after all.' She looked about her with weary loathing. 'I hate this place. I hate everything about it.'

'Why did you come back then?' Kirsty asked.

'Uncle Mervyn left the house to me and I'm the executor. I had to come back.' She walked into the kitchen, rummaged around under the sink and located a half-full whisky bottle. 'I think you need one of these. Sit down.' She inspected two mugs, grimaced, ran them under the tap, splashed in the alcohol and sat down opposite Kirsty. She had a long, shallow cut on her forearm.

'Did I do that?' Kirsty asked.

'Yes,' Angela told her. 'But it wasn't your fault. Drink. You look like death. And it seems we have a lot to talk about, so you'll need all your strength.' She folded her hands, looked squarely at Kirsty. 'What's she been telling you?'

'No. You tell me first.'

'You're sure? It's quite a tale.' Angela poured herself another drink. Kirsty watched, thinking that there was something overtired and slightly hysterical about her movements, her speech. As if she'd read her mind, Angela said, 'Don't worry, I'm not mad, or unbalanced or… I'm fucking tired is what I am, and ashamed and… yes, I am a bit hysterical, maybe. That's the word you were thinking, isn't it? But then, look at it from my point of view, it's a pretty hysterical situation. It'd be funny, if, you know… it *was* funny.' She passed a hand over her forehead. 'She told me that you've been blackmailing her for the last few months—'

'I've *what*—'

Angela put one palm up. 'Wait. That's just the beginning. She called me at about nine this morning saying that you came over last night demanding more money. You smashed her phone so she couldn't call me for help, you twisted her arm and bashed her round the head with a fire shovel.' She stopped, smiled quizzically. 'It's the little touches like that that give it the edge, isn't it? You hit her with a *fire shovel*. Anyway, she managed to talk you down by agreeing to give you five thousand pounds. She promised to deliver it to you at work today. As soon as you left she managed to get to a phone box in Beacon Hill and told me to come and get her. I took her back to my hotel in town and that's when she told me to get over here this morning and find the box while she was with you at the hospital.' She paused. 'Do you want to know what she said was in the box?'

'What?'

'Oh, it's gothic. A hank of hair belonging to a dead girl. A girl I killed. Is that what she told you too?'

'Yes.'

'Well, there's some consistencies in all this then. I had to find it before you did, so I'd be safe, and *you* had to find it so you'd have some evidence against me, is that about the size of it?'

'What would I be blackmailing her *about?* It doesn't make any sense...'

Angela spoke softly. 'She told me you knew I'd killed Lisa Cook.' The words stayed in their air, like lead with wings.

'Did you?' Kirsty asked slowly.

'Jesus, Kirsty! *No!* How could I have killed anyone? I was five, for god's sake! Could you have killed someone twice your age and size when *you* were five?' Angela almost poured herself another drink, changed her mind. Her tone changed too, from brittle facetiousness to something altogether more solemn. Her eyes were so large, so tired. 'But I can't blame you for believing it. I've believed it on and off myself for years, insane though it sounds. It's... complicated. The whole thing is... Gaslighting, they call it. It's when someone tells you things you know aren't true, but somehow they make you believe it through repetition, or they confuse you into believing it, or they bully you until you believe it. It gets so you don't know your own mind, your own memories, even. Cults work like that. Religions work like that. Families sometimes work like that. Though "work" isn't a very accurate way of describing it. A better word would be "survive". And Mum's all about surviving.'

'What are you talking about?'

'She's like a virus, she's all about surviving and thriving. She uses everyone around her to make sure she survives and thrives – that's all they're there for, in her mind. When I was little, she told me I was special.'

'All mothers say that.'

'Maybe, but not for the same reasons. I wasn't special because of *me,* I was special because of *her*. According to her, I was the last in the line, that four sisters had died before me, and I was the only one left to take care of her – she had to be taken care of, you see, and that's the only reason I was born. Plus I had four disappointments to make up for so I'd better do a good job. But I didn't do a good job. I was just another big disappointment. I was never good enough. I wasn't helpful enough round the house, or I was too tidy – "little-miss-nitpicker". I was so loud I hurt her head, or I was so quiet it gave her the creeps. I was gifted, but not as gifted as her and I shouldn't show off about it. *Lily* wouldn't have shown off about it. Or Jade, or any of the other dead sisters that were still, somehow, better than one live Me.' She smiled to herself. 'It took me ages to understand that she never wanted me to be anything but a disappointment – if I was good all round, what would she have to complain about? I tried so hard, Kirsty, for years, to make her proud of me because I thought that's what she wanted. When I started tarot, and I was good, she was pleased at first, and then she wasn't. I thought it was because I wasn't good enough and so I worked harder, but the better I got, the more she saw me as a threat.' She paused, put one finger in the air. 'For a long time afterwards I thought that my talent was a fault too – if I hadn't been demonstrably better at her when it came to tarot, she might not hate me as much as she did. Mum is a decent card reader – she's lazy, she cheats and she doesn't believe in it – but she's good when she tries. She taught me but I was better from the start and just got better still. The harder I worked, the more she took it as an insult. I'm genuine, she's a hack, and that was somehow my fault.'

'She read my cards, and they were spot on!' Kirsty put in stoutly.

'Let me guess. Empress for her, something of swords for Lee – the Nine maybe, or the King? Yes? Three of Cups to tell you that it was you, her and Lisa against the world?'

'How did you know?'

'Because it's an obvious spread to use make you go away thinking what she wanted you to think. An absolute amateur would have done the same thing. Tell me, did she even let you draw the cards? Shuffle them?'

'No.'

'Didn't think so. She just had them all arranged at the top of the deck. I've seen her do that before. Like I said, she's a hack.' Angela did pour herself another drink then. 'Can you imagine what that was like, Kirsty? Being trapped with her, in the middle of nowhere, never knowing what was real and what wasn't? Not knowing what you'd done to offend her this time and when the punishment would end?'

'Was this when you were in Ireland?'

'What?' Angela almost smiled. 'We were never in Ireland.'

'You lived in Galway! Before you moved here, she—'

Angela shook her head. 'We never lived in Ireland. I don't think she's ever been to Ireland, she's Beacon Hill born and bred, like me. Maybe she got that from my bio? My agent added that Emerald Isle stuff because it goes down well in America, that's all. She always told me her family was Scottish, but that's not true either – her real name is Sandra Pryce, not Sylvia McKnight.'

'Your dad must have been called McKnight?'

'Well, if you find out who he is or was, ask him,' Angela said. 'I don't know a thing about him, apart from rumours. I learned not to ask her about him either.' She took a drink. 'No, we lived here with Mervyn – well, when he wasn't in prison, that is. Just me, Mum, and the dead girls. There was no-one else to counterbalance things, you know? No-one to bring in a bit of fresh air and sanity, and so it was her little fiefdom; she could do what she liked. And what she liked was keeping me unsettled and pliable. She'd praise me for something and then when I did the exact same thing later, she'd tell me how terrible I was. Sometimes she'd tell me I'd said things I hadn't, had lied about things I knew nothing about and then, sometimes on the same day, she'd tell me how I was always truthful about those same things. It's… can you imagine how insane that is to live with? Especially when you're a child and she's the only person you ever see?' She shook her head. 'The longer you're with someone like that, the more you believe them… even if what they're telling you doesn't make sense, and you know it's not true and they've lied before, done awful things before… they still, somehow, convince you that you're wrong and they're right. You can start off *sure,* absolutely *positive* that what they're saying is a lie, but that truth gets chiselled away and chiselled away until… you don't know any more. That's what she did when Lisa was here.'

'*Here?* In this *house*?' Kirsty blurted.

Angela nodded. 'Mum sometimes told me she wasn't. She'd say it was a dream I had, or a lie I was telling, but I always knew she was here. I knew it then and I know it now.' She got up slowly. 'I want to show you something. It might not still be there, but if it is…' She walked towards the door, slow and heavy as a somnambulist. Then she was on her hands and knees, tearing up the linoleum by the door, levering up layers of it like flayed skin, until she reached the final layer – a pale patterned pink, stuck to the concrete floor – and what was there was obvious, even to Kirsty.

A long, dragged rusty scar, one small, smudged handprint, and drops of splashed red, faint but horribly vivid. With a grunt of effort Angela pulled the lino back even further to reveal more – an oval of deeper red, almost black at the centre, a human shadow, etched in blood.

'She didn't even get rid of it,' Angela managed.

'Oh Jesus…'

'Just covered it over. Layers and layers of covering up. That's a neat metaphor, isn't it? Can't change anything, she has to keep it all. Mum told me she'd never been at the house, that I was making things up or forgetting things… Sometimes she told me I'd hurt her, killed her, and sometimes, even though I knew it couldn't be true, I thought it was. That's why I ran away from her and never came back, do you understand? But I was five!' She looked at Kirsty, her face stained. 'I was only five, how could I have done anything to a big girl?' She patted the floor awkwardly, crying now. 'And I liked her! She was nice to me. She was so nice she even gave me this ring and she told me I could keep it.' From around her neck, she pulled out a thin silver chain, and there it was.

'The snake ring…' Kirsty whispered.

'Yes! With real ruby eyes!' Angela eyes were wet in red-rimmed sockets now. 'I didn't hurt her, I know I didn't, I *know* it!'

'Why was she here?' Kirsty crouched down now, too, placed her own adult palm next to Lisa's little handprint. 'What happened to her?'

CHAPTER THIRTY-TWO

Marie thinks big girls are fascinating. They're like home-grown angels. This girl smells of smoke and orange chapstick. Her cheeks are pink and her laugh is loud. She's standing in a ring of sitting boys, and she turns, revolves slowly, wobbling like the ballerina in Marie's musical jewellery box. From far away she's shining, but closer you can see that she's a bit grubby. There's a twig in her hair and mud on her socks. The boys laugh, and it isn't a nice laugh. Marie can tell it isn't, but the girl doesn't seem to notice. That's disturbing; big girls should know more than little ones – it's the natural order of things. The girl arouses a sense of awe tinged with protectiveness. Marie edges closer.

The girl laughs. Shrill. One of the boys mutters, 'Someone needs to shut that bint up, I tell you.'

What's a bint? Is it like the c-word? Is it as bad as that? Marie wants to ask, but at the same time doesn't want the answer. She doesn't want the big girl to be the c-word. Marie remembers her from the few months she went to school because she was the best skipper, and she won nearly all the races in Sports Day apart from Egg and Spoon. She has pretty hair, shiny. Marie bets it would be soft to touch, all lovely like fur.

Some of the Bad Lot Boys who hang around the youth club don't like her. What's she doing here? They chase her, and say mean things but it doesn't work. The girl stays. The boys are drinking lager from big gold cans, and the more they drink the less they chase her away. They laugh when the girl asks for a sip, laugh when she coughs and chokes, laugh while they pound her on the back and offer her more. She twirls and dances and asks for another sip and Marie notices, with relief, that they aren't mean-laughing any more, and that means they like her. Marie feels very strongly that the big girl must be liked because she's tried so hard and deserves to be rewarded.

Marie is in the park today because Uncle Mervyn is away. He won't be back for a while. How long? *Just a while, I said!* Mum answers. Will he be back for *EastEnders*? *If it's still on in eight months, maybe.* She's angry with Uncle Mervyn and says it's not fair that she has to pick up the pieces just 'cause Mervyn can't keep his mouth shut and Marie doesn't know what this means, but it's best not to ask. All she knows is that, since Mervyn's been away, Mum has had to spend a lot of time dragging things out of the youth club and taking them back home. She needs to sell them, she says. Marie can come too so long as she doesn't-make-a-nuisance-of-herself, and stays-out-of-the-way. She makes sure she follows these stern instructions because she likes being in the park because she gets to see people, listen to them, and that's good, better than being in the house alone because the house is scary when you're alone.

The big girl sips sips sips out of the golden cans like a little hummingbird, and the boys are getting rowdier. They ask her to strip. It's a joke, Marie can tell, because they laugh, but the girl doesn't laugh, instead she starts taking her skirt off. Marie knows this is a Bad Thing to Do, and she almost runs forward to say so, but then one of the Bad Lot Boys says, 'She's Bryan's sister, though. Fucking be careful, 'cause she's Bryan's sister.' And they tell her to put her skirt back on. The Bad Lot Boys seem scared of this boy Bryan, and this pleases Marie because it means that the big girl has Someone to Protect Her. Over the last hour it's become clear to Marie that the big girl shouldn't be here, and that she isn't actually that big. With every sip from the gold cans, she looks younger and younger. But that's all right, because when Bryan gets there, he'll take her home and tell her off in a fierce protective way before giving her a rough hug and vowing to Find Those Boys and Make Them Pay. Marie knows that's what big brothers do because she's seen it on telly.

But Bryan turns out to be a very disappointing big brother. He's not even that big. Marie notes with disdain his narrow shoulders, his little caved-in chest; she winces when he says bad words. Really bad words – even the Bad Lot Boys seem a bit shocked. He's angry with the big girl, but not because he's protective but because he wants her to go away. She's embarrassing, he says, but Marie hears something else underneath his words too – he's showing off in front of the others, and she gets a sudden, unwelcome, flash of adult comprehension; she sees that Bryan is a fool and always will be, that the big girl isn't afraid of him even though she pretends to be, that she pretends to be because she thinks they like it… What did *that* mean?… Marie can almost hear her thoughts, smell them, taste them, and when she closes her eyes, the vast swarm of drunken, scribbly little-girl ideas invades her.

The big girl is little… little like Marie but Marie knows that she will get larger, that her thoughts will expand, while the big girl will stay just like this forever and ever. Marie gropes along the edges of the feeling, looking for a trap door, a future for the girl. Her head feels hot and full and… she doesn't have the words to explain it, even to herself. Mum hates her being like this – she says she looks gormless and floppy, like someone turned her off at the mains, but it doesn't feel like that at all. It feels like the opposite – that every fibre, nerve and synapse inside her has been plugged into the mains and this energy, all the energy in the world it seems, has to somehow be contained in her small, fragile form.

This has been happening more and more recently, and when it does she sleeps for a long time afterwards, still as a carved thing on a tomb, and when she wakes she – mercifully – remembers very little.

Marie is called into the club then, and Mum gives her a bag of crisps and lets her watch the little black and white portable telly in the back room while she goes back home for the truck.

'And don't give me that look either!' she tells Marie. 'I can drive perfectly well without a licence, and how else am I meant to get these things back home?'

Should she answer? Is it the kind of question that needs an answer? Marie is still half in the fog of the big girl's mind, so she might have missed the cues… but Mum leaves without scolding her.

'You can have another bag of crisps if you want and there's a can of pop in the fridge. I won't be long.'

But she's gone for a long time, long enough to watch *The Muppet Show* all the way through and have three bags of crisps, long enough to get scared and cold. When she hears the little scrabbling knock on the door, she feels relief. But it isn't Mum. It's the big girl.

CHAPTER THIRTY-THREE

'She felt sick,' Angela said. They were sitting in the little dining room now, the same room where Sylvia had read Kirsty's cards that first time. 'And she *was* sick. All that Special Brew. I held her hair away from her face.'

'Was she hurt? Scared? Was Bryan still there?'

'She wasn't hurt or scared. After she'd been sick I gave her some lemonade and a bag of crisps.' Angela smiled to herself. Her face was losing years, by the minute. Kirsty had the strange sensation that she was simultaneously both here and then in some trance-like no-man's land of present memory. She closed her eyes. 'She asked me something that I didn't know how to answer. I'd never thought of it before.'

'What did she ask?'

'She asked me if I had a best friend.'

*

Marie almost says No. Then she remembers her sisters. 'Four of them,' she says. 'Ruby, Jade, Sophie and Lily. But they're all angels now.'

The big girl nods sagely. 'I believe in angels, don't you?'

'Of course I do.'

'Like that song? That old Abba song?'

'I don't know that song.'

'*Everyone* knows that song! Come here, I'll sing it for you!' And the big girl puts her arms around Marie, pats her head, and they rock gently from side to side and the big girl hums and sings half-remembered lyrics in a cracked falsetto and Marie is... *Marie is so...*

*

'Happy,' Angela breathes. 'I wasn't scared any more. And what was in her head didn't scare me any more. She was like my sister, or an angel. She was someone who wasn't meant to be here for long. She was like a gift.'

*

'Here's what we're going to be called. Lisa – that's me – and Kirsty – that's my best friend. Angels Times Two. Angels Times Two, get it? 'Cause there's two of us? And here's our song words…' Lisa's fingers are moving quickly over the book, flipping pages, scurrying down lines. 'And, look! Here's our logo – see? Two angels—'

'You're kissing.'

'When angels kiss it's not like proper kissing though,' Lisa explains. 'It's more… Have you ever kissed a boy?'

Marie almost laughs. 'No!'

Lisa opens her mouth, closes it, then cocks her head to the side, as if listening to some internal voice.

'Me neither,' she says. Then she gives a little flustered laugh, and Marie feels her emotions – embarrassment, fear, shame. 'Do you think lying is wrong?'

'Yes.' This is one of the very few things in life Marie is absolutely sure of. 'Telling lies is bad.'

'I told my best friend a lie,' Lisa confides after a pause. 'I told her I kissed a boy and did other things with him. A man really. And I said I was married.'

Marie can't help laughing. It was so silly! It was such a delightfully silly thing for a big girl to do! 'What did you do that for?'

Lisa looks taken aback, then she starts laughing too. 'I don't know! I thought it was fun, and then I just carried on!'

'You can't be married!' Marie tells her sensibly. 'You're a kid!'

'I *know*!' Lisa, still laughing, frowns. 'I don't know why I said it! I told her I was a princess and this was my engagement ring, look.' She thrusts her index finger out. 'I said it was from Oman but really I got it on the market.'

'Where's Oman?'

'I don't *know*! I just said it and then I carried *on* saying it.' She isn't laughing any more. 'And now my friend's mad with me 'cause she knows I lied.'

Marie's mind gropes for something helpful, finds it in Lisa's own mind. 'But you're Best Friends Forever. I *know* you are.'

Lisa looks at her sharply and Marie knows that she's scared her… *I've scared her because I knew what to say and now she'll hate me and…*

'You're right. We *are* Best Friends Forever,' Lisa says. 'We are, aren't we? And I mean, she already knows I've lied, doesn't she? What if I just went to see her now and explained it and promised not to do it again? That'd make it all right again, wouldn't it?'

And it should be simple to answer; one pert little nod and that would be it, but Marie can't because Lisa's words aren't like normal words that unspool in the crowded present and run towards the empty future in a straight line. With words like that, all you had to do was follow the thread to see the results, but… but… it wasn't like that this time. There was nothing to follow, nothing to pull on. The words were going nowhere. What did that mean? Where was her future? Marie shivers then, as if the cold dark from outside was inside and the dark would take her new friend and take her soon. The idea is so huge, so inevitable that Marie begins to shake. Lisa takes off her jacket, puts it around Marie's shoulders, and leads her into the back room, back to the TV and the half-eaten bags of crisps, and she fusses around, playing the role of Nurse, and Marie wants to tell her to stop acting now, because now is the time to be serious, now is the time to take care and watch out and keep her wits about her, keep safe, be careful.

'Look what I found!' Lisa pulls a bottle of brown liquid out of a cupboard. There are cobwebs in her hair. 'Brandy! Brandy's good when you're poorly. Have some brandy!' And she pours a little into the screw cap and passes it to Marie.

It's sour fire and it makes her gag. It makes Lisa gag too, but she manages a bigger swig from the bottle itself, and then another. Then she takes her ring off with a wobbly flourish. 'You can have this.'

Marie's head is fuzzy. It seems like a very bad idea to take the ring. She doesn't want the ring. 'No thank you.'

Lisa is hurt. 'Why not? Go on, take it.'

And Marie doesn't like to hurt people's feelings, and so she does take it, but it feels nasty in her hand, heavy and hot, a burden. Her mind, so young, struggles to understand itself, until a voice – a feeling really – tells her not to worry, that someday she'll understand what this means and how things came to be. She thinks of this voice as Lily's. Lily is stronger than her.

'I'm going to go to Kirsty's now.' Lisa takes the coat back, puts the notebook in the pocket. Then she picks up the bottle. 'Can I take this too?'

'It's Uncle Mervyn's though.'

'He's locked up in prison! He won't miss it. And I *did* give you my ring… It's got real rubies for eyes!'

'He's not in prison!' Marie feels scalding humiliation.

Lisa hesitates then and frowns, as if she, too, is consulting the advice of some inner older sister. 'No. You're right, he's not. I'm thinking of someone else,' she says kindly.

'He's on holiday!' Marie whispers, knowing it isn't true.

'And he'll be having a lovely time too, I bet,' Lisa tells her. 'Maybe he's swimming with dolphins? I've heard of people doing that. Maybe he's riding on their backs!'

Marie giggles, imagining Uncle Mervyn with his long sloping belly and his skinny little arms, hanging onto a dolphin for dear life. 'That's silly!'

'Or maybe he's riding camels in the desert. Camels fart all the time!' Lisa waves her hand under her nose.

'Ew!' Marie is delighted now. She kicks her legs and wraps her arms around herself happily. 'Where else could he be?'

'A gold mine in America? Maybe for a present he'll bring you back a nugget of gold.'

'What's a nugget?'

'It's like a brick. I think.' Lisa puts the bottle in her school bag. 'Where's your mum anyway?'

'Home?'

Lisa looks around the darkened club. 'I don't like leaving you here by yourself. You should phone her.'

'We don't have a phone at home.'

'Well, I'm sure she'll be back soon—'

'I don't want you to go,' Marie tells her suddenly, desperately. *I'm not afraid of being alone*, she wants to say, *I'm always alone; I just don't want* you *to be alone! I have to stay with you, to protect you.* Out loud she says, 'Can I come with you?'

'Won't your mum be back soon?'

'Please let me come with you?'

And Lisa puts out one hand. 'OK. We'll go to Kirsty's. They have a car and they'll drive you home. Kirsty's got a baby sister too and maybe you can play with her. But…' Lisa beckons impishly and Marie leans in, smiling. Lisa's breath smells of brandy, and up close her face is dirty, and there are spots under her skin and her eyes are a little bit unfocused. 'She poos her pants *all* the time!'

'Ew!' cries Marie delightedly.

Lisa, equally delighted, nods. 'I *know*!' She takes Marie's hand then. 'Ready?' When their hands touch, Marie tries extra hard not to feel Lisa's strange emptiness. She holds on tight, as if to squeeze extra life into her. 'I know a short-cut to Kwik Save, and Kirsty lives close to Kwik Save. We'll be there in ten minutes,' Lisa says briskly.

But they aren't.

*

'We walk for a long time, and it's cold and muddy, and she keeps drinking from that bottle.' Angela spoke with her eyes closed. Her foot twitched as if slipping in mud. One hand was curved, claw-like, around an unseen hand, the other lay loosely on her lap. 'She keeps saying we're near the path, but I know we're not because I know she's scared.'

'What was she scared of?' Kirsty asked.

'She's scared of the dark,' Angela answered. 'She's scared of being sick, too. She's drunk but she doesn't know it, she just knows she's wobbly and sick and scared. She feels very young and silly. She's just a little girl. I feel all that, but I don't understand it. She says we should maybe go back to the club and dry off, and she tells me not to be frightened, she tells me I'll be safe and warm soon, but she's talking to herself too, I can feel it. She asks me to tell her a story. She asks me to tell her about my sisters. She says, "Tell me a story and we'll be back at the club before you know it."'

'Your dead sisters,' Kirsty said.

Angela's eyes stayed closed. 'They weren't ever alive. They weren't ever real. Only Lily was real.'

CHAPTER THIRTY-FOUR

Marie had four sisters and she missed them terribly, proudly. She'd never met any of them, but they were always with her.

First was Ruby, so quiet in the womb, placid and dead two weeks before the midwife realised. Then, a year later, Jade fluttered on a scan, brief as a butterfly, before she too winked out of existence. Sophie, hot on the heels of Jade, put up more of a struggle: 'She kicked and she *kicked*! Oh, she wanted out,' Mum told Marie. 'She wanted to see me, I could tell.' But Sophie's little kicks grew panicked as she, too, failed to make it to the second trimester. Then it was Lily's turn – Lily, who wasn't expected, whose existence was only noticed at six months ('I'd given up hope,' Mum said solemnly) was born swiftly, early. She lay fully formed and quiescent in her incubator, each thin limb trembling as if a current ran through them. On the third day the trembling ceased, and she opened her eyes wide, blinked slowly, like a loving kitten. ('Oh! She had beautiful blue eyes,' Mum told Marie softly. 'She would have had the most beautiful eyes of all of you. They say all babies have blue eyes, but hers would have *stayed* blue, I knew it. That's why I called her Lily Blue.') But by the afternoon of that third day, Lily too had passed.

Lily's photo was on the mantelpiece, a small pastel smear behind the toughened plastic of the incubator, and next to it, no bigger than a pine cone, stood the urn holding her ashes.

'They said I couldn't carry a child,' Mum said. 'They told me that I'd never be a mum. Oh, I took it well, but inside a little part of me died. I believed them, you see, not myself. If I'd believed myself I would have had an easier time of it. I *knew*, deep down in my heart, that I'd have my daughter. The cards said it, it was in my palm. I *knew*, but those so-called experts said they knew better. Well, we showed them, didn't we? Because look what happened.'

'What?' Marie always asked the question despite knowing the answer. The answer was her favourite thing in the world.

'A miracle.'

'What was the miracle?' Marie would ask breathlessly.

'*You*,' Mum would say. '*You* were the miracle.'

And Marie would beg for the story, the whole story again, sinking into its folds, luxuriating in every sentence.

'Two years after Lily passed, two years to the *day*, you were born…'

Lily and Marie shared a zodiac sign, a birthstone, as well as a solemn birthday celebration. Every year, Marie's school picture was placed on the mantelpiece, next to the pine cone of ashes Lily in her incubator. When she was very small, Marie would confuse the two, fuse herself with Lily. That was to be expected, Mum said; Lily and Marie had a connection.

Mum was forty-three by the time she fell pregnant for the fifth time, and her age, combined with all those deaths, had convinced her that she'd miscarry.

'They told me I should prepare myself,' she told Marie. 'I thought, "Prepare myself? I'm prepared four times over!" This time I did everything differently. What's the point in making a meal for a guest that never arrives?'

And so she did everything, deliberately, wrong. She didn't keep up with her doctor's appointments, eschewed vitamins and took up smoking again, as if she could fool the hostile gods by appearing indifferent. She kept this up until the day labour began ('Early. Six weeks early. I thought, well, I know the drill, I know I'll lose this one too. But I still shed a tear') and calmly lay down, swallowed four co-codamol to mask the pain and tried to ignore the inevitable. 'I wasn't even going to call the hospital. No point.'

'But then you had a dream?' Marie would always ask then. The lines were the same, the emphasis the same, but the thrill of the tale always excited her.

Mum nodded. 'Yes. A dream.' When she heard those words, more often than not, Marie would close her eyes, sink down further into her seat. Mum always used the same words, the same intonation. It was like a chant. Or a prayer.

'I dreamed of a storm. Oh, a huge storm it was, with thunder and lightning. The lightning was so bright it lit up the whole house, and the thunder was as loud as the end of the world. And then, what did I see?'

'What?' Marie would whisper. 'What'd you see?'

'At the end of the bed was a baby in a cot.'

'Who was the baby?' Marie always asked.

'Its face was covered. I couldn't tell.'

'Then what?'

'Then I heard a voice – clear as mine is to you – but coming from the sky.'

'What did the voice say?'

Mum deepened her voice then, to sound like god did in those old Biblical films. 'The voice said: "This is your gift."'

At this point, Marie always wanted to open her eyes, because, even though she knew it was just Mum, the voice *was* a little scary. She never did though, because that would take away from the moment, and being a bit scared was part of the whole thing – a big part.

'And then what happened?'

'And then the lightning lit up the room as bright as day.' Mum's voice, the rhythm of that phrase, it never changed. 'And I saw all my girls around the cot, standing round it like guards, and the light was inside them, they were just glowing with love. They were angels. And then…'

'What?' Marie whispered. This was the best bit of all. This was the miracle that filled her with joyful fear, with such pride she could burst with it.

'Then the cover drifted away from the baby's face, and all my girls wept with happiness. Then the lightning flashed and the thunder roared again, and the voice told me you'd be mine forever and ever.'

'And how come I was all right? How come I lived and my sisters didn't?' This was the scariest, most thrilling part; this was the best part.

Mum turned her grave gaze towards the mantelpiece. 'Your sisters wanted you to, that's why. They wanted to make up for all the heartache. You lived to make me happy. That's what the dream was all about. Your sisters are always here, *always* here, to keep you on the right path, to make sure you look after me, always.'

*

It's the most beautiful story Marie can imagine. But maybe she got some of the words wrong, or wasn't clear enough because Lisa doesn't think so. She thinks it's creepy.

'So they're *dead*?' Her voice is slurred. 'They're all dead or never born anyway?'

'They're angels!' Marie protests.

'Who's their dad then? Who's *your* dad then?'

'I don't know.' Marie's own words surprise her. Why hasn't she thought of this before?

'Didn't you ever ask? I'd've *asked*!'

Asked? How to explain that asking Mum things is *Bad*. Asking makes Mum Sad, and if Mum is Sad, Marie is Bad. This is the circular logic that she is steeped in, that she can't question.

'Your mum sounds weird,' Lisa says. 'She sounds proper weird.'

'She's *not!*' Marie drops Lisa's hand. 'She's *not* weird and my sisters are *real* and they're *angels!*'

'You know what I think? I think Mervyn's your dad, that's what I think.'

Marie is confused by this. 'How?'

'I bet he is. Ask her.'

Marie feels around in Lisa's mind, and what she finds scares her. She feels hot then, and sick. She drops Lisa's hand. Lisa tries to take it again but Marie bats it away. 'Ow! That *hurt!*'

'Good!' Marie's voice trembles. She turns now and runs towards the club.

'What're you running for? I'm sorry about what I said about your sisters, OK? And your mum? Just, wait, will you? Wait for me.' Lisa is trying to run too, but the mud and the brandy slow her down. 'Wait!'

'There's my mum!' Marie sees headlights. The car is driving slowly, illegally, through the park towards the club and she realises that Mum will be Very Angry if she's not there waiting. What was she thinking? Going with this strange girl to another strange girl's house? When she should be in the club, watching TV and eating crisps like a Good Girl! She is going to be in so much trouble! Listening to these lies, telling her secrets.

'Wait, will you?' Lisa is far behind now, swallowed up by the dark. 'Wait! *Shit!*' Marie winces at the Bad Language, but stops.

'What?'

'I've fallen. My knee's all... come and help me! I'm stuck in the mud and my knee hurts!'

Marie looks towards the car headlights, closer now, and her instinct is to abandon Lisa and run to the club quickly to avoid a telling-off, but Lisa is her friend and gave her that ring (even if she didn't want it) and has looked after her (even if she was mean about the angels and said Bad Things about Mum) and... and so she turns back.

*

'I remember she flipped in the air like a gymnast. I thought she was doing it on purpose. I… I clapped.' Angela opened her eyes. 'And then, and then she lay on the ground and that's all I have. I can remember later, lying here, on the floor with her. I know she's gone, but I tell myself she's only sleeping.' Angela was speaking softly, almost to herself, and her eyes had that inward, trance-like look again. 'I stroke her hair and I sing something… I don't remember where I've heard it.'

> *Sleep my child and peace attend thee,*
> *All through the night.*
> *Guardian angels God will send thee,*
> *All through the night.*

She looked at the bloodstained floor rather than Kirsty. 'I hugged her as if I could keep the life in her. Here. I failed though. I thought that. I told myself that I could have kept her alive somehow if only I knew the right words or…' She trailed off, shook her head.

'She hit by a car?' Kirsty asked.

'By *Mum's* car. Yes. I remember running away from Lisa, and the car going past me and towards her, I remember her flying in the air, like an…'

'Angel.'

'Yes. Like an angel. But in the morning there was new lino down on the floor, and my top had disappeared and Mum said I'd dreamed everything. Later it got all mixed up with other memories. A few weeks later *I* was in an accident, you see. I was hit by a drunk driver in a car park. It turned out to be a policeman going off shift, and so Mum sued the council and got a pay-out. She told me for the longest time that what I thought I remembered about being with Lisa in the park was just my mixing things up in my head, not memories at all. I never met Lisa, she was never here, the new lino had always been there and I believed her, even though I had these memories, and I had the ring and I remembered hugging her and getting blood on my top. I remember her coat and the canal and… but Mum kept telling me it wasn't true, and I had no way of proving it…' She looked, suddenly, at Kirsty, with naked dread. 'Do you understand? I didn't *know* what was true and what wasn't. You don't know what it's like, to never be *sure*.'

'I do though,' Kirsty commented softly. 'I told the police I'd seen Tokki in the park. I said it because they made me think I had. I'm the reason they put him away.'

Angela nodded. 'Maybe you do get it then.'

'I've felt guilty for all these years… I've never stopped wondering what was true and what wasn't. Lisa told some lies, and the police made *me* lie and no-one seemed to want to get to the truth. It was as if the truth was too messy, not satisfying enough. It's easier to have a Bad Guy, you know?'

Angela smiled faintly. 'I do. It's child-like… it's *primal*. I've thought a lot about this. What I do, the people I help, that's what they're looking for too – they want to be told that they're good people, that they're forgiven, that death has kind of… smoothed the edges of life. They don't want grey areas. They don't want *doubt*. But, who does?' She shrugged, smiled wearily. 'Doubt is what kills you.'

'If you let it,' Kirsty said softly. 'And I've let it. Not kill me, but stunt me.'

'And I've spent the last thirty years trying to avert it all together. I tell people their dead dad approves of their career choices; I tell them that Grandpa says sorry, that their dead children forgive them. And it *is* true, but it's not *all* the truth.' She smiled crookedly. 'Grandpa really says, "I'm sorry, *but…*"; the son forgives but hasn't forgotten. It's more complicated than people can cope with, so why burden them? I know how terrible that is.' She shook her head. 'I've been back here for two months and she's managed to pull me right back, making me believe I did something I couldn't have, making me doubt myself and trust her, even though I know what she's like. God, she's good.'

She started to move her frozen legs, shuffled away from the bloodstain and started to get back on her feet. Her voice was broken, suddenly aged. 'Pour me another drink, will you? And you should have one too.' Angela pinched the skin between her eyes. 'It's… I don't know how to explain it. It's like an allergy almost, or like going back to a contaminated zone, like Chernobyl or something. I have this… propensity in me, this doubt, this *fear* of myself, that she planted years ago, and when I'm away it can't hurt me, but when I'm back, in the danger zone, it triggers, and I'm *lost*… things start falling apart in my mind again.' She turned weary, tearful eyes on Kirsty, and suddenly, she resembled the woman on all those YouTube videos again, a struggling, worn-down martyr of a woman. A good woman.

'There's always a bit of truth in the things she says, you see. Just enough to… When I told her that I smacked Lisa's hand, and I *did* smack her hand, Mum told me it was a dream, but then later, when she wanted me to believe I'd killed her, she'd say things like, "You *told* me you hit her." And I'd say, "I smacked her," and Mum would say, "What's the difference?" Later still, the whole conversation would be overhauled; she'd say something like, "Don't worry, I know you didn't mean to hit her that hard," and when I'd say, "I didn't hit her hard," Mum would get angry, or disappointed, tell me to tell the truth. And then she'd work on me, telling me what she said I'd said before, and even if I started out knowing what I'd said before, by the end of the conversation I wasn't sure at all any more. I wouldn't know, and I'd be tired and scared and I'd agree with her. That's what she did with the coat.'

'Sylvia told me that she was the "passer-by". She said it was to protect you.' Kirsty said.

'Because I'd hidden the coat there, and that proved I'd killed Lisa? She told me the same thing. Later she said I'd made her a criminal, and I'd better make it up to her somehow. At the time though, she just said it was a dream.'

'How did Lisa's coat get on the canal bank though?' Kirsty asked.

'It was a week after she disappeared. Early in the morning. She shook me awake…'

CHAPTER THIRTY-FIVE

Mum's hands are frantic, she smooths her hair back from her forehead, calls her darling.

'You were screaming! You had a nightmare!'

'I was?' Marie is confused. It's dark outside. 'What time is it?'

'God almighty, it was *horrible*. You were screaming like someone possessed! Like you were being... God, I don't even want to *think* about what it sounded like! Something about a big girl's jacket?'

'A jacket?' She's still partially asleep. 'Time is it?' Mum looks irritated.

' Forget about the time! *You* woke *me* up and you don't see me moaning about it! *Yes*, a jacket. Don't you remember? And water. Black water, you said.' She waits expectantly.

'I don't remember.' Marie yawns and sits up.

'Well, *try*. What big girl?'

'Girl?'

'What big girl? The one you say you saw in the park?'

'The girl who came back here? What *time* is—'

'Oh give over, there wasn't ever a girl here, stop being silly! Try to remember your dream just now! What colour was the jacket? Green, blue?'

'Blue?'

She must have said the right thing, because Mum's clutch loosens a bit. 'OK. Now let's think about the dark water. Was it wide like the sea? Or black and still like a pond or something?'

'I'm tired, Mum—'

'No, no no, this is important! Stay awake! You said "black water" in the dream. Like the sea or the canal?'

Marie yawns. 'Like the canal?'

Mum widens her eyes. 'The canal? The one in the park, where you saw that girl?'

Marie nods. 'Yes?'

'You're sure?'

'Yes.' She is.

'You better not be lying.'

'I'm not lying,' Marie assures her. She isn't either. She's making Mum happy with the right answers.

Mum nods seriously. She pats Marie's hand. 'I believe you. And you know what we should do?'

'What?'

'We should go to the canal right now. You and me. Like detectives! See what we can find.'

'Now?'

'Don't you want to be a detective with me?'

'Yes. Of course I do, but—'

'Right then. Let's get up and out.'

'It's dark though, Mum, and I'm tired and—'

'*You're* tired? You're the one that woke me up early, screaming and carrying on! If anyone's tired here it's me! Get up! Up up up!'

'OK,' Marie says weakly.

It's cold by the canal, and the heavy air feels like damp cobwebs on her skin. Every now and again Mum stops, asks her where they should go, and Marie isn't sure because she doesn't remember her dream at all, and there's a little falling elevator of helplessness in her throat. The idea of being a detective was exciting, but the reality is confusing. *What jacket? Why did they have to come here to find some old jacket?*

'Marie-Belle! Here!' Mum is on the other side of the bridge. A streetlight on the other side of the bank shines weakly on her hair, on her face. She looks serious. 'I think I've found it.'

'What?' Marie runs now.

'Keep your voice down, I said. And stay on this side of me, will you? Look…' She points at a clump of nettles with something poking out from them. 'Is that it? Is that what you saw in your dream?'

Marie peers at the bank obediently. 'Yes?'

'Well it was your dream, not mine!' Mum says sharply. 'So is it yes, or no?'

Marie makes her voice firm. 'Yes.'

Mum steps forward, uses one of the stiff handles of her shopping bag to part the nettles. 'Come here. Look.'

Marie does look, and she does recognise the coat. 'That's her coat! It *is!*' She feels triumphant now, because this means the girl was real after all!

Under the streetlight Mum's face looks very lined, very grim. 'And what's that on it? What's that stain? Don't get too close!'

Marie can't see any stains without getting too close. 'I don't know.'

'It's blood, is what it is.' Mum has a kind of sombre satisfaction in her voice. 'The girl's dead, you know that, don't you?'

'She's what?' Marie starts to cry. 'No she's *not!*'

'Oh but she is. And you were the last person to see her, and you know where her coat was, and what do you think that means?'

'I don't *know.*' Marie is badly scared now. All the breath has solidified in her throat, she can't breathe.

'It means they'll take you away. They'll take you away and send you to prison, that's what it means.'

'No!'

Mum nods. 'Oh yes. I've seen it before. They'll take you away, just like they did Uncle Mervyn, and then I'll be all alone! Oh, Marie-Belle, what did you *do?* Did she hurt you, this girl? Why would you *do* something like that?'

Marie is choking now, shaking. 'I *didn't!*'

'I'll say *I* found it.' Mum is talking to herself now. 'That's what I'll do. But if they arrest *me*, what will happen to *you*? You might have to go to a home—'

'No!'

'For orphans—'

'No! Mum!'

'Shhh! Calm down. I'll say I just found it while I was out for a stroll. I'll go there now, and you have a hot chocolate in the Tiffin Bar and wait for me, OK? If I don't come back, well, you'll know why.'

Mum tells morose Mr Speed who owns the Tiffin Bar that Marie is sad because her pet guinea pig died and could she leave her here for a bit while she arranges to get another one? Mr Speed keeps an eye on the catatonic, tear-stained child, reflecting that if she takes a guinea pig's death this badly she won't find life easy. When her mother comes back, the girl bursts into tears, hugs her as if she never wants to let go. He's so moved he brings them both another hot chocolate on the house.

*

'She put herself on the line for me. That's what she said. And over the years she'd come back to it, adding more details, hinting that she was being questioned by the police again, that someone was threatening her, trying to make her give me up. That's why those notes worked so well on me – the notes she said you were sending her? I was primed to believe that. She told me Bryan wanted to hurt me, that Peg would hate me, that I could never get too cocky, if I wanted to stay safe. Being too cocky was Mum-speak for rebelling.' Angela sounded bitter, for the first time. 'She planted this little seed in me from when I was tiny – and it's... anchored in me. I don't know it's there for years and then she'll give it a tug and before I know it I'm back in the past. But not *my* past, *hers.* The one she's concocted. She did it to you, too, didn't she? Before you knew it, you were slap bang in the middle of the world she'd created. Tell me, how did she get you to come here today?'

'She left me a message at work and when I called back she didn't answer, so I came over.' Kirsty's voice was small as a child's. 'I was worried about her.'

'And when you came over the place was trashed?'

'Yes, how did you know?'

'Because she told me you'd trashed it, remember? When you came over and hit her with the shovel? Go on, something else must have happened to make you scared. She never does things by half.'

'Someone in a car drove towards the house, and I was scared. I hid under the house. That wasn't you, was it?'

'No.'

'When I was under the house my husband – Lee – arrived and he was angry with Sylvia about something. We… we'd had a row so I didn't let him know I was there. Maybe it was him in the car?'

Angela shook her head. 'It wasn't Lee. Lee's been at your sister's for the last two days, worried for you. He told us that you'd been seeing a lot of Mum, that he didn't trust her, so I knew that she must have got into your head somehow… if he went round it was to tell her to leave you alone, but not to threaten anyone. Go on.'

'I went back home and then someone called me, saying they'd found Sylvia in the town centre. I picked her up, and she was bruised and limping and—'

'And *I'd* done that, right?'

'Yes, you. She told me you'd been there the night before looking for the box and you were violent and she'd had to play along until you calmed down and left. Then she walked into town and asked someone to call me.'

'What time did you get the call?'

'At about twelve thirty. I took her to my flat. She's there now.'

Angela pursed her lips. 'I doubt she's still there. You picked her up in town? Whereabouts? Parliament Street?'

'Yes, by the war memorial, how'd you know?'

'Because my hotel is on Parliament Street.' Angela almost chuckled. 'She didn't even have to walk far. She just waited until I left and got a friendly passer-by to…' She shook her head. 'Jesus. She's good. She hasn't lost her edge, has she? So, she gets both of us to come here at the same time, we're both afraid of the other, we both think we're defending her, and both of us will be in the same, small room with knives. If, that is, she ever expected you to get up the back stairs in one piece.'

'But how do I know it's not you who's manipulating me?' Kirsty made one last stand. 'At Vic's party, the first time we met, you tried to scare me away…'

'I didn't. I wasn't warning you about anything either. It may have come off like that, but I genuinely, *genuinely* saw something in you—'

'Oh, so you're a real psychic?' Kirsty said sarcastically.

'You *know* I am,' Angela answered with simple dignity. 'I saw a loss, and I also saw a child entering your life soon. The message was very, very positive and very strong.'

'Then why did you come to the hospital that time to threaten me?'

'I didn't. I came to see Peg. Peg more or less raised me in my teens, after things here got… too hard to handle. Peg is the only person who's always seen through Sylvia. She's smart. I owe her a lot. I ran into you by accident, but, yes, I *did* tell you to leave Mum alone. I shouldn't have, but I did, and for that I apologise. But, remember that everything she'd been telling *you*, she'd been telling *me* – she'd been telling me that you were frightening her, harassing her, and she showed me all those notes. I even saw you at the house that time, remember? I knew you were contacting her, and you obviously had a problem with me. That's why I was so harsh with you, and I would've been harsher, too, if I didn't know how much Peg thought of you. If you remember, when I saw you at the hospital I asked you to sit down and have a coffee with me, it was you who overreacted and started shouting. What was I meant to think after that?'

Just then Kirsty's phone rang. Both women watched the phone vibrate on the table like a trapped wasp, 'SYLVIA' flashing on the illuminated screen. They watched until it stopped.

'Wait,' Angela said softly. 'She'll call me, now. She'll want to know what's happened. She sent us here to kill each other and she won't care which one of us survived, but she needs to know so she knows how to play it. Shhhh… Look, here she is, right on time!' Angela took a deep breath, looked Kirsty in the eyes, and answered her phone.

'Oh! Marie-Belle, I've been so *worried*! What's happening?' Sylvia was a quavering old woman again, weak, frightened. 'Are you all right?'

'I'm fine, Mum. I'm—'

'Don't tell me you're not there yet?' The voice changed. Now it was querulous, despairing. 'She'll have been and *gone* by now! Bloody *hell*, Marie!'

'No, no, I'm here.'

'And what about *her*? What's happened?'

'Do you really want to know?' Angela drawled.

'No. No,' Sylvia said hurriedly. 'Just so long as it's… done, that's all. Where will you put her?'

Kirsty's mouth was opened with shock. Angela nodded at her, pressed her hand warmly. 'Where's best?'

Sylvia clucked her tongue musingly. 'Under the house? Wrap her up in lino and stick her under the house. We can move her later on if needs be. And make sure her phone's off, will you? We don't want her husband coming after her. He's a tricky one. Well, you met him, didn't you? Oooh, did you know he knew Bryan back in the day? That's a turn-up, isn't it?'

'He did?' Angela looked questioningly at Kirsty. Kirsty gave the briefest of nods. 'How?'

'*I* don't know. Bryan told me he'd seen him at the hospital, with Kirsty. I sent him over there to give Laini her present, and he ran into them both there. Small world, isn't it?'

Kirsty pushed her own phone towards Angela. On it she'd written: 'Ask her what the present was??'

Angela nodded, closed her eyes, swallowed hard. 'What did you give Laini?'

'A ring. Bryan didn't even know it was her birthday! I knew he'd forget.' Sylvia's voice rang with disapproval. 'So I told him he could tell her it was from him, not me.'

'That was nice of you.' Angela looked questioningly at Kirsty, but kept her voice level.

'Well, you do what you can.' The honeyed voice was back. 'I'll sleep better at night now, love, knowing there won't be any more nastiness. No more notes and *calls* and… all that. Not to mention the money…'

'How much did you end up giving her?'

'Oh, Marie-Belle, you don't want to know.' The old lady was back, vague, fretful, apologetic. 'Most of my nest egg. All that money you gave me to buy a house.'

'Well, don't worry about money, Mum,' Angela told her. 'I'll look after you, you know that.'

'You're a good girl. Now, how long will you be?'

'I'll pick you up within the hour. Are you still at the hotel?'

'Of course. I've been here the whole time.'

CHAPTER THIRTY-SIX

'What about this ring for Laini?' Angela asked.

'Sylvia told me that she'd had a dream, or a psychic flash or something, and she'd written down some... messages from Lisa. God, it sounds so *stupid* now!'

'She's very good at this, don't kick yourself. What did the messages say?'

'That I had to look out for a ring, and an old friend.'

'And the next day your old "friend" Bryan showed up with a ring?'

'Yes. It was shaped like an angel.'

'Angels Times Two.' Angela shook her head. 'I'm sorry. I'm so sorry she did all this to you.'

'She had the notebook. She even showed it to me! She knew about it all along!'

'Yes.' Angela nodded, and made a wide gesture, encompassing the whole house. 'She keeps everything. Even things that might make her look bad. She always finds a use for things. And the things she can't use, she covers up.' She inclined her head towards the bloodstained floor, got up, put on her jacket, picked up her car keys. 'I'm going to get her.'

'No! Call the police!'

'And tell them what? We haven't *got* anything, not yet!'

'What about that?' Kirsty pointed at the bloodstained concrete.

'Shit, that needs covering.' Angela pressed the lino back down again. 'Help me flatten it out, will you?'

'But that proves Lisa was here—'

'You're right, it does, but it doesn't prove that *Mum* did anything. It could still somehow end up on me. You've seen how convincing she is, so don't imagine that the police would see through her.' Angela pressed down one errant corner of the lino with the toe of one boot. 'I'm going to pick her up, right? Tell her I've… dealt with you. I'll record everything she says in the car over here. In the meantime, you stay in the room next to the dining room – hide behind the door, you'll be able to hear everything that way and you record it too, if you can. She can't play us off against each other if we're both hearing the same thing. She can't twist her way out of it, can she? And if we have recordings too.' She nodded, all exhausted excitement. 'It's our best shot.'

'I don't know, Angela, this is…'

'It's fucked-up is what it is.' She sounded more like Peg than ever. 'You've found out that this lovely old lady was playing you, and that's shit and I feel very sorry for you, but you've had it for a few months; I've had it for *years*, and it stops now. You need to help me stop it now.'

'Why has she *done* this though?' Kirsty's voice was small, child-like, full of uncomprehending hurt.

'You haven't figured that out yet?' Angela asked wonderingly.

'No, no I haven't. It doesn't make sense! Why ruin my life? Just for fun?'

'Not fun. Fear. You were necessary, that's all. You served a purpose.'

'What d'you mean?'

'Oh boy.' Angela sat down again, took her hand gently. 'Ask yourself, why does she live here?'

'Because of Mervyn—'

Angela shook her head. 'She didn't like Mervyn, and she didn't like looking after him when he was sick either. Listen, I've been sending her money every month. For years. She told me she lived in a little flat on the other side of town – I've been paying for this mythical flat for years! Then, Mervyn dies and leaves this place to me, and I find out there's no flat, she's kept the money I sent and has been here all along. She refused to even let me level this place and build her a new, decent house on the land.'

'But why?'

'Because she *can't* leave, Kirsty.' Her grip tightened. 'She. Keeps. Everything. Even bad things. Even… Lisa. Lisa's body is here, somewhere, it must be. That's why she won't let me sell the land, or build on it, because if that happens, there's every chance Lisa's body will be found. Do you get it now?'

'She's here? She's been here all along?' Kirsty cried.

'She used you to frighten me away. I wanted to sell the land, and she couldn't let me do that, so when we met at the party, and she found out who you were, she resuscitated the old story that somehow, at aged five, I'd killed Lisa. She worked on me hard, before telling me that this crazy woman – you – who'd stumbled on the truth, was gunning for me. She told me that I should just leave, go back to America, forget about the will and everything else, and just get away from you. It didn't work though, for once she overplayed her hand. She told me you were dangerous, that you'd hurt her, that you were extorting her; how could I just *leave* knowing that was happening? I told her I was staying longer. That's when her plan changed, that's when she decided to pit us against each other. She was desperate, and after all, if you killed me, she'd keep the house, the land and you'd be written off as this unbalanced stalker and put away. If *I* killed *you*, that would get me arrested and she'd still get to stay here. Whatever happened, Lisa would say buried and no-one would know what she'd done. Do you see what we're up against now?'

CHAPTER THIRTY-SEVEN

Kirsty stayed behind in the dark house in which lurked all the strange calamity of Sylvia's mind. Kirsty felt her own mind reach to the cleanest, most decent person she knew – Lee – and the humiliation, the too-sudden knowledge of her naivety, her own cruelty, stung horribly. Lee, her partner, the other half, a kernel of good, cynical sanity, had been thrown away on Sylvia's subterranean command. She thought of all those little hints scattered in their conversations: *I thought there were problems… does he often lose his temper?… He was a little forceful.* Then there was the tarot reading, which oh-so-neatly showed a man in a position of power, an inflexible, furious, scared man, a betrayer. Sylvia herself was a mother figure, kind and compassionate. *A wise counsel… she protects you, and loves you… She's on your side, come what may.* And, finally, Sylvia had added Lisa into this toxic mix… a silent partner keeping the circle together, all the while knowing that she was here, rotting away, or burned, or… Kirsty had to call Lee, tell him she was OK, that she'd been wrong. Even though she was alone, she kept her voice low.

'Lee?'

'Shit, love, where've you been?' Lee's voice boomed in the silence, all honest relief and love. 'Are you OK? Are you sick? I called the hospital and they said you hadn't come in today.'

'I'm so sorry, Lee,' she was sobbing, 'I'm so sorry, I said all those things to you and I, god, I'm *sorry*!'

'Hey, hey, love, come on, come on, now.' His voice was gentle, reassuring, as warm and alive as this room was desiccated and dead. 'Where are you? What's happened?'

'I'm at Sylvia's. You were right about her, Lee, she's *awful*. She *lied* to me and—'

'Come home now!' he told her.

'I can't.'

'I'll come and get you then! I'll come right now—'

'No, Lee, you can't. It's dangerous and you can't—'

'What d'you mean, dangerous?' His voice was panicked now. 'Are you hurt? What's she done to you?'

A car was approaching. 'They're coming back now. I have to go. Lee? I love you! And I'm sorry! I'll… I'll call you back when I can. I promise.'

The car pulled up, the doors opened and slammed. Kirsty took up her post behind the door, put her phone on silent, and waited.

*

'It's warmer in here,' Angela said. 'I left the gas fire on.'

They were in the little dining room now. Kirsty pressed record on her phone and very slowly, very gently, placed it on top of a pile of newspapers by the door. She could see, through a tiny crack in the door panel, Sylvia sitting on the sofa, rubbing her hands together.

'Cold out there.'

'Take your coat off. Sit closer to the fire. Do you want tea?' Angela was unctuous. 'Will that help?'

'Oh, that'd be lovely.'

It was… bizarre. There they were, each convinced – one of them correctly – that the other was a killer, and they were chatting about the weather like nothing had happened, like they were a normal mother and daughter. They sat and drank tea in what could easily pass as an amiable silence, and Kirsty felt a sudden, sick fear that somehow this was part of her torture, that nothing Angela had told her was true, that *she* was the master manipulator after all, that the whole thing would never be resolved, the truth would never be known.

Then, as if she sensed her despair, Angela glanced at the door and nodded, just over Sylvia's head. 'Will you tell me now?' she asked Sylvia.

'What about?'

'About Lisa Cook, what happened to her?'

'Oh lord,' Sylvia said with mild irritation. 'Why do you have to ask about all that for?'

'What harm can it do now, Mum? Look, I did… this thing, for you, right? Well, can you tell me what happened to Lisa? I know it wasn't me, but, you know, you must have had a good reason for saying it was. I just want to put it behind us.'

Sylvia sipped her tea meditatively. 'It *was* your fault,' she said eventually.

Even from the next room, Kirsty could feel Angela's exasperation, her despair that Sylvia was just going to trot out the same bizarre lie.

'How was it? What happened? Mum, please? Come on…'

'Well, maybe you're right.' Sylvia sounded a little bit satisfied, as if she liked to be begged, liked to show mercy every now and again. 'It's not like you can drop me in it any more, is it? And it *was* your fault, in a way. What were you doing running around in the dark with her anyway? I told you to stay in the club.'

'You hit Lisa with the car?'

'And you were lucky I didn't hit *you*. I swerved when I saw you, and I hit her. Like I said, it was an accident, and if you hadn't been out with her in the first place it would never have happened.'

'I remember her being here though. In the kitchen?'

'Well, that was your fault too. I thought I'd just leave her in the park, but you were crying and carrying on and so I put her in the back seat, brought her here.'

'Why not the hospital?'

Sylvia stared at her. 'I didn't have a driving licence, did you forget that titbit? Imagine taking her to hospital and them going,

Oh, how did you get here then, and me saying, *Oh I drove.* Then they get a statement from me, find out I'm illegal, look at the dent in the car, and lock me up for murder and dangerous driving and I don't know what else. And where would you have been then? Who would've looked after *you*? What was I supposed to do?' She shook her head.

Kirsty pressed her lips together, trying not to make a sound as the tears rolled down her face, dripping off her chin. Angela, too, was having trouble controlling her face. Kirsty watched as she got up, ostensibly to turn the fire down, but mainly to wipe away her own tears. Still with her back to Sylvia, she managed, in a remarkably steady voice, to congratulate her on having such good sense.

'Well one of us had to.' Sylvia was warming to the conversation now. Proving her own logic against others' sentiment was obviously a favourite topic of hers. 'Left to your own devices, you'd have told everyone and anyone about it.'

'Is that why you… you had to tell me I'd hurt her? So I wouldn't—'

'Ruin it all? Yes. And, when all's said and done, you *did* hurt her. I mean, it was your fault, wasn't it? If you hadn't been running around with her in the dark…'

'And the coat? Did you put her coat by the canal?'

'Yes, and I'm glad I did because they'd just arrested that man – the black man – what was his name?'

'Toqueer Al-Balushi.'

'God, that's a mouthful, isn't it? Well, they'd already got him, and so I thought the coat might push things along a bit.'

'And it did.'

'Yes, it did,' Sylvia said with satisfaction. 'Thank god.'

'Where is she? Where's Lisa's body now then?' Angela managed. Her voice was fogged with pain now, but Sylvia was too carried away with her own cleverness to hear it.

'Under the house!' she said triumphantly. 'Where you put Kirsty! That's quite neat, isn't it?'

'Neat.'

'Scuppers the plans for building too, doesn't it? Not moving now, am I? Can you imagine? The diggers uncovering that? We'd both be buggered, wouldn't we?'

'And Kirsty? How did she find out about Lisa?'

'God knows! She was mental, that girl. Did I tell you she came round here a bit back, trying to break in? I was round the back and I saw her. I gave her the shock of her life though!' She chuckled.

'What'd you do?'

'Well, Mervyn's old Ford Focus is back there, so I jumped in it and I drove right at her! She got the shock of her life!'

'And she didn't see it was you?'

'No, she was too busy crawling under the house like a rat. And I was too quick and my hair was covered, and—' She cocked her head to the side. 'What's that?'

'What?'

'Cars.' Sylvia walked into the kitchen. Angela cast a panicked look at the door, flapped one hand at Kirsty – *Come!*

'Marie? *Marie?*' Sylvia, panicked, called from the kitchen. 'Tell me those cars aren't coming this way! Ma*rie*! Oh for god's sake, where are you?'

And she came bustling back into the dining room, to find Angela and Kirsty standing side by side. Those cheeks, pinkened by unveiling her triumph by the humid gas fire, quivered, the colour drained, her face fell, like slack dough, from absolute control to pure shock. From behind her, the sound of the approaching cars was louder, their blue, flashing lights an ever-encroaching glare, and Sylvia stood absolutely still, rigid with rage, with cold, passionless hatred..

'You. Fucking. Bitches,' she muttered. Then she turned, snatched Angela's bag from the table, and sped out of the front door. They heard the BMW jerking into life, the gears crunching, the skid of mud, and then the sirens started as one pair of blue lights turned to follow Sylvia, while the other stayed on course, the beams finding and settling on the still figures of Kirsty and Marie, standing together at the doorway, the rain pounding the mud before them.

CHAPTER THIRTY-EIGHT

It's a strange thing to have lived through a catastrophic event that never actually happened. The ripples extend over years, until more suffering stems from yet more nothing. A fire destroys a building; an innocent man is imprisoned; two girls are condemned to years of fear and doubt; hundreds of people on the internet put their heads together to Solve the Case. So much guilt, so much hate, so much… *noise* is generated from one small horrible truth that no-one could know. But once this false narrative is ripped apart, what can fill it? Yet more narratives, of course.

According to the police report, Sylvia lost control of the car just as she was about to get onto the main road running into Beacon Hill. With the police car behind her, she made one desperate attempt to make a swift right, the car skidded across the tarmac and hit a row of garages, sending the door of one straight through the windscreen and straight through Sylvia. This 'Serious Incident' in police parlance, became a 'Tragic Accident' in the unlikely words of an anonymous Beacon Hill resident to the local paper. By the next morning, local radio were calling it a 'Desperate Police Chase Ending in Tragedy', and by the evening it was snatched up by Dark Hearts as 'New Lead in Cook Case? Car-chase drama may be the clue we've been waiting for.' The story that unspooled over the next few weeks was dubbed 'insane', 'confounding' and 'fucking nuts' by all media, from the *Guardian* to Reddit. It was a bizarre, slow-burn shocker with something for everyone.

Tokki was immediately released and quickly married one of the women who had faithfully written to him for years. He gave one newspaper interview, in which he put the swift turnaround of his fortunes down to the direct intervention of Jesus Christ (he'd recently, at the urging of his fiancée, converted to Christianity). The accompanying photo showed that he was bald now, fat, and seemingly all-contentment, despite those scars – the self-inflicted throat wound, the missing finger from an attack ten years ago, the deep hatching of scars on palms and forearms from fending off another. There were other, hidden scars too, shakes, nightmares, cold-stored hate for the people who did this to him and those who let people do this to him. It was rumoured, and then confirmed, that he would sue the police for an undisclosed sum in compensation. Nobody gets out of things whole, after all, but maybe money helps heal some of the wounds.

Lisa's body – dust and bone now, wrapped in linoleum and stuffed under Sylvia's house – was retrieved with as much reverence as a forensic team could manage. A catastrophic head injury, a crushed ribcage, a dislocated shoulder. She had died immediately, long before Sylvia and Marie had got to the house, long before Marie, sobbing, was singing her to sleep and stroking her pretty hair. The funeral was very private, just Denise and Kirsty. Bryan was back in prison for breaching Mona's prevention order in a typically self-indulgent, stupid way – throwing rocks through her window in full view of the neighbours. Denise was relieved he wasn't there, Kirsty could tell. She sat rigidly through the short service and shed no tears, just clutched Kirsty's hand, quickly, spasmodically, as the coffin trundled away and the red curtain drew around it. Kirsty dropped her off at home and offered to come in, but Denise said she had to get the lodgers' tea ready, and she walked down her pathway squaring her broad shoulders, a solid, intensely private woman. People grieve differently, and Denise, as ever, grieved alone, silently. It was her way, too, of getting out whole.

Angela and Kirsty had a different method. They knew that they wouldn't be granted the luxury of privacy, and so they allowed their names, their faces and their life stories to be pored over. They posed for photographs and gave interviews – not many, but enough to prove that they had no regrets, no doubts, nothing to hide. Angela in particular was good at this; the transatlantic drawl was back, she knew how to stand in front of cameras with her back straight, her chin up. She knew how to look into a lens and tell it to trust her. Angela happily took the lead and Kirsty was grateful to her, grateful to be relegated to the role of Brave Sidekick, Plucky Assistant. Angela was so glamorous and Kirsty so honestly self-effacing that they were universally admired – even the grumpiest of trolls in the deepest crevices of Dark Hearts couldn't fault either of them. Kirsty was – in a roundabout way – apologised to in a special posting entitled, 'Why We Should Learn from Kirsty Cooper and Look Before We Leap (to Conclusions)'. Kirsty never read that post though, because she had no need to; the truth – most of it – the parts the public would want to know anyway – was out there now, and the ball was rolling. The press was already calling for a public enquiry, the tapes of Kirsty's and Tokki's questioning were already being pored over by the IPCC; heads might roll, pensions might be questioned, and papers would sell. As for the rest of the truth, Kirsty and Angela spent hours piecing that together, finding fact in the lies and the lies in… bigger lies.

'Tell me about Star Child,' Kirsty asked.

'What?'

'Star Child? The organisation you went to when you were five? They taught you about tarot and crystals and—'

'There was no Star Child,' Angela told her. 'She made all that up.'

Later, Kirsty checked, and there was no evidence of any organisation called Star Child anywhere. It seemed that Sylvia had concocted it from half-read articles on Indigo Children and Scientology.

'I suppose it gave the whole story a bit more colour,' Angela said. 'After all, she got to be the Mum Trying to Do the Right Thing

Up Against a Shadowy Evil Cult. It's… compelling, you have to admit. She was good at telling stories.'

'I don't know how you're so calm about this,' Kirsty said. 'I don't know why you're not *angry* all the time.'

'I used to be, but I turned it all in on myself. But then Peg stepped in. Once she's on your side, she's *on your side*, you know?'

'Like a mum.'

'Like a mum, yes. Peg arranged for me to do a few tarot readings in the back room of the pub she worked in – The Fox? Rough place then, probably still is, but to me it was like an extended version of Peg's living room; everyone sat around having a laugh and knocking back Guinness and everyone knew I was Peg's niece, too, and that was nice. I felt welcome. And I started to understand how strange people thought Mum was – you mentioned her name and it was all raised eyebrows and wry grins. It made me feel bad at first, like I was betraying her a bit, but at the same time…'

'It was fun?'

'Yes! It was good to hear that not everyone took her seriously, they just thought she was silly, you know? It felt cheeky… blasphemous almost. So I started questioning things a bit more, asking Peg things, and that's when I started finding out about some of the weirdness.'

'What things?'

'Well, she hadn't pulled me out of school for violence, for a start. I remember Peg saying something like,' she lowered her voice, amping up her accent, to sound exactly like a younger, bullish Peg, '"Well that's bollocks, right there. I don't know why she took you out, but I told her it was a bad idea at the time. You were so shy, you wouldn't say boo to a goose. Being in school would've helped you out, if you ask me. Fights? You? Nah. Ask Mona if you don't believe me. I told her to keep an eye on you when she was in the last year, and she never saw you in any trouble at all." Mum had just taken me out for her own reasons. Then I asked what Peg knew about my sisters, and she told me that there'd been no dead babies, no miscarriages—'

'What? She told me all about the miscarriages, and she was so—'

'Believable? Well, in fairness there was one. Child though, not a miscarriage. Lily was real, according to Peg, but the rest of them, no. That was just more… colour.' She smiled bleakly, put on Peg's voice again. '"Marie, what your mum *says* and what's *true* are very different things. She's tapped maybe. Got a want in her."'

'How old were you then?'

'Sixteen. I left home then, just left and didn't tell Mum, not for a year. Peg gave me enough money to go to London, and I worked in bars and read the cards, and managed to get on a few psychic fayres, and hen parties. I saved my money and did every course I could at the College of Psychic studies, mediumship and remote viewing. Peg kept on at me, telling me I was daft not to charge money: "If you were a mechanic you'd get paid, wouldn't you? Or a dentist? You wouldn't see them spending all that money on training and not wanting anything at the end of it. Get your coin, 'cause I'm telling you now that Sylvia'll leave you fuck all when she goes. If she ever goes. That bitch'd survive a nuclear strike."' She smiled wryly at Kirsty. 'And she wasn't wrong, was she?'

'But why did she let you go?' Kirsty wondered. 'Someone that controlling… it doesn't fit.'

'I've wondered that myself,' Angela said. 'I think she didn't have a choice. She could only make me do things or believe things if I was with her – it was like really strong magnetism, but it didn't work when I was with Peg, it was like Peg jammed her circuits. When I left I didn't have a phone. When I got a phone I didn't call Mum from it. I never came back, I never let her know my address, I changed my name, just like she had, but I wanted to go the opposite way – Night to Bright.'

'Why Angela?'

'Angel. Like Lily. Like Lisa. A homage, almost. When I moved to the States, I called her more often because I thought I was so absolutely safe – I mean, I was a different hemisphere away – I… relented. And she seemed to have mellowed too. She seemed… changed. I let my guard down. I started sending money. I figured I could afford it, and I was worried, you know, about her rattling around in that house, full of trash, with Mervyn getting older and sicker. She said she'd bought a flat for them both and I thought I was paying the mortgage. I thought that flat existed right up until I came back for the funeral, and I didn't find out the truth until just before Vic's party, where I first met you. I was livid, I felt conned and *stupid* and… *small*. And there she was, playing the lovely old lady who's so proud of her daughter, it made me sick. That's why I probably came across as so weird.'

'What did she tell you about the money, where did it go?'

'She said she was saving it up in case I made her homeless. She told me that she didn't trust me to look after her in her old age, that I was cruel and distant and that she needed her own "nest egg". You "took her nest egg", remember?'

'Ah, yes. I forgot I'd done that.' Kirsty allowed herself a rueful smile.

'When Mervyn left the house to me, that tipped her over the edge I think. She saw the house and the land as hers; she was bitter, angry. The body under the house didn't matter so much as me getting one over on her; that's how her mind worked.'

'Why did Mervyn leave everything to you, though?' Kirsty asked delicately. 'I mean…'

'*Was* he my dad, is that what you mean?' Angela's face wore a smile, bitter, stoic, challenging. 'That *is* what you mean?'

'Well—'

'I don't know why he left it to me.' Angela answered flatly. She was, for a moment, the same aloof professional she had been at the party. 'And as for the other…' The tight mask cracked just a little, into pain, into disgust.

'Did you ever ask Sylvia?'

'No. What would be the point? What answer could I have trusted? I don't *want* to know, anyway. Would *you* want to know? If you were me?'

Kirsty hesitated. 'No. No I don't think I would either,' she admitted.

'Families are best left alone.' Angela said softly. 'They're dangerous. For me, anyway.'

'Vic wanted you to be Milo's god-mother.'

'Well, she can keep on wanting.' Angela shook her head. 'Clients like her always get too attached.'

'She's moving onto religion now anyway,' Kirsty told her. 'She did one of those DNA tests and she thinks we're descended from an ancient tribe of Israel. She's talking about Kabbalah now.'

Angela smiled broadly at that, looking more like Peg than ever. 'Well, that gets me off the hook, eh?'

CHAPTER THIRTY-NINE

And then there was Lee. Lee, who distrusted Sylvia from the start, who watched aghast as his wife wandered back into her personal hell, Lee who possessed such a stubbornly faithful spirit that he refused to give up on her.

When Kirsty had called him from Sylvia's home that last night, he'd immediately called the police and deliberately exaggerated his knowledge of what was going on.

'I told them you'd gone on a client visit and you were being kept against your will. I told them they'd got violent. They couldn't very well *not* send a car over then, eh?'

'You could've been charged. You could've been arrested for wasting police time,' Kirsty told him.

He shrugged. 'Maybe. But what did I care? I had to get you out of there, didn't I? I had to get you back.'

Lee was just ten minutes behind the police that night, driving through Beacon Hill. He saw Sylvia mount the pavement, though Lee had his doubts about how accidental it was.

'I saw her face for a second, and she looked right at me. I'd pulled to the side of the road by then, when I saw the blue lights, and then suddenly, out of nowhere, this massive Beamer charged out of the field, right towards me.' Lee paused then, and his eyes were far away, almost frightened. 'She sped up when she saw me, I really believe she did, and I could see it was her...' He laughed. 'It was almost funny, there she was, sitting up all prim and straight like Miss Marple or someone, and yet she was staring at me like she wanted to kill me. I floored it then, and moved up the road as quick as I could, and she turned to follow me, got up on the pavement to try to get alongside me, I'm sure of it. That's when she lost control and hit the garage.' He was pale, now, ruminative. 'The sound of it, Kirsty… the crash like… thunder, and then the car alarm, this high squeal like something trapped, and then the garage door slicing through everything. I could even hear the tyres losing air, the suspension going, like something alive dying, like a big beast.'

He shivered, then smiled, shook his head, and Kirsty could tell he was trying to gather up some protective facetiousness.

'Hark at me, being all lyrical.'

'You don't have to do that, you know. You don't have to pretend it wasn't scary.' Kirsty was very serious. 'She was a pretty scary person.'

Lee was very serious now, grim. 'She was a pretty evil person.'

'I don't know about that, and I know you're thinking that I'm being too nice and I'm trying to see the best in her and all that, but I'm really not. I just think "evil" is a bit too simple, it almost lets people off the hook, d'you know what I mean? We say Hitler was "evil" – and that's true, but it means all the bad stuff starts and ends with him, but all the other people – all the thousands of little people who did what he told them to – did it because they believed him. But we don't call them "evil", do we?'

'They were misled, hypnotised almost. I mean, there's loads of factors—'

'Yes, I know. And maybe that was a bad example. But with Sylvia then – to call her evil lets me off the hook. I went along with her, didn't I? I might even, if Angela hadn't stopped me breaking my neck on that staircase, have hurt her. I might even have killed her. And all because I let myself be carried along by… trust, I suppose. Blind trust. It's terrifying when you think about it.'

'Well, you see, that's where I think she *was* evil. To make someone trust you and manipulate them into doing things that are so out of character, so damaging? How can that not be evil?' Lee said.

'Well, we don't know what happened to her. Maybe she had a terrible childhood, or a mental illness or—'

'A brain parasite? An evil twin?'

'You know what I mean. There must be a *reason*.'

'That's where we differ. I think, sometimes, there isn't a reason. These people just emerge like a virus, take as many people down with them as they can, and then either go dark or die,' Lee said seriously.

'That's bleak.'

'Maybe it is. But it's true.'

CHAPTER FORTY

'I agree with Lee.'

It was Angela's last day in the country, and she was in the hospital overseeing Peg's triumphant return home. She'd managed to talk Mona into letting Social Services inspect her newly adapted living room; she'd bought all the much-needed equipment as well as a ludicrously large flatscreen TV that was already screwed to the wall at an angle to suit Peg even when she was lying flat on her back. She'd also – discreetly – arranged for some of the money from the land sale to go to Peg and her family in small, regular payments for at least the rest of Peg's life (and probably Mona's too if she carried on smoking the way she did). Angela and Kirsty were sitting in her office, or what was her office only for the next week, because Kirsty had given in her notice and was moving back to London with Lee.

'The problem with trusting someone bad, bad like Mum, is that it carries on damaging you. What they do to you, it doesn't end when *they* end, the poison is long-acting, and if you're not careful, you never really trust anyone again.' Angela tapped one beautifully manicured nail against the scarred desk. She was once again the slick, groomed woman she'd been at Vic's party. 'You can't let that happen to *you,* Kirsty.'

'Lee thinks I trust too much.'

'And he's probably right. You trust not wisely but too well. So don't stop trusting, just trust better.' She smiled. 'I'm the opposite. The only person I've ever trusted is Peg. And, now, you.'

'I trust you too,' said Kirsty, and both women felt the same; an awkward and peculiarly British sense of warm, happy, discomfort.

Then Angela stood, hefted her Birkin bag, and Kirsty stood too. They faced each other a little shyly.

'Have a nice flight,' Kirsty told her.

'I won't. I hate flying.' Angela smiled.

'Will you come back for a visit?'

'No. No, I don't think so.' Angela shivered. 'I hate it here. It's a bad place. There's something wrong with this town. And don't you come back either, Kirsty, promise me? You're an unfinished meal for this town, just like me. If either of us come back again, we'll never leave.' Her face was grim.

'It's just a place,' Kirsty countered weakly, but she knew Angela was right. She could feel it too.

'Trust me, there's better places. Come and see me in Los Angeles,' Angela said briskly and leaned in for an equally brisk hug. 'And if I'm in London I'll send you some free tickets for the show.' She looked at her watch. 'Right, I'm off. Oh, and, here.' She handed Kirsty a small lilac envelope. 'Open it with Lee. Just a thank-you card with my address in, that's all. Take care.' She turned, and walked quickly down the corridor, into a waiting lift. As the door closed she smiled a bright smile, and her eyes were shiny and wet.

CHAPTER FORTY-ONE

Kirsty had nothing to pack from her flat but clothes. She and Lee got into the van and wordlessly headed towards the motorway, cheering when they saw the sign marked simply 'SOUTH', and it wasn't until they were back in London, tired but grateful to be back home, Kirsty remembered the note in her pocket.

Dear Kirsty

Please find enclosed a cheque for £300,000. It's two-thirds of the money I expect to receive from the land sale. The remaining third, as you know, is going to Peg and her family. I didn't want to give it to you in person because I know you'd be embarrassed and refuse to take it. I figured that if you opened it with Lee, there'd be a better chance of you seeing the sense in taking it without question. Lee is eminently practical like that.

Why am I doing this? Well, because you need it and I don't. Also, you earned it. Without you, I wouldn't have been able to get to the truth of what happened to Lisa. I may even have stayed in that hellish place being slowly digested by my own mother. You understand? This is not a gift, or charity, or any of the other things you may be thinking. It is your due. You lost your friend, your life was damaged, you've suffered, so look on this as compensation.

There's also this: do you remember when we first met? I told you to prepare for someone coming, that you had to be careful, and get through a bad time, and then she'd appear. You thought I meant Lisa, and to tell the truth I wasn't sure what it meant, but it was strong, it was something I had to tell you right then, even if I didn't understand it all at the time.

Well now I can tell you. You're pregnant with a girl, about twelve weeks, it was her I felt, it's her you've been waiting for. She's already a happy person, Kirsty, a good, strong person, like Lee. Like you.

Use the money, put it towards a house, spend it on your daughter. You've earned everything good that is coming to you, Kirsty, I promise.

With all love
Marie

A LETTER FROM FRANCES

Hi!

I hope you enjoyed *Two Little Girls*.

If you did enjoy it, and want to keep up to date with all my latest releases, just sign up at the following link. Your email address will never be shared and you can unsubscribe at any time.

www.bookouture.com/frances-vick

Two Little Girls completes the quartet of novels (*Chinaski*, *Bad Little Girl*, *Liars* and *Two Little Girls*) that are all set in and around the same imaginary unnamed city, sharing locations, characters, events and themes. For five years I've lived in this city, where mysterious, sometimes nasty, and sometimes lovely things happen in the strangest of ways. I know every street, every pub, every estate in the place, but there are surprises around every corner. It's that kind of town.

This is probably my most personal book. For a long time now I've been fascinated with memory, with how memory can be manipulated. So much of our identity relies on what we remember about ourselves, but how much of that memory is real? How much of it has been imparted to us by those who think they want the best for us, or, possibly, those who want the worst?

Kirsty, struggling to free herself from her memories, only traps herself further. Angela/Marie thinks geography will do the trick, but she's just as trapped. Lee lies about what he remembers, and pays dearly for that denial. Bryan's memories are resolutely self-serving. And Sylvia? She weaponises the memories of others to survive. There are more Sylvias out there than you'd think…

I'd be interested in what you think about memories. And about psychics for that matter. Is Angela a 'real' psychic? Did anything happen to make Sylvia so manipulative, or was she – as Lee believes – born that way? Can Kirsty recover? I hope so. She's a good soul.

Once again, thanks for reading. Feel free to get in touch with me on Facebook, Twitter or via my website: www.francesvick.com.

A new book will be out just as soon as I move away from this strange concocted city. Maybe somewhere bigger, brighter? America?

Cheers!
Frances

🖥 www.francesvick.com

f francesvickwriter

🐦 @francesvicksays

ACKNOWLEDGEMENTS

As ever, huge thanks to all the team at Bookouture, especially my editor, Kathryn Taussig, Noelle Holten, Kim Nash, Maisie Lawrence, proofreader extraordinaire Liz Hatherell (good catch on Grange Hill), my agent Kate Barker and everyone who works so hard to get my nasty little books read and (hopefully) enjoyed. My incredible family also deserve a medal for putting up with my deadlines/insecurities/strange working hours. Shout out to my Constant Reader Elvie Ashton. Finally, everyone who has picked up this book or any of my others and thought, 'What the hell, let's give this a try.' You're gold. Thank you.

Printed in Great Britain
by Amazon